FOCUS

BAD BOY BILLIONAIRE SERIES

MICHELLE LOVE

HOT AND STEAMY ROMANCE

CONTENTS

Made in "The United States" by:

Michelle Love

© Copyright 2021

ISBN: 978-1-64808-772-1

❀ Created with Vellum

ABOUT THE AUTHOR

Mrs. Love writes about smart, sexy women and the hot alpha billionaires who love them. She has found her own happily ever after with her dream husband and adorable 6 and 2 year old kids. Currently, Michelle is hard at work on the next book in the series, and trying to stay off the Internet.
"Thank you for supporting an indie author. Anything you can do, whether it be writing a review, or even simply telling a fellow reader that you enjoyed this. Thanks

BLURB

Lust. Betrayal. Passion.

Talented engineer, Gia Flynn, finds herself in the middle of a tug of war two billionaires are playing with her.

Her family's financial security is cemented if she stays with Damien Markov, a Russian Space Industry Magnate.

Her heart belongs to Ryker Crawford, another Space Industry Magnate from America.

Who will she choose or will the race to get to Mars leave her alone on Earth?

Ryker Crawford is a new billionaire who's taken over the CEO position of his dearly departed grandfather's company, Apollo Engineering.

Gia Flynn is a young woman who's a talented engineer. She's been lying dormant for three years as she's become the girlfriend of space engineering magnate, Damian Markov.

When Ryker lays eyes on her at a fundraiser, he finds her boyfriend ignoring her as he pays attention to his cell phone instead of the young, dark haired beauty.

Can Ryker lure the brilliant woman away from the Russian Billionaire?

1

PART 1 - THE SPOTLIGHT

RYKER

Flames explode out of the bottom of the new rocket boosters that Ian has developed. Applause spontaneously begins as we all watch the large screen at the front of the meeting room. *We're one step closer to making getting to Mars a reality.*

APOLLO ENGINEERING WAS STARTED by my grandfather ten years ago. He passed away a little over a year ago, cancer took him from us, before he could see his dream of becoming one of the first settlers of Mars, come true. He's turned that dream over to me.

"Ryker, tell me what you think," Ian says as we all sit back down after watching the video he recorded when he tested the rocket booster in Cape Canaveral.

"I think you're a genius. But what else is new?" I ask, drawing chuckles from the other board members. "My one question is, when can you get this into production? With fifty ships to build, we need to get at least one of them done within the next three years, so we can test before sending people off to outer space in the things."

"Here's where you're going to decide to give me a monster bonus, Ryker," he says with a smile. "I've got the approval to produce these things in Russia. The government is willing to let us use their facilities in exchange for the technology. It's a fair trade, I think. But what matters is what you think, Ryker."

"The Russian government, huh? I'll have to consider that. There's a fundraiser tonight. I might be able to pick the brains of some of the privately owned Russian space exploration companies' top guns, to see how much they would trust their government with their own technologies. So, I can get back to you on that soon, Ian." I look around the board table. "Does anyone have anything they'd like to add to Ian's presentation?"

Sandy looks at me as she says, "I'd like to know why he wants to use a Russian facility to build the boosters when we have facilities here in the U.S. that could be used."

I turn to Ian to allow him to answer that. "Ian?"

"They'd make us pay. I know the company has plenty of money but why pay when we can get them made for free?" he asks, raising a good point.

"The money goes into our economy, though," Sandy retorts.

I raise my hand to stop any further arguing. "Let me talk to some people first, before we go into this. It may not be a thing we need to argue over at all. If that's all, we can adjourn this meeting."

With everyone nodding, I get up and take my briefcase with me to my office. Ted comes to my side as we all leave the boardroom. "Mr. Crawford, I think you should know there will be some very big names in our industry at this fundraiser. Damien Markov, the CEO of Markov Global, is in town. He's sure to be there. You should pick his brain. His family has been in space exploration since the Russians sent Laika on Sputnik 2. He's a natural born leader in our field."

"I'LL MAKE sure to introduce myself to the man. Thanks, Ted." I leave the young man to go into my office to find Bridget leaning over my desk.

"Is the meeting over already, Mr. Crawford?" she asks me, as she straightens up and smooths out her knee length, pencil skirt.

I close the door behind me, locking it. My tie is constricting me, so I take it off after I place my briefcase of the chair next to the door. Her smile is sexy and smooth. That cherry red lipstick is about to leave glossy marks all over my desktop.

"Please remove those documents from the desk, Bridget. I have an urgent need that you, as my personal assistant, need to help me with." I pop the button on my pants and watch her push the papers into a drawer then lean over my desk.

Her thigh is silky as I run my hand up one of them to push her skirt up. Pressing my cock to her ass, I lean over her and tie my tie around her eyes. My cock is pulsing as I push the other side of her skirt up. Moving her panties to one side, I hesitate for only a moment as I look at how creamy her ass is.

THE SOUND of the buzzer of my intercom has me jerking my head up. "Mr. Crawford, a Mr. Markov is here and requests a meeting with you. He says it won't take long," the receptionist, interrupts my plans.

With a sigh, I step back, put myself away and pull my tie off Bridget's eyes. "I guess I'll be seeking your services another time. How about you take off for lunch now? I was going to let you go afterward, anyway. Take the rest of the day off. I have to get out of here early to get ready for the fundraiser."

"I could go with you, Mr. Crawford," she says as she smooths out her skirt. "If you'd like me to."

"My dear, Bridget," I say as I put my tie back on. "That would have pictures of us taken together. People would think we were on a date. You know I don't date members of my staff." I tap the button to reply to the receptionist. "I'll send Bridget out to escort him to my office, shortly, Veronica."

With a nod, she makes her way to the door. "I'll bring him to you, sir."

"Thank you," I say then take a seat in my chair and think about stock prices, the tyranny in Afghanistan, and orphaned children, in an effort to get my cock to go back down. It's never a good idea to meet someone for the first time with a hard-on, after all.

The things my mind conjures up help ease my situation and I find the door opening and Bridget gesturing for a tall, muscular man to enter my office. "Mr. Markov, Mr. Crawford."

"Thank you, Bridget," I say as I get up to shake the man's hand. "You may go now."

THE BLONDE MAN with piercing blue eyes, the color of ice, is a large man. Only slightly smaller than myself. Our hands meet in a firm shake as we size one another up. "You must work out," he says.

"I do and it seems you do to," I say as I release his hand. "Have a seat, Mr. Markov."

"Call me, Damien," he says as he takes a seat.

I go around my desk to take mine and say, "Then you must call me, Ryker."

"Good, I abhor formalities, Ryker. I am here because I saw a little thing on the internet about new boosters your company was testing in Cape Canaveral."

"Wow!" I say, stunned. "That's top secret. Did you say you saw it on the internet?" I pull out my laptop out of one of the drawers and open it. "Where might I find this?"

He pulls the computer to him and taps in something then turns it back to me and I see the same damn video that we just watched in the boardroom. "This is where I found it."

I see the video has been up for one day and that lets me know Ian's either leaked it or he's been hacked. One can never tell with these things and it's not worth the time to interrogate Ian about it. It's out, that's a fact.

"So, why are you here, Damien?" I ask as I put the laptop away.

"I'd like to offer my production company's services, of course. I can offer you a great deal for us to produce them. It will only cost you information." He taps the desk with long fingers as he eyes me.

"Russia certainly wants every tidbit of information it can get its hands on, doesn't it?" I ask him as he sits back in his chair, crossing his arms over his chest.

"I am not Russia, Ryker. I am one man with one company and I want to get to Mars just as badly as you do. It's been my dream for a while now. I want to start a new life on a new world and your rocket boosters can help me get closer to that reality."

Drumming my fingers on the desk, I ask, "What's your deal, Damien?"

"We will produce your boosters in exchange for the technology that you used to make them. That means..."

I interrupt him. "I know what that means. You want to be listed on the copyright. Your company and mine will be the only two to use the boosters."

"That's right. So, what do you say to such an awesome deal?" he asks as he smiles, revealing very white and perfect teeth.

"I say, I have a board that has to make that decision together. I will tell you that we have an offer exactly like yours, though. And already one of our board members has expressed concern."

"If you allow me to approach the board, I assure you, I will get their approval. I can be a very forceful man when I need to be, Ryker," he tells me and I feel a bit like he's threatening me.

"How long will you be in Florida, Damien?"

"Two weeks. So, let's not waste time." He gets up to leave, abruptly. "I have a lunch appointment. Will I see you at the fundraiser tonight?"

"I'm going," I say as I get up to escort him out. "And I'll talk to the engineer who invented the boosters. It is him who has been approached with the other offer."

"Let me leave you with one thought, Ryker. If it's my government who made the offer, you need to know this. They share their technology with all Russian companies."

With a nod, I open the door and lead him to the elevator. "It was nice to meet you and I look forward to seeing you this evening."

With a nod, he gets on the elevator and I find myself wondering what I should do.

What can I do?

~

GIA

"Yes, mother, we're in the states. We're in Orlando, there's a fundraiser tonight. I'm at the spa, being pampered right now. My feet are soaking in a gooey substance and my face is covered in mud. Damien is spoiling me again."

"Are you going to be able to come to Nebraska for a visit?" she asks.

I hem haw around, as I say, "I'm not sure. Damien said our stay is only two weeks. He's got some new thing he really wants from another company. I foresee him spending the majority of his time here, in Orlando."

"What about you, Gia?" she asks. "You could come for a visit on your own, couldn't you?"

I know I can't. Damien would never let me go. But she'd hate to hear me say that. "I'll see. He needs my help, Mom."

"Oh, good," she says, enthusiastically. "It's nice to hear he's letting you use your brain again. You were such a talented engineer. What are you helping him with?"

"Um, well, it's top secret," I say as I'm not helping him do anything. He doesn't let me. But Mom sounds so happy, I can't let her down.

"Top secret! Wow! A Russian top secret project, how exciting for you, sweetie," she says as I see Damien come into the spa.

"Gotta go, Mom," I say. "I'll talk to you later in the week."

"You do that, Gia. We all miss you. Your sisters, your father, and I all would love to see you. It's been a couple of years, you know."

"I know, Mom," I say as Damien comes my way. "I have to go. Love you." I end the call and put my cell in the pocket of the white robe the spa puts their clients in.

"They say you have two more hours. I am going to lunch with a comrade from back home. An old school pal. You will go back to our suite when you're finished here and put on the dress I had hung in the closet for you. I've instructed the woman at the front desk on how I want your hair done. Be ready by eight," he snaps at me.

"Eight? You won't be back from lunch until tonight?" I ask as that's insane.

"I am catching up with my old friend, Gia. I don't know how long that will take me. You will be fine. I'm going to take my tux with me, so I can get ready."

"Where? Where are you going to get ready at?" I ask as he's making no sense.

"The hotel room where I am meeting my old friend. Have no worries. I will be at the room at eight to get you. Be ready." He spins around with nothing else and leaves me.

I WATCH him walk away from me. Damien is tall and built like a brick house. His light blue eyes seem to see right through a person. He's handsome and commands respect. And he's mine. My boyfriend of three years.

I was fresh out of MIT when I met him at a space fair in Washington. It was about the idea of going to Mars in the future. He sought me out when he found a project I had made. It was a capsule with nutrients enough to sustain a human body for three days. An invaluable thing for the long journey to the planet.

He thought I was a genius and his company bought my patent and they will be the ones who will sell the capsules when space travel begins. It's odd to me how he thought I was so smart but once we really got together, he had me stop working and devote myself to him.

At first, I was so enthralled the magnificent man wanted me to be at his beck and call, that I gave myself to him, entirely. It was a novel, the man wanted me around him all the time. He showered me with gifts and attention.

His attention in the last year or so has been lax. He's always on his phone. He leaves me at home on his vast estate, in Saint Petersburg, Russia, when he goes to his office. I used to go with him but he started leaving me behind and that became a trend.

He only brought me with him to the U.S. because I'm not a Russian citizen and I have to leave from time to time. I thought, by now, he'd have asked me to marry him. *But that's never been discussed between us.*

I OVERHEARD him and his father talking once, in Russian, that Damien should marry a Russian woman. His father told him that he could keep me as a mistress. Damien didn't say anything back to his father. I have no idea if that's a thing he thinks I will allow or not.

I wouldn't, though!

IF HE WAS to go that far then I would definitely leave him. Even though he has helped my parents, financially, since he took me with him to Russia. He's even made sure my twin sisters and their husbands are taken care of.

He bought them homes, cars, and puts money in an account for them all. They want for nothing. If I left him, they'd lose it all. I don't want that.

He's not mean, abusive, or anything like that. Just neglectful. I don't think that being neglected is a reason to end a relationship. *Especially one that affects my whole family.*

"TIME TO WASH this stuff off and do your hair and makeup, Miss Flynn," the attendant tells me.

I watch her as she pulls my feet out of the gel and wipes them off then slips on a set of thin slippers. At least once a month, Damien makes sure I'm completely pampered. He's not neglectful in that way.

I drive an expensive car, wear expensive clothes, and have tons of jewelry. I have all the money that I want. He's a wealthy man and has no problem spending money on me or my family. It's his time, he's stingy with.

But this old friend of his has managed to get an abundance of his time for some reason. I'm lucky to get ten minutes with the man before we go to bed.

He does pay attention to me in bed. He always has. Only, this last year, he's changed. It's pretty much wham, bam, thank you ma'am, now. No soft words, and no exciting lust-filled nights, either. Just plain old, roll over and let him hurry up, sex.

HIS DREAM of going to Mars is his reason for the change in him. He's in a rush to get there. There is a small fact about Mars that I have a problem with. I don't want to go, not that he's invited me.

He's never asked me, even once, if I wanted to go with him. I'm unsure if he just expects I will or if he doesn't even want me to go with him. He and I haven't talked much, lately.

He tells me what he wants and I do it. Like tonight, for instance, he has to have me at this boring fundraiser. I did tell him I'd rather not go and he said I must. He said it looks bad for him to go to such things alone.

All I know, is I'm not looking forward to staring into the crowd as he ignores me. I know it'll happen that way. *It always does.*

RYKER

The place is packed as I enter the gazebo of the Central Florida Zoo. Only the wealthiest people were invited. Thanks to my grandfather, I joined that list of the elite a couple of years ago. I'm one of the youngest men here. At thirty, I'm a baby, compared to most of the people here.

When I took over my grandfather's job as CEO of Apollo Engineering, I gained a massive amount of money as well. The responsibility is high and the anxiety I can get at times is hard to handle.

Hence, my need for a personal assistant who can handle all my personal needs.

Bridget was sent to me by one of the other board members when he saw me struggling in the early days. I was a mess and he sent the woman to my office with a note that said she was my assistant and I could use her anyway I needed to. He added at the very end, even sexually.

She was fine with the arrangement and I use her about three times a week to ease my frustration level. It's great. *No commitment, no drama, no worries!*

I HAVE women I mess around with. One night stands, mostly. I don't like getting too close to anyone. I plan on leaving this planet as soon as I can. Getting attached to someone here would be dumb.

My plan is to find someone and settle down after I reach Mars. That way, I can be part of populating that planet. It fills me with a surge of energy to think about being such a huge part of the beginning of a new place for humans to reside.

Who knows, maybe one of my kids will end up as the king of Mars? I have no idea how we're going to rule that planet. But I like the idea of kings and queens. I'm old fashioned that way.

The gazebo is lit with white Christmas lights and I see a monkey is in a nearby cage. The zoo is special to me. They have a breeding program and plan on sending some of their animals to Mars too. It's going to be so exciting!

"That's Rufus," a woman in a long white gown tells me as she walks up and hands me a flute of Champagne. "He's one of our ideal Columbus monkeys. It's his sperm we're collecting and keeping for the mission to Mars. It will be some of his descendants that make Mars their home."

"And I suppose the retrieval and storing of that sperm requires money," I say as she nods and sips the bubbly liquid.

"Lots of it." She slips her arm through mine. "I'm Claudette, a breeding scientist, here at the zoo. Let me show you some more of our prime animals, Mr. Crawford."

"And just how do you know who I am?" I ask her as this is my first function of any kind since I took on the CEO position.

She produces a pamphlet from a pocket on her dress. Along with several other wealthy men, my picture is there with my name and what company I represent. Underneath my picture is Damien Markov's. "We were all given these to make sure you each had five-star treatment."

"I see. And where can I find this man?" I ask as I point to Damien's picture.

"Mr. Markov is sitting at a table over here. Come on, I'll show you to his table." She takes me with her, heading through the crowd. "He's brought a woman with him. She introduced herself as Gia Flynn, so you'll know who's with him. I suppose you two have business dealings."

"We might," I say then see him sitting at a table, talking on his phone. "I'll take it from here, Claudette. You don't have to worry about my donation, it will be a great one."

With a smile, she leaves me and I look back at the table to find a young woman with dark hair, held up in a loose bun with shiny tendrils falling out of it, sitting down at the table with Damien and he's not paying one bit of attention to the rare beauty who seems to be in the middle of a spotlight.

Nursing a drink in her hand, she looks at the floor then glances around the place. She seems to be lost. And it's a shame that she's being ignored like that.

Her skin is a pale creamy color that her pink lips accent perfectly. I watch her take another drink and wish I were the glass that touches her sweet lips. She can't be Damien's date. *He's not even looking at her at all!*

· · ·

But why would she sit at a table with him if she isn't here with him? Why would she be fine with being ignored? Why am I standing here when I can go talk to her?

I move one foot in front of the other and make my way across the floor, only to be stopped by Gary from Sim Corp. "Ryker, great to see you here," he says as he shakes my hand and claps my back. "Come here, I have some men I'd like you to meet. I brought my team of engineers tonight. I know they'd love to pick that enormous brain you have."

I go along with him as he takes me to a group of men who all wear expensive tux's like I do, only most of them seem uncomfortable in them. They fidget as I come up to them. One calls out, "Hey, it's Ryker Crawford!"

A laugh erupts out of me as I had no idea I could command that much excitement from a group of guys. "It's nice to see you know about me."

They seem in awe now and converge on me in a circle, fencing me in and keeping me from getting to the gorgeous creature perched on the edge of her chair at Damien's table.

She just can't be his date!

I'm trying to give this group my full attention but can't seem to focus on them as I'm so focused on the woman who's looking sad and lonely. Damien is still on his damn phone and I watch her as she gives him longing looks then looks away when he doesn't notice her at all.

One of the guys asks me a question about my plan to go to Mars, so I have to answer him. "Yes, I want to be on the first mission. It's my dream to see the red planet and tame it for future Martians."

The men laugh a little and I see the woman place her hand on Damien's arm. He looks at her hand then gets up and walks away. Shaking his head at her.

I find the way he's treating her, appalling and excuse myself to go talk to the woman, now that she's alone. I make sure Damien is all the way out of the gazebo before I get to her. I pick up a couple of drinks from the bar and go to her. "Hello, gorgeous."

She looks up and stares at me. "Who me?"

I place the drink on the table in front of her. "Mind if I sit down and introduce myself to you?"

"I'm nobody," she says. "I'm here with Damien Markov."

"I'm sure you're somebody. No one is a nobody. And I don't see Damien around. Are you supposed to be on a date with him?"

"He and I are a couple," she says, shocking me.

"For how long?" I ask as I reach out and twirl a tendril of her silky hair. "I knew it would feel this soft. You are a rare beauty, Gia Flynn."

"How do you know my name?" she asks with surprise.

"Oh, I have my ways. When one sees such a beautiful woman, one finds things out about her. Your name was first on the list. And now that I know you, I have more I'd love to know about you. Like why you're sitting here, being ignored by any man." I take a seat, even though she's not offered one.

"Damien's busy with a call from an old friend he met with today. I suppose it's quite important." She takes a drink and I reach out and touch her arm.

"Since he's so busy, would you care to take a walk with me? Touring the zoo in the twinkling lights looks fun. But I don't want to do it alone," I tell her as I stand and pull her up with me.

"Damien should be back soon," she says as I tuck her hand into the crook of my arm.

"I'm sure he will. And he can wait on you, when he gets back. Don't worry, I'll explain things to him when I return you to him. If you want to be returned to him, that is."

HER GIGGLE SENDS chills through me. "You're funny. And your name is?"

"I am Ryker Crawford of Apollo..."

"Oh, I know who you are. Apollo Engineering was a company I was going to see about interning with before I met Damien," she says.

"I'm sorry about your grandfather. His mission to see Mars populated is what started that company. He was a true revolutionary man. The space community misses him, dearly."

I smile with her sweet sentiment. "Why didn't you still apply for an internship? Meeting Damien shouldn't have ended your career."

"No, it shouldn't have," she says as her brows furrow. "But it did. I moved away to Russia with him. I thought I'd work for his company. You see, I designed a capsule with enough nutrients to keep a human body nourished for days at a time. It would be useful..."

I cut her off as I know what it would be useful for, "...Moving people and animals to Mars."

She stops and nods as she smiles, broadly. "Yes! But I haven't made one for animals yet. Each animal has different needs. I was going to work on that and develop them for each kind of animal. That way, they would be ready for when the first mission takes off."

"What stopped you?" I ask as she seems brilliant.

"Damien," she says and her smile fades away. "I sold the patent to him. He has his own people working on doing that. They've yet to come up with anything as good as I did for humans. I'd love the chance to work on the project but he likes me to be available to him."

"Not to be nosy, but available for what?" I ask, wondering if Damien Markov is keeping this woman as his sex slave. She's far too smart to allow that to happen to her.

"Just be available. Not exactly in a sexual way. Just be around when he comes around. Which isn't a lot, anymore," she mumbles.

"Where are you from, Gia?" I ask as I move us along. *I'd love nothing more than to hide her away from the man all night long.*

"Nebraska, Blue Hill, Nebraska, to be exact. My father was a farmer," she says as we stop in front of a cage that supposed to have a bear in it but he seems to be sleeping.

"He was a farmer?" I ask as I move us along to the next exhibit.

"Since I got with Damien, there's no need for him to farm his land. Damien gives my family more money than they know what to do with. Dad's land is just sitting there. He keeps it fertilized but that's all," she says then points to the back of an enclosure. "See, that?"

I squint to make out the shape of the animal she's pointing at. "What is it?"

"A lemur," she says. "Can you imagine a day when these creatures will be on a new planet?"

"I can and do, all the time," I say. "It's my dream to go on the first mission. I suppose you'll be accompanying Damien on his first mission."

"I don't know about that." She walks away from me to the next cage.

Getting back to her side, I take her hand and tuck it back into the crook of my arm. "And why don't you know about that?"

"I don't want to leave our planet. I'd like nothing more than to help people and animals to get there, though. You know, like the ground crew." She looks up at a sleeping Eagle in its huge nest. "Eagles flying in a red sky, how cool, huh?"

"We do need people here to make it all happen. It's admirable of you to want to help people get there. I want to be there. I want to have one of the first children born on the planet," I tell her and find her smiling.

"So, where is Mrs. Crawford?"

"There's not one," I say. "There won't be one, here on Earth. I'm waiting to meet a woman on Mars. It's there I want to make my life. It's there I want to raise a family."

"And you'll leave all your wealth to who, here on Earth?" she asks as she peers into a dark cage and jumps back when an owl swoops out at us, screeching to let us know he dislikes being disturbed.

I find her in my arms and hold her tight as I look down at her sweet face. "I don't know. I've never even thought about it. I suppose I could donate it to a deserving charity or several of them."

"You're very generous," she says as she moves out of my arms. "Sorry for jumping into you like that."

"Not a problem," I say then take her hand again. "I didn't mind at all. So, tell me more about yourself. Are you a scientist?"

"No, I'm an engineer. I graduated from MIT." She looks away like that's not a huge deal.

"Why would you be wasting away in Russia as Damien Markov's toy? You're much too talented to do that. I'd like to offer you a position with Apollo Engineering," I say, without hesitation.

"My only idea, I've sold to Damien's company. What good could I even do for your company?" she asks me as she looks away, shaking her head. "I've wasted my chances."

STOPPING HER, I turn her to face me, leaving my hands on her narrow shoulders. "Gia, you said you don't plan on going to Mars. Damien is going to go. So, what's your plan when he leaves you here, all alone?"

She seems to be thinking about this for the first time ever. "Um, I guess I don't know. I kind of thought he'd make sure I was taken care of."

"Is that all you want out of life?" I ask her as she doesn't seem the type to be so shallow. "To be taken care of?"

"No," she says then looks down. "Oh, I don't know what it is I want, Ryker."

"There you are," Damien says as he walks up behind us. "Are you trying to steal my girl away, Ryker?" He laughs with a deep sound, as if that could never happen.

I let Gia go and she steps around me and goes to him. "He was keeping me company while you were busy, Damien. Do you know this man?"

Damien looks at her with surprise. "Oh, he didn't tell you about the business deal we discussed at his office earlier today? I thought that was why he came to introduce himself to you." His ice colored eyes dart to mine. "Why else would he take someone else's woman off?"

With a chuckle, I say, "I was on my way to talk to you when I was ambushed by a pack of engineers, trying to pick my brain. I saw you leave, just as I got free. It was my intention to tell Gia why I had made my way to her. But we got to talking about other things, like how wonderful she is, smart she is, and talented she is. I could go on and on, obviously."

"And taken she is," he adds. "Perhaps I could join you two on your little walk?"

Gia holds tight to his arm as she senses his jealousy. "Please do, Damien. It's nice to know you want to do business with Ryker. He seems to be a nice man and a generous one too. Much like yourself."

I watch her smooth his rumpled feathers, expertly. She must be used to him getting pissed when anyone wants her attention. *Not that he does!*

GIA

DAMIEN'S PULSE is rapid as I hold his hand. He's never had to see me with another man's hands on me. It seems to be doing something to him. Maybe he'll see he should pay more attention to me or someone might swoop in and take me away from him.

"Which one of you would care to tell me about this deal?" I ask. "Or is it top secret?"

"You don't need to worry yourself with it, my darling," Damien says then kisses the top of my head.

"I don't see why she can't know," Ryker says. "You see my company has developed a highly effective rocket booster. Damien would like to manufacture it. All he wants in trade for his work, is to have rights to it."

"Not exclusive," I say as I look at him, worried Damien will make a deal with him the way he did with me not truly understanding I would never get to work on my project again. "You'll keep your rights too, won't you?"

"What does that matter to you, Gia?" Damien asks me. "This is none of your concern."

I've pissed him off by asking something and I don't care. "Look, I just don't want him to lose something that's so important. The way I did."

"You know, in light of you and she being a couple," Ryker says as he turns to continue our stroll through the zoo. "Couldn't you, at the very least, let her work on the other capsules for the animals? She said your people haven't come up with anything yet. We really could use that sooner rather than later, you know. You have a diamond there, Damien. You seem to be covering her with dirt, though."

Damien starts to walk too, taking me up next to Ryker who looks at me from the corner of his eye as Damien says, "Gia has no reason to lift a finger. I take excellent care of her and her family. Has she explained to you all I do for them?"

"Yes, she has. You've taken care of their finances. Given them more money than they know what to do with. But aren't you going to be going to Mars?" Ryker asks, making Damien sneer.

His pulse goes insane as he says, "So what if I am?"

"She'll be left here, alone. Those who have grown dependent on you would be left with no idea how to take care of themselves. What you see as a service, I see as a disservice." Ryker stops and takes my other hand. "What do you think, Gia?"

My eyes go wide as Damien's hand squeezes mine. His hand is hot and I know he's about to blow a gasket. So, I ease my hand out of Ryker's and smile. "I think this conversation is taxing, to say the least. Damien is a man I can count on."

"And who needs any more than that?" Damien asks then starts walking again. "No need to worry over Gia, Ryker. She will have my portion of my family's wealth when I leave. She can dole it out to her family as she likes."

"No want to take her to Mars with you, Damien?" Ryker asks and I find myself looking at Damien to see what the hell he says about that.

"She's much too fragile to go to Mars. She's allergic to everything and fights with anemia. Her family also has a history of mental illness which would block her from going anyway," Damien says and I am shocked.

"What are you talking about? My family has no such history!"

"But they do," Damien says. "You have an aunt no one talks about. She was institutionalized when she was twelve."

My jaw drops as I stare at him. This man must've done some extensive research into my family's background to come up with this. And for what?

"You and I will discuss this later," I snap then spin around and run away from them both.

I've never been more humiliated!

"GIA, WHERE ARE YOU GOING?" Damien shouts.

"I can't understand why he's with me if he has no future where I'm in it." And everything is spinning in my head. He was all about me for the first year and a half. Suddenly, he became distant and forgetful where I was concerned. And I bet it has everything to do with finding out I can never go to Mars with him.

Not that I was ever going to go. He'd know that if he ever bothered to talk to me about it. Instead, he played detective to see if I was worthy of going in the first place. He's impossible and I have no idea why I'm staying with him.

A hand on my shoulder stops me and spins me back around. "Hey."

I find Ryker is the one who came to stop me and look around him to see Damien is nowhere in sight. "Where'd he go?"

"He made a phone call and walked away. Don't let that shit about your aunt get to you, Gia. We all have a squirrel or two in our family trees," he says then grins at me. "I have five in mine."

His silly grin makes me laugh, despite my anger at Damien. "I'm sorry for how I'm acting. I really am. I wasn't this person."

"Let me guess," he says as he takes my hand. "Before Damien Markov."

"Yes," I confess. "I was different before him. I was strong willed and sure of myself and now I'm neither of those things."

"Well, damn!" he says as he pulls me along with him. "And those are great things to be. What made you change?"

I find him taking us to one of the bars and ordering something pink and fruity then he hands it to me. "Thank you. And I don't know why I changed. I don't want to blame Damien. It was me who changed. He never tried to change me. It just happened, somehow."

"He's overbearing," Ryker says as he picks up a Scotch and takes me with him to a table.

I nod. "I agree."

"Do you love him?" he asks me and I freeze.

"We don't use that term. We never have." I sip the delicious drink. "Yummy. How did you know I'd like it?"

"It's got strawberry liquor in it and cream, what chic wouldn't?" He moves his hand over my cheek and his smile is devastating.

Ryker is taller than Damien by about an inch. His shoulders are a little wider but his build is a touch smaller. His jaw is rugged and he keeps a five o'clock shadow going, making him look darkly handsome.

"You're thoughtful," I tell him as I watch his plump lips form another heartbreakingly beautiful smile.

"Sometimes I am. I'm not a saint. I have my bad points too," he says then licks his lips, picking up every last drop of the Scotch he's just drank.

"And they are?" I ask as I have to think something bad about this perfect man who's paying so much attention to me.

My body trembles as he leans in very close and whispers in my ear, "I have a penchant for corrupting gorgeous, smart, talented women, like yourself." I go wet as his lips touch the place just behind my ear. "Have you ever fucked around behind Damien's back?"

Jerking my head back, I hiss at him, "No! Ryker! I'm not that kind of woman!"

. . .

SITTING BACK, he grins at me with a sexy stare. His dark eyes penetrate mine as he licks his lips once again. "Pity."

My heart is racing and my body is shaking. "Ryker!"

"Say it again, Gia," he says under his breath. "Say my name, baby."

I hate the fact I'm on fire and he has me this way in mere seconds. "Where's the nice man I was talking to? Do you suffer from split personality?"

He shakes his head, sending his dark waves dancing around his face. "Nah, I have a naughty side, that's all. I can be a little naughty and a little nice, can't I, Gia?" He leans forward, putting his elbows on his knees and jerks his head toward one side of the gazebo. "You're in need of some attention and I can give it to you. Damien has no future plans for you. Dump him. Or don't. That's up to you. I want you, either way. And you need me, baby."

"Ryker, you're being too forward," I say as I look around to see if anyone can hear what he's saying.

"I know. It's a byproduct of being so damn smart. I'm quick to act. I'll be in that private bathroom, if you care to join me." I watch him get up and stroll to a door just off the wood floor. He leaves it ajar and I find my body is trying to get up and follow him.

Holding myself back, I take the rest of my drink down in one gulp to douse the fire he's started inside me. I look around for Damien and don't see him anywhere.

With the realization that Damien will leave me all he has and I will one day be without him anyway. I get up and walk across the floor to let Ryker do to me what he wants. Because I want it too. *I want it more than I've wanted anything.*

MY HEELS CLICK as I cross the wood floor. My ass shakes as I feel radiant and confident. That gorgeous man wants me. He hardly knows me and he wants me. It's been a few weeks since Damien's touched me. I am ripe for the picking.

My hand hovers near the door knob. My body breaks into a sweat. My mind stills as I touch the door knob.

"Let's go, Gia," Damien's voice comes from behind me. "I've made my donation and I have plans for later on tonight. I need to get you back to the hotel suite."

"What?" I ask as he takes my hand and pulls me away with him.

He hurries away with me in tow as I look over my shoulder and see Ryker walking out of the bathroom. He must've heard Damien talking to me. He eyes me as he knew I was coming to him.

I turn back around and run a little to keep up with Damien as he says, "My old friend is having a crisis of sorts. I need to go and see if I can be of help."

"Take me with you," I say. "I might be able to help. What's the crisis? Women problems? I can help."

"No, you can't. My friend is shy. Very shy." He waves at a waiting cab and we get inside of it.

He moves me all the way over, sliding his body with mine to get me on the other side of the bench seat. I look at him as he slides back to the other side of the car. I feel cold and somewhat ashamed of what I was about to do.

"Damien, don't leave me. Please, don't leave me alone for the night." My hands knot in my lap as I can't stand the thought of being alone.

"You'll be fine. You can drink the wine I've had delivered and eat the cheeses and fruits I've told room service to bring to you too. Order a movie on the television. You'll be fine. I should be back before the morning."

I feel deflated and look out the back window to see Ryker walking into the street. "Just leave me here then. I'd rather be here than in our room, alone."

His eyes narrow as he turns his head to look at me. "Gia, that man is a whore. The woman who took me to his office was his slut. Is that what you want? To be a notch on his extremely notched bedpost? I thought you were better than that?"

"How do you know it's Ryker I want to see?" I ask him as his glare turns into a smile, an evil one.

"Do you think I don't know you were about to walk into that bathroom he'd gone into? Do you think I didn't see that exchange between you two when he kissed your neck? Do you think I don't know what will happen if I let you out of this car?"

"Please take me back to the hotel and stay with me then. I need to feel like I'm one with another person, Damien. I feel alone. Look what I nearly did." I glance back again and find Ryker is no longer in the street, waiting to see if I'll get out of this cab and go to him.

Why would he wait for me?

DAMIEN'S RIGHT ABOUT HIM. I know he is. It's possible, if I wasn't so damn lonely, that I would see right through him and not want a thing to do with the man.

Ryker is exactly like Damien. He's leaving this planet on the first ride out of here. He's going to make his life on Mars. I have no place in either of the men's lives.

Yet, Damien promises to leave me his wealth. That money will make sure my family is taken care of for the rest of their lives and then some. Once he leaves, I can move on as a rich woman. I can find a man to love me then.

Now is not my time, I suppose. Damien is taking care of me. For that I should be grateful. And not be thinking about giving my body to another man.

Tears fill my eyes as I look at Damien. "I'm sorry. That was wrong of me. I felt hurt by what you said about finding things out about me that you've never even told me before. And I feel so lonely. You've taken your attention away from me."

"I give you all you need and more. I am leaving you everything I have and this is how I am thanked?" he asks as he looks at me with sadness in his blue eyes.

"I know," I look down and shake my head. "I'll shut up."

He looks out the window as he sighs. "I wish I could feel more for you, Gia. I do. The fact is, I need you here with me now. I know I can't make you any promises about always being with you. I won't be. But you will have my money to keep you warm. I'm merely asking for your faithfulness while I'm still here. That's all. I just need you to be my companion."

I nod. "I can do that."

But I don't feel like I am his companion. I don't feel like I should be here for him just so me and my family can keep his money. But I don't know what else to do.

The cab pulls up to the hotel and Damien looks at me. "Go on. I'll be up when I get done."

Sliding out of the cab, I walk into the hotel. From what I've heard, it could be ten years or more before they begin taking people to Mars. For ten years, I could be stuck in this life.

Money certainly has taken hold of my life.

STOPPING to watch the cab with Damien in it pull away, I find my heart heavy and turn back around to go into the lobby. My head hung low as I make my way to the elevator.

"Miss Flynn?" I hear one of the desk clerks call out. "Can you come here, ma'am?"

Looking up, I walk over to the counter. "Yes?"

The young man slides a card to me. His hand covers it. "Mr. Markov isn't coming in, is he?"

"No," I say as I look over my shoulder again. "Not until later, he said."

"Okay, I was instructed to give this to you, only if he wasn't with you." He slides his hand off the card and I see his cheeks go pink. "And you have nothing to worry about, Miss Flynn. We're a discreet bunch of people here."

I nod and take the card then walk to the elevator. My heart is thumping as I squish the thing in my hand, balling it up. I have a feeling I know what it is and I don't want the temptation.

In the elevator, I think about what I'd be giving up by messing Damien over. What I'd lose for my family. And it's just not worth it.

As I leave the elevator, I toss the waded card in the trashcan, just outside of it. "Thanks, Ryker, but no thanks."

All the way to our suite, I think about his dark good looks. His dancing eyes, his kissable lips. And I know I will never allow myself to taste his kiss or feel his intimate touch.

Opening the door to our room, I feel a warm breeze move over my face. It brings to mind how his hot breath would feel as he kisses my body all over. His hands would bring heat to my skin as he grazes them all over me.

Pulling my clothes off as I go into the room, I find the bottle of wine and retreat to the bathroom. A bath is in order. A nice, long, hot bath might help me to forget about the handsome man who wants me.

Something has to help!

RYKER

"I thought you hated him, Ryker?" Ian says as I address the board about letting Damien's company make our boosters.

"I hate the way he treats his woman. But this is business. I did my research and if we let the Russian government make them, they can and most likely will, give our technology to all companies in Russia who make these kinds of things. If Damien makes them, only his company and ours will have this booster."

"Should I even try to talk about using an American company?" Sandy asks.

I smile at her. "What do you have for us? Anything near this good?"

"No, but Steel Corp will make them for only ten million each," she says, knowing there's no way in hell I'll pay that over nearly free.

With a shake of my head, I look at Ian. "We can take a vote if you like."

"No," he says as he admits defeat. "The fact is, I didn't know the Russians could do that. It would put us nowhere near the lead in the race for Mars. Go with Markov Global. It makes the most sense."

"It does," I say and have to smile. "Meeting dismissed!"

Making my way to my office, I open the door to find Bridget sitting in my chair. She jumps up as I come in and I laugh.

"Sorry, sir."

"Not a problem. Get Damien Markov on the phone. I have great news for him and I feel a celebration coming on," I tell her as I toss my briefcase on the chair by the door and head to my private bathroom.

IT'S QUITE likely Damien will bring Gia to dinner when I invite him to meet me, so I can tell him the good news. I know I should bring a date and I have no idea who I should bring on such short notice.

When I walk back into the office I see Bridget has the phone in her hand. "Mr. Markov is waiting on the line for you, sir."

"Good," I say as I walk over and take the phone out of her hand.

"Should I leave, Mr. Crawford?"

Shaking my head, I point at the chair for her to take a seat. She does as I say, "Hello, Damien. How's your day going?"

"It's alright. Are you about to make it better?" he asks.

I want to ask how Gia is doing but I know that'll piss him off, so I just say, "I can try. How'd you like to meet me for dinner at The Capital Grille at eight tonight? I'm bringing a date, so bring Gia along, if you'd like."

"I don't like to mix her into my business," he says, making me mad in an instant.

I chill, though. I want him to bring her. I've been thinking about her nonstop since I left my number with the front desk and she never called it. I know she was going to come into that bathroom two nights ago, I heard her outside the door.

. . .

"Tonight, business will be short and celebrating will be long," I say as I watch Bridget fidget in her seat.

"I will see if she cares to come with me," he says and I find that's not enough for me.

"Reservations have to be made," I say. "Is she around? Ask her if she wants to come."

"You said you're bringing a date too, right?" he asks.

"I am," I say and my eyes settle on Bridget. "I'll be bringing my personal assistant, Bridget. You've met her."

With a laugh, he says, "Her? Okay, I'll bring Gia. We will see you there at eight. Is it formal?"

"Yes, see you at eight," I say and end the call with so much cheeriness, it's slipping into insane proportions.

"You're bringing me?" she asks as she looks at me with wide dark eyes.

"Do you mind?" I look at her and think she's surprised.

"No! Not at all. I just thought dates weren't a thing you wanted to do with me." She gets up and paces a little. "You see, here's the thing, well, how do I say this?"

"Just spit it out, please," I say, feeling a bit annoyed.

"I have a girlfriend now."

"Huh?" I ask as I'm more than stunned. "You're a lesbian?"

"Bi,' she says. "And my girlfriend is jealous. She doesn't know just how much I assist you. I tell her I'm on birth control to keep my monthlies in check."

"You're bi-sexual and you have a girlfriend?" I ask again, in disbelief.

"Yes, Mr. Crawford," she says as she looks a bit nervous.

"For tonight, it's Ryker. And only for tonight. Is this girlfriend going to be anywhere near that restaurant tonight?"

"No, she works at a bar. As long as I'm home by two in the morning, she'll be none the wiser." She offers me a weak smile. "But, no sex. If you get me home too late to take a shower, she'll know and boy will there be hell to pay. That woman loves my ass."

"Noted," I say as I didn't plan on doing much with her anyway. "Can I ask you something, Bridget?"

"OF COURSE," she says as she stops her fidgeting and pacing.

"Do you like it when I fuck you?"

"Of course!" She fans herself. "Your great, sir!"

"But you'd rather be with a woman. Are you with any other men?"

Shaking her head, she says, "For the last five years, it's been strictly women. And then you, when I was hired for you."

I feel more than a bit sick as she gets nothing out of it and now I can see that as clear as the nose on my face. I don't want to tell her she's no longer going to be needed for my frustration releasing any longer. I need her to go with me to the meeting. But it is over.

How blind am I?

～

GIA

"HE'S BRINGING HER?" I ask as Damien tells me we're going to meet Ryker and the woman he said was Ryker's personal assistant and his slut.

"Yes, so you will get to see the man for who he truly is. I hope this will settle you about him. Talking in your sleep, has me knowing that you think about him," he tells me, shocking me.

"What? Why are you just now telling me that I've talked about him in my sleep?" I ask as I cringe at the memory of the steamy dreams I've had every time my eyes close.

"What did you want me to say to you, Gia? Hey, what's up with you screaming obscenities that end with that man's name on your lips? You bitch about not getting enough sex, but you seem to be getting plenty, in your dreams." His light eyes hold mine as he looks at me like he's caught me in a lie or something.

"I can't help my dreams," I say as I go to look in the closet for something nice to wear. "Should I go to get my hair and makeup done, Damien?"

"WHY, you want to look nice for your dream lover, Gia? Of course, by all means, please go use my money to pretty yourself up for the man who would use you and toss you away like he does all the rest."

I ignore him and go to the closet. "Red or blue?" I ask him as I hold out a couple of dresses."

"Black should work," he says as he walks past me to pull a tux out of the closet. His face is near mine, his cheek, nearly touches mine. "Like your soul."

"Damn it, Damien!" I toss the dresses to the floor and hurry to the bathroom. "I can't help my damn dreams!"

"But you can stop thinking about the man. You can think about me and what I've done and will do for you. You could think about pleasing me, sexually, instead of him."

I spin around and glare at him. "You're never here! How could I even do that?"

"Are you telling me that you've forgotten how to be spontaneous? Are you telling me, you've forgotten how easy I am to please? You don't try, Gia. You never try anymore."

"Because you ignore me, almost entirely," I shout at him.

"Shouting at me, is not a thing I allow. You know this. So, lower your voice when you speak to me," he says as he begins to pull his clothes off in front of me. "I am here now. There are hours before we must leave. Are your hair and makeup more important than pleasing your man?"

I tremble with how I'm going back and forth with what I should do. Damien's right about Ryker. The man is bringing his tramp to dinner. And the man who takes care of me is open to sex right now.

So why do I feel torn about what to do?

2

PART 2 - THE TARGET

Waiting in the bar area for Damien and Gia to show up at the restaurant, I feel the air stir as the door opens. A chill runs through me as I turn back to find them entering the dimly lit room. "They're here, Bridget."

We get up to meet them as the hostess leads them to us. "Your guests have arrived, Mr. Crawford. Would you like to be seated at your table now?"

"Yes, please," I tell her and reach out for Gia's hand first.

She places it in mine. "Ryker, how are you doing this evening?"

"Better now," I say then leave a kiss on top of her hand. I let her hand go and nod in gesture to my date. "This is Bridget. Bridget, this is Gia Flynn. You've met Mr. Markov."

"Of course," Bridget says as she lightly shakes Gia's hand and then I find Damien giving her a hug.

"Nice to see you again, Bridget," he says. "Please call me Damien."

"I will," she says as he lets her go.

He shakes my hand with a quick movement. "Ryker."

. . .

"DAMIEN," I say then extend my arm toward our waiting hostess. "Shall we?" Placing my hand at the small of Bridget's back, escorting her out of the bar.

"This is a very lovely restaurant," Gia says as we walk through the entry way to cross from the bar to the restaurant. "Thank you for inviting us, Ryker."

"Thank you for coming, Gia. I was worried Damien was going to leave you at the hotel," I say as I look at her, over my shoulder. "It's nice to see you again."

"You, as well, Ryker," she says and gives me a smile.

Turning to look back in front of me, I feel my heart beat a bit faster. The woman certainly does more for me than I can recall feeling for anyone else. *Too bad she's wrapped herself around that man.*

THE BLACK DRESS, she's wearing, holds her body in a way that makes every curvy stand out. The neckline is deep, separating her perky breasts. There's no way she has a bra on, underneath it.

It has me wondering if she has any panties on as the dress is tight and I think I'd see the lines of them if she did. The thought of how available she might be right now has my cock stirring.

I'm thankful to get to our table, so I can hide my reaction from them all. Holding out a chair for Bridget, I help her to take the seat then take my own. Damien holds out a chair for Gia and leaves a kiss on top of her head after she sits down.

I watch the act too closely and he catches my grim look. "Ryker, should we order Champagne?"

With a nod to our hostess, I say, "Have our waiter bring a bottle when he comes to us."

Curtly, she nods and leaves us. I can't stop looking at Gia. Her hair is down, flowing in dark waves over her nearly bare shoulders. The dress has short sleeves that hang at the very edges of her shoulders. The length is short and her red heels are high. I can picture one of her legs wrapped around me as I push her against a wall.

"I can't wait to hear what you have to say, Ryker," Gia says as she looks at me then gestures to Bridget. "How long have you two been seeing one another?"

Bridget looks at me with the same expression a deer gets when headlights hit it. "You answer that one, please."

WITH A CHUCKLE, I say, "She's been with me only a few weeks after I took over the CEO position. But dating is new to us."

Bridget sighs and looks at Gia. "Very new."

"First date?" Gia asks as she looks at us.

Bridget nods and I find Damien smiling. "Good for you, Ryker. Making an honest women out of her."

I don't even care what he means by that as I look at Gia and find the red lipstick looks great on her plump lips. She used a silver eyeshadow along with blacks to make a smoky eye. "Tell me, Gia, are you going to go see your family while you're here?"

"We don't have time for that," Damien answers for her.

I watch her look down with a frown on her gorgeous face. "No time?" I ask. "I can send you on my private jet, if you'd like."

She looks up at Damien with hope. "Can I do that?"

His jaw tightens then he looks at me. "That would be nice of you. But it's not necessary."

"When was the last time you saw them, Gia?" I ask her.

"Two years," she says and that just pisses me off.

Letting it go, for now, I see our waiter coming with the bottle of champagne and four flutes. "Here we go," I say as he places the glasses on the table.

"I am Devin, I will be your server this evening. Your Champagne is on the house tonight, as we've been informed we have not one but two very talented men at this table tonight. I'd like to welcome you both, Mr. Markov and Mr. Crawford, to our fine establishment, this evening. I'm on the list for the Mars population program, you two are a couple of heroes in my book." He pops the bottle open and fills our glasses.

"I am hoping Mr. Crawford here, has some great news for me, this evening that will get us that much closer to getting there," Damien says.

I hold up my glass and say, "Devin, you might like to stay for this, it's a momentous occasion, after all." I turn my eyes to Damien. "Apollo Engineering has decided to accept Markov Global's proposal to manufacture our new rocket boosters."

DAMIEN'S SMILE is huge as he lifts his glass and clinks it to mine. "That is something to drink to, Ryker. You will be happy with our work, I promise you."

The ladies join us in clinking the flutes of golden bubbly and then we all drink to the new deal. Gia's eyes rest on me and she gives me a smile. "So, you will be coming to Russia to visit then?"

"My engineer, Ian and I will be coming," I tell her. "Along with a few others."

Gia's eyes move to Bridget. "You as well, Bridget?"

Bridget's hand flies to her throat. "Oh! I doubt that."

Damien is quick to say, "You should bring her, Ryker. The nights get cold in Russia. I'd hate for you to sleep alone."

Gia looks away as if the thought bothers her, which I love. So, I test those jealous waters a bit. Putting my arm around Bridget, I lean in close. "Maybe you should come."

The way Gia's head snaps back to look at me with wide eyes has me nearly laughing. She watches, closely as Bridget fidgets, not knowing what to say. "If you need me, sir."

I tense at her reaction. She's not getting that I need her to play a part. And Gia's eyes narrow, telling me she's getting wise to my ploy. There's a dancefloor not too far away, where some other couples are dancing. "Dance with me, Bridget." I get up and take her hand, leading her out to the dancefloor, away from them, so we can talk.

When I turn back to take her in my arms, I see Damien leaving Gia alone at the table as he has his phone to his ear and is walking away to make a call.

· · ·

"I DON'T WANT to explain everything, Bridget. I need you to pretend we're more than we are. And leave the 'Sir' out of things, please. Just go along with anything I say. I won't be taking you to Russia when we go. But you act as if you will be going with me. Do you understand me?"

"Yes," she says. "You like her, don't you?"

"I'm not about to answer that question, Bridget. Now, please leave me and go to the restroom, so I can take the opportunity to have words with Gia, alone." I let her go and she nods as she leaves me on the dancefloor.

Making my way back to Gia, I find her looking up at me when I get to the table, alone. "You seemed to have lost someone," she says.

"As have you," I sit down and run my finger around the rim of the glass in front of me. "Did you get the message I left for you the other night?"

Her smile lets me know she did. "No."

Pink fills her cheeks as I say, "Lies are easily read on your beautiful face, Gia. Why didn't you call me?"

She meets my gaze. "I knew what you wanted."

"So, again, I am asking you why didn't you call me?" I grin at her. "You were about to meet me in that bathroom."

"But I didn't and the man, who has done so much for me, got me out of there, so I wouldn't make a fool of myself. I'm quite thankful for that. I'm not interested in becoming a notch on your bedpost, Ryker." She picks up her drink and I notice the slightest tremble of her hand.

Getting up, I walk over to her and pull her chair back. "Dance with me."

"That's a bad idea," she says but then Damien walks up behind her. I had seen him coming and made my move on purpose.

"Nonsense," he says. "Dance with him, my darling. I trust you."

Gia eyes him as she gets up. "As you wish, Damien."

He winks at her as I take her hand in mine and lead her away from him. "I promise I won't bite, unless you ask me to," I whisper as we get to the dancefloor.

She gasps as I jerk her body into my arms, making sure our bodies touch, so she can feel my desire for her.

GIA

I GASP as Ryker pulls me so close to him, I can feel his bulge pressing against me. "Ryker!"

"Say it again, Gia," he whispers as he nuzzles my neck.

"Stop that!" I hiss at him as I look back to find Damien on the phone, not looking at us at all. I thought he'd be staring a hole in me but I was wrong.

Our little spat at the hotel turned into a hot bit of passion, he must feel he's adequately fulfilled my needs. But he's wrong. *Ryker brings out needs in me only he can fill.*

PULLING HIS HEAD BACK, he looks at me as we sway back and forth to the slow song. "If you don't want to become a notch on my bedpost, as you said earlier, what would you like to become?"

"I don't know why you'd bother asking me that question. You told me you were going to Mars and that's where you'd be getting serious with a woman. You know I'm not going, so what the hell does it matter what I want?" I ask him as he smiles at me and I hate how attractive I find him.

"I'd just like to know," he says then spins us around. "Humor me, will you?"

I decide to scare the man off. "I want you to fall in love with me, Ryker. I want you to marry me and forget about going to Mars. Stay here with me, forever. Leave that dream behind you."

He chuckles then says, "You don't expect much, do you? Have you asked that of Damien?"

"Why would I?" I ask. "He hasn't asked me what it is I want."

"You know, Gia. The Russians may not be going to allow people with imperfect backgrounds to go to Mars, but America holds no such regulations. You could go with me." His dark eyes glisten as he looks at me and waits for what I'll say next.

"You and me, Ryker. Like a team?" I ask, as if I'm really contemplating going with him.

"Something like that," he says then we spin around again. "So, what would you think about doing that? I mean, he'd be gone on the first ship out of here. I could wait for you to get to me."

"You seem like you're being serious," I say with a laugh. "Ryker, you know I can't do that."

"You can," he says. "Those things Damien said about you, don't make you unable to go. You should think about it."

"Let's just pretend for a moment that I'd do that. You and I get to Mars where Damien is and then what?" I ask as he spins us again.

"What will he care?" he asks as he smiles, wickedly. "He'll have left you behind."

"With all of his money," I say as he seems to have forgotten about that.

"Money?" He shakes his head. "You are worth more than that. Why do you insist on thinking more about the financial gains that come with Damien than anything else? You're brilliant and Mars could use a mind like yours."

"And it will get it. But from Earth. I can make things for the people and animals here that I couldn't up there. Don't you see the big picture? There won't be labs to work in. Plants to manufacture things in, won't be available there. Everything will have to be shipped in. With the money he leaves me, I will be able to help the beings that go to Mars. I will be able to make the things that will make life there, better."

One of his dark brows cock up. "I never thought about that."

"I HAVE," I say and find him slowing the dance.

"You are very smart." He licks his lips as he looks at me. "That's very attractive."

"Ryker, I know that woman you've brought with you is your personal assistant and your lover. I have no idea what you want with me, other than a quick roll in the hay. But I have my plan and I'm sticking with it. Damien is part of that plan."

"I could be the same thing for you. Only better." He looks at me as if that's really a thing I might consider.

"I don't trust you. I trust Damien," I say then find the song has ended and yet he still sways with me as if music is playing. "We should take our seats, Ryker."

Reluctantly, he lets me go. "Perhaps, if you'd just allow me to have a taste of you, then I could get you out of my head, Gia."

I laugh as we walk back toward the table where our dates are waiting on us. "I'm afraid you'll have to figure out another way to get me out of your head, Ryker."

I too have to figure out a way to get him out of my head. Having sex with him will only plant him in my head that much deeper. *And I can't have that!*

RYKER

As our waiter takes the order, I find Damien's dominance over Gia infuriating. "No, you won't have the shrimp. Gia. Bring her the filet mignon and broccoli, no butter or cheese, steamed only. She can have a small amount of whole grain rice as well. She's had too much alcohol tonight, so bring her water. I'll have a lobster, baked potato, loaded with everything, a steak kabob on the side and a Long Island Iced Tea."

I don't say a word as Gia looks down. Then the waiter looks at me and I gesture to Bridget. "Go ahead, Bridget."

She rattles off what she wants and I can't stop looking at Gia and how she's fidgeting in her seat. After telling the waiter what I want, I find Damien pulling his cell out, yet again, the fifth time already, and holding up a finger as he gets up and walks away from the table.

"Will that be all?" the waiter asks us.

"No," I say. "Gia, order whatever the hell you really want to. It's not as if Damien will be paying any damn attention to what you're brought, anyway."

She smiles at me. "Do you really think so?"

"I do," I say as I look at her and see her eyes brighten up. "Get what you want."

"Okay, the shrimp and a loaded baked potato and a glass of white wine, please. I hate broccoli." She smiles as she looks at the waiter.

He nods and off he goes. I watch her face begin to glow. "You should learn how to tell him to shut the hell up, Gia," I tell her then lean over to Bridget. "Can you leave us alone?"

"I need to powder my nose again," she says as she gets up and leaves.

"I should learn how to do that," Gia says then I find her looking out the door to the balcony.

"Would you like to check that out?" I ask as I get up to take her outside. "It's nice out, tonight."

"I should wait for Damien," she says and I pull her chair out anyway.

"You'd be waiting all night," I say as I take her hand and tuck it into the crook of my arm. "And I'd like to get a breath of fresh air myself."

"You have a lot to say about Damien but you too are neglecting your date, Ryker."

"I have danced with her once," I say, in my defense. "And she's not really into me. I can tell."

"So can I," she whispers as she leans in close. "What's the real deal between you two?"

"Kiss me and I'll tell you all you want to know," I tell her as I open the French doors to the balcony, finding no one else on it.

She bats my chest, lightly as she giggles. "Why are you so silly?"

"Why are you so beautiful and smart in all the right ways, save one?" I ask her as I close the door behind us and move her to the railing. Leaning her back against it, I wrap my arms around her. "You feel perfect like this."

"But you need to let me go. This isn't okay, Ryker," she says as she pushes at my chest.

"I'm not doing anything I wasn't doing on that dancefloor, Gia. The more I'm around you, the more I find fascinating about you. You have to know that Damien is messing around."

She stops pushing me as she looks into my eyes. "What makes you say that?"

"Who the hell does he talk to on the phone that much?" I ask her as she looks to one side of me.

She pushes my chest hard. "Here he comes!"

I STEP BACK and watch him open the door. "There you two are. Dinner is served and we need to eat and get out of here."

"What's the rush?" I ask him as we make our way to the door, my hand on the small of her back.

He looks at where my hand is as we pass him. "I have to get to my friend. Another crisis, I'm afraid."

I don't say a word as we go back to our table but one thought is floating into my brain. *Gia will be alone in their hotel room!*

"TOO BAD," I say. "I had planned on having a long evening. But I understand. Friends take precedence."

"Over everyone, it seems," Gia says as she takes the seat he holds out for her.

I sit in my chair and elbow Bridget, gently. "Seems we should hurry, Damien has things to do."

"Okay." She leans over and whispers, "I can take a cab home."

"That would be best, wouldn't it?" I ask her and she nods her answer.

With her off my plate, I can focus on getting Gia alone. Pulling my phone out, I discreetly tap in a message to my secretary, telling her to get me a suite at the same hotel they're staying at.

Gia seems pissed as she stabs a piece of shrimp. "Will you be gone all night long again?"

"I might. Why?" he asks her as he barely looks her way. And just like I thought, he doesn't notice she doesn't have the meal he ordered for her.

"No reason. A girl just likes to know when her boyfriend will be coming home, that's all," she says and stabs another shrimp. It's plain to see, she's pretending the shrimps are him.

"If I told you an approximate time, I'd be lying. You don't want me to lie to you, do you?" he asks her and I see my secretary has replied back that she got me a suite and I can check in when I get there.

I smile as I put my cell back in my pocket and ask, "If you're in a hurry, Damien, I can have my driver drop Gia off. It's not a problem. I can also get you one of our private cars to take you where ever it is you're going."

I have a million dollars that says he won't take the car I'm offering him!

HE HESITATES as he was about to eat a forkful of lobster. "Are you taking Bridget home with you for the night?"

"Yes," I lie. "We could drop Gia off before we go back to my place. I promised Bridget she could stay the night with me."

"Sure, you can give Gia a ride to the hotel," he says then takes the bite.

"And should I call my service about getting you a car?" I ask and watch his head shake.

"I'll take a cab. Don't worry about me," he says as he gestures to Gia. "Just drop her off for me. That'll be enough. What time should I be at your office tomorrow to get to the paperwork on our deal?"

"Whenever you'd like to. The earlier the better," I tell him as I watch Gia becoming angrier with him.

He's oblivious to it or doesn't give a shit. *The latter I bet.*

. . .

"I'LL SHOOT by the suite in the morning and change my clothes then be there about nine thirty. Will that be fine?" he asks as he doesn't realize he's just told us that he'll be spending the night with his friend instead of Gia.

She got it too and is looking at her plate like she wants to pick it up and throw it. "Shoot by the suite?" she asks between gritted teeth.

He looks at her and then down at her plate, finding five shrimp tails and three uneaten shrimp, and her half-eaten baked potato. His eyes roam to the glass of white wine instead of water and his cheeks go red. "When did you change your order?"

"When you left the table," she meets his icy stare and the two have a silent war, using only their eyes. He wins when she averts hers.

"Please see that she has no more alcohol. It gives her a headache in the morning if she does," he says as he looks at me. "She forgets that so easily."

"It happened once," she says then takes a long drink from the glass.

"And you'd have that happen again?" he asks as he glances sideways at her. "Foolish of you, don't you think?"

Her eyes roll to one side as she sighs and places her napkin over her plate. It's plain to see she's lost her appetite. And who could blame her?

GIA

STANDING OUTSIDE OF THE RESTAURANT, I watch Damien get into a cab while we wait for Ryker's driver to bring the car to us. He doesn't even bother to wave goodbye, he just gets on his phone as the cab pulls away.

"Have you met this friend of his?" Ryker asks as another cab pulls up and I watch Bridget get into the backseat. Ryker hands the driver some money and waves at Bridget as she leaves.

"I thought you were taking her home with you," I say as a black BMW pulls up and Ryker opens the back door.

"Get in and I'll explain why I lied to Damien," he says as he pulls my hand to make me move.

"But I don't understand and I don't think being alone with you is a good idea, either."

He slides in beside me and closes the door. "We aren't alone. The driver is here."

"Where to, sir?" the driver asks.

"The four seasons," he answers and leans back, laying his arm along the back of the seat. "I took a room there for the night. The long drive back to Sebastian isn't a thing I'm up for tonight."

"Sebastien?" I ask. "You don't live in Orlando?"

"No, my estate is on the coast. You should come for a visit. Oh, and Damien too, of course." He smiles at me and I find it to be sexy with a side of contriving.

"And you lied to Damien, why?" I ask him as I move over a bit.

It does no good as he moves too. "So, he'd let me take you home."

His hand moves over my knee and I shiver with how it fills me with heat. "And you wanted to because?"

"BECAUSE I WANT to be with you for a while longer. I enjoy your company, Gia. And I'd like to pick your brain some more. I bet you're full of ideas. I need ideas and you have them. Get it?" He chuckles. "You have other things I need too but you seem not to be interested in that. Yet, anyway."

"I really don't have any more ideas. I'm afraid to disappoint you."

His hand moves off my knee to stroke my cheek. "You can't disappoint me."

"Ryker, you need to keep your hands to yourself." I take his hand away from my face and place it on his leg. "You seem to forget your place."

With a groan, he looks away from me. "Why couldn't I have met you first?"

"It doesn't even matter." I turn a bit to lean more on the door, so his leg isn't touching mine. It's making little zaps of lightning go through me and is very unnerving. I don't know why that's happening.

"I don't know why you're saying that. If I would've met you first, then I know I'd have you talked into going to Mars with me by now. You and I would make some nice looking kids, Gia."

Heat fills my cheeks at his words. "Ryker, stop!"

"No," he touches my cheek and I look at him. "We would. You should think about that. You and I, populating a new world."

IN HIS DARK EYES, I see excitement. I never see that in Damien's. I only see determination in his icy eyes. And Damien's touch has never stirred me the way Ryker's does.

"Well, I'm not going." I turn away from him and look out the window.

The hotel is just ahead and the driver slows to turn into the parking area. I feel Ryker, staring at me. When we stop, he takes my hand and pulls me with him, out of the car. "Come with me to check in. I want a room near yours."

"That's not going to matter. I'm not coming to it," I let him know.

"Oh, but you will. You see, I have things to offer you that Damien won't."

My body goes electric as my mind flies to what he could offer me that Damien won't. But my mouth flies open, "I don't care for anything you have to offer."

"You will," he says as he tugs me along.

The desk clerk looks at me with a grin. "Miss Flynn. Is your evening going well?"

"Sure," I say as Ryker won't let my hand go.

"I want a room near hers. I have a reservation," Ryker tells him.

The clerk looks at me and grins even more. "Okay, and the reservation is under?"

"Ryker Crawford." He gives my hand a squeeze.

He's more than excited and I hate the fact I'm going to ruin his little party idea. I really do hate it. I'd love to see what he has to offer me. I would. But I can't do that. I can't cheat on Damien.

Just as he finishes signing the paper, his phone rings and he takes it out as he accepts the keycard the clerk gives him. Pulling me along, he smiles as he answers the call, "Hello, what do you have for me?"

I hear nothing as he pulls me onto the elevator. "You can let my hand go, Ryker," I whisper, after we're on the thing and I'm trapped with him and couldn't go anywhere if I wanted to."

He shakes his head as he talks on the phone, "Fantastic. Take them to my place. My staff knows what to do. And thanks for doing that so quickly, Stella." He looks at me with a huge smile. "Don't you want to know who I'm talking about, Gia?"

"It's not my business." I look away from him.

He takes my chin and pulls my face back. "Don't you care at all?"

"No," I say and watch the elevator doors open. "Come on."

We walk out of the elevator and he pulls me to his door. "Well, I wouldn't tell you, even if you did ask me. It's a secret. Just make plans to spend tomorrow night at my place in Sebastien. And Damien too."

"Of course," I say as he opens his door and pulls me inside his room.

"This is a nice suite," he says as he pulls me along and I stop him.

"I'm going to go to my room. The one I share with Damien."

"Why are you so faithful to that man? He isn't to you." He looks me dead in the eyes, testing me, I'm sure.

"You don't know that." I twist my hand until he lets it go.

He's in front of me, getting between me and the door before I can make it out. "Wait, I'm going to order us a bottle of wine. I really do want to talk to you."

"I can't have anything else to drink," I say as I huff.

"Because the master told you not to?" he asks as he picks up the phone in the room. "One bottle of red wine and two glasses please. Make it the best you have."

I'm angry he's said such a thing and glare at him. "No, not because Damien told me not to. Because I don't want to get tipsy around you."

"Don't trust yourself, huh?" he asks as he takes off his jacket then his tie. I watch him unbutton the top few buttons and stop breathing. "I have to ask this, as it's been biting at my mind since you walked into the bar tonight. Do you have on any panties?"

"Ryker!"

WHAT? I have to know. It's killing me not to know." He kicks off his shoes then sits on the bed and takes off his black socks. "So, do you think people on Mars will feel the same thing when they have sex that we do on Earth? I'm dying to feel that. The gravity is different, so the sex has to feel different too."

"Is your mind always in the gutter?" I ask with a laugh.

A knock at the door signals the wine is here and I should be going. But I sit on the edge of the bed, instead. Not really knowing why, but I just don't get up.

Ryker answers the door and thanks the man for the things then closes the door and locks it. I watch the way he moves with fluid motions, taking the wine and glasses to the small table. He opens the wine then I see him taking his shirt off.

Averting my eyes, I find my body burning. "I should leave. You want to get comfortable. I'll leave you to that."

"I do want to get comfortable. I've been in monkey-suits all day." His pants drop, leaving him in loose boxers and I can't breathe any more.

His body is tan and toned and hot as hell. "You know, Ryker. You won't have any trouble finding yourself a woman on Mars. You'll be fine."

Walking into the bathroom, he comes back with a fluffy white robe on and tosses another one to me. "Get comfortable with me, Gia."

Shaking my head, I get up and go sit on the small sofa in the corner of the room. "I don't think so, Ryker."

He laughs as he goes to pour the wine into the glasses and comes to sit right next to me, instead of across from me on the other sofa.

"Here you go, Gia. I was talking to some of my food engineers today and they told me it would be great to get to work with you."

"I'm going back to Russia with Damien."

"I know that. I'm only asking you to brainstorm with them about some ideas they have. Damien will be at the office too. You can come with him, get a consulting fee from my company and help out the space program. Please." He looks at me like a little kid, asking for a lollipop.

"If Damien says, I can then I will."

His cute face turns hard in an instant. "I hate that, Gia. I fucking hate that!"

"What?"

"You can make your own decisions. You just don't. Do you want to do this or not? It's as simple as that. Don't tell me a fucking thing about Damien. Tell me if you want to do it or not!"

His face is red and I can't believe how mad he is over what I've said. "I want to. You don't seem to understand. Damien doesn't like me in his business."

"This doesn't have a thing to do with him. This is a consulting deal between you and Apollo Engineering. You want it or not?" He gets up and when he does, his robe opens and he takes it off, tossing it on the other sofa. "That thing's too hot."

"I think your temper has made it that way, not the robe. I can't answer you right now about if I'll do that or not. I have to talk to Damien about it."

"Then take out your phone and call him." He goes to get my clutch purse off the bed and brings it to me.

"Pushy much?" I take my purse and pull out my cell.

"Pushed around much?" he counters. "And, for the record, you calling him is even pissing me off. You shouldn't have to ask him if you can use your fucking brain."

I stop trying to get my phone out as what he's saying resonates in my head. "I shouldn't, should I? I'll do it, Ryker. And thanks."

His sigh is over the top and the next thing I know, he has me in his arms and is hugging me. "Finally!"

RYKER

AFTER BREAKING THROUGH TO HER, I find her eyes are beginning to open to what she's allowed to happen to her, so I dig in and forge ahead. "Go to your room, change out of that tight dress, get comfortable in whatever you want and come back, so we can talk."

She looks at me for the longest time before she says, "Promise me you won't make any moves on me."

"Not unless you ask me to," I say as I raise my two fingers. "Scouts honor."

She gets up and walks to the door then turns back to me. "Were you even a scout?"

SHAKING MY HEAD, I laugh and watch her leave my room. Gia is beautiful inside and out. Her mind is being wasted and I find that the worst kind of negligence. She was given a gift for the world, and it's being squashed because of one man and her willingness to do whatever he says to.

After fifteen minutes, I get worried that she's not coming back and get up to go bang on her door. As I open the door, I find her with her little fist raised to knock. "Oh, there you are. I was about to come get you."

She rolls her eyes as she comes in. "I had to use the bathroom."

"Okay, too much information," I say with a chuckle.

I put the robe back on, so she doesn't have to be distracted by my body while we talk. But she's distracting the shit out of me with a cute pajama set with teddy bears all over it. It's silky and looks soft and I want to run my hands all over her body but I won't.

Sitting down across from her on the opposite sofa, I lean up and push her glass of wine to her. "Here you go, Gia. Now tell me how you came up with this nutrient packed capsule of yours."

She picks up the glass and takes a sip. "It's not mine anymore." I watch her go into another place in her head and want to stop her from doing that.

"Ignore that fact. Just tell me how you went about making that. It's a great idea, you know. I want to know what made you think it up." I take a drink of my wine and see her face change with her thoughts.

She's so delicate, mentally speaking. I would blame Damien for it all, only she has her part in it too. *She allows it.*

He's not a mean man. He's not threatening to her. He is overbearing but she could handle him if she wanted to. There's not a doubt in my mind. *She's handling me and I'm hard to handle!*

"It all started when I read a paper on nutrition and how our bodies need certain things. Supplements can keep us going when food can't be ingested," she says.

"And having enough food for the trip and when we first get there is going to be hard to do for such a high number of people," I add.

"Yes, exactly." She sips her wine and looks at me with wide eyes. "If a person consumes normal foods every fourth day, the supplement can be taken three times, every eight hours, for three days and no negative effects were found. I need to do more testing and where animals are concerned there's all the testing to do. And we need this for animals too. If I could just work on the project, I know I could get it done."

"Okay, so you sold the rights to that particular supplement to Markov Global. Are there slight changes you could make in a new product that would allow us to get another patent? We could make it in a pill form or even a powdered form that could be added to water. It's not the exact same and we could leave your name out of the patent, to make sure you couldn't get sued over it."

Her chest rises and falls, rapidly as she looks excited. "We could do this in secret?"

"We could. No one needs to know that you and I are working together on this. And you would get the money paid to you under consulting, instead of engineering."

Her eyes go back and forth as she thinks about what I'm offering her. "I could stay in Russia and work with you online."

"If you wanted to." I take a drink and think about how to word the next thing. "As a consultant, I could have you flown in once a month to consult with my company. Put you up in a nice hotel, you know, the usual we do for all of our consultants."

Her cheeks go pink as she gets excited. "I could do that, couldn't I? I have to leave Russia several times a year anyway. And Damien will never marry me to make me a citizen. I could come here to consult. And I could bring new ideas too." Then her face falls. "He'd want my new ideas, Ryker. I know he would."

"Our information has to be kept secret. You will be under a contract not to talk about anything we talk about in our consultations with you. Especially anyone in the space industry. Surely, he'd understand that."

"And surely, he won't want me to do this," she says then takes a drink. "Thanks for the opportunity but I can't."

Getting up, I slam my glass on the table between us and go to her, taking her by the shoulders, pulling the glass out of her hand, and making her get up. "You need to see something."

I take her to the bathroom and stand in front of the long mirror. "What are you doing?" she asks as she looks at me in the mirror.

"Don't look at me. Watch yourself. Watch your reactions. Answer this question. Do you want to use your brain?"

"Of course," she says but her eyes go to mine in the reflection of us.

"Look into your own eyes, Gia. Do you want to make a difference in this world, using the brain you were given to do such a thing?"

"I do," she says as she looks into her eyes.

"Gia, do you think anyone has the right to ask you not to help others with your brain?"

I catch her eyes falling away. "No."

"Look at yourself!"

Her eyes dart back to meet her reflection. "Why do I look like that?"

"I think it's because you've made an idea in your head that you have to be weak where Damien is concerned. His hold on you, with the money he's giving your family, is making you give into him. I don't even think he wants you to give into every little thing he asks of you. You do it on your own."

"Do you really think so?" she asks me as she turns around.

"I DO. And I think you need to practice doing what you want to." My hand moves up her arm, over her shoulder, and I take the back of her neck, holding her still. Her eyes dart back and forth as I hold her steady and ease my lips toward hers. "Do you want this?"

She looks at me with wide eyes as our mouths are so close, we're exchanging breaths. "Not while I'm still with him, I don't. I'm not that type of person."

I back away and let her go as she's told me what I needed to hear. She does want me. She just has to make a decision. And I can help her make it.

GIA

HIS TOUCH IS AMAZING. He is amazing. And I am in a relationship that I know is going to end.

Yes, it's going to end with me having a lot of money but it is going to end!

. . .

"WHY ARE you bothering with me, Ryker?" I ask him as we stand toe to toe in his bathroom.

"Because I see inside of you. I see a scared woman who needs to stop being afraid. I know I have a lot of money and my family has always been wealthy, since before I was born. But money isn't everything."

"It brings security," I say as I search his dark eyes for more.

He steps back, and I feel the absence of his energy. He takes my hand and leads me back to the sofa but he stops and leads me over to the bed. I hesitate as he sits down, pulling me to stand between his legs. Then I move in between them as he looks at me on my level.

"If your family saw you this way, would they still want you to continue what you're doing?"

"You know I've stayed away from them, just so they wouldn't see me like this, don't you?" I ask him as he moves his hands up and down my arms.

He nods and I look down. "What would they say to you, if they knew?"

"They'd tell me to stop. They'd tell me they could handle things on their own. But I want to give them more. I have an opportunity most never get."

He touches my chin and smiles at me. "Gia, you were given an opportunity most never get when you got that brilliant mind. I want to see you use it. I bet that's a real thing of beauty."

I can see myself falling for this man. This man who sees in me something no one else has. But this man, who is sitting on this bed, wants more than to see me work my mind. He wants me to work my body for him too.

"If I consult for you, do you promise to stop chasing after me?"

"No," he says, bluntly.

I smile with his honesty. "I see."

"But I will keep our work connection, professional. If you want me to." He grins and tickles my chin.

"It would be very nice to be treated professionally again. It's been three years. I've missed it." I run my hands through his dark waves and knew they'd be this soft. "For the record, I find you attractive."

"And you love me," he says then chuckles.

"You love me," I say with a giggle. "But I am with another man and I'm..."

"Not a cheater," he interrupts me. "I got it. I'm just happy you're going to work with me. I'll try not to dance around when you tell Damien about it."

"Yes, please try to contain that joy." I step back away from him as he's just too comfortable to be with. "I should go to bed. Apparently, I'll need to be using my brain the remainder of my time here."

"That you will, Gia." When I turn to walk away, I feel a slap on my ass and spin around as I gasp. "I had to. It was right there. I promise to behave at work."

SHAKING MY FINGER AT HIM, I back away to the door and give him a wave before I leave. "Good night, rogue."

"Good night, ravenous. I'll see you in my dreams."

My heart stops as I think about the dreams I've been having about him and they're sure to be glorious tonight. I hope Damien doesn't come back tonight. I can relish the dreams, for once.

Leaving his room, I make my way across the hallway and go inside the room to find Damien watching the door. "And where have you been?" He holds up my cell phone then drops it on the bed.

Well fuck!

RYKER

THE AIR IS fresh and I've never felt more enthusiastic than I do today. I got up at the crack of dawn and went to work out at the gym. I keep a suit there, just in case of overnight stays in town and am striding into my office, ready to see Gia and start this thing with her.

I can't wait to see her in action. I know she has to be even more gorgeous when her brain is firing those neurons, creating great ideas, and forging the future.

A temp is at my receptionist's desk and I wave a hello to her and stride on by then turn around. "I'm expecting a Mr. Markov and a Miss Flynn soon. Send them in as soon as they get here, please."

"Yes, sir." She makes a note of the names and I walk into my office with a grin on my face that won't go away.

I see Bridget, waiting in my office and am reminded that I need to make her useful elsewhere. "Good morning, Bridget."

"How'd it go, Mr. Crawford?" she asks as she pulls my chair out and stands behind it.

"Well. I'd like to ask you about something and I need you to be honest with me." I take the seat and find her trying to sit on my lap. "No, no." I gesture to the seat on the other side of the desk.

She looks a little bewildered as it is Friday and we do usually start the day with a bit of play but not today, or ever again. Now that I know she's not into it at all and only doing it because she's paid to.

"Honest about what, sir?" she asks as she takes a seat.

"What would you like to do with your professional life?" I ask her and see her mind go blank.

"This."

"No," I say. "You see, this is no longer an option."

"Is it because I'm bi?" she asks with a frown.

"No, it's because I have a conscience and I don't want this to go on any longer. I'm not going to fire you. I want to know what else you'd like to do here."

"I can type, I guess. I could do that. You don't like the way I..."

I hold up my hand to stop her. "It's not that. I promise you. So, you can type. I can put you into data entry. I'll make the call and you can get over there today and start. It'll be the same pay and everything. Okay?"

"Well, yes, sir. I guess so. Are you sure you no longer need my services?" She looks at me with a blank expression. "Did that Gia woman become your girlfriend?"

"No, it's not about her. It is and it isn't. Anyway, get your butt down to the third floor and ask for Cindy. She'll get you going." I pick up the phone as she leaves my office and find her turning around.

"Thanks, Mr. Crawford. You really are a good guy."

I GIVE her a thumbs up and make the call to our data entry department. "Cindy, I'm sending my personal assistant, Bridget, to you. Put her to work in your department. Her pay will stay the same, so don't bother with payroll. Treat her well, please."

After a promise that she will, I hang up and find my intercom buzzing. "Mr. Markov to see you, sir."

"Send him in." I jump up and go to open my door and great them. When I open it, I only see Damien. "Where's Gia?"

"Not coming. You and I need to set some ground rules." He moves past me and walks into my office as I stand, stunned.

I close the door and go to sit down as he's already planted his ass in a chair. "Is she okay?"

"Why in the hell would you think it's okay to have her in your hotel room?" he asks me.

"We were talking business," I say, as it's true.

"In her pajamas?" He looks at me, like he's looking right through me.

"It was late." I take my seat and square my shoulders. "She and I had a consulting deal and I'm holding her to her word."

"No, you aren't," he says and squares his shoulders too. "She's not going to be involved in this thing we have going on, any longer."

"Tonight, I wanted you two to come out to my estate. I wanted you to spend the night," I tell him as he shakes his head.

"No, that will not be happening."

"I'm having my lawyer meet us out there. He's from Sebastien, where my home is located. That's why I set it up out there. It's necessary, Damien."

"I know you want her. Okay? I know this. And I'm no fool. You think just because I am going to Mars and she isn't that I should have no problem letting her go. Well, I do have a problem with it."

"Look, I'm going to Mars too and I get your point. You want a companion while you're here. The thing is, Gia's smart. She can really be a help to the future of space travel. Let her use her brain, Damien. That's all I'm asking."

"You want to fuck her!" he shouts.

I stop and think about what the hell to say to that. *It's true, after all.*

"SHE'S VERY COMMITTED TO YOU," is all I can come up with.

"I can't trust you to be professional with her," he says and gives me a look that tells me, I might not win this battle.

"I will. I promised her that. I want to see her use that talented brain of hers. I swear that I want that more than anything else from her." I look straight into his eyes, so he knows I'm telling him the truth.

"I tell you what, Ryker, we will go out to your place for the night. If I can see you treat her professionally, I will reconsider letting her consult for you. If you flirt at all, I will not allow her to work with you."

Standing up as his words have pissed me off, I say, "Allow her? You don't own her!"

"I pretty much do. Can you act professional or not?"

"I can and will. We will all ride out to my place together. I've hired a limo for the trip," I tell him and watch his eyes glow.

"You best have your own woman, Ryker. Mine is no longer an option."

"Don't worry about me. Now, would you like to go and see the prototype that was tested?"

He gets up and follows me out. I have to admit, I've never felt more tested than he's making me feel. *And I pretty much hate it!*

GIA

THE CAR RIDE OUT to Ryker's is deathly quiet. I sit next to Damien while Ryker sits across from us and looks everywhere but at me. "So, you said you have guests at your home, Ryker?" I ask as he's been way too quiet with me.

"Yes," is his one word response.

I knew Damien was going to tell him that I couldn't take the consulting job, as we fought like cats and dogs over that last night when he caught me coming into our suite. But I didn't know he'd be this mad at me over that.

"Are they nice people?" I ask, just to get him to talk to me more.

"I hope so," he says. "I don't know them."

"Then why did you invite them?" I ask as he's very nervous and acting so oddly.

"I have my reasons," he says then opens the mini fridge and pulls out a beer. "Beer, buddy?" He holds one out to Damien, who shakes his head.

Ryker close the fridge without offering me a thing. "I'd like one, Ryker," I tell him.

He looks at Damien, instead of me but he doesn't say a word. Damien nods and Ryker hands a beer to him and he hands it to me. I take it and get the feeling Damien told Ryker some shit about leaving me alone.

Sitting back, and taking a long drink of the beer as I look out the window at the sun setting, I wonder if I like that he did that or hate it.

It's bad enough he refused to let me take the job but now he's gone and made Ryker afraid to speak to me. So, I push it further and keep talking to Ryker. "Were you mad when Damien told you I couldn't work for you?"

"Hell no!" he says, way too fast.

"Really?" I ask as I know he had to be. "I told him you'd be mad."

"Nope. He's the boss, Gia. He's your boss." He takes a long drink and I know it's to keep him from saying what he really feels.

I look at him and keep looking at him and find there's no way he'll look at me. Then I find Damien's hand on my leg. "Leave him alone, Gia."

I shut my mouth and want to knock the shit out of them both. "This is stupid," I say then down my beer. "Can I have another, Ryker?"

"If Damien says you can," he tells me as he finishes his too and holds out his hand for my empty bottle. "I'll throw that away for you."

I lean forward and hand him the empty bottle and graze his fingers as I do. "Can I have another, Damien?"

"No," he says and I sit back with a pout on my lips. I catch Ryker barely glimpsing at me and he doesn't get himself another beer, either.

SOLIDARITY, I suppose.

The rest of the ride is made in silence as Damien texts someone and Ryker stares out the window and I stare at him. I will find out what happened between them. *If it kills us all, I will find out!*

THE SMELL of the ocean comes through the air conditioning vents and I find we're turning and following the shoreline. After a while, we make another turn and go into a gate. When we pull up, the outside is all lit up and palm trees blow in the constant breeze. "Here we are," Ryker says as we pull to a stop in front of the large house.

It's nowhere near as huge as the mansion Damien and his family live in but it's big. Another limo is in the driveway and I find myself feeling a little anxious about meeting more new people.

With the way, Damien is acting, I pray no handsome, charming men are here. *He seems to hate that kind of man!*

"YOU GUYS CAN GET OUT FIRST," Ryker says and Damien hurries to get out, holding my hand, and keeping me close to him, for a change.

He must really be worried about Ryker stealing me away. I wonder what the hell they said to each other this morning.

A happy dog comes running around the corner with his tail wagging and looking happy. "Toby!" Ryker says as he holds out his arms for the large Yellow Lab.

The dog runs right past him, coming straight to me. I smile as I pet him. "Are you named, Toby? Hello, big boy." I scratch behind his ears as he licks me and paws at me for more of my attention.

I can see the exchange of looks between Damien and Ryker then Ryker says, "Come on, boy. Leave that nice lady alone."

"I don't mind. I love dogs. It's been forever since I've seen the one I had to leave behind when I moved away with Damien. Lady's a Brittany Spaniel and I missed her so much at first."

The front door opens and I look at it to find a white dog with brown spots hauling ass out of it. "She heard your voice, sweetie."

I look up and see my mother standing in Ryker's front door. "Mom?" the Brittany Spaniel jumps up and down at my feet. "Lady?"

"Surprise," Ryker says, "I flew your whole family in for the weekend."

"What the fuck?" Damien says.

"Oh, my God!" I scream as I pick up my dog and run to hug my mother. Tears are stinging my eyes as I collide with her and hug her and the dog. "I can't believe you did this, Ryker! Thank you!"

I can hear Damien as he says, "Yeah, thanks a lot, Ryker." Sarcasm isn't a thing a Russian man hides well.

Damien can be pissed but I'm not going to let that get in the way of enjoying the weekend with my family and my dog!

My twin sisters come out and join our hug then I hear my daddy say, "Leave a few kisses and hugs for your old man, sissy."

Mom and my sisters, Fancy and Nancy, let me go and I put Lady down and go to my dad. He takes me in his arms and I find myself bawling like a baby as he hugs me and whispers in my ear, "It's been too long, string bean."

And I know it has. Two years is far too long to stay away from those you love and who love you too. When Daddy lets me go, I find myself turning around and through the tears I see two hulking men standing behind me.

I move so quick, he doesn't have a chance to get away from me. Throwing my arms around Ryker, I say, "Thank you, Ryker. You've made me happier than I've been in forever!"

I kiss his cheek and then I see Damien's face as I wipe away my tears. And I know there will be hell to pay for this.

3

PART 3 - THE ABANDONED

RYKER

Gia's lit up like a firework, yet Damien still doesn't pay a bit of attention to her as she sits between her mother and father, stroking the spaniel on her lap. She's smiling bigger than I've seen her smile. Damien frowns as he taps at his cell, ignoring everyone.

"Apollo Engineering, huh?" Gia's sister, Nancy, asks me. "Are you planning on going to Mars, Ryker?"

After placing my dirty martini on the coffee table that separates the twin burgundy leather sofas in the main living area, I answer her, "I will be going to Mars. I wanted to be on the first mission my company sends but lately I've been thinking about taking a later mission. Your sister has spoken to me about being of use from Earth. I'm beginning to see I might be of more use on the ground, in the beginning anyway."

Nancy's identical twin sister, Fancy, takes over the conversation that Damien has taken a sudden interest in. *He's put his phone down and everything!* "Our little sister has influenced the likes of you, Ryker?" Fancy asks me with a surprised expression.

. . .

"SHE HAS. She's a genius, you know," I tell her and find Damien getting up from the chair at the far end of the large room, to take a martini off the tray full of them my cook delivered to us while we wait for dinner to be prepared.

"Genius is a bit more than she is. I have six, verified geniuses I employ at Markov Global," Damien says as he sits on the opposite end of the sofa I'm sitting on.

Fancy and Nancy have taken places on the bar stools at the bar to one side of the living area. With a quick glance across the table, I notice Gia is completely in another world with her dog and parents. She's paying no attention to us what so ever.

"Would you two consider yourselves to be in competition to see who can get to Mars first?" Nancy asks then sips her martini, peering over the edge of the glass at me.

With a nod in Damien's direction, I say, "We all are competitive. You have to be in the space industry. But we're helping one another as well."

"And I thought we'd be on Mars around the same time," Damien says then looks at me. "I don't see why you'd let a female change your mind about being on the first mission. The first people there will be the hierarchy of the new world, Ryker. I thought you and I were like-minded in that respect. Don't you want to secure a position of power on the planet?"

"I do," I tell him and find him seeming a bit prickly. "But I think I'd like to be sure the missions have everything they need to build on Mars too. I may have more work to do here before I leave Earth."

His icy eyes level in mine. "Are you sure it's merely for the space travelers you are thinking about and not a woman who will be left behind?"

"It's only because I want it to work on Mars. I don't want the missions to fail because of a lack of support from Earth. And on that topic, I'd like to add that Gia would make an excellent scientist to have on the ground. Since you have no intention of using her gifts at your company, you should allow her to join mine," I say and watch Damien's face go red.

"This is not the time to discuss business, Ryker. Gia can do as she pleases, once I leave. But she will be a wealthy woman and working won't be a thing she needs to do," Damien says and I see Nancy looking worried.

"Ryker, I'm sure our sister will do what she feels is right," Nancy says as she looks from me to Damien. "Damien makes sure we're all taken care of, after all. He's a generous man who loves our sister with all his heart. He'd take her with him to Mars if she'd go."

"Oh," I say as I look at Damien. "You didn't tell them about their faulty DNA?"

"Faulty?" Fancy asks.

And with the word, DNA, said, Gia and her parents look up and join the discussion. "There's no need to talk about that," Gia says then puts the dog down and smooths out her black skirt, a nervous habit I can see she has now. "Ryker, you're playing dirty. You need to stop."

Looking down like a scolded child, I know she's right. "I apologize. I'll check on how much longer dinner will be." Getting up, I find Fancy's hand on my arm as I pass by her and her sister.

"We have children, Ryker. What about our DNA?" she asks me.

I look at Gia, instead of answering her sister. "I will leave that up to you to share or not, Gia." Then I leave the room and feel a weight on my shoulders for some reason.

MAYBE IT'S because of how Damien won't let Gia do what's best for herself. Maybe I feel like I should be doing more to stop the man from squashing her. But she is the one who allows it. And now that I can see how her family is about the man, I am beginning to understand it a lot better. They all are depending on him. Their financial security is all on Gia's back and I find that unfair.

Instead of going to the kitchen, I sit at the dining table in the dark and empty formal dining room. Placing my head in my hands, I find myself feeling desperate. I desperately want Gia to find her true self and I might be pushing too hard at her to do that but I don't know any other way to get her to see what she's doing to herself.

The click-clack of high heels echoes through the hallway and into the room comes Gia, her eyes are searching and I know she's looking for me. "Ryker, there you are. I have to make this quick as Damien has excused himself to freshen up."

Getting up, I meet her in the middle of the room and place my hand on her arm. Just to touch her sends millions of tiny sparks through my body. The way her eyes move to where my hand is, tells me she feels something too. "Gia, you look lovely. I've wanted to tell you that. I looked forward to meeting with you this morning and when Damien came alone and gave me the news that he wouldn't let you work for me, I nearly came unglued."

"That's what I wanted to talk to you about. See, he was in the hotel room when I left your room and we had a hellacious argument. He gave me the chance to walk away from him last night. He told me I could leave him and go to your room and he'd never bother with me again."

"You should've done that," I say as I move my hand up her arm until I find her soft cheek and stroke it.

She leans into my touch then looks up at me with shining eyes. "But I didn't. I have more responsibilities than most. My entire family relies on Damien. And I do respect the man."

My lips quiver as they ache to touch hers. Her body is close to mine and heat fills me. Taking her hand, I take her with me to go to one of the spare bedrooms on the first floor. "Can we be alone for a little while?" I ask her as I tug her along with me.

"No," she pulls up short, stopping me. "Ryker, you have to stop this. I'm not about to go anywhere private with you. Damien and I are on shaky ground. Did you hear what I just told you?"

"I did." I turn around to face her and see a shadow moving down the hallway. Letting her hand go, I whisper, "Someone is coming."

She steps back and says, "So, when is dinner going to be ready? Daddy has to take his medication soon. He needs to eat."

"Clever," I whisper. "Soon. Come with me to the kitchen and let's get a definite time on that. We can grab him something to eat if it'll be much longer."

"Ryker," Damien calls out as he comes into the dining room. "Just what do you think you're doing?"

Great!

~

GIA

"I CAME to find out how much longer dinner will be, Damien!" I snap as he's made me mad with his accusing tone. "And I can talk to Ryker if I want to."

His eyes pierce me as he says, "That is all you two can do. You do recall our conversation last night, don't you, Gia?"

Ryker huffs and turns away from us. "I'm going to the kitchen if you two care to come."

I follow behind him and Damien takes my hand to slow my hasty retreat. "Surely, you understand why I feel I can't trust you two together. We did talk about this," he whispers in my ear. "You are a treasure to me. I do not wish to lose you."

"You won't."

LOOKING AHEAD, I see Ryker turning a corner and a light comes on. "This place is like a maze," Damien says. "So many twists and turns."

"It is easy to get lost in here. Keep your phone with you at all times, so you can call me if you find yourself lost in my home." He looks over his shoulder at me. "Or take your dog with you, she'll make sure you find your way back."

"Thanks for bringing my family to me, Ryker. Too bad the kids had school and had to stay home with their fathers, instead of coming. Maybe my next trip back to the states will have me seeing them too," I say as I miss the little rug-rats.

He pushes a door open and we're in a bustling, huge kitchen. "Connie, when will you be serving the first course?"

"Fifteen minutes," a woman near the back of the kitchen shouts out over the noise of the ten or so people who are working like crazy.

"You keep this much kitchen staff?" I ask as it seems a bit much.

Ryker smiles as he turns to look at me. "This isn't my staff. This is the staff from Per Se in New York. I flew them in for the weekend to cater to us all."

"That must've cost you a fortune, Ryker," I gasp.

One of the women working at a table nearby says, "It did."

My heart swells with all he did just for me to get to spend the weekend with my family. I want to give him a hug but Damien has a death grip on my hand.

"It's a shame we won't get to spend more than one night here, Ryker. You really should've spoken to me about it. I have to be back in Orlando first thing in the morning," Damien says, crushing me.

RYKER GESTURES for us to leave the kitchen, leading us back through the maze to get to the living area my family is in. "Gia isn't a part of any of your business. She can stay here and see her family. I'll send you back in the limo if you want."

Damien's grip tightens to the point I have to let him know he's hurting me. "Ow," I hiss at him as I shake my hand.

He eases his grip then says, "Would you want to do that, Gia? Would you want to stay here, without me?"

With a shrug, I say, "I'll be alone in the hotel most of the time anyway. I can stay here and bunk with my sisters. Like a slumber party. It'll be fun. You go ahead if you have business to see to. Although, with it being the weekend, I don't see who you're going to meet with."

"That's not the kind of business I was talking about," Damien says as we enter the living area. "My friend was feeling worried with me leaving town."

"So, you want to go back for this friend?" I ask him then pull him with me to a remote corner of the large room, so everyone doesn't hear us talking. "This friend keeps taking precedence over me for some reason. Damien, is this friend of yours a woman?"

When he glances to the side, I have my answer and walk around him, angrier than I've been in quite some time. He grabs me by my arm, pulling me back. "It's nothing you can imagine, I promise you."

Glaring at his hand on my arm, I jerk out of his firm grasp. "Then what the hell is it?"

He looks down as he whispers, "She's the mother of my only child."

It feels like a brick wall has caved in on me. I can't breathe. I can't think. *He has a child!*

"You and I need to talk, alone, Damien," I say then turn away from him and see Ryker, talking to my sisters. As I walk to him, Damien follows me closely. "Ryker, we're going to our room to freshen up. You all feel free to start eating without us. We'll catch up."

Ryker stands up and looks me over. "Are you feeling alright? Do you need anything? Medicine of some sort?"

Shaking my head, I walk away from him. "No, I just need to freshen up, that's all."

I can feel his eyes on me as Damien and I leave the room. Neither of us say a word until we're in the guestroom and he closes the door behind us. "Now you can understand things better, Gia."

I hold up my hand to stop him from going any further. "How old is this child?"

"Two," he says and I stumble to sit on the bed.

"That means you were with someone when we first got together," I say as I think about the timeline. "And you've been hiding this for three years. Why?" I look up to find him looking worried. *The man never looks worried!*

. . .

"I HAVE my reasons for hiding this from everyone. You see, my family would never allow her in their midst. She was a common prostitute. I had hired her for the night. I knew the chance I was taking when I did it. It was two days before I met you, Gia. It was a horrible mistake and I will pay for it forever. I don't take care of her for her sake but for my son's I do." He sits on the bed next to me and runs his hands over the tops of his legs.

"They are from Russia, right?" I ask as I'm not sure how much of what he told me about this old friend is true.

"They are. I keep them in a small home not far from our estate. At home, I have to keep my visits limited to the night hours when most people are sleeping," he tells me and now I know why I'd wake up so many nights to find him gone. He'd tell me he couldn't sleep and went to work early but he lied about that, I see now.

"In Orlando, you can go to them more often," I say. "And you have spent the majority of your time with them since we've been here. I get why you can't tell your family but I don't understand why you couldn't tell me. She happened before us. I can understand that. I'm not a monster. I'd have accepted the fact you had a child and I would've encouraged you to know and care for the kid."

"I just thought it would be best if no one knew about her and the boy. I have more I should tell you, so it doesn't hurt you when the time comes."

I hold up my hand to stop him, I know what he's going to say, so I say it first, "The reason you aren't taking me to Mars is because you will be taking them."

"Yes," he says, sending me into a spasm of pain. "But I need you with me until that day comes. Otherwise, my family will be on me to marry a Russian woman, the way they were all over me to do before I met you."

"I am merely a distraction for your family. I get it now."

"And you will be greatly rewarded, Gia. I take care of you very well, do I not? And your family, as well. I am giving you a future of wealth. And all I am asking is for you to stay with me until I leave for Mars, taking my little secret family with me."

"This is beyond hard to take, Damien. Do you have sex with this woman?" I look at him to try to see the truth in his eyes.

"Once a week," he tells me and I double over with a pain in my gut. "It would be cruel to leave her sexually frustrated. Don't you agree? I don't love her. But I am going to have her in my life forever. I will not see another man raise my son. Surely, you can understand that, Gia. I take good care of her but I take excellent care of you."

"Damien, this is too much for me to handle. I can't..."

HIS HANDS ON MY SHOULDERS, stop the words from coming out as he pushes me back on the bed and kisses me with a hot passion. I press my hands against his wide chest to make him get off me but he won't.

When his mouth leaves mine, his hot breath on my face makes me feel even sicker than I did before. "I love you, Gia. I will marry you. I will make you a Markov by name. I will give you all you want. Just allow me to keep my little family, my love. Please, I am begging you."

"You never had any intention of taking me to Mars," I say as I glare at him.

"You never had any intention of going," he says with a cocked brow. "Don't act like you did. And I cannot leave my son behind. And children need their mothers, Gia. What else would you have me do?"

"Marry her," I say. "Make a respectable woman out of her. For your son's sake, do that."

He shakes his head but he still won't let me up. "I cannot do that in Russia. She is a known prostitute. My family would cut me off without a cent if they knew of her and the child. I'd be thrown out of the company too. I have no idea how to be poor. I have no idea how I'd make a life for us. I just need your help for a while longer. I foresee the first mission leaving within five years. After that, you will be free to do what you want. Until then, I need you to be with me."

All I can do is stare at the man I've been with for three long years and all I see is a stranger in front of me. *What the hell am I supposed to do?*

~

RYKER

With dinner over and the hour growing late, I find everyone retreating to their bedrooms to get some sleep. More than once, I've caught Gia looking at me with a forlorn expression. She hasn't been the same since she and Damien went off to their room for nearly an hour. It's doubtful they were in the room doing anything physically stimulating!

Heading to my bedroom at the opposite end of the house from the guestrooms, I overhear Gia say, "I have to let Lady out to use the bathroom. I'll be back inside in just a bit, Damien."

"Okay, I'm going to take a shower anyway," he says and then I hear the sound of the door closing.

Heading back to the entrance room, I find Gia with her dog, Lady, just like I expected to. "Hey," I say as I step in front of her and open the door.

She nods and walks out with the dog who runs off to sniff around. "You should be in bed, don't you think?" she asks me as she leans on a palm tree near the front door.

"I think you look troubled, Gia. I think I wouldn't catch a wink of sleep if I did go to bed. Tell me your troubles, doll," I say with a chuckle then lean against the tree too. Our shoulders are nearly touching and I can feel her energy from here.

"On the upside, I will be staying the weekend here. And thank you again for that, Ryker. Really, thank you," her eyes convey to me more than her words. She is thankful.

"And how did you accomplish that feat?" I ask. "How did you get Damien to decide to stay? Or dare I ask?"

She giggles and a blush fills her cheeks, turning them a light shade of pink. "He's not staying. He will be going back to Orlando to hang with his old friend. But I got his approval to stay here. And a stern order to watch myself with you. You, my friend, are not to be trusted. Can you imagine him thinking that about you?"

"Me?" I ask with a high pitch to my voice as I press my hand against my chest and give her a devilish grin. "Oh, you can trust me."

Her eyes hold mine for a long moment then she looks away. "I bet I can."

The sense she has a lot on her mind is a thing that has me asking more, "So, why the long face?"

She touches her face as she answers, "Is it that obvious?"

"To me it is," I tell her then take her hand away from her face and hold it. "You should talk about it."

"It's not my story to tell," she says then looks away again.

"Did he tell you something that upset you?" I watch her closely and see her eye twitch. That answers my question but I wait to see what her response will be.

"Sometimes things happen that are out of our control. And sometimes we find ourselves in situations that benefit all while being painful for some. Do you understand what I'm saying, Ryker?" She looks at me with the need to be understood.

"You are the one who's being caused that pain," I say and she nods.

"But I'm okay with that. It means more to me that a certain person has someone in their life. My part in it is a bit like a martyr but I'm okay with that." She looks at her hand, the one I am holding and adds, "Damien told me he loved me. He told me he'd marry me." Her eyes move to mine. "What do you think about that, Ryker? The man will definitely be leaving on the first ship out of here but he wants to leave me here, carrying his name and fortune. I have but one, very simple, task."

"And that is?" I ask her as she doesn't look very happy about things.

"I am never to get pregnant by him and I am to remain faithful and a dutiful wife. In return, I will have myself and my entire family taken care of, forever. A cheap price to pay for such a grand thing. Don't you think?"

"You don't want me to tell you what I think about that." I let her hand go and walk around the tree to come up behind her. My hand at her waist, I whisper in her ear, "And did you tell him that you loved him?" My lips graze her ear and she shivers.

"I don't lie," she says with a sigh.

"So, the man knows you don't love him and yet he still asked you to marry him. That's unusual, isn't it, Gia?" I ask as I move my arms around to encircle her and draw her back to me. The shadows hide me, so even if anyone looks out a window, no one will see me, holding her.

She doesn't try to get out of my hold and leans her head back to rest on my chest. "Unusual and complicated, as well, Ryker. It seems I am to live my life in limbo until a way to get to Mars is found and Damien leaves this world to go to another."

"Seems kind of unfair," I say then venture so far as to leave a kiss on her neck. "Seems like you should get more."

"I'm getting plenty. I'm getting more than most have, for our deal. And that's exactly what it is. It's a deal and nothing more than that. But I will have to keep up the appearance of being a happy couple, a doting wife, a vision of what his family wants."

"I could give you more, Gia. I want to give you more," I whisper as I kiss along the length of her neck. She reaches back to run her hand through my hair as she sighs.

"Ryker, were I a lesser woman, I would give into you in a heartbeat. I hold my family close to my heart. And you are a playboy with one thing on your mind. Once you've had me, you will lose interest and I will have lost everything. If it wasn't for my family, I might risk it. You seem to push all the right buttons. Your touch is like fire on my flesh. Your lips feel sinfully sweet as you move them over my neck. And I am sure to fall head over heels in love with you, while you will have your taste of me. All too soon, you'll be moving on to the next delicious female who catches your attention."

Her idea of me pisses me off and I pull away from her. Staying in the shadows, I hiss, "Your assessment of my character isn't a thing I like."

"Am I wrong, Ryker?" she asks as she looks up at the night sky, full of bright and twinkling stars. "You too will leave this world and I will be right here. Am I to pine away for you when you go? At least I can honestly say, Damien's leaving me to go to Mars won't hurt that badly. If I allowed you to get as close as you'd like, I have a feeling your leaving would devastate me."

"You act as if you can't go. You can. I've told you, I will take you. Why do you have to be so stubborn about it?" I ask her as she's making me furious.

"You are the one who is being stubborn. It's you who is trying to force something. I've made my pact and I will stand by it." She turns and looks at me. "That's the kind of person I am, Ryker. If I tell you I will do something, then I will."

"Tell me you won't marry him," I say as I reach out for her to come into the darkness with me. The tips of our fingers touch, I maneuver them up until I have a solid hold on her hand and pull her to me. Holding her close as I lean against the wall to stay hidden from prying eyes, I find it hard to stop myself. "I want to kiss you, Gia. I want it more than I've ever wanted anything."

"But you won't, unless I give you my permission," she says as she looks at my lips.

Resting my forehead on hers, I say, "Give it to me, Gia."

"I can't. Even now, I feel my heart pounding harder than it ever has. You are my one temptation, Ryker. You are the one thing I have to learn to deny myself. For my family's sake."

"I can take care of them. I will take care of them," I tell her as the need to feel her mouth is overwhelming.

"I don't trust you," she says then I feel the dog at my feet, bumping against our legs and yapping that she's ready to go back inside.

"But you trust him," I say as I graze my lips over hers. Her sweet breath is intoxicating to me and I feel light headed and want to fall into a drunken state as I taste every inch of her.

"I do. We should go inside now. I've been too long out here."

Holding her tightly, I say it once more, "Tell me you won't marry him, Gia." I meant my voice to come out much stronger. Instead, it comes out like a plea. *I've never pleaded with anyone!*

"I'm not going to marry him. I don't have to. He merely wanted to let me know he would if I needed that from him, which I don't. I have no want to try to divorce a man who's left the planet, so I can one day marry a man I love."

Her words send me to a place of joy and hope. "Good. I'm glad you're being smart about that. You're an extremely smart woman, except where relationships are concerned."

"And I'm sorry you don't understand me. Let me go inside first, just in case Damien is waiting and watching." With that, she leaves my arms, opens the door and she and her dog go inside, leaving me alone in the dark and feeling sick at my stomach.

My head is spinning and my world feels as if it's coming undone. *If this is love, it certainly sucks!*

GIA

The touch of Damien's hand on my stomach makes it tense. Lying in bed, next to him, I'd rather be anywhere else. But he needs me, so I stay.

With a kiss to my cheek, he moves his hand lower and I see where he's headed and can't believe the man. "Damien!" I hiss at him. "Do you think I actually want to have sex with you, after what you've told me?"

"Gia, nothing has changed, except now you know the truth. It doesn't mean anything needs to be different between us. As a matter of fact, you knowing what you do and still staying with me actually, makes me care even more for you." His lips run over my shoulder as he turns over to lean his head on his hand and look down at me. "The same way I don't expect the mother of my son to go without sex, I don't expect you to, either. And seeing as you won't be getting that anywhere else, per our agreement, I am here for you. Take advantage of that."

"Look, I have no idea how you don't understand how I'm feeling right now but you are clueless, so let me educate you," I say as he does seem not to understand me at all. "The man I have thought was faithful to me has just told me he's slept with another woman every week during our relationship. The kid I can get past, the sleeping with another woman, I can't."

"Are you telling me that you and I aren't going to be having sex again because I can't take that?" He looks at me with a grin on his face, as if he's being cute. "I like your body and I like the way you make me feel." His finger trails between my breasts. "Are you going to lie to me and tell me you don't like it too?"

Measuring my words, as I don't want to annihilate the guy, I tell him, "It's a thing I find satisfying. That said, I don't feel like doing it at this time. When my emotions are all over the place with your news and I feel like crying."

His smile grows and I find him more than a bit insensitive. "You care about me, Gia. I can see it now. I mean, I knew you had to care about me to stay with me all this time but I wasn't sure how much you were staying because you liked me or if you stayed so I'd take care of your family. What you're saying now means you have real feelings for me. And that's sweet." He leans down and kisses me.

I don't stop him. I should but I don't. I can't even explain to myself why that is. I can't seem to do anything but give to this man. *Whatever he wants, I just give it to him.*

MY BODY GOES numb as he moves forward with his sex plan. I suppose he needs it to feel like we've made up. But we haven't exactly done that. I'm going to accept the fact he has a kid and another woman who will be on the sidelines while I get to take center stage, where his family is concerned.

And as he kisses me and nudges me to bend to his will, I do as I've always done and bend any way he needs me to. And for what? For the financial safety, my family gains from this?

When it ends, he rolls off me with a deep sigh. I roll over and close my eyes and try to fall asleep to end this hell of a day. Tomorrow morning, he will leave and I will be alone with my family, thankfully. I need some time to think.

I should be getting more out of this deal. Ryker is right. Perhaps I should get my own side relationship, no one needs to know a thing about. *It's only fair, after all!*

~

RYKER

"GOOD MORNING, RYKER," Gia says with a smile as she comes into the breakfast nook. "Thanks for shoving the map and note under the bedroom door this morning. I would've never found this room on my own." Her hand flows along my shoulders as she comes to take the place next to me. "The rest of the family isn't far behind me." She kisses my cheek and I find a smile moving over my lips. "Thank you again for this. You're one in a million."

"Damien got off early this morning," I say as I fill her juice glass. "Is that why you're in such a good mood?"

After taking a long drink, she places the nearly empty glass on the table where I refill it for her. "Not exactly. I just feel kind of fantastic today. That's all. Most likely it's due to you bringing my family in for me." She leans over and plants another kiss on my cheek, making me wonder what the hell happened to make this drastic change in her.

"Well, I'm probably going to make you do flips with this," I say then take her shoulders to keep her seated. "I'm taking you all to the beach today."

Her eyes go big and she claps her hands and I get another kiss on the cheek. "Thank you! You are the best, Ryker!"

"You're welcome. And I'm happy that you're happy, Gia." I kiss her cheek and find her moving at the last second and my kiss lands on her lips.

"Oops," she says as she turns her head.

I kiss her cheek and have an odd feeling that wasn't an oops, at all. The sound of her family coming down the hallway has me leaning back in my seat and in no time the small breakfast nook is buzzing with excited conversation as we all talk about going to the beach on such a sunny and gorgeous day.

Gia's nearly glowing as we leave the room after enjoying the delicious breakfast that was prepared for us. And Gia took the reins easily when I handed them to her. She made the order for what food they'd be preparing at the beach for us for dinner.

Lobsters, clam, shrimp, and Mahi Mahi will all be made for us on a grill down by the water. I foresee a moonlit stroll with her this evening. *I know I'm happy to have Damien out of our hair for the next two days!*

As HER FAMILY goes off to dress for the day at the beach, I take Gia by the hand and lead her with me on the pretense of helping me get together leashes and other things for the dogs, so we can take them with us.

"Lady's never been to the beach," she says as we look through drawers for the elusive leashes I know I have but can't recall where I put them. "I bet she'll love it."

I find a black leather collar, studded with rhinestones and hold it up, "I have **your** collar, now to find a couple more for the dogs."

She laughs and bows. "You want to me my master, Ryker?"

She's joking, of course. The fact she lets Damien rule her isn't a joke, though. I take her chin in my hand, lifting her back up to eye level. "You don't need a master, Gia. You're perfect just the way you are. No training is required."

Her lips quirk up on one side as she looks at me. "Thanks. You know, I have to say I think you're pretty perfect, yourself." Finding the errant leashes and collars has her opening another drawer and she quickly takes out a handful of leashes and holds them up while eyeing me. "You certainly have a lot of these things. You sure you're not into some kinky stuff, Ryker?"

"I've been known to dabble on occasion. If you care to come with me to my bedroom, I could show you a thing or two." I chuckle but I mean it. *If she'd go, I'd be down for that.*

"Not right now. We're supposed to be getting ready for a day at the beach, remember?" she asks as she picks out a red leash for her dog and a blue one for mine.

I follow along behind her, admiring the view and happy to know I'll soon be seeing her nearly naked. "I had something delivered to your room," I tell her, making her stop and turn around.

"What?" Her eyes sparkle a bit with curiosity.

"Something I want you to wear today. It's tiny and red and will look great on you." I push a lock of her hair off her shoulder and let my hand rest there.

"A bikini?" she asks with a frown. "Because I only wear one pieces."

"Why is that?" I ask her as I move my hand down her arm then over to her waist. "You have a smoking hot body, Gia."

"Damien..." She stops herself.

"Damien doesn't like you to wear bikinis?" I ask her as I pull her close to me. She nods and I lean in close. "He's not here, is he? And I won't tell on you. Can your family be trusted?"

She giggles and says, "I suppose you're right. Don't take any pictures, though. He'd be furious."

"And we can't make Damien mad, now can we?" I stare into her eyes until she closes hers.

"You don't understand."

"Educate me, Gia." Letting her go, she takes a step back and shakes her head.

"Maybe another time. I honestly, don't want to think about him today or tomorrow. It'd be great if you wouldn't talk about him at all. I need a little Damien-free time." And with that she turns and walks away, leaving me wondering what the hell has gotten into her.

GIA

SALTY AIR and warm sun seem to be just what the doctor would've ordered, had I went to one to get a cure for what ails me. The addition of Ryker has made it a day I will remember for quite some time.

My dog is playing with his in the gentle surf. My mother and father are strolling, hand in hand, along the shoreline. My sisters are gathering shells to take home to their kids. And I am sitting on a lounge chair under the cover of a giant umbrella. I can't recall a time when I've felt so relaxed.

"How about a walk?" Ryker walks up and asks me. "The sun's getting pretty low in the sky. A walk, on the beach, at sunset, no less. Well, I won't blame you if you accidentally fall in love with me, if you come with me."

Pulling my sunglasses up, I look right into his eyes. "What if I've already fallen?"

He chuckles and takes my hands, lifting me up. "You most likely have. Come on, walk with me. I want to delve into that brain of yours."

"I don't want to think today," I whimper as he keeps hold of my hand as he leads me to walk in the shallow water. Our bare feet make tiny splashes with each step and I find it odd how much I like the way our feet look, walking side by side like this.

"Can you imagine what it will be like to swim in water that no one or thing has ever swum in before?" he asks me and I see he's going to talk to me about going to Mars with him again.

"Ryker, I want to ask you something. And I want you to be honest with me."

"I always am," he says then pulls our clasped hands up and kisses mine. "Ask me anything."

"Is it selfish of me to want what Damien has?"

"His money?" he asks.

"Well, that and one other thing," I say, careful not to spill Damien's secret to Ryker, who would most certainly not keep it to himself.

"What's the other thing?"

"No, I can't tell you that. I just want to know if it's selfish to want the same thing your boyfriend has."

"Like, he has a motorcycle, so you want one? That kind of thing?"

I weigh that idea then nod. "Yes, he has something and I find it unfair that I don't get to have one too. If that's how he wants to be."

"Come on," he says as he stops and takes both of my hands and turns me to face him. "Tell me what he has that you want too but he won't let you have."

"Just something. I really can't say. But I have no choice except to let him keep this thing he has. If I was to get something like it, it would have to be kept a secret. I'm not a liar, so that may well be impossible," I tell him as he looks at me with an odd expression on his handsome face.

"I think it's fair for you to want the same treatment you give. I think it's fair to want things that your other half has if you want them. Is this a thing you two could share?"

A laugh jumps out of me, without me knowing it was going to happen. I jerk my hands out of his and cover my mouth with them. "Sorry."

"What would be funny about that?" he asks as he eyes me, suspiciously.

"Nothing. So, if I did get something along the lines of what he has, you're saying I wouldn't be an awful person?" I ask him to be sure of what it is he thinks.

I care about what he thinks of me. I don't want to come at him with my idea and have him think me trashy or a person with bad moral character.

"I'll get whatever it is for you," he says and I laugh again. "You're making me crazy. What is it? Is it some kind of weird sex toy?"

"No. Not really."

Taking my hand, he starts walking again and shakes his head. "So, what will I be getting you?"

"You." I leave my answer short as I have no idea of what else to tell him.

He laughs and looks at me out of the corner of his eye. "Me?"

I nod and bite my lower lip as I wait to see what he thinks about it. He looks down and doesn't say anything, making me think this was a huge mistake. So, I add, "It's just for sex, Ryker."

"DAMN!" He makes a nervous laugh and then stops. "Gia, what is this about? You told me you are no cheater and now you openly ask me to have sex with you. That is what you're asking, right? For us to have sex but tell no one about it? And just what are we talking about, once? Or is it more like an ongoing thing that we have to hide? Because I'm not into sharing. I'm not into lying and hiding, either."

And just like that, I know I've messed up. "Forget I said anything." I pull my hand out of his and try to walk away from him but he grabs my arm, pulling me back to him.

"If you've found out Damien is screwing someone else, why aren't you dumping his ass?" he asks me as he glares into my eyes.

He's furious!

I DID NOT SEE this coming at all. I thought he'd just agree to a simple affair and be happy about it.

"Because it's complicated. And you can't tell a soul. You have to promise me."

"Gia, you aren't being true to yourself. There's no good reason for him to have an affair and you stay with him. Get out of this relationship. You're not even married, for God's sake! Is it financial security? I can give you a job that will pay you a lot of money. Don't do this to yourself. End it with him."

I look at him and know I'm breaking the agreement I made with Damien by doing this but I can't seem to stop myself. "He got a woman pregnant on accident a few days before we met. She has his son. He's taken care of her and the boy but she was a prostitute and his family will never allow him to marry her. If they found out about her and the boy, they'd cut him off without a cent."

"And that's your problem because?" he asks me with squinting eyes.

"Because I want financial security for my family. It's a trade-off. I keep his family off his back by portraying his loving girlfriend or wife until he leaves on the mission to Mars. He'll be taking the woman and boy with him but his family won't be aware of who they are to him. I'll get to keep his money, making me and my family set for life and then some."

"You're selling yourself to him, Gia. An MIT graduate, a brilliant person, and you are selling your body to a man." Disgust covers his face then he lets my hand go and walks away from me.

I'm stunned. In silence, I stand and can't comprehend what just happened here. I was offering him exactly what he's wanted from the beginning. Sex with me.

How could he judge me so harshly?

RYKER

Rain has set in as I head back to Orlando. I politely left Gia and her family alone at my place and told them I had pressing business to see to in Orlando. I told her family goodbye and told her I would send a car for her and make sure she was returned to the room she shares with Damien at the Four Seasons. *I don't want to see her anymore.*

She may be brilliant but she's so broken I don't think it's possible to fix her. I've made arrangements to go out this evening with a young woman I met at a club a couple of months ago. I need someone to take my mind off Gia.

The driver pulls to a stop in front of the restaurant I'm meeting Yolanda at and I get out. I put on one of my best suits before I left my home. Gia looked at me with a sad expression and told me goodbye. She could tell I was going to go out once I got into town.

Her face is haunting me and I have to do something to get it out of my head. *She's a terrible person!*

Just as I walk into the place, I see Damien and he has his little, secret family with him, it looks like. Making quick strides to him, I decide to see what he tells me about the woman and child who are with him.

He scans the room then he sees me, heading his way. "Ryker, hello."

"Damien," I say as I gesture to the short woman who is nowhere near as pretty as Gia is. "Who do we have here?"

He doesn't falter, used to this, I suppose, as he says, "This is Svetlana and Friedrich. My good friend from back home didn't feel well, so I took his wife and son out for dinner."

The woman looks down at her son and I can see she's also used to being introduced this way. "Nice to meet you, both," I say and pat the little boy's head. The child looks just like Damien. How he's gotten away with this in his hometown with his family around, is shocking.

"And you're back in Orlando, because?" he asks me.

"I have a date I forgot about. She's meeting me here. I'm going to send a car for Gia on Monday when her family leaves. She'll be delivered to the hotel," I inform him then see my date waiting at the bar for me.

"You seem agitated," he says. "Did anything happen that I should know about?"

I want to blurt out that he turned a fantastic woman into a blithering idiot by what he's done but I can't do that, so I say, "No, the trip was long because of the rain. I felt bad for leaving my date waiting for me. I'll be staying in town for the rest of the weekend."

"I'll see you on Monday to finish hashing out our deal. You should make time to come to Russia, later in the month," he tells me.

"I will," I say, knowing I will have to see Gia now and then with this business he and I have. But I'm not liking it one bit.

WITH A WAVE, I leave and go to the bar. "Took you long enough," Yolanda says as I approach her.

"It was raining. I'm sorry. Did you have more important plans?" I take her hand and lead her to the host, so we can be seated.

"I might have. Why such short notice, Ryker?" she asks me.

I stop and pull her close to me. "I needed someone to help me get some other person out of my head and your name came to mind."

She slides her hand over my shoulder and coos, "Lucky me."

She may not feel so lucky when we're done. *I have some major aggression to work out!*

GIA

"I'D RATHER NOT, DAMIEN," I tell him as he's getting ready to go to see Ryker for a lunch meeting that he wants me to go to with him. "I just got back and I need to rest. My family said to tell you goodbye. They hope to see us soon."

"Maybe you should invite them to see us. Maybe they could do that sometime," he says as he straightens his tie. "I saw Ryker at a restaurant on Saturday night. He was on a date."

My heart falls because I had a feeling he was going out. "Oh, yeah?"

"I had them with me, Gia. He may tell you about that. That's the reason I'm bringing this up. I told him they were my sick friend's family."

"What are their names?" I ask him as I fall into a chair.

"Svetlana and Friedrich," he tells me. "I'm sure Ryker will use that to try to get at you. Tell you I'm on the prowl."

"I wouldn't worry about that," I say then look around the room for something to drink. I've spent every waking moment rethinking what I told Ryker. And in none of the scenarios did I envision him going out with another woman and seeking her attention, instead of mine.

"Was she pretty?" I find myself asking him.

"Svetlana?" he asks me.

"Sure," I say but I meant the woman Ryker was with.

"She's not unattractive. You have more beauty than she does."

"And the woman Ryker was with?"

He looks at me with a frown. "Why would you care?"

"Why not?" I ask him and get up to go to get the bottle of vodka I see on the small dining table. "Vodka, Damien? Did you bring them to our room?"

"Yes," he comes to me and pulls me into his arms. "I feel much better being honest with you." His lips touch my cheek and my stomach cramps.

"I need to go to the bathroom. I'll see you when you get back. I think I'm coming down with something," I lie and get away from him and go into the bathroom.

"I'll see you later," he says then I hear the door shut and I explode into tears.

Nothing is fair! Damien is getting everything he wants. Ryker is too. *And I'm getting nothing!*

. . .

WELL, I am getting money and lots of it but nothing else. And now that Ryker has pointed out that I'm no better than a paid whore, I feel as if I'm losing more than I'm gaining.

My hurt and anguish spin in an instant as I realize I am furious at Ryker. I head back out of the bathroom and grab my cell out of my purse and call him.

It rings four times before he answers it, "Gia."

"Ryker, why did you go and find another woman?"

"I'm a free man, Gia. Is that all you wanted to know?"

"How can you judge me? You're a whore, yourself!"

"I'm not taking anyone's money in exchange for anything of a sexual nature. If you don't like being called that, simply stop being one, Gia. Shit!"

"Did you fuck her?" I ask and can't breathe while I wait for his answer.

"That's none of your business. I have a lunch meeting with your man. I need to get where I'm going. And just a note for future reference, when I have business with Damien, I'd rather not see you."

"Ryker, you have no right to be like this! I'm nothing to you. You can't treat me this way!" I scream at him.

"You know something, Gia," he says, "You can manage to bring up an anger in you where I'm concerned but not where Damien is concerned. You should really think about that. Why do you suppose that is?"

"Because I love you and I don't love him, Ryker," I say and then end the call and throw the phone at the wall, busting it. "I love you! Damn it!"

Running to the bed, I throw myself on it, face first and cry like I've never cried before. I've never been this messed up over anyone or thing. Not even when I didn't get asked to my high school prom and that was a real boohoo-fest.

I cry until I can't anymore then I lie still as I think about what the hell I just did. Stone cold sober, I just made a huge-ass mistake of epic proportions.

I told Ryker that I loved him!

. . .

I've gone crazy, that's what's happened to me. I'm insane. *Clearly!*

Ryker is going to meet with Damien and I know he'll tell him what I said. I know he will. He's that kind of guy who will do that just to split me and Damien up. And he'll state that he did it for my own good.

I know he will!

I need to tell Damien first. That's what I need to do. But I broke my damn phone. Looking around the room, I see the hotel land line and pick up the phone. It's been forever since I used one of these and I have to really think to remember what Damien's cell number is. I finally remember it and call him.

He answers on the first ring, "Hello?"

"Damien, it's me, Gia."

"Why are you calling me from this number? Where is your phone?"

"I broke it. I tripped and it flew out of my hand and hit the..." I stop lying and think about what I'm going to say. "That's a lie. I threw it at the wall. I've done something stupid, Damien."

I hear a voice in the background say, "Is that Gia?"

"Is that Ryker?" I ask him.

"Yes, he just walked in. Why did you throw your phone at the wall and break it, Gia?"

"I'll tell you why," I hear Ryker say and I fall to my knees.

"Gia, why does Ryker know why you would throw your phone?" he asks me with a stern tone.

"I don't know what to say, Damien. This should be discussed between you and I. Tell him not to talk about it," I say and hope Ryker will do what Damien asks him to.

"I should let him tell me, Gia. Goodbye." He ends the call and my hope of telling him before Ryker does.

An odd sensation washes over me, fear mixed with relief. Damien will end this thing we have. I won't be looked at by my family quite the same way anymore. Their worlds will be turned upside down, as will mine.

Dad will have to scramble to get the farm going again. I have no idea what my sisters' spoiled husbands will do to make money. I won't have the option of working for Apollo Engineering any longer.

Getting up, I go and get my purse to look inside of it. I find my wallet and see all I have to my name is two hundred dollars. I'm broke. I have no place to go and no way to get anywhere anyway.

My eyes go to the vodka on the table and I make my way to it. Filling a small, clear, plastic cup, I sit in a chair at the table and try to think about what my next step will be.

I've never felt more alone. *Abandoned.*

It occurs to me that I should just leave before Damien gets back and we have one ugly scene. I need to pack and go. But to where?

My family is in Nebraska. So far away.

Why did I do it? Why did I say those words to him? Why would I sabotage myself this way?

I've never made bigger mistakes. I've always calculated my plans and actions and this time I went off without thinking and I've cost me and my family everything.

The vodka burns as it goes down my throat. Then the pain of it ebbs and I begin to feel a bit numb. I want this feeling. I don't want to feel a thing anymore.

I don't want to feel unloved anymore. I don't want to feel used anymore. I don't want to feel anything anymore.

How could I have gone and screwed up so badly?

4

PART 4 - THE CONCERNED

RYKER

My temper flares at Damien, who seems unmoved by what I've just told him about Gia. "Did you hear me?" I ask him. "She loves me, Damien. Has she ever told you that?"

"That's none of your business, Ryker. The fact is, she belongs to me. I have no idea what's going through her mind right now. I'd imagine you threw yourself at her, flirted with abandonment, and cajoled her into thinking she has feelings for you. Her life, for now anyway, is with me. She knows that," he tells me then sets his briefcase on the small table in a private section of the restaurant we're having our meeting at.

His blatant disregard for Gia's feelings is anything but okay with me. "You speak as if you own her, this is the second time you've said something like that. You do realize I can pay her too, don't you?"

His laugh is making me even angrier at him as he says, "She knows I will provide. Where you are concerned, I doubt she believes in you enough to take that chance."

"You've turned her into nothing more than a prostitute, Damien. How can you justify doing that to a woman of her intelligence?"

His icy eyes narrow at me as he says, "And you have just said you would do the same thing to her. Offer her money to take care of her family. So, tell me again how I'm a terrible person and you're not."

"I SAID I could pay her, I never said I would. For a moment in time, I contemplated it and even offered that to her. But since then I have taken that offer off the table. I wouldn't hand her one dime. But I would offer her a job. One that pays her what she's worth and not a penny more. You see, she needs to learn her self-worth. You took that away from her when you pulled her into your life, her and her family. You surrounded her with all you think she and they will ever need and you did it for your own selfish reasons. Love not being one of them."

He looks at me with a lack-luster expression that tells me he's not worried one damn bit about me as a rival. "You tell me why she'd leave me for you then. If you don't plan on giving her all I have, then why would she put her family in that precarious position, Ryker? The answer is, she won't."

"You have her bound to you and it's unhealthy for her." I take a seat across the table from him where he's taken one and try to get into his head. He has to have a soul in there somewhere, so I push the parent button, he doesn't know that I know he has. "If you had a child and someone was crippling them the way you have done to Gia and her family, what would you do?"

"I don't think of what I'm doing as crippling anyone. I have a vast amount of money that will be left here when I go to Mars. Someone should have it. And she is my companion in the meantime. I offered to marry her, did she tell you that?"

"She did and she told me she wouldn't be marrying you," I let him know. "Did she tell you that?"

· · ·

HE LOOKS AWAY for only a moment, letting me know she did not tell him that. "She hasn't told me one way or the other. It matters not. It's a thing I was doing to make her feel more secure. Did she tell you that I told her I love her?" His eyes cut to mine with a curious expression filling his face.

I nod. "And she told me she did not tell you those words in return. She does not love you, Damien. She is in love with me. Yet, you want to keep her. You want to keep her dependent on you. And you expect me to sit back and accept it all."

"If she wants to leave me, she can. I won't stop her. If that's what you mean. But when she finds you offer her nothing, I don't see that happening. Do you?" he asks then opens his briefcase and pulls out a ton of papers. "Here is the contract for manufacturing the boosters. This is the real reason for our meeting this afternoon. Gia was never on the agenda."

Tapping my finger on the table, I pull the contract over and begin to read it. I have to let this thing with Gia go. He's right, she won't leave him for me. Not when I will refuse to hand her or her family a damn thing. It's not that I can't, it's that it's not good for any of them."

"My lawyer will have to read this first before I sign it. I'll take it home with me and read over it then get it to him and then back to you. You will be leaving at the end of the week, right?" I ask him.

"Yes, on Sunday. Can you get it back to me by then or will I need to extend my visit?"

"I'll have it to you. But I want you to know that I'll be sending Gia a formal letter, asking her to join my team and work for Apollo Engineering as a food engineer. She will have this week to make a decision about taking the job or not. And I will not be talking to her on my own. I want her to know she has other avenues she can choose, without sex being a part of it."

His eyes close as his face goes red and now it seems I've made him angry. My offer must be a thing he's worried she will accept. When his eyes open, his color has returned to normal and his words come out clean and crisp, "Do what you want."

With a nod, I open my briefcase and put the vast amount of

paperwork the contract consists of into it and close it. "Thank you for allowing me to treat Gia like a fellow human being, Damien."

"Sarcasm is not a thing you wear well, Ryker. You and I both know she won't take the job. She has no place to stay. The money my company paid for her invention was spent long ago. Her only money is the small amount of cash I have given her. She has no car, no home, and no way to put a roof over her head to stay here. And if you offer her those things, then it will be you who is taking care of her the way you are accusing me of doing. It will be you who makes her your prostitute. I don't look at her in that light. Gia means more to me than that. You wouldn't understand, though."

"People helping people?" I ask him as I get up to leave, tired of him and this conversation. "I suppose that's how you think of what you're doing."

"It is. We're here to help one another. I can help her and her whole family. She can help me with mine. It's a win-win. We enjoy each other's company and we enjoy having sex with one another. Another win-win. I can see you enjoy digging into her. You enjoy watching her squirm with your flattery and flirting. But you offer nothing deep, the way I do. You offer her no security, the way I do. You only offer her cheap sex and a job. Go ahead, make her your offer, Ryker. I'm sure your heart won't be broken when she turns the offer down. You do have other women who tend to your needs, after all. Your heart isn't in Gia's hands."

"Your heart isn't in her hands, either." I watch him as he blinks a few times as he realizes he doesn't have anything more than a financial hold on her. "And apparently, I hold her heart in the palm of my hand. What should I do with it, I wonder?"

LEAVING THE ROOM, before he can say another word, I find him coming up behind me at a fast pace. "Get in touch with me as soon as you have the contract signed."

I nod and he walks faster to get ahead of me. He seems to be in a hurry to get somewhere. Back to his hotel room, no doubt. Back to work on Gia's head, so she won't want my offer.

It wasn't my plan to make her one. But his actions and words had me thinking she needs to know she has other things she can do. But the problem of not being able to give her a place to live and upfront money is an issue I didn't foresee. But then again, the woman is smart and I'd assume she's resourceful when she needs to be.

All I can do is put the ball in her court, I can't make her hit it!

GIA

My body being shaken, has me waking from my drunken slumber. I have no idea how much vodka I drank but I drank it until I passed out. "Gia! What have you done?" Damien shouts at me as I find it's him who is shaking me.

"Damien," I mumble as I'm still drunk. "I'm sorry." I start crying again.

He wraps me in his strong arms and holds me tight. "I didn't know you'd take this all so hard. I really didn't. I had hoped you could cope with it all. I hoped you and I were close enough for you to handle my real life. Was I wrong, Gia? Are not strong enough to handle this?"

"Strong?" I ask then hiccup.

Pulling back, he looks at me and nods. "I know you're a strong person. That's what first attracted me to you. I thought you'd under-stand what it is I have to do to make sure my son has me in his life."

"You aren't mad at me?" I ask him as I was sure he'd show up and tell me to get the hell out.

"I'm not happy with you, right now. I mean, you've obviously been seeing Ryker behind my back. But you can stop doing that, can't you? He's just a playboy. He's not ever going to be the kind of man you need. The kind of man who offers you a lifetime of security for you and your family."

"What did he tell you?" I ask as my stomach feels terrible and I hold back a wretch as my tears stop falling.

"He told me that you told him you loved him." His eyes pierce mine. "Now, I know you don't really love him. You might like the attention he's been pouring on you. The flirting, the flattering. I know, you and I, don't do that. We're beyond that point in our relationship."

"A relationship that's going nowhere," I say then burp. "I think I need to get up and throw up."

He helps me off the bed and holds me tight to his side, taking me to the bathroom. Grabbing a rubber band off the vanity counter top, he pulls my hair back into a high ponytail. "Now you won't get anything in your hair. Should I leave you?"

I NOD and he goes out of the bathroom, closing the door behind him. Getting on my knees in front of the toilet, I let it all come up. I don't know what I was thinking with drowning myself in alcohol. It didn't solve a thing and now it seems Damien isn't tossing me away like the rubbish I feel like I am.

When I get it all out, I wash my face, brush my teeth and go back to find him watching television. He smiles as I come out and pats the place on the sofa next to him.

Taking the seat, he's offered, he puts his arm around my shoulders and pulls me closer, giving my cheek a kiss. "Do you feel any better?"

"Not really. How can you be okay with what I did, Damien?"

"For the same reason, you will become okay with what I did."

"Do," I correct him. "You're still doing it."

"For my son, Gia. Only for him," he reminds me of how noble he is.

Leaning my head on his shoulder, I think about what I should do. I was set to run away from them both. Instead, I drank myself into oblivion and stayed right where I've been the last three years. Dependent on Damien and still on board with being his companion until he leaves Earth.

Only now, I know he has other obligations he's been worried

about and I also have the knowledge I am not the only woman he's sharing a bed with. Somehow, I think this should hurt worse than it does.

I'm hurt by it but I don't feel the stab of jealousy I did when I found out Ryker went out with another woman. I saw red and went out of my mind over that.

"THAT MAN KNOWS how to work women up into a sexual frenzy. He's a master at it. He did that to you. I don't blame you. I blame him. But if you continue to allow him to talk to you in such a way then I will blame you," he tells me as he strokes my arm with his fingertip. "He will never do the things I do for you. He may say he loves you but I show you that I do."

"And for that, I haven't even returned those words to you." I think about that for a moment then pull my head off his shoulder to look at him. "Does it hurt you that I care for you but I don't love you?"

"It should hurt worse than it does. When Ryker told me that you told him those words, I was a bit taken aback. But then I thought about it and I believe you merely said those words in a fit of retaliation. My news hurt you worse than you want to admit. You haven't known that man long enough to know if you love him or not. And I can tell you now, he's shallow and not a person you can count on. He's all talk and his only actions would be sexual. You're better than that and smarter."

"I am, aren't I?" I ask him as I search his eyes for the truth. "That news did mess me up. And I did a stupid thing and now that I think about it, it was because I wanted to let you feel what it feels like. But I don't need to do that to myself. I need to make this situation work."

"Do you trust me to do what I've told you I will for you and your family, Gia?" he asks me as he squeezes my shoulders.

"I do."

"Do you feel like you are selling yourself to me, the way Ryker says he thinks you are?"

"Do you?" I ask as I bite my lip.

He shakes his head. "I do not feel that way."

"I never did, until he threw that at me. He thinks I'm a whore, a paid whore, Damien. He told me that to my face."

"He's wrong. You and I know we are much more to one another than something that simple. And now I think you and I need to make this thing even deeper. I want you to meet Svetlana and Friedrich. I want us to be more like a little family. I would have much more time with my son if we could figure out a way for her to be incorporated into our lives."

My stomach lurches again and I jump up and run to throw up in the bathroom again. Damien just keeps pushing me one step further. I swear the man isn't going to stop until he has us both in his bed with him every night!

After another bout of nausea, I clean my face again, brush my teeth again and go back into the room to find him watching television, like nothing is wrong.

"Vodka doesn't agree with you, Gia. I suppose you forgot about that." His eyes cut to the side to look at me. "It's so unattractive."

"I'm sorry," I find myself apologizing. "Damien, I need to be honest with you. This thing with the other woman is a thing that's hard for me to take."

"I NEED your help and you're telling me you won't give it to me?" he asks me as he turns off the television. "After all I've done for you? I take care of your mother and father. Not to mention your sisters, their husbands, and children? And all I am asking is for you to make nice with Svetlana. Pretend you want her to be our personal maid. That way, she and Friedrich can live in our part of the estate. I can see my son every day. But you don't want to do that for me or for a young boy who needs his father?"

My stomach twists with what he's asking of me. Then I make him an offer. "If I do that, then I will take a bedroom away from yours. You and she can share a room and be what it is you will be when you leave anyway. I'll be what you need me to be in front of your family but nowhere else. I don't want sex to be involved. It's making me feel bad about myself."

"You don't care that I want you in that way?" he asks me then gets up and takes me in his arms, swaying a bit with me then placing his lips on my forehead. "I don't want to lose what we have, at all. I merely want to add to it."

"Are you telling me that one day you will be wanting to add her to our bedroom?

"No, I'm not saying anything like that. I will still keep you two separate in that way. I'm not trying to make you do sexual things you don't want to. I don't want you both at the same time, anyway."

I shudder as I think about what he's asking of me. "I am to let you have your cake and eat it too?"

"AND IN RETURN, I will leave you billions of dollars to ensure you and your family have more than a lifetime of monetary gains. I just want more time with my son. Like I told you before, I don't think it's fair to leave any woman sexually frustrated. Especially if you're asking her not to look for that attention elsewhere."

I nod, even though I don't understand entirely. I get that he's from a place where families rule over everyone in them. I get that he needs help and that he's willing to pay for that help. I get it all but I don't know if I can do this to myself.

What I was putting up with, being in a loveless relationship for my family and myself was hard enough. Putting up with a man who is sleeping with another woman may be the straw that breaks the camel's back. *Or my sanity!*

RYKER

AFTER CHECKING WITH A FEW PLACES, I've found that if Gia looks into it hard enough, she can find places that will let her live for free until she gets on her feet, especially if she has a job and Gia will have a great one that will pay her after two weeks of working for my company.

She can get on the state's food program and will be able to eat. The places that will give her shelter will also give her a free bus pass. Her life won't be that easy for the next couple of weeks if she takes the job offer but then it will be fine and she will see that she can do this on her own.

I think it will bring her to a place that's much more mentally healthy for her. Her parents have the family farm they can get back to with a little ingenuity. There are grants her parents can get from the government that I can help them find and fill out.

I'm sure her sisters and brothers-in-law can figure out how to get jobs. Surely, those men worked somewhere before Damien took over their lives, spoiling them. The whole family will be better off than they were.

Well, not financially, but they will be better off than they are now, mentally speaking. That's if she decides to turn over a new leaf. I might be disappointed in her. I most likely will. I know that. I know that chances of her walking away from all that money are slim. There's just something about her that makes me want to help her find the woman I know she's lost.

I'm sure that woman is remarkable. Smart, funny, secure!

I don't care if she never wants to get together with me. I just want to see her become the woman she can be. *The woman she should be!*

AFTER HAVING my secretary draft an invitation to interview for a food engineering position, I had a messenger take it to Gia at the hotel. I made sure she could see, she has a deadline. By Friday I will need her answer. She has five days, including the rest of today, to make a great decision that will change her and her family's lives.

Now to see if she does it...

GIA

A KNOCK at the hotel room door has me wondering who it could be as Damien goes to answer it. A frown is on his face for some reason. It makes me think he has an idea of who it is.

As he opens the door, I see a young man at it with a large manila envelope. "This is for Miss Flynn." He hands the thing to Damien and leaves, leaving me wondering even more.

"For me?" I ask as he brings me the package.

"Ryker sent it. To lure you away from me," he says then tosses it on the sofa next to me. "Here, look at it, don't look at it, I don't care. I'm sure he thinks he can offer you more than I can but can he be trusted?"

LOOKING at the envelope but not touching it, I think about how Damien will really feel if I open it to see what Ryker is offering me. "I'm sure you're right, Damien. Just throw it away. The man has caused enough trouble as it is. I need to learn how to ignore him. He has my head a mess, after all."

"That he does," Damien says and comes to pick up the thing and takes it then throws it in the trashcan near the door. "I'd like to invite Svetlana and Friedrich over to the room, so you can get to know one another."

Swallowing hard, I find myself feeling ill again but say, "Okay." *Why do I do shit like that?*

I DON'T WANT to deal with this right now. *Maybe not ever!*

BUT THE WORD just slipped out of my mouth, even though I don't mean it at all. I can't think of how I'll take being around her. I know she has a place in Damien's life but damn!

"They're just a few doors down. I'll go get them," he says then leaves.

I jump up and go to the bathroom. I look kind of crappy with being hungover already and feeling so unsettled. And what about the thing Ryker offered me? Why was I so quick to chunk it? Why did I leave that up to Damien? *What's wrong with me?*

I run back out and take the thing out of the trash and hide it in a drawer. Maybe I will look at what it is later. When Damien's not around to watch me.

The door opens just as I close the drawer and I turn to find Damien coming in, carrying a little boy who looks so much like him there's not a doubt in my mind the kid is indeed his. A short woman, plain, and looking more than a bit sheepish is following them.

Damien beams at me. "This is Friedrich."

The boy is shy and hides his face in Damien's shoulder. "He's adorable," I say as it's true. Then I look at the woman who won't look up at me. "Svetlana, it's nice to meet you."

She looks up at me, revealing dark eyes with shadows beneath them. Life must not be as easy for her as it has been for me and that makes me feel sorry for her. Hidden away, like she's been, must be hard.

"It is nice to meet you also, Gia. Damien has told me all about you and how you are helping him to keep us in his life. I too appreciate you and what you are doing. I am sorry for the conditions."

At least she understands there are hardships on my part. It's not all roses and cherries. "Thank you for understanding. This is an odd situation. And I think we can all agree this child and his needs outweigh all of ours."

Damien's smile doesn't fade as he says, "See, Svetlana, I told you, she's one in a million."

I don't feel like one in a million, I feel like a pushover. Walking away, I take a seat on the sofa and they follow. Damien coaxes the two-year-old to shake my hand and he finally does. "Hello, Friedrich. My, how handsome you are."

He nods and lays his head back on his father's shoulder and I find it sweet. And I also find myself feeling like a third wheel. If the place was bigger and there were more rooms, I'd excuse myself and go hide away from the little family that is Damien and these people.

"What you are doing is beyond selfless," the woman tells me. "I can't say I'd do the same if I was in your shoes."

"Nonsense," Damien says then gives her a stern look. "And what have I told you about talking that way?"

So, he rules over her too. *Interesting.*

"WE SHOULD all go out to dinner," I say as I get up to find some clothes to change into. "I'm starving and we might as well start being seen in public together. Once we go back to Russia at the end of the week, this charade will begin. I think it's best that way. We can say I found her here. We can say she was working for Ryker's staff and I asked her to come work for us."

"You're getting ahead of yourself, Gia," Damien says. "She has family in Russia. I will come up with a plausible story."

"He already has," she says as she looks at him with a frown. "You have not told her everything?"

"Not everything." He looks at me with a grin. "You see, I've already called home. A place has been readied for them. I told them you hired her and had her brought to us, in America, to interview her. She filled out an application at a temp agency and I answered it, under your name, back in Russia."

"My name?" I ask as I feel a bit violated.

"Yes, I wanted nothing to come back to me. So, the story is that you hired her and we will bring them back with us on the company jet."

"What does he call you?" I ask Damien as I gesture to his son.

"Mr. Markov."

I find that appalling. "Yet, he knows who you are to him, right?"

"No," Damien says then looks at the child's mother. "I am merely his mother's friend who comes around a lot and pays special attention to him."

"But when you leave to go to Mars, you will tell him the truth, right?" I ask.

The boy's mother nods. "That is when he will be told. So, you see, that's not to be talked about. You do understand."

I nod and say, "Well, with the story told to me then we can still go get something to eat."

"And you need a new cell, don't you?" Damien asks as he sets the boy down and hands him something out of his pocket, a little toy to play with.

"I could use one," I say then go into the bathroom to freshen myself up.

I can hear them mumbling and can't quite make it all out. I know she's about as happy with this, as I am. She's not keen on another woman being around her son. I can hear her telling him that I am not to get close to their son.

Damien is agreeing with her and I feel left out. Why bring me into this and make it where I have to virtually ignore a child? Why do this to me at all? *Why am I allowing it?*

I GRIT my teeth and look at myself in the mirror. "What's wrong with you? Do you think you deserve this?"

A light knock on the bathroom door has me looking at it and I open it to find Damien standing there. "She'd rather not join us. She wants to keep things very separate. I think she's afraid our son will get close to you. The same way I want no other man in his life, she wants no other woman."

With a sigh, I walk out of the bathroom, finding them gone, and say, "How is this supposed to be, Damien? Am I to ignore the kid and her or what?"

"Treat her the way you'd treat any of our maids and their children." He takes my hand and leads me out of our room. "It'll all work out. You'll see."

I'm not happy with this situation at all. But I can't seem to tell him that. I can't seem to find my voice. I can't begin to understand when I lost myself. I guess around the time he gave my family all the money he did...

RYKER

It's Wednesday and not a word has been heard from Gia. My lawyer has told me to sign the contract for Markov Global and I've done that and am waiting for Damien to show up to pick it up.

I don't have to wait for him. I could leave and go home for the day but I'm interested in seeing what he has to say about the proposal I sent to Gia. I did expect something out of her by now. I'm not sure why I did but I did.

"Mr. Markov is here, sir," the secretary tells me over the intercom.

"Send him in," I say as I push the button.

He strides into my office with a certain confidence that seems more on the cocky side, in my opinion. "Ryker."

I get up and shake his hand. "Damien."

"I see you've signed the contract. Good," he says then sits down and picks up the stack, going through each page to be sure they're all signed.

"I will be coming to your factory at the end of the month. Will that be a suitable time to see how things are going?" I ask him.

He nods and puts the contract into his briefcase. "That will be fine. I can make arrangements for that."

Walking back to my chair, I find myself bristling with curiosity. "Did Gia get my package?"

"Yes," he says then gets up. "I have a lot to do. I'll keep in touch."

Just before he walks back out the door, he just came into, I ask, "What did she think about the offer?"

"She tossed it into the rubbish bin without opening the envelope." And with that, he walks out the door, leaving me with my mouth hanging open.

She didn't even open it!

. . .

ANGER RISES inside of me so fast, I find myself throwing a paper-weight off my desk and it hits the wall, leaving a dent in it. "Shit!"

Jumping up, I begin to pace and wonder why the hell I'd even give her a damn offer in the first place. *She's obviously happy right where she is.*

SHE DOESN'T SEEM happy but she must be. Maybe she's one of those idiot savants. Clever in some ways and daft as hell in others. *Whatever she is, I'm done with her!*

LEAVING MY OFFICE, I get to the elevator bank and stop when I see Damien with that woman and kid again. They must've been waiting for him. He gets onto an elevator with them and I take a different one down.

Tailing them, secretly, I see them get into a cab and get into one too and tell them to follow the one Damien and his family got into. When I see them going somewhere to eat, I know I can find Gia, alone.

"The Four Seasons, please," I tell the driver.

I shouldn't care. I really shouldn't. I should leave her the hell alone and never think about the woman again. But there's concern building in me for her.

Can she be into something with the man that has him holding something over her head? Maybe something as sinister as killing her family?

Nothing she's doing is making any sense to me. I know I've had money my whole life but would middle-class people really go this far to ensure great wealth for them and their family?

I can't see it. I just can't. Not when her father was a successful farmer and she could be a successful food engineer. Now, if everyone was stupid, I could see it. But none of them are.

There just has to be more to it than what she's told me. *There has to be!*

. . .

THE CAB PULLS UP to the hotel and I pay him then get out. Going straight up to their hotel room, I knock on the door and finally can breathe normally when I hear her say, "Hold on a sec."

I don't say a word, worried she'll hear my voice and not open the door. When it opens, I can see by her surprised expression that I was right on the money. "Gia."

"No!" she snaps then tries to close the door. It's too late, I'm inside and have a hold of her arm.

"You didn't even open my letter?" I ask as I kick the door closed behind me.

"Let me go!"

"No. Why would you not even look at what I have to offer you?" I ask her as I shake her a bit then stop myself and let her go. I'm between her and the door, she's not going anywhere.

"I saw no reason to see what you wanted to give me. You told me what you think of me." She turns and walks away from me. She's wearing a tiny little dress that leaves nothing to the imagination and some sky-high heels.

"And where might you be going all dolled up like that?" I ask her as I follow her.

"Out later. With Damien." She stops and spins around to glare at me. "And you can see your way out, I'm sure."

"Do you know where your man is right now, Gia?"

She nods and turns away from me again. "I know everything."

Taking her by her arm, I flip her back to look at me. "And this is all okay with you?"

"No, but it is what it is," she says and I can see behind the face full of makeup that she's conceded to the man. She'll do whatever he wants her to just as long as in the end, he pays her.

"Gia, I'm concerned about you. You're too smart to do this."

She looks at me with shining eyes. Her arm is quivering and I notice she's broken out into goosebumps. Her breathing is heavy and her chest is heaving.

When her lips part, I find I can't stand it any longer. She is easy to pull into my arms and as our chests collide, I can feel just how hard her heart is beating.

She's completely still as my hands travel up her back and one takes her neck and holds her while the other moves back down and I cup her ass. When she licks her lips, I can't take it anymore and I kiss her.

She wants it too as her mouth opens for me and her tongue goes to work on mine. Her hands move up my back and tangle in my hair. She moves one foot up the back of my leg, opening her body to mine.

The bed isn't far and I move back with her until it stops us. I fall onto the bed with her and kiss her harder than I've ever kissed anyone. She wraps her legs around me as I grind into her.

Her moan makes my mouth vibrate and I can't stop myself from groaning in response. Finally, I pull my mouth off hers and find her looking at me with wide eyes. "If I take you, you will be mine and only mine," I tell her and her eyes close.

"No," she whispers. "If it has to be that way, then my answer is no."

I roll off her, madder than hell. "Gia, why? Why can't you admit you have feelings for me?"

SHE LEANS up on one arm, her dark blue dress is bunched up around her waist and her black panties are making my mouth water. She doesn't even try to get herself back together as she licks her lips. "I have admitted that to you, Ryker. You have yet to admit that to me."

"You want me to tell you that I love you?" I ask her. "And if I do then will you be mine?"

She shakes her head. "No. I belong to Damien until he leaves this planet."

"I can't have a mere piece of you. I want you all!"

"And why is that?" she asks as she pushes down one side of her dress, revealing to me one perfect, naked breast. The nipple looks as if it's pulsing and I find I'm trembling.

"I don't know if I love you yet. Do you want me to lie?" I ask her as my mouth is watering like crazy to taste that pert tit.

"I want you to tell me the truth. If you don't love me then why do you want me to yourself?" she asks me then runs her hand over her tit the way I want to run my mouth over it.

"Stop," I moan as I watch her. "I can't explain why it is I want you to myself. I just fucking do."

"You should leave," she tells me as she uncovers her other breast. "You want more from me than is mine to give. You have my heart, Ryker. When he leaves I can come to you. And in the meantime, we can play around. He doesn't need to know."

AND JUST LIKE THAT, she's pissed me off. "What has gotten into you? Put yourself away. You're making a fool out of yourself!"

She sits up and tucks her boobs back into the dress and pulls it back into place to cover her panties back up. "Ryker, you are all over the place with yourself. You flirted with a woman who was obviously with a man. You baited and tempted me to no end. And now that I'm willing to give you what you want, you want more. More than I have to give."

"Leave him," I tell her. "Leave him. Take the job I offered you."

"I can't." She gets up and walks to the dresser and pulls out the opened envelope. "I read your offer when Damien wasn't around. I suppose he told you at your meeting that I didn't read it but I did. I just didn't tell him anything about it. I'm not dressed like this for him. I knew you'd come looking for me. It was me who told him to take his kid and the kid's mother out for the evening. I feigned feeling sick."

"Damn, you're devious," I say as I'm seeing her in a light that I don't much like.

"I wouldn't say that. I'm just going out of my mind with what life has thrown at me. I need a quick fix. A roll in the hay with you might right my head again. Or it might just kill me. Either way, something changes. I'm not in control and I know that."

"You are in control," I tell her and see she is swaying in the breeze here. "You can have a job. I want you to do the rest on your own, to prove to yourself that you can."

The way she looks at me has me worried. Her chest rises and falls with her breathing. Like the process is almost too hard for her. "If you could feel the weight I carry, you might understand me better. It feels like an elephant is on my shoulders. There's not just my family to think about any longer. There's this little kid. A kid I feel so sorry for because he can't know that Damien is his father until they leave this world. All because of money."

"That isn't your problem," I tell her and go to take her in my arms again as I can't seem to stop myself from doing it. "Baby, listen to yourself. You're letting him make you think only you can help him with the shit he's gotten himself into."

"The poor kid, Ryker. This poor, little, innocent kid will live in poverty. Sure, he'll have his mother and father but at what cost? It's a few years of my life. I can handle it. I know I can. But it would be so much easier of I had you as my little hidden secret."

"I am not a man who hides," I tell her as I cradle her in my arms. "And you should not be a woman who martyrs herself for anyone. Not even a child. Has it ever occurred to you that Damien isn't being honest with you? Have you not thought about asking his family some, what if, questions to see what they'd really do?"

"He'd kill me if I did," she says and shudders. "Ryker, why can't you work with me? Why can't we just have one another and keep this all to ourselves? Please. You have no idea how much easier that would make my life if I knew I had you, in secret, but that I had you."

"You make it sound easy. But it's not. I'd go insane with the thought of him touching you. Being intimate with you. Can you tell me you wouldn't hate the fact I would be with other women too?"

Her eyes fall away from mine as she nods. "I'd hate that."

"Your quick fix isn't what you think it will be. And I know better than to do that to myself, whether you do or not." I kiss her again. Long and slow. I hold her in a loose grip, running my hands up and down her sides.

. . .

WHEN I END THE KISS, I feel more than I did before and my heart races as I say, "I do love you, Gia. Leave him."

Looking into each other's eyes for the longest time, she finally says, "I can't."

"Then neither can I," I tell her then let her go.

My heart feels awful. It' filled with love and hate at the same time. I didn't know this was possible. Each step I take toward the door has me feeling more and more weak.

"RYKER," she whispers. I stop and wait to see what she's going to say. Her hands move over my back. "Please tell me you love me again."

"Why, it won't change a thing?"

"I love you, Ryker. I will be yours alone as soon as he leaves. I can make it where he and I don't have sex at all. I can pull that off. Then once he leaves, you and I can be together."

"I'm leaving too, you forget that." I turn around and find her looking down at the ground.

Her eyes cloud and she steps back. "Oh yeah."

"Oh yeah," I say and step forward, taking her back into my arms. "We have limited time if you refuse to go too. Or we can have the rest of our lives if you'll come to Mars with me."

"I don't want to leave my family," she says. "That's the reason I won't go. I'm giving up time now, so I can have time with them later."

"Has it ever occurred to you that you should give the people you love your time now? You never know when that will be taken away from you. Your way of handling life will bite you in the ass if you keep it up."

"What are you offering me, really, Ryker?" she asks as she gazes at me. "Are you offering me marriage?"

"Marriage?" I ask as I wasn't looking that far ahead. "Can't we get to know one another better?" I laugh a little and watch her frown.

"You're a risk and Damien isn't."

"Damien is a sure thing," I tell her. "Sure, to leave you with you not knowing love for years. Sure, to leave you feeling used and abused. Sure, to hurt you in ways you can't even imagine. You think you feel broken now, wait five years."

"And you?" she asks as her hand moves over my cheek. "You are sure to do what?"

"With me, you get uncertainty. You get it in spades, baby. Will we work out? Who knows? Will we travel to a new world together? Who knows? Will we fall so madly in love that I stay here with you? Who knows? It's a gamble. I will admit that to you. I can make you no promises because I refuse to lie to you. But I can tell you that I've never felt more of a connection to anyone in this world than I do with you."

She moves in for another kiss and this one sends me to another place and time. It's soft, sensual, and the easiest thing I've ever done. Our hands flow over each other's bodies as the kiss grows deeper.

My feet move backward until I find the sofa behind me. I sit on it and put her on my lap, so I can move my hands over her pert breasts and then in between her legs.

She's warm and open to me as I move my hand over her mound of flesh that provokes me to no end. I pull my mouth away to see if she's ready to concede to me. "Be mine, Gia. Be only mine."

Resting my forehead to hers, she gasps for air. "Ryker, please. I can be yours and yours alone but I have to live with Damien. Please understand."

The pain in my heart is too much to take. "No."

Gently, I pick her up and place her on the sofa and get up to leave. I won't let her stop me this time. I can't. She's made up her mind and I can't take what she has to offer me.

"Ryker!" she shouts but she doesn't get up.

"You know what I want. I will take nothing less than that. I hope you take my advice and get up on your own feet. Stop playing martyr, stop playing victim, stop playing house with Damien. And stop playing with my heart, Gia. Just stop it all and take your life back."

Then I walk out the door and down the long hallway to the elevator. When the doors open, Damien and his little family come off it.

"Ryker?" he asks me with concern. "You look like you've been hit by a truck."

I can't even look at him or say a word to him. I get onto the elevator and push the button that will get me the hell away from them all. That man will never do what's right for Gia and God knows she won't help herself, either.

I know I should be happy I know that, without a shadow of a doubt now. But I don't feel happy at all. I feel crushed by the knowledge. Crushed that she'd do this to herself. I am but a by-product of her self-annihilation.

At least I know there's nothing I can do anymore. That should help but it doesn't...

~

GIA

LYING in a crumpled heap on the sofa where Ryker left me, I find myself in a puddle of tears, yet again. I'm so tired of crying and feeling sorry for myself.

The door opens and in steps Damien then he steps right back out. "She's a mess. I don't want Friedrich to see this. I'll come to you soon."

He comes back in and I shout at him. "Go with her. Leave me alone!"

"What did he do to you? Why did you let him in? What the hell do you have on?" his questions pepper me in rapid succession.

"Just leave me alone!" I shout at him again.

"He's ruining everything," he says then begins pacing and throwing his arms up into the air. "Three years we have managed to keep it together. Less than two weeks this man has come in and made you doubt everything we've built. You, my dear woman, are a billionaire. Your family will be taken care of forever. That was great with you, just days ago. Then he came along and you have been a wreck ever since. He does strange things to your mind."

"Yes, he does. He tells me things that are true. He tells me I'm smart. No, brilliant. He tells me I'm worthy of love. He tells me he wants me but he won't share me."

"Neither will I," he says, infuriating me.

"Yet, I must share you!"

"You've just recently found that out and it's a shock to you, I know. But the money..."

I SLAP the hell out of him and he recoils. "Damien!" I hurry to run my hand over the red mark I've left on his face. "My God! Damien, I'm sorry! I am. What am I becoming?"

"Erratic," he whispers as he looks at me with hurt in his eyes. "You need to step away from me."

I step back as he's asked me to. "I am sorry. I am. Ryker makes me crazy."

"Yes, he does. His influence on you is appalling." He rubs his cheek then goes to sit down on the edge of the bed. "I need to think about things, Gia."

I can see it running through his head. He's worried I can't stand up to the pressure of this situation and I suddenly find a river of strength that's been dormant inside of me. "You can count on me, Damien. I'll get a grip. This thing with the new woman is going all over me. I'm a mess. Ryker is pushing buttons and it's all been too much. When we get home, things will even out. I can pretend I don't know a thing about Svetlana and your son. I need to act like that, anyway, don't I?"

"We need to get you home sooner rather than later. I don't think Ryker will ease up on you. Not the way I saw him looking. He's fallen for you." He gets up and walks into the bathroom as he rubs his cheek.

My heart pounds like crazy in my chest and I wait to see if it will hop right out and leave me, chasing Ryker down.

He's fallen for me!

. . .

How can I leave here? How can I turn my back on him?

I have my family to think about. Ryker said it, himself. He's a gamble and Damien isn't. Ryker isn't promising me a damn thing and Damien is. I have to get back to my life in Russia with Damien.

He walks out of the bathroom. "The only way this is going to work is if you never see him again. Once I'm gone, I don't care what you do. Until then, you will stay away from that man. He will have to come to Russia at least once. At the end of this month. When he is coming, I will send you to see your family. I don't want you two in the same place ever again, until I am gone. Do you understand me, Gia?"

"Yes," I say and fall to my knees as I look up at him. "Thank you, Damien! Thank you for not giving up on me. Love is fleeting and financial security is forever. Thank you."

His face is stern as he looks down at me. "We will need stricter rules. I'll need your cell and you will only be allowed to call your family when I'm around to make sure that's who you're talking to. Agreed?"

I nod. "Yes, agreed."

"Get it for me. I want it now. You are weak, where he's concerned."

I get up off my knees and hurry to get him the phone, he just bought me, from my purse. "Here," I say as I hand him my phone.

"I'm sorry I'll have to be so strict with you. This is too important not to be. My son is at risk."

"I understand. I do. I never understood more than I do right now. Ryker is making me something I'm not. When I give my word, I mean it. I never go back on it. I gave it to you. I am yours until you leave. Whatever that entails."

"Yes, whatever that entails. Now, it means you must ignore the fact of what I will be doing under the roof I share with you and my family. You must only think of the money and not your foolish pride."

The term, foolish pride, echoes in my brain. Is it really that, I'm feeling? I don't think so. I think it's more than pride. But I'm not about to argue with Damien about the words he's used. *Not after all I've done.*

. . .

"GO WASH YOURSELF. I'm going to make the arrangements to leave as soon as possible. I have to go to help Svetlana get the things together. You can handle getting our things together. I'll be back soon. I can't wait to leave this place and that man. It's amazing the change he's made in you in such a short amount of time. I can honestly say, I never saw this coming from you. You're always level headed and business minded."

I nod and watch him leave as he shakes his head in confusion. I too am confused. Why would I let anyone get in my way of what my goal has been?

Secure the wealth then let my real life begin. That's been the plan since Damien told it to me.

As I go to wash away the makeup my tears have ruined, I have to face myself in the mirror. Turning a blind eye to the weak-ass person I'm looking at, I wash the black trails of mascara off my cheeks. The smudged red lipstick, Ryker helped to destroy, is washed away too.

My stomach clenches when I see a red lip imprint from his lips after he kissed me and got my lipstick on him. Across one cheek, the mark is there. Perfect and memorable.

I fall against the wall, my back to it. Staring at the place on my cheek, I close my eyes and relive the kisses, the touches, the feelings I've never had before and may well never have again.

His touch made my body hot and liquid in an instant. His mouth on mine felt like I was attached to an electric socket that filled me with its energy. Only it was Ryker filling me with something I didn't know existed. *Raw power and what has to be love!*

BUT IF IT'S really love I feel and that he felt as well, how are we walking away from it? It is rare, isn't it?

Filling the sink with cold water, I plunge my face into it. I have to stop thinking. I've kept my brain shut off for three years, what's five or so more?

When I come back out of the water, I dry my face with a hand towel and feel my mind has gone quiet. It took some time to silence it in the beginning but I must've gotten used to it. I can do it again. It shouldn't be a problem. All remnants of the man who has messed up my head are gone. I see no traces of him and with no traces, I can put him out of my mind.

I step out of the bathroom and freeze as I see him standing in the middle of the room. "I will not give you up without a fight."

"Ryker, we're leaving. All of us. I have to get away from you."

"I won't let you go."

"Ryker," I whisper as he falls to his knees.

"Stay. Please, stay, Gia." Tears fall from his dark eyes and I don't know what to do.

"If Damien comes back in here and finds you, I don't know what he'll do," I tell him as I stay right where I am.

"I'm not afraid of him or what he'll do. I'm deathly afraid of you leaving with him and me never seeing you again."

"It's been less than two weeks, Ryker. We're being delusional. We don't love each other."

"We do," he breathes out. "I've never been more certain of anything."

"I'm going with him. I've made up my mind. I've been weak, where you're concerned. I have to stop being weak."

"You are being weak where he's concerned, Gia. It's not me, it's him who is baiting you, leading you, manipulating you. It's him, not me."

My mind is spinning and a part of me wants to run into his arms and go away with him. But that part of me knows better than to do such a thing to my family.

"I'm sorry, Ryker. You have to go. We're leaving soon. I'm going to Russia with him. There is nothing you can say or do to stop that."

"Marry me. I will make sure you and your family are always taken care of," he says and for some reason, it makes me furious.

"Get out! Get the fuck out, now! You've called me a whore for what I'm doing for Damien, yet you want the same damn thing. Get out and leave me the hell alone! I never want to see you again!" I spin around and go back into the bathroom and lock myself in. I won't come out until Damien comes back in and he can deal with Ryker.

I hear the door close and peek out to find the room empty and then I wonder how the hell he got in here in the first place. Damien is right, we need to leave quickly. Ryker has designs on me that border on psychotic.

5

PART 5 - THE REACTOR

RYKER

Wafting trails of smoke dance around the dimly lit bar I've found to drown my sorrows in. Gia is leaving and there's nothing I can do about it.

"Another shot, mister?" the bartender asks me as he picks up the empty shot glass.

"No, I think a nice large glass of bourbon with a splash of Coke is in order. I need to erase someone from my brain. You're a professional, do you think that will do the trick?"

The pale barkeep chuckles as he goes to get me what I've asked for. "It sounds like it might work." I watch him fill the glass with ice then pour the amber liquid over the clear cubes, making them crack and pop. Fissures are left behind, marring what were perfect blocks of ice. Adding a touch of coke, he brings the drink to me and places a straw on the bar next to it. "So, who needs to be erased?"

"A female who has given away her soul, so her family will never have to worry about money again." I take a small sip of the liquid that's still warm despite the ice.

The skinny man pushes a bowl of peanuts toward me but I

merely look at them, not taking any. "I know who you are, Ryker Crawford, CEO of Apollo Engineering. And I know you are planning on being on the first mission you're able to get going, out of here. So, what do you care if some woman has sold her soul to make sure her family is well off?"

"I shouldn't. I know this. But she's a brilliant person and she's squandering her gifts. And she's leaving true love behind for the sake of money." I take another sip then pick up a handful of peanuts.

"You are her true love?" he asks me as he sweeps away some dust that came out of the bowl as I picked up the peanuts and I place them on a nearby napkin, instead of eating them.

"I am. And she's admitted her love to me. But she's still going to be with the man who will see to her financial security."

"You're a rich man, yourself. Why not offer her what he has?" he asks me as he makes his way to serve another patron who looks to be enjoying themselves as they tap away on their cell.

"I did and she got mad at me. But, I can't blame her for that. I did kind of let her know I thought it was wrong of her to let the other man buy her like that. I'm at a loss with this woman. She has me turning myself inside out over her."

As he comes back my way, he says, "You should stop doing that. She's going to do whatever it is she wants to. It sounds as if you need to let it all go."

I nod and take another drink. The alcohol isn't burning my throat anymore, the numbing action has set in and I feel unsettled still but that's begging to wane. "I should let it all go. I should be thinking about better things. More important things. I have more to do than most."

LOOKING AT THE GLASS, I find I've drank more than half of it and I should stop while I'm still functioning. Placing a hundred on the bar, I get up and give the man a nod then leave the bar and walk out into the sunlit day that's went on as I've wallowed in self-pity.

People walk up and down the sidewalks as I watch life go on. And

I know my life will surely go on without Gia in it. But I'd love it if she'd never leave it.

Walking toward my office building, I find my mind wandering and the thought of making a fuel out of corn moves in and settles there. The fuels we're working with now are burning at a fast rate. Diesel is the slowest burning fuel but we need to add more to it, to extend it even further. The addition of a corn, biofuel might be the key. The missing link!

My steps increase with my excitement and I hurry to get to my office and my computer to research the different types of corn that could be used to make the new fuel. As I step off the elevator, I get an idea.

Johnny and Donna Flynn!

GIA'S PARENTS! They have farmland that is lying dormant but has been kept fertilized for a few years. That land would be perfect to try out a new breed of corn!

Getting into my office, I quickly turn on my laptop and get busy looking up information about corn and its use as a biofuel. Then I make a call.

"Hello, Ryker," Johnny Flynn answers his phone. "How are you doing on this fine day?"

"I'm doing fine, Johnny. I was thinking today about corn and you happen to have an unused farm that might just help me to develop a crop that could be used to make what we'll need to get us to Mars. What do you say to me and some of my engineers making a visit to your place to see what we can do with it?"

"That sounds exciting," he tells me. "When would you like to come? As you know, we're wide open."

"This weekend sounds good to me. And I want you to know this could be a very profitable thing for you and your family. If we get the results I think we might. Can you handle that?" I ask him and wait to see if he's as dead set on not using his brain as Gia seems to be.

"Do you really think so, Ryker?" he asks me and I can hear a bit of nervousness in his voice. "I wasn't doing so hot with my farming before."

"This will be different. Your crops will be in a contract. We will buy the product at a specified price, no matter what. You see, it will be our engineered seeds that make the corn. You won't be expected to make anything, we will do that and take care of all the work that goes into raising the crops. We'll lease your equipment and employ the people you trust to do the work the right way to ensure a healthy crop."

"By God, I think I'm loving this idea, Ryker! I really am. This sounds exciting and to be in on the Mars missions is a thing that'll go down in the history books. Count us in, son. You come on up here to Nebraska whenever you want to. We have a big old farmhouse, we can put you and up to ten more people up while you're here. Donna and the girls will love cooking for you all. So, don't you dare think of booking yourselves a motel? You hear me?"

His hospitality is overwhelming and I find my heart is pounding with his generosity. "Will do, sir. Thank you. I'll be in touch later today to let you know the whole plan. This is exciting!"

"It is. It's not the money I care about but being a part of the process to get people to another planet that has me so enthusiastic," he says.

"I know money isn't an issue for you. And this may well ensure it never is, Johnny. Talk to you soon. Bye." I end the call and have a river of energy flowing through me.

IF THIS CAN HAPPEN, Gia's family can depend on themselves to make a legacy and financial security all on their own. Eliminating, at least, that weight. I don't know how long she'll see Damien's illegitimate son as her burden to bear but at least the major one may soon be lifted.

And now I think I need to fix the damage my emotions have caused. I've never had any trouble keeping my head on straight before. I can't blame Gia, entirely for how I've acted. I need to make amends with her.

Calling her next, I wait to hear her shriek at me or curse me. "Ryker?" Damien answers her phone. "Gia isn't a person you should be calling."

"I had something I wanted to say to her. I'd like it if you gave her the phone, please." I tap my finger on my desk as I wait to see if he'll do as I've asked.

"No," he says, very simply and it makes me mad but I hang onto my temper.

"Damien, I know about your secret family. I don't want to let your secret out but if you keep me from speaking to Gia, I will."

"She told you?" he asks me as if that's inconceivable.

"She did. So, give her the phone or the media will get wind of what you're hiding," I threaten him.

When he hangs up on me, I look up the phone number for one of the local television stations. He will not get away with what he's doing if he expects to take Gia down to do it.

GIA

AFTER A SHOWER TO clear my head, I've started packing and have gotten my head back on straight. This nonsense with Ryker got out of control and I feel much more put together.

The door to our hotel room opens and Damien strides in, tossing the cell phone at me. "Call Ryker and see what the hell he has to say. You told him about my son. He's threatening to go to the media about it. I don't know why you did that but it will be up to you to fix it."

I catch the phone and feel frozen inside. "Damian, I..."

"Save it. Call him and hurry up about it. And be nice."

His pacing is making me nervous as I find Ryker's name in my contacts and call him. "Gia?" he asks as he answers the phone.

"It's me."

"Ask him if he's called the media yet," Damien directs me.

"I heard him," Ryker says. "Tell him I haven't yet."

"He hasn't yet, Damien," I relay the message. "Ryker, why would you threaten that?"

"I'll do whatever I have to, Gia. But that aside, I didn't want you to leave thinking about how we left things. That's not who I am. I think you and I are kind of a mess about one another. I don't like to think of myself in that light and I'm sure you don't like it, either."

"I don't like it at all," I tell him as I watch Damien take a seat, visibly relaxing with the information that Ryker hasn't played that card yet.

"Glad to hear we're on the same page about this. I wanted you to know I called your father..."

"You did what?" I ask him as his words have sent a chill right down my spine.

"Not about you," he assures me. "About making a special crop of corn to use as a biofuel. I wanted to tell you about that before you left for Russia. I also would love to have your input on that but I won't force your hand about that. If you do have any idea or knowledge about corn being used in conjunction with other fuels, I'd really like to have your help with this. If we find something that will work, it will mean we're that much closer to getting a mission underway."

"I see. Well, thank you for asking but I'm afraid I'll have to leave myself out of that."

"Out of what?" Damien asks me, suddenly looking nervous again. "Give him what he wants. Gia!"

Putting the phone on mute, I hiss at him, "He's not forcing me to do it, Damien. Chill out!"

HE GIVES me a harsh look then says in a low voice that has a lot of menace behind it, "You will do as he asks. You are the one who told my secret and you are the one who will have to accept the consequences of that. It means you are in that man's hands now, just as much as you're in mine."

A shiver runs through me at what he's just said. And I have to shake my head to clear it, then answer Ryker who's calling out, "Gia? Are you there?"

Taking the phone off mute, I answer him, "I am here. Sorry, I accidently hit the mute button. About your offer, can I think about it?"

Damien narrows his eyes at me, letting me know he expected me to take the offer. But I'm not about to fall into Ryker's hands. Damien has no idea how hard it is for me.

"You can. And I don't even need you to be here. You can simply help by emailing me your findings. I know you want to be with Damien," he says and I find that odd because he knows it's not what I want, it's what I have to do.

"So, I can work from Russia?" I ask him and nod at Damien who nods back. "I can do that."

"Great," he says. "I'm going to your family's farm this weekend. It's a shame you're leaving so quickly. It'd be great to have you there."

I look at Damien and relay that information. He huffs then says, "You can go. I will stay here with my son and his mother. We will all leave, once you get back. He has us over a barrel. We have to do what he asks."

I MUTE the phone again to say, "Damien, he doesn't sound like he's threatening anything. He's asking and being very cooperative."

"He's going to get what he wants. You don't see it but I do. Go with him to Nebraska, Gia. There's no other choice, no matter what he's telling you."

Taking the phone off mute, I say, "Ryker, Damien thinks I should go with you to my family's farm, so I will. You do understand this is strictly business, right?"

Damien pulls his hand over his face then gives me another dirty look along with a scowl. *He's pissed!*

.   .   .

"Yes, I do realize that, Gia. Thank you. This is for the better of our people, after all," he says. "If it's okay, I'll call you this evening after getting with some more of my engineers. I'll bring by a consulting contract for you to sign this evening. Or better yet, I'll send a messenger with it."

"You do that, bye," I say and end the call to deal with Damien who seems furious. And he's right to be. "I am so sor..."

"Don't! Don't say you're sorry, Gia! You have me by the balls." He gets up and starts pacing again and I cringe and move to sit on the edge of the bed.

"It's not me..."

He spins around and is up in my face, his words are hot on my face as he says, "It is you. You gave that man enough information to ruin me. Completely! And it will be you who caters to his every want where you're concerned. It will be up to you to make nice with the man, so I don't lose everything. Because if I lose it all then so do you. And your family will as well."

"I don't think I like the way that sounds, Damien. An hour ago, I was to never talk to him until you leave the planet, now it sounds as if you're saying if he wants me in his bed then I damn well better get my ass in it."

Gripping my chin, he speaks through gritted teeth. "That's exactly right, Gia. You've put yourself into a precarious position by running your mouth. Telling business that was not yours to tell. And spare me the attitude of prudish concern for being taken by the man. We both know you want it, anyway."

I shy away from him as I move further back up on the bed to get away from him. "Not like this," I say. "Never like this. Not with your downfall being held over my head. I hate this. I never meant to get you in this position."

"Everything has to be rethought," he says as he steps back. "You may have ruined it all."

A sudden pain shoots straight into my heart. "Damien! What do you mean?"

When he looks at me, it's as if he's looking right through me. "I mean, I can't afford to step on his toes where you're concerned. The thought of you being with him and me too, isn't a thing I can take."

"Damien, I can make this work. I can! Let me try. Don't drop me."

"I can't drop you. I still need you. I just don't want you sexually if he insists on having you that way." He looks at me with disgust and it makes me mad but I hold my tongue.

"He's not that kind of man. He'd never want me like that as he holds something over my head for it. You have nothing to fear. I'll stand by our deal, Damien. I will."

"I have a lot to think about and I need to tell Svetlana that we're not going anywhere just yet. We'll have to unpack and that will take a while. You stay here." He walks out of the hotel room, leaving me with a mess in my head.

My phone is lying on the bed. I am now at Ryker's beck and call, thanks to my mouth. And Damien's constant security I've grown to rely on, seems to be skating on thin ice.

Now, what am I supposed to do?

RYKER

Feeling much better about things, I make the call to Johnny Flynn to give him the great news that even his daughter will be attending our meeting. "Ryker?" he answers the phone. "What did you come up with?"

"Johnny, I have great news, Gia is on board as a consultant with Apollo Engineering now. I've just received the signed contract back from her and we're all set up to leave on my jet on Friday. We'll be staying two nights with you and I will have seven in the party. Is that going to be too much on you?"

"No, not at all. And you said Gia has signed on with your company?" he asks, sounding surprised.

"She did," I hold up the contract in my hand the messenger just returned to me. "Isn't that great?"

"It's surprising," he says. "She's never worked since she and Damien got together. I though he didn't want her to."

I'm sure he didn't. "I managed to sweet talk him into letting her do it if she wanted to. It seems she wanted to work. She's brilliant, you know."

"SHE IS. And it's going to be good for her to work. She didn't act like the same old Gia when we spent the weekend with her. Thank you for that, by the way."

"I think all Gia needs is to use that brain of hers again and that girl you knew will be coming right back to the surface. She's just buried her true self to morph into what she thinks Damien wants. But Damien can take her for who she really is or he can move on," I say as I run my finger over her signature at the bottom of the contract.

"Move on?" her father asks. "Is that something that might happen with her taking this job? I don't want to interfere with anything between them."

"I didn't mean it the way you took it. They'll be fine," I say but I'm pretty damn positive they won't. And they shouldn't be. Gia shouldn't be a pawn in the man's ploy to distract his family from what he's done. "I'll have a car bring us in from the airport. See you around five or so, I'll call you when we hit the ground."

"Great, bye."

With the call ended and all my plans settled, I sit back in my chair and put my hands behind my head. Things may work out after all. Putting one's mind to work and shoving emotions to one side really works much better than living on emotions alone.

GIA

DAMIEN HAS LEFT me alone most of the time in the last two days. His disappointment in me isn't an easy thing to take. I find myself feeling like a child who has misbehaved when he has come to see me for shorts amount of time.

I asked him if he wanted to end it all and he told me he didn't. He said he needed me and I am to still play the part of loving girlfriend, even though he doesn't wish to touch me anymore.

Deep inside, I feel like I did what anyone would do, being put in that position. People need to vent, every once in a while. It's been years since I've vented about my situation with him. When you add in that he's been unfaithful the entire time and is using me as a cover, well, I had to vent!

But to tell Ryker was stupid. I could've talked to my sisters about it. I told Ryker for my own selfish reasons. And now my selfishness is going to bite me in the butt.

My cell rings and I see that it's Ryker's new assistant, Tony. Ryker, himself, hasn't spoken to me. He's let others do that for him. He's keeping things very professional. I like it but then again, I don't.

BEFORE I CAN SAY a word when I answer the phone, Tony starts talking, "Miss Flynn, I hope you're having a pleasant day. I'm calling to let you know a car is being sent to get you and take you to the airport where the company jet is waiting. You need not bring a thing. Like I told you on Wednesday, Apollo Engineering is providing everything. Your uniform has been tailored to the measurements you gave me. The other women have been asked to gather their hair into a neat bun. We do expect paparazzi at both airports as this is an open topic. You are to wait for the driver to bring up one of the uniforms to you, so you can wear it. You will be expected to wear the uniforms you are given for this entire, two-day meeting, excluding bedtimes, of course."

"I understand, Tony. I'll see you soon," I say just before I get off the phone.

It feels odd talking to Tony instead of Ryker. I feel very much a part of the group but not a part of Ryker. I find I miss him. More than I should. The man is my boss now. I should put my feelings for him, away.

When my cell rings again, I look at it to find it's Ryker and my heart jumps. I swipe the screen. "Ryker! Hi!"

"Hello, to you too, Miss Flynn." His voice is deep and smooth as it falls on my ears that missed hearing it so much.

"Miss Flynn?" I ask as I look in the mirror to make sure my makeup still looks right.

"I like to keep everything very professional during company outings when the press is around. In private meetings, I'm more lax. So, Miss Flynn, you will call me, what?"

"Mr. Crawford. I get it, Ryker. Professional." I find a smirk moving over my lips and try hard to stop it. *It's just so damn good to be talking to him!*

"GREAT," he says. "See you on the plane."

Before I can say another word, I find he's ended the call and a knock comes to my hotel room door. "Miss Flynn, I have your clothes," a man's voice calls out from the other side.

Going to the door, I open it and take the black garment bag. "Thank you. You can come in and take a seat while I change."

The man nods and comes inside. I retreat to the bathroom to put on the clothes. In the privacy of the bathroom, I unzip the bag and pull out a skirt that looks to be knee length and pencil shaped. A military type of jacket is to be worn with it. The letter, A, is embossed on the silver buttons of the rust colored suit and the Apollo emblem is on the left side just above the pocket with my last name embroidered on it.

A small black bag is in the bottom of the bag and I pick it up and untie it to find a matching rust colored bra and panty set. Picking up my cell, I tap in a text to Ryker.

-I see you felt compelled to send me lingerie.-

He texts back right away.

-Not me, my assistant. Didn't he tell you the company would be providing everything? That includes your underwear, Miss Flynn.-

. . .

My cheeks heat with embarrassment and I don't text back as I feel like a fool. It seems he intends on treating me professionally. Like we never meant a thing to one another.

The thought has me feeling sad but as I get dressed and look in the mirror, I find a woman looking back at me that I haven't seen in years. A real professional. The uniform makes me feel like part of a team. A team with a huge mission on its hands. *A mission to get to Mars!*

∿

RYKER

Sitting at the back of the cabin, I watch Gia as she comes aboard. Her dark hair is slicked back into a tidy bun, just like the rest of the women I have on this team.

Tony hops up from his seat at the very front and quickly introduces her to everyone as he leads her back to sit across from me. She was the last to get here, meaning we'll be leaving soon.

Looking at my tablet, I pretend not to notice her as she shakes everyone's hands and greets them. I can see a rosiness to her cheeks that's been missing. Her smile is confident and so is her grip.

It's been such a short amount of time but I see something inside of her shining brightly. She's in her element. For the first time in years, she's where she belongs.

I offer her a curt nod as Tony says, "You'll be sitting here, Miss Flynn. Once we're in the air, drinks will be served. Do you have a preference?"

"Red wine," she says then I cut my eyes at her.

"Try something different, Miss Flynn. Something you might have wanted to try for some time and just haven't yet. Tony was a bartender while he went to college. I made sure we have a full bar on board for him to work with."

Her eyes dart to mine, as she asks me, "Any suggestions?"

I look at Tony and nod. "Give her some ideas."

"How does aged rum, ginger, and vanilla sound to you?" he asks her.

She smiles at him. "Very good."

"Then I'll bring you a drink called, Midnight Oil." When she nods, he leaves us and goes back to his seat, just as the pilot comes over the speaker to let us know we're taking off.

"It's a pleasure to be working with you, Miss Flynn. I'm looking forward to it."

She nods and smiles, shyly. "I look forward to working with you too, Mr. Crawford."

WE PUT on our seatbelts as we've been instructed to do and I find myself thinking about her and I, leaving on the first mission to Mars and how I wish she'd consider it. But I hold my tongue. I'm determined to treat her with respect and let her see how that feels. I know she'll like it.

She seems calm as we start to taxi down the runway, so I ask her, "Are you okay with flying?"

"I am. Damien and I fly a lot."

"Of course," I say, forgetting about that.

With her looking the way she does, professional and part of my team, I seem to be forgetting that she's with the man. And I'm kind of glad to see that happening.

I want to reach out and hold her hand but I push that urge down and close my eyes, doing what I do many times when we're taking off, pretending it's a rocket ship. Once we level off, I open my eyes and see her looking at me out of the corner of her eye.

"You like to think about going to Mars more than you like to think about anything else," she says.

I nod. "That's true."

"And anything anyone can do to help you see that dream come true makes you pretty happy," she says as she smiles at me.

"Very happy, Miss Flynn. Having you with your exquisite brain on my team is a Godsend."

PINK FILLS her cheeks and she looks away. "I hope I don't disappoint you."

"You won't." I reach over and pat the back of her hand. "I know you won't."

A flash of anger moves through her eyes as she looks at me and whispers, "Is that because you have me over a barrel?"

I'm surprised by her actions and words and shake my head as I whisper back, "I don't have you over anything. I asked you to join us in this endeavor because I need your expertise and I thought you'd like to be a part of something. Especially since it's your family farm that will be included in this. If you thought I meant to use what I know if you didn't accept my offer, you're mistaken. I used that threat only to get to talk to you. I won't be using it anymore."

Her eyes go soft and she whispers, "I'm sorry I said that then. I had the wrong idea."

"Most likely because it was planted there," I say as I think about Damien and his influence over the poor woman. "I want you to know, I believe in you. That's why I asked you to come work with us."

She nods and looks down at her hands then smooths out her skirt and bites her lower lip. I know she wants to say more but she's stopping herself. This isn't the time or place to get into any of our personal business and she knows that.

Tony starts serving drinks and conversations start to pop up as everyone begins to loosen up and move around a bit. The young woman, sitting in front of me, turns to look at Gia. "Mr. Crawford told us about what you invented. I think that's fantastic. I too am into the food sciences. Hence, my presence on this team. He also said it's your family's farm we're going to be using. Do you, by chance, know what the soil samples have in them?"

Gia lights up as she begins to tell the other scientist about what kinds of things her father has used to increase nutrients in the soil that's gone unused for three years. I sit back and enjoy how animated and excited she is about this and I know I did the right thing by using that threat when I did.

It may seem unethical but I don't give a crap!

GIA

Sipping on some coffee after eating Mom's homemade apple pie for desert, I find myself feeling more than I've felt in what seems like, forever. Sandra, Tabitha, and I have formed a special team, within the team, to research everything we can about corn and its use as a fuel.

Dad is talking to Ryker and some of the other men about the machines he uses to do what he does with the soil and the crops. While my mother and sisters take care of cleaning up after dinner. I offered to help but was quickly told by Ryker that I was here on his team and he expected me to work with his other scientists on this visit.

To the side, he told me he'd bring me back anytime I wanted, to make a normal visit with my family. I love that he did that. I'm a viable asset to the mission, is what he told me. It made me feel pretty damn special and I haven't felt that way in a very long time.

"What if we infused nitrates into the seeds?" Tabitha asks as she writes things down on a tablet in front of her.

"It could be done," I say as I lean forward and tap into my tablet and bring up a site that shows every part of the seed there is and just how others have engineered them before. "I think I can get us some time at the local co-op. I worked there one summer when I was in high school. The old men there have more knowledge than we'll ever get out of the internet."

The girls hold up their hands for high-fives and I give them what they're looking for. Our attention goes to Ryker as he stands up and announces, "Bedtime, troops. We'll get at it again at first light."

Murmuring is all I hear as everyone gets up and heads to the bedrooms my mother doled out to us all. I got my old room, of course. Before I head out, I go to find myself a bottle of water to take up to my room and find Mom in the kitchen.

"HEY, MOM," I say as I come in. "Thanks for doing all of this."

She nods then I see her gesture behind me and find Ryker is there, which I didn't know. "Apollo Engineering is paying us well to host this conference. No thanks are necessary."

"You are?" I ask Ryker as he moves past me to get a bottle of water himself.

He reaches into the fridge and pulls two of them out, handing me one. "Apollo is," he corrects me. "This is business, Miss Flynn."

Mom laughs at him calling me that and she shakes her head as she leaves us alone in the kitchen. "Goodnight guys. I'm headed to bed."

We both say our goodnights to her and I open my water and find Ryker looking at me as he takes a drink of his. "I think I like you calling me that," I tell him as I turn to head up to bed.

"Good," he says as he follows me. "You liked today, didn't you?"

"I have to admit that I did. I liked it very much. I never said I didn't like to work or use my head, Ryker."

"YOU JUST DIDN'T DO IT," he says as he moves up the stairs one step behind me. "I'd like to make sure you know that you have a place at my company, Gia. If, for some reason, you decided not to go back to Russia, I could advance you your first month's salary. Our human resources department could help you find an apartment, there are several really nice complexes that give our workers discounts on the rent. And you would be issued a company car, as a traveling consultant."

"That's a lot to think about. But I will think about it, Ryker," I tell him as I stop at my bedroom door. "This is me."

He smiles as he looks at my old bedroom door. "Did they leave it just how it was?"

I nod. "Would you care to see how teen me lived?"

"Would I?" he chuckles as I push the door open, revealing lavender walls with pink accents.

"Don't touch my collection of my little ponies, Ryker, they're priceless to me," I tell him as I laugh and we walk into my old bedroom.

"There's a lot of fluffy pink material on that bed, Gia. One could get lost in there," he says then goes to sit on the bed and looks surprised when he is enveloped in the goose feather mattress. "Whoa! You really could get lost in here."

"The winter nights can get cold," I explain about the mattress. "That helps you stay warm. And in the warmer months, it does the opposite, making the bed cooler." I watch him as he tries to escape the thing and reach out to help him out of it. "One rolls out of this kind of bed."

Once I have him up, we stand toe to toe and I find myself wanting to kiss him, so I back up and walk to where the suitcase is. "Are there even pajamas in here?" I ask him to help me think about other things.

"There are. Apollo PJ's." He comes up behind me as I find the top and pull it out.

"Rust colored again and little planets all over it. Sweet," I say as I hold it up to me. "And it'll fit too."

"Just like everything else. We run a pretty tight ship. How do you like everyone?" he asks me and I find a grin taking over my mouth.

"I really like everyone. I'm going to miss them when I have to leave." I toss the top on my old dresser and find the bottoms that are black. "Why black?"

"To represent space," he says as he takes them out of my hands and places them on the dresser too, then I freeze as he pulls me into his arms. "Gia, I want nothing more than to treat you like I do everyone else but I'm finding that impossible, now that we're all alone."

My heart pumps and bumps and sputters as he holds me close then rests his forehead on mine. "Maybe this was a bad idea."

"It was," he says then lets me out of his arms. "I shouldn't have come in here. I wouldn't do that with any of the others. Goodnight, Miss Flynn. I will see you bright and early. Put on your sleeping cap and in the morning trade it out for your thinking cap. We have much work to accomplish."

I wave as he leaves me. "Night, Mr. Crawford." He smiles at me just before he closes the door behind him and I find my body aching for him while my mind is forming a new kind of respect for the man.

As I STRIP out of my Apollo uniform and put on my Apollo pajamas, I can't stop humming with happiness. It's fantastic to know Ryker still wants me. Even after our horrible fight and all we said to each other, he still likes me and the man respects me now. A thing I know he didn't before.

But then again, I'm not so sure I respected myself the way I should've. Climbing into my old bed, I feel at home. My eyes close without a problem and I find sleep is close by and I feel better, more secure, and happier than I have been. Since I made a life with Damien, that is.

RYKER

"I DON'T KNOW what any of you guys think but that damn rooster is an idiot and he's mentally living in another time zone, it seems. He went off way before dawn," I say as I sit down at the breakfast table.

Gia laughs then says, "That kind of sound is what you will most likely wake up to in the mornings on Mars, you know." She moves around behind me, placing a cup of piping hot coffee in front of me. Her breast barely grazes my shoulder as she does and it sends heat all through me.

I want to grab her and pull her onto my lap and give her a good morning kiss but the uniform she has on reminds me of why she's here and I give her a nod, instead. "Thanks for the coffee, Miss Flynn."

"You are welcome, sir. My mother said to tell you all the eggs are nearly done then breakfast will be served," she takes the seat next to mine and I can smell her clean, fresh scent wafting into my nostrils and making me have a hard time thinking.

"Miss Flynn, since you grew up here, do you know how to drive any of those big machines we saw in that barn out back?" one of the men asks her.

She smiles and nods. "I can probably get my father to show you how to drive them if you guys want."

A COUPLE of the younger guys nod enthusiastically and I look back to see Gia grinning like crazy. Again, I am reminded just how in her element she is with all of this.

As her sisters come in, bringing platters of food with them, I watch Gia as she starts to get up to help. I touch her arm as I say, "You're with us."

She nods and looks down and smooths out the skirt of her uniform. "I keep forgetting."

"You'll get used to it," I tell her and then I realize my hand is still on her thigh and I move it.

And I have to get used to treating her with the same respect I treat everyone else who works for me in a professional sense. Nancy gives me a pat on the back after she places the platter she carried, on the table. "Morning, Ryker. How'd you sleep?"

"Like a baby, Nancy," I say and find Gia gasping. I turn to look at her. "What's that for?"

"It's just that you knew that one was Nancy. Not many people can tell my twin sisters apart," she says as she looks a little stunned.

"I'm not most people," I remind her.

SHE NODS AND NANCY SAYS, "Damien has never been able to tell us apart."

With a nod, I get her reaction now and am not surprised to hear that at all. Leaning over I whisper, "Has he called you?"

Shaking her head, she whispers, "I told him not to while I'd be working. He distracts me."

"That he does," I agree. "Smart of you, Miss Flynn."

"I thought so," she says then she ventures further as she looks around the long table at the other members of the team. "How do you all put your relationships out of your mind to do your work?"

"I don't have one," one of the younger guys says as he laughs. "That's my secret."

"I don't put mine out of my mind," Tabitha says as she looks at Tony who is sitting across the table from her. She gives him a wink. "But while we're working, I treat him like the coworker he is."

Tony smiles at her and winks back. "Vice-versa."

"I had no idea about you two," Gia says and I find her eyes going to me. Then she looks away.

I caught that look. The one that says, maybe that could be us someday. And I think it could be if she'd ditch the man who's keeping her for his own selfish reasons.

"There are quite a few couples in our industry who are in working relationships with their better halves. They all maintain professionalism while at work," Sandra tells Gia.

"I see that now," Gia says.

Nancy chimes in, "Gia's boyfriend doesn't think that way. He's kept her cooped up."

.   .   .

GIA BLUSHES and looks angrily at the table in front of her, I'm sure she's furious at her sister for revealing too much about her personal situation. But Sandra saves her by saying, "Well, she's out of the coop now. Miss Flynn is going nowhere near that coop anymore, we won't let her."

Gia's blush disappears as she realizes her coworkers like her and like working with her. A smile moves over her face as she says, "You guys are great. I have no want to go back to the coop. And I won't be."

My heart does a bit of a dance as I wonder what that really means. *Is she done with him?*

EVERYONE BEGINS to make their plates, passing around the platters but all I can think about it what Gia is talking about. If she's dumping him, I'm going to throw a party!

"So, are we going to that co-op after breakfast?" Sandra asks Gia.

"If you want to, we can," she says then turns to look at me. "I'm sorry, unless you have other things you want us to do, Mr. Crawford."

"No, that'll be fine. Find your niche and explore it. That's what we're here to do. Figure out things then go back into the office on Monday and share our ideas and how we can put them all into action," I say then take a bite of bacon.

"Monday?" she asks and I nod. "I'll just make sure the other women have my notes. I have to leave for Russia on Monday morning."

I nearly choke on the bacon as I thought she just said she wouldn't be cooped up anymore. She pats me on the back as I cough then she picks up my juice glass and hands it to me. "You should drink this."

Taking the glass from her, I take a sip to calm myself. "That bacon went down the wrong way."

She smiles, clueless as to why I had the choking fit. "You should chew more," she says then turns her attention back to her plate.

I'm not sure how to ask her without sounding whiny. With her, I can't always trust my voice to come out with authority the way I can with everyone else. So, I keep my question to myself, for now.

With breakfast finished, we all go our separate ways but not before I tell everyone to meet right back at this table for lunch at noon to discuss what we've accomplished.

As we all walk toward the front door, I find Gia walking next to me at the back of the pack and place my hand on her arm. "Can we talk sometime today? Alone?"

SHE LOOKS at me with a bit of worry in her expression. "You sure that's a good idea?"

"Not really," I say. "But I need to talk to you."

"After lunch?" she asks me.

I nod and we get out the door, parting ways as she and two of the women go with her on their fact-finding mission. I follow her father with the rest of the team to check out the soil.

Her head is held high, her confident demeanor is radiant, and she is still going to leave this all behind her and go back to Russia with the man who took this all away from her in the first place.

The thought goes flitting through my head that I could easily stop that. She told me she thought I was going to tell the media what I know about Damien's son to have a power over her. Which I know I could do.

But should I do that to get her to make the right decisions? Or would that make me just as bad as Damien is?

"Ryker," her father calls out to me. "Come here, son. You're the only man I trust with something this precious of mine."

He's talking about one of his many tractors but his words bring back into my mind that Gia is also a thing he holds precious to him and I decide to let her make her own choices without my interference.

If this is meant to be then Gia will come to her senses and decide to stay. Maybe I need to commend her more to make her see just how essential she really is to us.

Maybe I need to let her know that she has me in more ways than one.

GIA

The day was so full and busy that Ryker and I never had a free moment to talk about whatever it was he wanted to talk about. And even though I know this is most likely going to test my self-discipline, I'm heading to his bedroom to see if he still wants to talk to me.

With a quick tap on his door, I whisper, "Ryker?"

The door opens and he's standing there in just his PJ bottoms, looking sexy as hell and I turn around to leave. *If I stay, I'll throw myself into his arms!* His hand on my shoulder stops me. "What did you want?"

"Um, uh," My train of thought went right out the window as my libido took over. "Never mind."

Gently, he pulls me into his room and closes the door. "Gia, what is it?"

"Could you put your shirt on? You're very distracting," I say then close my eyes, so I can't see him anymore as heat courses through my entire body, settling in the intimate area, I'd like to see him be a part of.

He chuckles with a deep sound and moves away from me. "There, you can open your eyes now."

I sigh as I feel both relief and sadness at the same time as I see he's put the pajama top on. "Thank you. I'm trying hard to make changes in myself. I don't want sex to rule me, where you're concerned."

"We haven't had sex," he reminds me.

"Yeah, I know that. It's just," I stop and shake my head. "Let's talk about something else. What did you want to talk to me about, this morning at breakfast? We never had time to talk."

He takes my hand and pulls me along with him then sits on the bed and I have to sit next to him. "I'm feeling concerned about you. You seem to be very happy doing this with us, yet you plan on going back to Russia. I told you all the company would do for you and you want to leave, anyway. I know you have your deal with Damien. Here's the thing. He can't make you go with him. You have options, where he's concerned. You can keep your deal with him about his money and you can make appearances in Russia to do that, while still working with us."

"He'd never go for that," I say as I know he won't.

"He would if I told him to. I think you know that," he says as he takes my chin in his hand. "But I would only play that card if you wanted me to. I'd much rather you take the option of letting him and his money go. You see, your family will have financial security with this project. If we can make fuel out of what your family grows, they will make a ton of money. And so will you. My scientists are some of the top paid people in this industry. Gia, you are qualified to get that huge pay too."

"His son," I say and know he doesn't care about that at all.

"I get it. I do," he says. "But he really isn't your concern."

I nod and know he's not my concern. "Ryker, you might think I'm crazy but I'm afraid. I'm afraid things might not work out in this industry."

"Things will work out in this industry. That aside, Gia, there are no promises in any world. There are always gambles. It's the people who work hard and can accommodate themselves in any situation, who have fruitful lives. And I want you to know that I have more to offer you than just a career. I want you to know that you have me too. If you want me, that is. If you want time alone, I can give you that too."

"I have you?"

He nods. "You hold my heart in your hands, Gia. I'll walk through fire for you."

"You would?" I ask as I've never known a man who'd do or say that. As he nods and moves in close, I recall that he's leaving when he can and I put my finger up to his lips. "But you will leave me."

HE SIGHS and stops trying to kiss me. "We can see what the future holds. I want to go to Mars and you don't. But what about our time here? What about we take this time and see what happens?"

"I'll tell you what will happen. I will never want to leave and you will. End of story. And when you go, there is every chance your company will begin to decline and all who work for it will go broke. Now, I'm not saying I might not change my mind someday about Damien and his money. As a matter of fact, he and I have had a parting of the sexual ways and there may be more parting to come."

He stops me with his finger on my lips as he asks, "You two aren't having sex anymore?"

"Thanks to you," I say and give him a smile. "And I'd like to say, thanks, to you for that. I haven't wanted him at all since I found out he cheated on me this whole time. But he was adamant that we would continue with our physical relationship too. Once you threatened him, his tune changed quick and in a hurry."

"What does he think?" he asks me. "I mean, what does he really think?"

"He thinks you're holding his secret over him. He told me I was to make nice with you and do anything you say to." I watch him go pale and he moves to the floor on his knees and takes my hands.

"Gia, I never want you to think you ever have to do a thing with or for me. I really only meant that threat to get him to let me talk to you. I'd never threaten you with a thing. I swear that to you."

Taking one of my hands out of his, I run it through his hair. "I know that now. I didn't ever think you'd do such a thing. I know you're a better man than that. But you know Damien isn't a man to be argued with. He told me that he knew you'd want me to have sex with you and he told me I had to do it if you asked for it. Then he said he couldn't touch me if he knew you did, so he wouldn't be touching me anymore. Which is great with me."

"Let him go, Gia," Ryker says with a tremble to his voice. "Please. I don't care if you want me or not. Just let that man go. I can't imagine anyone telling a person they care for to have sex with anyone, to save their own ass."

"And I am seriously considering it. But I must go back to Russia this time around. I have to see how things are. I have to do this for me. For my sanity."

"Are you, at the very least, telling me you won't be having sex with him?" he asks me as he stays on his knees.

"If you don't mind it," I say. "I'm thinking I'm going to tell him that we did have sex, just so he'll stay with that idea of not touching me."

He laughs and says, "That's cool with me. Just so you know, though. You and I aren't going to be doing a thing unless you and he are over."

"You know something, Ryker, I thought you were just being controlling at first. But I can see now that you're deep. You're so deep that you're not looking to do a thing except help me be me again. And for that, I have tremendous respect for you. So much respect that I'd never want to be with you without ending things with Damien first."

His eyes close and he lets out a breath as he takes my hands and holds them to his heart. "You have no idea how good that is to hear, Gia." When his eyes open I can see how glassy they are and it makes my insides melt.

"You do love me, don't you?" I ask him as I can nearly see the love that glows around him.

"I do," he says with a nod. "And I've never known this kind of love before. Gia, everything I've done lately, is for you. There's not a thing I've done without you at the forefront of my mind. That's how come I know that something will work out for us in the long run. I have not one fear about that."

"My only real fear is that you will try your best to bend and shape me into doing and being what it is you want," I tell him, finally being honest with myself.

He looks down as if contemplating what I've said. When he looks back up at me, he says, "You may well be right."

Biting my lip, I know I'm right. "So, you see, there's not a hell of a lot different between the two of you."

"No, you're wrong," he says as his grip on my hands grows tighter. "You see, I will never force you and I will always keep watch over you. If I think you're caving to me, I will stop what I'm doing. I want you to do whatever it is you want in this life. But I want us to spend at least a piece of this lifetime we have, together."

"That's almost like a proposal, Ryker. A very sweet and honest proposal and I wish like hell I had my shit together already. But I don't."

HE NODS and lets my hands go then gets up and stands in front of me. "So, I will be waiting for you until you come to me or tell me not to wait anymore. In the meantime, I will keep you to your contract with Apollo Engineering. I get you for a week out of each month. So, you go on back to Russia if you want to but I will see that gorgeous face at least once a month."

With a smile, I get up and make my way to the door. "If I was completely out of this thing with Damien right now, I'd be all over your ass, Ryker. You're caring ways have me flowing hot."

"Then you better hurry your hot ass out of here and lock your door because it's taking everything I have to hold myself back from throwing you over my shoulder and taking you to the bed and showing you just what you mean to me."

I giggle but when I turn back around to look at him, I can see that lustful look in his eyes and the laughter stops. "Oh, you're for real!"

"I'm for real. Run, baby," he growls and starts moving toward me.

Part of me wants to run right into his arms but the part of me with what's left of any morals that are trying to come back to the surface, turns and I go out the door, run to my bedroom and lock the door behind me.

Falling back on the closed and locked door, I laugh then hear a thud on the door behind me and the door knob wiggles. "Damn!" I hear him say.

Resting my head on the door, I want to open it more than I've wanted anything. "Goodnight," I whisper.

Then I know he's still there as he whispers back, "Goodnight, Gia. Can I hear you tell me the words?"

"I love you, Ryker."

"Yes," he hisses. "And I love you, Gia. With my whole heart and soul, I love you. Make the right decisions, baby. Make the right ones with me in mind, please." Then his steps can be heard, walking away and I walk to my bed.

Sleep might come or it might evade me but one thing is certain, I have to make some drastic changes to my life. For my sanity and Ryker's, my mind has to be made up and that has to happen sooner rather than later.

6

PART 6 - THE DEPARTURE

S tepping off one jet to get right back onto another, I look over my shoulder to find Ryker wearing a frown on his handsome face. Looking forward, I see Damien has stepped out onto the stairs to look for me.

Sandra and Tabitha come up on either side of me, Sandra whispers "You hurry back to us, Gia. We really need you."

Tabitha pats me on the back. "You're the major brain in our trio, Gia. Please do hurry back to us."

"Gia," Damien shouts as he waves at me. "Come, we need to be on our way."

"I'll try," I tell them as I quicken my steps to get to Damien.

"Gia!" comes a shout from Ryker as he hurries to get to me. I jerk my head in Damien's direction to see what he thinks about this and find him frowning. "I need to tell you one more thing before you leave us."

I stop and wait for Ryker to get to me and find him taking my hands in his and looking at me with more than a bit of fear in his dark eyes. "Ryker, you know this is going to get me into trouble with Damien."

"Good," he says then grins. "Gia, I want you to be confident. I'm not going to ever use the information I know about Damien's son. Don't let that affect your decisions. No matter what Damien thinks, I'm not that kind of person."

"That's great to hear, Ryker. For the record, I knew you weren't."

"Gia, promise me you'll come back soon." He looks into my eyes and I see the worry in them.

"I'm going to see about things. I'm not making you any promises. The only one I will make you, is that I will be returning next month as the contract states I will."

He nods but my words have done nothing to comfort him. "Don't let him treat you like shit."

"I won't."

"You say that but you've always allowed it," he says then pulls me very close to him. So close, I'm afraid he's going to kiss me.

"Ryker," I say but it does no good.

HIS HANDS LET mine go as they move up my arms. I should step back but I stay right where I am. My body tingles with his touch and when he takes my face between his hands, I melt into him.

Our lips touch and a fire rips through me. *I'm kissing Ryker Crawford in front of his employees and Damien!*

THE WAY his thumbs rub my jaw has my lips parting for him and he comes right on in, like an old friend. Our kiss is long and speaks to me just as clearly as any of his words could possibly do to make me see what he feels for me.

I can hardly breathe when he ends the kiss with light pecks. "I love you, Gia. I don't care who knows that. Come back. Whether you come back to me or not, just come back."

I can't talk as I look into those sad, dark eyes of his. I nod and turn away from him. Tears blur my vision as I walk to Damien's jet. I wipe them away as I walk up the stairs and find him still waiting at the top of them.

"That was going too far, Gia," Damien hisses at me. His hand closes around my upper arm then he jerks me inside the plane.

I see Svetlana and Friedrich sitting in the back as Damien manhandles me to a seat in the front. He, not so gently, pushes me down to sit and I look up at him. "You need to stop with the physical shit, Damien."

Leaning over, he whispers in my ear, "You and I will be going into the bedroom as soon as this plane is in the sky and you will learn who you belong to, Gia."

My stomach knots then it quickly goes away. "No, we won't. I don't belong to anyone. Not anyone, Damien. I'm going back with you for my own reasons. None of them have to do with you."

"Do you really expect me to give you what I leave here, if you don't do what I ask of you?" he asks me as he takes the seat across the tiny aisle from me and belts himself in as the plane is readying for takeoff.

"I'm not going to talk to you about that right now." I close my eyes and lie my head back to rest as the captain speaks in Russian over the speaker system.

"You seem confidant," he says then makes a huffing noise. "Let's see how long that lasts. I will be reminding you of what I have to give you."

"Yes, the palatial estate in Russia. The mountains of money."

"The jewels, the cars, the purses, and shoes. The designer clothing, the fancy creams and lotions. All those things you now have are really mine, Gia. You came to me with the clothes on your back, which are long gone now. I promise you, you will not leave with any more than you came with."

I open my eyes and level them on his. "I bet I will."

His right eye twitches a bit. "He has turned you completely against me, hasn't he?"

"You have done that on your own." I lie back and close my eyes again in an attempt to keep my relaxed composure.

. . .

MY STOMACH IS DOING a dizzying dance of knotting up then relaxing as my body goes between full on panic and trying to keep control of my emotions. I will not go back to the weak woman I have been these last three years. But it's an internal battle that's going on inside of me.

"We will talk, you and I," he says as the plane starts to take off.

"Yes, we will," I agree. "I will talk."

"Your head is held high now," he says under his breath. "But how it will soon fall."

My heart clenches as I fear what he's going to do but then it eases as I tell myself, he can't do anything to hurt me. He only has the power I give him and I am no longer going to give him any.

I can hear poor Friedrich crying as we make our ascension into the sky. His cries stir my soul and I feel terrible about him and what he came into. But he carries the genetics that make up Damien too. I'm sure, as he grows up, he will have that same strength the whole family of Markov's possess. And I remind myself, he is not my burden to bear.

My family is not my burden to bear. I have but one and that is myself, for now, anyway. One day, there may come more people into my life that I hold dear enough to make sacrifices for. These people are not them.

Spending time with the team has taught me loads about life. I was hellbent on taking what Damien offered me and making sure my life as well as my family's was stable, secure, and one of great wealth.

I spent the weekend with people who are striving to make it possible to leave this planet, with all of its material things, to go to a place with nothing. Sandra was talking about doing a camp out once and thinking it was hard and she'd never want to do more than a couple of days of living like that. But she wants to go Mars, where living will be a hundred times harder than camping anywhere on this planet is.

I suppose that's where I'm at right now. I thought I couldn't do without the money Damien would be leaving me. I thought my family could never make it without that security. But I'm about to leave that security blowing in the wind as I take off to another place. A place of uncertainty and hard work.

There's never been a time that I felt so close to the brink of disaster and I love it in this place. There will be no wobbling back and forth, where Damien and his money are concerned. I'm set on the path I have planned out for myself.

Two men will not be happy about what I've chosen to do but I will have to learn how to deal with men who are unhappy with my decisions.

~

RYKER

IT'S BEEN two weeks since Gia left with Damien to go back to Russia. And she's not contacted me even once. I've given her space and left her alone but my heart is aching to hear her voice, so I'm calling her on the pretense of work. While the work day is over, being it's six in the evening here, it's just beginning in Russia, where it's eight in the morning.

"Gia Flynn's assistant, can I take a message?" a young woman asks me as she answers Gia's cell.

"Uh," I stammer as I have no idea what the hell is happening or who this is. "This is Ryker Crawford."

"Oh, yes. Mr. Crawford, Miss Flynn has a consulting contract with your company, Apollo Engineering. What may I do for you today, sir?"

"Can I speak with her?"

"She's in court today. That's why I have her cell. I'm not sure when she'll be out. I will leave her a message to call you. Is this an important matter that needs immediate attention, sir?"

"No, not really. She can call me back whenever she gets time. Where is she?"

"I'm not at liberty to give out that information," she says with quipped words. "Will there be anything else, Mr. Crawford?"

"Is she in the states or Russia?" I tap my finger on the desk, as not knowing is making me crazy.

"That is not my information to divulge."

I TURN on my charisma and charm to see if I can get more information out of this tight-lipped woman. "You sound pretty. Mind me asking where I might find you? It's nearly lunch and I've yet to find a lunch date. Maybe you..."

"Sir, I am well aware of your relationship with my employer. If you would refrain from speaking to me in a flirtatious manner, that would be appreciated. Also, I am quite smart and am completely aware that you are seeking information about my whereabouts so you can obtain Miss Flynn's. She will be given this message when she gets out of court. Good day, sir."

"Good day," I say as she ends the call.

WELL, I'm not stopping there. I call her father to see what he knows about his daughter and her whereabouts and why she's in court. "Ryker," her father answers. "How's it going, son?"

"Great here. How about with you, Johnny?"

"Fine, just fine. Did you get those soil samples back yet?" he asks me.

"Still waiting on them. I needed to make sure you emailed your banking information to payroll, so they can set up the direct deposit for you."

"Yes, that was done already," he says.

"How's Gia?" pops out of my mouth.

"Good, I suppose. I haven't talked to her since you guys left that day. I thought she was working with you, Ryker. You should know how she is."

"I haven't talked to her since that day, either. Do you know if they made it back to Russia?"

"Well, now that you're saying something about it, no. You don't think something's happened, do you? A plane crash!" he says.

"No!" I stop his bad train of thought. "No, I talked to her assistant. She's fine. Alive, no crashing. It's just that I don't know where she is."

"Her assistant?" he asks. "Your company gave her one, or what?"

"Or what," I tell him. "She must've gotten one on her own. I called to discuss some business with her and the lady who answered her phone said she was in court. And I suppose you don't know anything about that, either."

"No, not a thing."

"Well, okay then. I guess I'll have to call Damien. I need to set up the dates I'm going over there at the end of this month, anyway."

"You do that. Let me know what's going on with my baby girl. We've gotten used to not knowing anything or hearing from her for months at a time since she's been with Damien. It sure was nice to get to see so much of her while she was in the U.S. this last month. Thanks for that, Ryker."

"Yes, sir. You're welcome. I'll let you know what I find out. Bye." I end the call and make the next one to Damien.

His cell rings and rings then goes to voicemail. So, I call his office phone. "Markov Global, Mr. Damien Markov's office," a secretary answers.

"Is Damien in?" I ask.

"Not today. He is out for the entire day. May I take a message?"

"Let him know, Ryker Crawford called to set up the dates for my visit at the end of the month."

"You can give me that information," she says.

Crap!

"I would but I needed to see what's good for him," I say, stalling to get to talk directly to him.

"All days are good for him," she says. "So, give me your dates."

Taking the calendar that's in the top desk drawer, I pick the last three of the month and she sets me up but I still don't know a thing about Gia. Hanging up the phone, I don't have anything else I can do.

This is sure to drive me nuts!

GIA

My heels click along the marble floor as I make my way out of the court hearing. The sound of men's shoes, coming up behind me, has me wanting to run but I maintain my steady gait.

"Gia, wait," Damien says as he catches up to me. "You won the case against my company, and rightfully so but what does this mean for us?"

I stop and look at him with a stern expression. Then wait for my lawyer and the one for his company to pass us by before I say a word. "Tell me who, us, is?"

He points to me and then himself. "You and I."

"Oh, I have to ask because you have two of us. Tell me what I mean to you, Damien."

"You mean security to me the same way I mean that to you and your family."

"I don't mean the world to you, do I?" I ask as he looks at me with confusion riddling his handsome face.

"I don't know what you mean. I need you and you need me."

"Not anymore, I don't. Not since I'll be getting what's fair for my invention that I sold much too cheaply to your company. I'm about to be a very wealthy woman, and I've done that entirely on my own. No help from a soul. So, please tell me what it is you and I have."

"I need you," he says then looks down. "It's me who needs you to portray my girlfriend. You know that. So, I am asking you, will you still be doing that for me and." He stops and looks around to make sure no one is around us. "My son, needs you too, Gia. Don't forget about him. He needs this more than I do."

.   .   .

"THAT'S SUPPOSED to pull at my heartstrings, isn't it?" I ask him as I smile. "It's not accomplishing what you intended it to. Sorry, Damien. That deal is off. No hard feelings, I hope. I'm sure you can find another woman to fill my role in what's left of your life, here on Earth. Mars will mean different things for you. And I wish you and yours, the best. My assistant will be helping me pack my things later this evening. I will be staying until I've made arrangements back in the states. My assistant is also going to be staying too. I've made arrangements with your mother about that already."

"And you think I'm going to allow that?" he asks me as he pulls himself to stand up straight and tall.

"I know you will, Damien." I offer him another smile and walk away from him. "See you at dinner."

HE HURRIES to catch up to me. "And you told my mother what?"

"That you and I are parting on amicable terms." I stop and face him. "She told me she was glad to hear that. Want to know why?"

He looks at me with his mouth hanging slightly open. "Why?"

"Because I looked sad all the time. She told me I looked happy for the first time in three years. What do you think about that?"

"Are you blaming me?" he asks as he looks a bit shocked.

"I could," I say then smile at him. "But I'm not. I'm the one who lost her voice, her spirit, her pride. You didn't take it, I misplaced it. But I've found it and I'm not about to let it get away from me again."

I take off again and find him right next to me. "Gia, I don't want us to end. I really don't."

"I'm sure you don't. In my opinion, there is no, us. There never has been. You see, you both have to be invested to call yourselves something that contained. Us, means you think of yourselves as a whole being. You and I both know we're not nearly that close."

"You and Ryker are, though?" he asks. "That's what you're saying."

I stop and see his eyes are narrow and he looks like he's caught me cheating. "No, we are not an 'us', either. I don't know if we ever will be. I love that man, though. I do. If it weren't for him and his incessant pushing, I'd have left the real Gia Flynn right where she was shoved when I made plans with you and shoved her into a closet and locked her away. I almost forgot where I'd put her."

"You will be with him, though. Won't you?" he asks me and I can't stand to leave him wondering.

BUT I HAVE TO. "I'm not sure what I'm going to do. And I'm not sure you need to know anything else about me. Your world is elsewhere, leave me out of your head. It shouldn't be very hard. You did it most of the time anyway."

We both get into the company car and I take the place across from him. He looks me over and says, "Confidence is sexy on you, Gia. What do you say you let me come into your bedroom until you leave me?"

I lean forward, making sure my cleavage is revealed. "No." Then I sit back and smile to myself about how good it feels to say what I mean and mean what I say.

∿

RYKER

MY EYES FLY open as my cell makes a dinging noise that tells me I have a text message and I roll over to pick it up off my bedside table. I have to rub my eyes to get them to focus and see a text has come in from Gia.

I hurry to open it and read it.

-I know it's late, so I didn't want to call and wake you. Things are great with me. I will be seeing you the first week of next month. I'm making huge changes and I have you to thank for helping me find myself again. I love you to the moon and back!-

.   .   .

I CALL her since I know she's available to talk and sigh as I hear her sweet voice say, "Ryker, I woke you up anyway, didn't I? Sorry."

"Don't be. I've been wanting to hear your voice. So, you're doing great?"

"Better than great. I've turned over a new leaf and no one will ever be taking advantage of me again. I'll tell you all about it when I come for my monthly visit. I've added in a couple of more clients that I'll be consulting for. Don't worry, boss, they aren't in the space industry. I won't be sharing our secrets with them."

"You've certainly been busy in the last two weeks, Gia," I say as I am more than surprised.

"I really have. But not to worry. You're my number one client."

"Am I your number one guy?" I ask as I can hear the strength in her voice and I know that might mean she needs time away from men.

"If you want to be," she says. "I'm not going to lie to you and tell you that I'll be right there under your wing. I'm going to be doing what I need to do to fulfill myself. That means I'm jumping headlong into a career where I can use the information I've collected in my life to make a difference in this world and in your company's case, other worlds too."

"I want to be your number one guy and you can be my number one girl if you want to. Because I love the way you're thinking, baby. Do you need any help? I mean, I know I told you to do it all on your own but if you need help, I am here for you."

"That's really nice of you to offer. I know I can count on you for anything. I've got it handled, though. I've gotten my shit together. With the help of a lawyer, I renegotiated the sale I made to Markov Global. Let's just say, I'm catching up to you very quickly, financially."

"Wow," I say, more than a bit stunned. "I'm glad to hear you've righted that wrong. So, money isn't a worry for you any longer?"

"No, it's not. And I've moved the burden of my family off my shoulders as well. They all have ample opportunities with Apollo Engineering and it will be up to them to make that work for them or not. I'm not going to sell my soul for them any longer. If they realized

I was giving up myself for their financial security, they'd tell me to stop, I'm sure."

"I am too. They really do love you, baby. I can't wait to see you again. I miss you in a way I didn't know was possible. And I'm proud of you in a way I never knew was possible too."

"Thank you. I'm pretty damn proud of myself too."

HER VOICE IS SO confident and strong, it's hard to believe it's only been a couple of weeks that's made such a change in her. "I'm going to get some rest now. I can finally sleep well, now that I know you are more than okay."

"Ryker, I guess I could use your help," she says.

"Anything."

"Do you think you could find me a place to rent in Orlando? I'll want a home there since I'll be spending at least two weeks of each month there. I've already found a flat in London for the other two weeks I'll need to be there every month."

"Why rent when you can stay with me?" I ask her and kind of hate the laugh she gives me in return. "Is that a, no?"

"I'm not ready to move in with you. So, if you could send me some ideas about what's available there, that would be great."

"Price range?" I ask her.

"I want something upscale and cutting edge, price isn't an issue," she tells me and I am again surprised.

"Did you really gain that much wealth, Gia?"

"I did, Ryker. So, make sure you find something very nice. I'll be having clients over at times. I want something that says I'm cutting edge and successful."

"Can do, Gia. Anything else you might need?"

"I could hear you tell me that you still love me."

"I love you, Gia."

"I love you too, Ryker. See you in a couple of weeks. Bye."

"Bye, baby." I end the call and feel a million times better than I have since she left.

She sounds like an entirely different woman. *I wonder if this means she might join me on Mars.*

GIA

THE FUNNY THING IS, I was more than a little worried about facing Ryker again after making my miraculous transformation. I came in from Russia and took a cab right over to Apollo Engineering with my assistant, Viola. She's thirty, a perfectionist, and professional at all times. She's also a lesbian who lives with her life partner in Vermont, when she's not traveling with me, that is.

"After this initial meeting with the team I'm working with at Apollo, you can go back to Vermont for the remainder of this month. You can do everything I'll need you to via the internet and phone," I tell her as the cab stops at the front entrance to the massive building that is Apollo Engineering headquarters.

"Lois will be pleased to hear that," Viola tells me with a stoic face. Her dirty blonde hair is pulled back into a very tight bun and her gray pantsuit is impeccably pressed. Her ever-present clipboard is in her hand as we slip out of the cab.

"I'm sure Mr. Crawford will allow you to take the company jet back home," I tell her as we walk to the elevator bank in the main lobby.

"Baby!" I hear coming from the left of us. I turn to find Ryker with his arms outstretched and I find myself frozen.

"Oh, my God, he's even more gorgeous than I recalled." I move in slow motion as he hurries to me and find myself enveloped in his strong arms and warm embrace and I would love it if I never had to leave it. "Ryker, I've missed you."

"You better have!" he says then he gives me only a quick kiss. He looks into my eyes and his twinkle with excitement. "I'll give you a better kiss when we don't have so many people staring at us."

. . .

I cut my eyes to either side of us and see that we do, indeed, have many onlookers. "I'm going to hold you to that, Ryker."

He smiles and lets go of only one side of me, keeping me locked tight to him with his right arm as we walk back to Viola who is busily ignoring us and tapping something into her cell. "And you must be Viola," he says as he lets me go to shake her hand.

"I am, Mr. Crawford. It's a pleasure to finally meet you."

"And you as well. You are certainly extremely capable. I think Miss Flynn has made a wonderful choice in making you her right hand," he says as he gestures to the elevator that's just arrived. "Please step inside and I will take you where the others are waiting."

He chats away with her, telling her all about the things he thinks I'll do for his company and the venture to Mars. I can't speak as I breathe him in and relish the citrusy, musky scent that's coming off him. If we were alone in the elevator, I'd have myself wrapped around him right now.

My blood is boiling and I have no idea how long I can wait to really let myself go with the man. When we get off the elevator, he takes us to another area that I've never been too and we go into a lab to find my partners Sandra and Tabitha in lab coats and both are glad to see me.

"Gia, finally!" Sandra calls out as we come inside. "How we've needed more than your phone calls. I hope you're ready to work your ass off for the next week."

"I will leave you all to your work," Ryker says then gives me a gentle squeeze before releasing me entirely. "And you and I will be eating lunch together. I'll be back to get you at noon."

I smile and nod then remember what I wanted to ask him. "Ryker, do you think you could have the company jet take Viola to Vermont? I'm releasing her for the remainder of this month, to work from home. I need her for only a couple of hours then she can go if you have the plane available."

"I do and I'll get that set up right away. I'll come back in when I have it all set up and I'll have one of our cars take her to the airport and see her to our jet." He looks at me with a certain depth to his gaze. "It gives me another chance to stop in and look at you, anyway." With a kiss to my cheek, he turns and leaves and I'm left breathless, with a foggy brain.

"I wonder just how long it will take," Tabitha says.

I shake my head to rid the cobwebs that have taken it over. "How long what will take?"

"For you two to make it official," she says then all of them giggle and I look at them with what is sure to be a dumbfounded expression.

"I'm going to take at least a year to be myself," I let them all know and find them laughing openly. "I am! Now, let's get to work. My time is money, you know!"

We get down to business, the laughing done away with and the importance of the project taking our complete attention. Until he comes back in to get Viola.

"Hey," he says with a deep, brusque voice that comes from near my ear. "You all were in such deep conversation, none of you seemed to have noticed that I came in." His hand barely touches the small of my back and I find my body is going loose and my mind is too.

"Huh?" I ask as I turn to look at him. His hand trails over me as I move and he leaves it, resting on my hip.

His smile is cocky and he looks like a man who knows he has me right where he wants me. "I'm here to take Viola down to the car that's waiting to take her to the jet. And then, in an hour, I'm coming back for you, Miss Flynn. So, get to a stopping point by then. K?"

"K," I say and sigh. *I didn't mean to sigh, it just came out.*

Giggles start up again but at least they're quiet ones that Ryker doesn't seem to notice. "K." He turns away from me and gestures for my assistant to go with him. "This way, Viola."

"Call or send me an email," I tell her. "I want to know when you've made it home safe and sound."

"Will do, ma'am," she says and gives me a little salute.

"Viola, what have I told you about that?" I ask her.

"Sorry, ma'am," she says and puts her hand down. "Left over from my military days. I'll stop doing it someday."

"I hope so," I say and turn back to my work. "Bye now."

"Goodbye," she says and leaves the room with Ryker just behind her.

He turns back and I can feel his eyes on me and turn back to see he is looking at me. "One hour, Miss Flynn. Not one minute longer."

I give him a nod. "I won't keep you waiting."

The women erupt into giggles again and I find my cheeks heating with embarrassment. "Oh, you have it bad," Sandra whispers, so Ryker doesn't hear her.

I look up at her and ask, "Does it show that badly?"

They both nod and I know I'm going to have to fight myself where Ryker Crawford is concerned.

RYKER

PUSHING open the lab room door, I announce, "Lunch!"

Gia spins around with a giant smile on her beautiful face and comes straight to me, ditching the lab coat along the way. "I'm starving."

"Take a two-hour lunch, girls," I tell the others and they nod at me.

I can't help but run my arm around Gia's waist as she gets to me. Taking in a deep breath, I inhale her essence. She smells like love and sunshine and I don't know if I can ever get enough of that scent.

It feels as if I'm walking on air as I lead her back to my office. "Did you forget something?" she asks me as we head in the wrong direction from the exit.

"No, I made us a picnic," I tell her and open my office door.

A red and white checkered blanket is lying on the floor. A wooden picnic basket is sitting on one corner. A bottle of red wine and a couple of glasses are next to it. I have soft music playing on a speaker that my cell phone is playing songs I picked just for this lunch.

I dim the lights a bit before I close and lock the door. Her eyes are wide as she looks at the pristine scene. "Ryker, this is lovely."

I CAN'T WAIT ANY LONGER and push her long hair to one side and press my lips to the side of her neck as I run both arms around her and pull her back to me. "Nowhere nearly as lovely as you are, Gia. I have missed you more than I knew was humanly possible. It was made worse by knowing you were merely a few doors away from me but I had to give you time to work."

I turn her around in my arms and look at her. Trailing my finger over her plump, pink lips, I sigh as I have missed seeing her face. "Ryker?" she asks as she draws my attention from those luscious lips to her sparkling eyes. "You do realize I have to be true to myself, don't you?"

"Whatever that entails," I say. "I have to tell you how much more I feel for you, now that you've made such huge strides. I'm not about to get in your way. I only wish to be at your side."

She blinks a few times then says, "That's beautiful."

"You are," I say then I can't wait one more moment and I kiss her.

My mind goes to another place as her kiss takes me away. Her touch does something to me no one else has ever done before. She tastes like mint as we exchange hellos with our tongues.

And just as I'm about to do something vulgar, like grind my blossoming manhood into her, I stop my kiss and rest my forehead to hers. Our breaths mingle as the kiss went deeper than I believe either of us knew it would. "It's been some time since I've felt this way," she says, quietly. "You won't make it easy for me to live life as a single woman, will you?"

"I don't consider you a single woman, even now," I say and pull her along with me to the little picnic. "I'm not trying to be a Neanderthal but I'd kill any man who even thinks about hitting on you. Just so you know."

"Oh, thank you for letting me know that," she says with a giggle. "And may I ask if you have been out with anyone since I've been gone?"

"I have not." I help her to take a seat on the floor and join her on the blanket. "You see, you have stolen my heart. Taken my attention, completely. I see no reason to even look twice at anyone else. My heart is set on you, my one and only."

"And my being in Orlando only two weeks out of each month isn't a thing that detours your feelings?" she asks me.

"Why would it?" I ask her as it makes no difference.

"I won't be at your side all the time," she says.

I open the basket that I had a local restaurant deliver and find the cream cheese and salmon appetizers I ordered and place the small tray on the blanket. Taking one, I put it to her lips. "Gia, I don't need you right at my side all the time. I do want you and I to have a serious relationship, though. I want us to be exclusive. But I also want you to use that brilliant mind you have. And I know you have to go to other places to do that."

Her eyes go dark as she looks into mine and takes the bite of food I've offered her. She gazes at me as she chews then swallows. "I know you're going to leave me to go to Mars." I open my mouth to argue but she places her finger to my lips. "Ryker, it's okay." Her lips quirk into a crooked smile. "I want to be with you. I want to have you in my life while I can. And the fact you want me to use my mind just makes things even better."

"You are surprising, Gia. I don't know exactly what clicked in you but I'm damn glad it did. You radiate confidence and I can't explain to you exactly how sexy I find you now. I also can't stop myself from being forward with you. I want you. I want to make love to you. I want that so damn bad, it's almost all I've thought of."

"Honesty, huh?" she asks then leans in close. Her lips move softly over my neck all the way up to my ear. "I want that too."

"Forget lunch," I growl as I grab her and push her to lie back on the blanket.

OUR MOUTHS COLLIDE as I unbutton her clothes as she does mine. Our shirts are off and lying where ever they were thrown as our kiss grows more intense. I planned on taking my time but things are progressing all on their own. Our bodies are making the decisions and every single one of them are right.

My hands grab her tits as her chest heaves with each breath. I knew they'd feel perfect in my hands. Her hands fumble with the button on my pants until she frees me, sending them into my pants along my hips to get rid of them for me. I do the same for her with her pencil skirt. Her body arches up as I unzip the back of it and shimmy it off her.

I groan as one of her hands moves into my underwear and grasps my rock-hard cock. She moves it up and down the length and moans. Our mouths part as I have to rid us both of what's left of our clothes.

Our eyes stay glued on the others. Our breathing is hard and our bodies shimmer with sweat. "I have a shower in the connecting bathroom. You don't have to worry," I tell her as I pull her panties off then kiss her in a way I've only dreamt of.

"Ryker!" she yelps then her hands move into my hair, tangling up in it as I kiss her, intimately.

Her hips gyrate, as I take her with my mouth. Her moans never stop, they only increase until she's wrapping her legs around me as she can only groan with her release.

I can't possibly wait another second and move my body up hers until I find myself buried in her hot, tight, wet tunnel. I groan with the first stroke, "Baby, my God! You feel like Heaven!"

Her arms wrap around me as she coos, "You feel like home."

I've never experienced such intense emotions before and when a single tear falls from my eye and lands on her cheek, I know, without a single doubt, she is the one who was meant for me.

And I have no clue how I'll be able to leave her when things are ready to go to Mars!

GIA

THE WAIT WAS WORTH IT!

I've never felt as much as I feel with Ryker. Our bodies seem to be going on their own. I move without thinking about it. Arching when he tries to leave me, he holds me down to make smooth and deft strokes that send me to new heights of pleasure.

Our eyes hold the others as we make love. It's as if we're speaking to one another, using no words. I don't doubt that he cares for me. I also don't doubt that I care more for him than I even realized. *I'd kill for this man!*

WHEN THE FIRST quivers of pure bliss run through my body, I shudder as I don't want this to end. But I can't hold back the torrent of desire, lust, and love, that's a tangle of emotion that's just as tangled as our bodies are.

My release has him gasping for air as he tries hard to hold back, to make it last. He too loses his battle and we end up in a spent heap. Our breathing echoes off his office walls. Our combined sweat fills my nostrils, making me feel animal-like.

"I love you," he whispers in my ear as he kisses down my neck. "I love you more than I knew I was capable of loving."

My hands move over his back as I hold him tight. "Me too. I can't even explain this. I think love is too subtle a word. I adore you."

He pulls back to look at me as he brushes the hair off my face. "And I, you." His lips barely touch mine, with the tiniest of pecks. "I'm so damn glad I found you. My missing half."

I feel exactly the same way. How could I have thought I could wait years to feel this?

I was a fool. I have no idea where my head was for the last three years. I just know I want this man for as long as I'm allowed to have him. However long or short that is.

But I pray it's a long time!

"GIA, I need you to make me one promise," he says as he looks intensely into my eyes.

"Ryker, please don't ask too much out of me. I'm really stretching myself as it is."

His smile is sweet as he says, "I know that. I only want you to promise me that you'll never lose yourself again."

With a laugh, I say, "Not to worry. I will be holding on strong to the woman I've found again. And I think I love you even more for wanting me to stay strong and independent."

"But always know, you can have your weak moments with me and I'll never take advantage of you when they happen. We all have them, you know. It's just making sure we're not around the wrong people when it happens that's the key."

Moving my hand over his cheek, I find myself lost in his eyes. "Thank you, Ryker. I don't think I can ever thank you enough."

HIS LIPS TOUCH mine and our bodies ignite all over again. I hope this is a sign of things to come. Things like lying in bed all day on the weekends, just enjoying being with one another. Not doing a damn thing but this.

I can see a happy future with this man. And I am happy, even though I know that one day it will end when he leaves me to go to Mars. But for now, he's mine and he's here with me. I can't ask for any more than that.

RYKER

As the rain makes the tin roof of the shed we're standing under sing, I hold Gia's hand as the rocket lifts off the ground and heads up into the sky. It's the third test of using the new rocket boosters with the weight the actual ship will weigh.

A year has flown by and we're getting closer with each passing month. Gia and I, along with about a hundred others on my staff, turn to watch the large board with the statistics on it that's telling us the speed and altitude of the weighted down rockets.

The first two attempts had the rockets giving out before leaving the Earth's gravitational pull. With some major tweaking, we are hoping we've finally got it right.

Gia's hand grips mine as the numbers climb to near where the first test ended when the rocket started to fall back to land in the Atlantic Ocean. She breathes a sigh of relief as it passes that mark and keeps going at full speed. "No loss of speed yet," she says.

I give her a sideways glance to let her know not to say another word, lest she jinx it. I'm not normally a superstitious man but I'm on pins and needles here and grasping at anything. "Be careful, Gia."

She nods, knowing how I feel about things and keeps her eyes on the board. The mark where the second test failed comes up and the thing is still moving on. Three minutes later it's reached the outer atmosphere and the rockets go out as there's no need for them any longer. Gravity is no longer pulling at the cylinder they took up.

Cheers ring out and Gia jumps into my arms. I feel the wetness of her tears as she cries with what I hope is joy at the fantastic step we've taken. When she pulls her head away from my neck, I see the tears streaming down her pink cheeks and kiss her. "It's going to be okay, baby. We're still a few years away from being ready to go."

"I know, I do. It's just that it brought it all home, that's all. I'll stop crying. I will." She buries her face in my chest as her feet touch the ground.

Everyone's so excited no one notices how she's reacting to what all consider great news. I pull a handkerchief out of my pocket and give it to her. Discreetly, she wipes away her tears and blows her nose.

She's yet to change her mind about going to Mars and I've yet to change mine. We both know this thing we have will only last so long but it doesn't do a thing to help either of us deal well with that fact.

Once I'm sure she's alright, I take her by the hand and lead her to the control tower to make the announcement to the waiting media about how well the test went. "You don't have to say a word, Gia. Just stay by my side while I answer the reporter's questions. Okay?"

"Okay," she says. "I'm sorry for crying."

"Don't be." I run my arm around her shoulders and give her a squeeze. "It shows me just how much you love me."

She nods and looks down. "It shows me that too."

As SOON AS we enter the tower, the questions are fired at me. "Mr. Crawford, do you think with the success of this test that you've moved the send-off date any closer?" a small woman with black-rimmed glasses and a large microphone asks me.

"I have no idea about that yet," I answer her, truthfully. I have no idea what other problems we will encounter after all.

"Aren't you Gia Flynn?" one of the male reporters asks Gia as she holds tight to my hand.

She looks at me with surprise and I answer for her, "This is Gia Flynn. Do you have a question for her?"

"I do as a matter of fact," he says then looks at her. "Miss Flynn, it's been published recently that you have worked not only on the fuel for the missions but also supplements to sustain life in both the human travelers and the animals as well. My question to you is, how are they to maintain nourishment while on the planet? And will they be able to manufacture more of the supplements when they get to Mars?"

"I'm working with a team on that. You see, we will be sending drone-operated cargo ships to the planet at three-month intervals. More supplements will be sent with each shipment. I'm going to stay here, on Earth and continue to work on developing things to help the pioneers make a life on the planet. And all of our new inventions will be sent out to them."

His eyes move to me and he asks, "Mr. Crawford, it's long been known that you will be on the first mission to leave for Mars. It's also been obvious that you and Miss Flynn have a strong relationship. Have you changed your mind about going to Mars with Miss Flynn staying here?"

I look at Gia and find her looking down with a sad expression on her pretty face. I hate to see it. "I'm still going to Mars." And her expression only looks sadder. "Miss Flynn and I have discussed things. And we prefer to keep our personal lives out of the news."

More questions come and I answer them as I notice Gia's hand go loose in mine. She inches away from my side until suddenly, she's no longer there and I'm looking around to see where she's gone.

"Mr. Crawford, is it true that Markov Global is using these rocket boosters too?" a tall lady asks me.

"They are. We shared our technology with them so they would manufacture the rockets for free. I expect them to be near the same timeline as our company is. And that's all the questions for today. The next thing we're working on is the actual ship. A test will be done when that's accomplished and then we'll be getting ready for the actual trip to Mars. Thank you all for coming today." I leave the tower and find Gia sitting on a bench, alone.

She's soaking wet as she's sitting in the pouring rain. I go to her and lift her up, then take her to the car and find she's in the poorest of moods. "Baby, there are still years before I leave."

"But you will leave," she says as rain water drips off her and onto the leather seat. "I think I've been like an ostrich with its head in the sand this last year. I haven't let myself think about you leaving at all. And now it's obvious to me that you will leave me. You will leave me alone here and I don't know how I'm going to take it. I'm taking the thought of it very badly."

"You could always come too. There are others who can do what you do here on Earth. You could start training people to take over. You should do that. You should teach others, so you can come with me."

When she looks up at me, I see how red-rimmed her eyes are and it physically hurts me. "I don't want to go. I don't have that pioneer spirit a person needs to do well there. I think I'd go insane in a place like that. I'm not exactly spoiled rotten to the basic things like running water and electricity, but I am spoiled to things like technologies and access to information. And I do know that I'd be more help from here."

I know she's right too. That's what makes this so damn hard. She's always on the internet, searching things. She has a mind that works almost constantly. And I know she will be more help here than there. We just have different paths and that's hard to take.

"Can we put this conversation to rest?" I ask her as I take her hand away from smoothing out her soaking wet skirt and hold it. "It really isn't a thing we should be talking about just yet. We still have years to go. And who knows what will happen in that amount of time?"

"Ryker, should we end this?" she asks as she looks at me with confusion riddling her pretty face.

"You know it's going to hurt me to leave you behind too," I tell her as the driver takes us back home to Sebastien. I just recently talked her into moving in with me and letting the rental in Orlando go. She's only been living with me for the last two weeks and now she wants to end it!

"I know that. That's why I think we both might be better off ending it now. Before we fall even more in love with each other."

"I don't want that. Why should we hurt ourselves like that?" I ask her as I take her face in my hands. "Anything can happen. Neither of us knows for certain what the future holds. I know this, though. I love you now and I always will. I don't want to live my life without you, not ever. I'm positive about that, when the time comes, both of us will know without any uncertainty what the right thing to do will be. Please don't talk about ending what we have, baby. That would kill me, I'm pretty sure." I leave a kiss on her cheek and she finally smiles.

"Me too," she says then wraps her arms around me. "I know it is years away. I'm being foolish. I'll stop. We have each other now. That's what really matters."

"It is what matters." My cell rings and we both look at it as I let her go to pull it out of my pocket. "Damien."

SHE SIGHS and goes to look out the window. "Tell him I said hello."

I chuckle at her sarcasm then answer his call. "I just heard the news," he says before I can say a word.

"That traveled fast," I say in surprise.

"I pay one of the reporters to send me information immediately. You will be sending a complete report to Markov Global, won't you? It is part of our agreement."

"I will. It could take a week or more to get all the data but you'll get your report," I tell him.

"I saw a picture of you and Gia during the press conference. She looked terrible. How's she doing with this?" he asks and something inside of me spikes. *I hate it when he asks about her!*

"SHE'LL BE FINE. It just brought things home to her," I say as I reach out for her and pull her to my side again.

"Being with you has done nothing more for her than when she was with me. She will lose you too. In the end," he says and she over-hears him as she's so close to me and looks up at me.

"He's wrong. Being with you has made my life into something I didn't know it could be. I'm thankful for you, Ryker. I'm thankful for every moment I get to have with you. And I'm sorry for saying anything stupid about ending it before we have to. I love you." She kisses my cheek and I know things will work, somehow. *They have to!*

.   .   .

"I'll get that report to you as soon as I can, Damien," I say then end the call, so I can pay attention to the most special person in the world to me. "I'm thankful for you too, baby."

Her hands flow over my shoulders to hold me tightly. "Ryker, tell me one thing."

"Anything," I say as we look deep into each other's eyes.

"Tell me that you'll never forget me and what we shared while we had the chance."

"How could I ever forget this?" I ask her then kiss the tip of her nose.

"I can see it happening. I can see you getting to Mars and being excited about that. I can see you finding a woman to be with and making a family with, there. I can see time going on and you moving on. I can see it all and it's like a burr underneath my skin. It pricks at me at times like these. I just need to believe that you will always keep me with you in your heart. And in the end, when we both leave our worlds, maybe we can meet in the place all souls go to when our lives are over."

Her words are making my heart ache. I can't even think about making a family with anyone but her. Yet I know we'll never have that. Not when I'm leaving. I'd never leave a family here. One of the reasons I find it so easy to say I'll go to Mars is because I have no close family left in this world. But suddenly I'm seeing that I might.

Gia is as close as any family I've ever had. Falling in love with her just may have been a terrible mistake, taking me away from what has been my goal since I found out it might be possible to go to Mars during my lifetime.

"Gia, I don't think it's possible to forget a love this strong. And you've brought up some other things that don't seem possible to me. Our relationship has spun things in a direction I didn't see coming."

"I know that. I can see it in your eyes. You will have trouble leaving me," she says then looks down. "Like I said, if you think we should end this..."

I stop her with a kiss then end it and say, "I think we might think about ending what we currently have."

Her body sags as she leans against me. "I thought as much."

WITH A CHUCKLE, I add, "Not in the way you're thinking. In the way of making this more permanent. I want to start a training program for those going to Mars. Set up a desolate spot where we will have to learn how to adapt and live in an environment like the one on Mars. And you could be right there with me, learning how to acclimate yourself to it as well. I think if you knew more about what to expect, you'd find a sense of adventure and join me."

Her head shakes but I see a little light in her eyes as she makes the gesture. "That's crazy."

"Is it?" I ask. "Or is it genius? I'm going with the latter. Come on, Gia! Think about it. We can set up something that will really be of help. And you've always said you want to help the people who go to Mars. Well, how can you really be all that much help if you lack the basic understanding of how life there will be? And your expertise in doing research will be invaluable to this project."

Her eyes dart back and forth as her mind is sparked about what I'm saying. "I think there definitely needs to be a training program."

"AND I THINK you'd be perfect to help me and some others set it all up. And I think you just might find that you might like to go with me." I hold her tight as I can see it there inside of her. She might find it not as bad as she thinks it will be.

"Sandra and Tabitha would love to help," she says. "We could effectively test the supplements too. Even on the animals! Ryker, now you do have me excited. I don't think it will make me want to go to Mars but I am excited about working on this project and experiencing it all. I'm in, baby!"

"Yes!" I say then kiss her again to seal our deal.

I just might make a Martian out of this woman yet!

7

PART 7 - THE LIBERATION

GIA

Red-orange light filters into the dome, making a pretend Martian daytime for the test site. Ten acres have been stripped of anything but dirt. A dome made out of reddish polymers was constructed to cover the area. We arrived yesterday with nothing more than one backpack each, filled with essentials. And the other things that each pod can hold. Which isn't a lot.

I watch Ryker, as he's in his element. Sheer joy is the expression on his handsome face. The men are overseeing the building of the tent system. It's large and each couple or individual has separated, private rooms. A huge tent with a bunch of smaller tents inside of it, essentially.

There are fifty people, all scientists or engineers, who signed up for the six-month test. I was a lead developer in the plans to make this test, we hope will be a success.

Six of the women are in charge of digging the two latrines. Three more are putting up the mechanism, which one of Apollo Engineering's top engineers came up with, to pull water out of the air. Now, we know the conditions won't be exactly the same but the idea should work on Mars. Maybe the quantity of water might not be the same but there should be water, an essential part of life anywhere.

I'M WORKING in the group that's making the garden. This will be our primary food supply. All of us went on vegan diets to ready our bodies for the change in the foods we eat. It was discussed at a world forum about how people should eat on Mars. The overwhelming decision was made that only plants such as herbs and spices, vegetables, and fruits are to be taken to the planet.

No meat will be eaten there. The protein the body needs will be provided by spinach and beans. Until our garden grows, we only have supplements to live on and freeze dried meals that have been specially prepared with the vegan diet in mind.

To be sure no one was sick or had any disease of any kind, everyone had to get a physical and undergo an extensive examination and testing. And, here's the hard part, as there are no pharmacies on Mars and may never be, a new birth control concept had to be developed.

Each female was given a device she must urinate on, daily. It reads the hormone levels to determine if she's in a fertile state or not. If she is, then she's to refrain from sex, unless she and her partner want to have a child. There are three couples here who are pregnant right now. They'll all be delivering within the six-month period, so we can see how all that goes.

The first woman is due in three months, two of the people who signed up for this test have been trained in basic medical services and have delivered babies at the local hospital to gain some experience with that task.

Cloth diapers and breastfeeding will have to be done by them all and all who go to Mars. Back to the old ways of doing things, a thing I'm not keen on but the pregnant couples are all looking forward to that, for some strange reason.

My eyes wander around, looking at all the people, working busily to get things set up. Last night we all slept on the ground and that was not comfortable at all. Ryker cradled me in his arms the whole night, keeping me mostly off the ground. I think he's trying to show me just how much he'll take care of me if I'll go with him.

He gives me a smile and a wave as he catches me gazing at him. With no shirt on and the light glistening off his magnificent body, he's something to look at. I blow him a kiss and he acts like he catches it, making me smile and my heart skip a beat. *He's just so damn cute!*

Settling into a squat, I get back to planting the seeds for the lettuce down one long row. One of the women who are in charge of the cooking calls out, "Breakfast!"

Everyone stops what they're doing and heads to the area where the make-shift dining area has been set up. Ryker meets me there and takes my hand, delivering a kiss to my cheek. "You look pretty today, Gia. I like what you've done with your hair."

I giggle at him and pat the bun on top of my head. Most of the women opted for the bun style. A few got theirs cut really short, which I thought was kind of dumb. As it grows out, it'll look pretty bad.

Ryker got his cut a bit but he's going to let his hair and beard grow out, he says. I expect to have a caveman by my side in no time. I run my hand over his still short hair. "I like what you've done with yours too." I kiss his cheek and love the way he's smiling and smells kind of musky from all the sweat he's built up while doing all that manual labor on the tents. "You love this, don't you?"

He nods as he picks up a tin plate with some unappetizing white and gray food on it. Plus, the pill that will add some real nutrition to the meal. "Here you go, baby." He hands me the plate and gets one for himself then we go to get our cups of water to drink with it.

"Thank you," I say as I laugh. "And to think just yesterday, we were eating at a five-star restaurant and look at us now."

We walk over to where everyone has sat down together, on the ground and take a seat, Indian style, to join them. Chatter is all I hear as everyone talks about the progress they're making.

"The tent will be up before night falls. And the solar panels seem to be charging, even in the dimmer light. Have you checked yourself today?"

With raised eyebrows, I ask, "What do you mean, checked myself?"

HE GRINS, sheepishly and whispers, "You know, with the stick? Have you checked your urine? Is tonight a go for us?"

"Oh, no I haven't yet. I'm kind of waiting on the latrines to be built. Most of the females are waiting on that. We're not like you guys who don't seem to mind trotting over to the edge of the area to let it all go."

He nods as he takes the pill first. "I get it. But you will make sure, right? I'm kind of red-hot for you, baby. Something about all this hard work and the idea of you and me working together on this has me kind of crazy for you."

I'm not extremely happy that this is making him so hot for me. I can see it in his eyes, he thinks this might make me change my mind. *I know it won't.*

"I'll make sure I get that done before we retreat to our little cubby-hole in the tent."

As he takes the last bite of the tasteless food on his plate, he leans in and whispers, "And cleaning up after our long day will probably have you aching for me too."

I laugh a little as he's just being so cute and adorable. "So, you think a little sponge bath from you is going to make me ravenous for you?"

WITH A LOW GROWL, he nips my neck. "I hope so."

"Hey, Gia, do you think we'll be able to send larger trees to Mars?" the cook, Jana, asks me.

"I think we should make a companion drone full of larger trees that can go with the first shuttle. The ones we brought won't make fruit for at least a year. And that environment will be different. At least we can streamline the cross-pollination process with this test."

"Great idea, babe!" Ryker holds up his hand for a high five and I laugh as I give him one. "You're already learning from this experience and it's only been a day. What else will your brilliant mind figure out? I can't wait to find out." He gives me a quick kiss then gets up and holds his hand out to help me up. "Back to work."

I nod and go with him to put our plates and cups in the tub, so the kitchen staff can clean them up for lunch. We only have the exact number we need, nothing will be wasted. I get another quick kiss then Ryker heads out with the other men to finish up the tent and I head back to my garden work.

Looking around as everyone gets back to their specific tasks, I have to admire everyone here. They're all so dedicated and excited. It's rubbing off on me. But I still can't think about leaving my family behind. It's bad enough I have to stay away from them for six months.

Don't even get me started on what would inevitably happen if I did go to Mars when I had to have a baby, sans pain meds and technology!

RYKER

WATCHING GIA, skipping with a couple of other young women, makes me smile and laugh. She's so laid back, here in the dome. She thought not being able to have her computer would depress her. *She's anything but depressed!*

THE EVENING IS SETTING in fast and dinner is being served. The other couples are taking theirs to their new bedrooms, to eat them alone. I pick up the vitamin supplements and put two servings of food on one plate, then pick up a cup of water and make my way to our finished personal chambers.

Catching Gia looking at me, I give her a nod. She picks up our ration of bathing water that was made fresh today and heads my way. I wait for her in the open living area of the giant tent and she steps in next to me as I show her to our new little home.

"At least our shelter is finished," I say as I take her to the third personal tent, within the huge tent that is home for us all for the next six months.

With a gesture for her to step through the unzipped opening, she smiles and goes inside. "No way!"

"You like?" I place the plate on the small table and pull out the chair for her. "Our personal dining area."

She takes the seat after placing the bottle of water on the bathing stand. Everything is small, lightweight, and portable, while being very efficient. And she seems to be amazed at all the things in our tent. "A chandelier, Ryker? How?"

"It's collapsible. And it runs off the solar panels that cover the top of the main tent. So, we have electricity. Once you pour that water into the bathing station, we'll have a type of running water." I point at another zippered door. "And behind that door is our very own portable toilet. Now, it will have to be taken to the latrine and emptied every morning but we have one. I'll handle that unpleasant task."

She can't stop smiling and that has my heart filling with hope. "I can't believe this. It's amazing." She points at the door I've left open, by pulling back the two sides of the zippered door. "And what's back there?"

I chuckle and take her hand. "Let me show you our bedroom for the next bit, baby."

When we get to the opening and she can see inside, she gasps and I find my smile just won't fade. "Ryker! How?"

"The mattress can be rolled into a tight cylinder. When unrolled, the material inside of it can be fluffed up, so you have yourself a very comfortable bed. Nice, huh?"

She nods and looks up. "And yet another chandelier. And you picked out my favorite shade of blue for the blankets and pillows too.

Ryker, this isn't what I pictured at all. I... I...." She turns to me and wraps her arms around me. "I love it!"

Rocking her in my arms, I whisper against her cheek, "I thought you would."

"Let's eat and then get down to washing this dirt off us," she says as she pulls back to look at me. "I kinda have the hots for you right now, my caveman."

Chuckling at her name for me, I take her hand and lead her back to the table to sit down. "And just what does that mean, Gia?"

"It means, you are much like a caveman, an extremely capable one. And all too soon, I know I'm going to lose sight of your handsome face as you grow out your beard. But I'm beginning to think I just might like that."

"Are you also beginning to think you might just like to go to Mars too?" I cross my fingers and hope she is.

Her laugh is light and airy and even though she's shaking her head, I know she's thinking about it. *She can't fool me!*

TAKING OUR CHAIRS, she taps the tabletop and asks, "And how about when children come along? What would you do to make this place bigger, to accommodate them too?"

"Excellent question and on that subject, are we good for tonight?"

She nods and sips her water. "For tonight we are. So, expansion, how would you do that?"

"I think it would be easy to make orders of more tents from Earth that could be brought in on the supply shuttles that will come. Why? You planning on coming with me and giving me a bunch of Martian babies?" I laugh but I hope she'll think about doing just that.

"Martian babies!" She laughs and shakes her head. "I don't know about that. Now, Earthlings, I can do."

I stop and look at her to see if she's serious. "You'd have my kids, Gia?"

Her eyes cut sideways as I think she didn't mean to say that. "I would if you were going to be around to help me raise them. But you won't, so I guess I shouldn't have said such a thing. I'm sorry."

PLACING the nutrient pill on her tongue I hand her the glass of water. "Drink up your nourishment, baby. I have big plans for you."

She takes the pill down then picks up mine and places it on my waiting tongue. "Your turn." Our eyes hold while I swallow the pill then she leans in and kisses me. "I love you so much, Ryker. I don't think you have a clue how much I do."

All I can do is look at her. I want to tell her, for the thousandth time that we can be together forever if she'll just come with me. But I know I'm beating a dead horse when I use my words to coax her. So, I decide to use a bit more than that.

I pull the band off the bun it's holding her hair in and run my fingers through it to loosen and free the dark waves of silkiness. "No makeup, hair in a tasseled state, yet you're still every bit as beautiful as you've ever been. How do you do it?"

Her smile devastates me. "Ryker, I know you're full of crap but I do love the way you make me feel."

"This stuff is going to taste the same whether it's cold or warm," I say as I stroke her cheek. "How about we forgo dinner for now and get cleaned up then I'm going to get you all dirty again."

She nods and gives me a shy smile. "Let's do that."

Pulling her up as I get up, I take her to the middle of the room and unzip her blue jumpsuit. We all wear the same thing, a uniform made out of a dirt resistant material. Placing it in the cleaning closet, I turn to look at her as I take mine off too and place it next to hers.

Pressing the button, the vacuum system begins the process of pulling away the dirt and sweat off the uniforms to make them good as new for tomorrow. There are no night clothes. Our birthday suits will have to suffice for this test, anyway.

The washcloths have built in microbes that will clean our skin when mixed with a small amount of water. She takes her place on the bathing mat while I get the cloth ready with a bit of water. Starting at her toes, I move the cloth in a circular fashion, ridding her body of the dirt and perspiration after a day of hard labor.

I find her watching me as I take my time to make sure every part of her has been cleaned then she gets up and I take the place she left vacant. With a new cloth, she cleans me up and leaves me wanting her more than I knew possible.

Grabbing her wrist as she places the cloth on the edge of the wash basin, I get up and throw her over my shoulder, igniting laughter from her as I carry her to our new bedroom. "Caveman!"

"I'M ABOUT to show you how caveman I am, baby!"

Tossing her onto the bed, I gaze at how gorgeous she is then I dim the light and crawl over the bed to get to her. Again, I start with her little toes and kiss them, trailing kisses all the way up until I'm right where I want to be. Hovering over her and already feeling my breath going ragged with desire for her.

GIA

I CAN'T IMAGINE why my body is reacting to Ryker's so much more than it ever has, and it has reacted to him a lot!

His dark eyes hold mine as he moves his body over mine, only slightly allowing our bodies to graze against the other. "Tell me," he whispers.

Reaching up to try to pull him down to me, to cover me with his body, I find him taking my wrists in one of his hands and holding them down, over my head. I suck in my breath as he looks at me with dominating eyes. "I love you," I say in an attempt to soften him.

"Tell me who you belong to," he says as he moves his hard cock over my sex, sending sparks all through me.

"You," I breathe out as I arch up but find him staying just above me. I can feel the heat from his body and I'm dying to have him all over me. "Ryker, please."

His mouth takes mine, but he still keeps his body just out of my reach. When I try to wrap my legs around his waist to pull him to me, he pulls his mouth from mine. "Stop."

I do as he says and put my legs down on the bed. "Please, Ryker," I moan.

HE GIVES me an evil grin then kisses my neck, driving me even more insane with his little nips and sucks. I wiggle a little and find him giving me a hard bite. "Be still, Gia!"

With great frustration, I groan and give up, letting him toy with me until I'm quivering with need. When my body starts shaking, he stops his delightful torture and lets my wrists go, so he can pull my legs up to where he wants them. My feet on either side of his head, spreading me open for him.

He locks eyes with me as he pushes his large hard erection in. His eyes close as he relishes the sensation. With an easy movement, he slides back out of me, all the way then makes another easy stroke.

I moan as he's still toying with me. I want him all, I want it fast and hard and he's not about to give me what I want. He pulls all the way out with every slow stroke, making me miss him for a few seconds before he eases himself back into me. Over and over, he slowly tortures me until my body goes into an orgasm of unbelievable proportions.

Biting my lower lip to keep myself from screaming with the deep sensations that rage through my entire body, I find his body shaking as he's held himself back for such a long time, too.

When he pulls all the way out of me, leaving me under the pressure of my climax and yearning to have him back inside me, I cry out, "No!"

.   .   .

HE LOOKS at me with wanting eyes and rolls to one side, looking at me as he uses his hand to hold himself up and strokes my stomach with the other. He just looks at me until the intense orgasm is over then he smiles at me and takes my breast in his mouth as he plays with the other one.

I struggle to catch my breath and feel as if I'm a mouse beneath the claws and mouth of a playful cat. His tongue moves in deft circles around my taut nipple. He pinches and pulls at the other nipple, making a mixture of pain and pleasure.

When his hand travels away from my breast, down my stomach, my breath hitches in my chest as he plunges two fingers into me, then slides them up to play with my clit.

The sucking and the rubbing have me going over the edge again. I buck as I climax again and groan with frustration. "Please, Ryker. Please!"

He eases his sucking and stops playing with my clit, allowing the orgasm to wane. Again, he watches me. When I reach out to take his face and pull him to kiss me, he leans back to avoid my hands.

"Naughty girl," he says with a smile and rolls away from me, getting on his knees and tossing me over on my stomach. With a hard pull at my waist, he pulls me up on my knees and I'm on all fours, waiting for him to plunge into me, and gritting my teeth in anticipation.

Instead of that, I feel him moving around and the next thing I know, he's underneath me, kissing me intimately and further arousing me. His hands grip my ass, pulling me down to him as he eats me like I'm the best tasting thing he's ever had. His growls and moans let me know he's in a sexual rage.

When I come for him, he goes even more ravenous, sending me into a frenzy of sensations. I gasp as he stops and find myself yanked back as he takes a chunk of my hair and thrusts himself into me with a loud grunt. "Baby, yes!"

I moan as he fills me and push my ass back to him. "Ryker!"

Savagely, he takes me, making me burn with passion. The raw emotion fills me and tears spring from my eyes as he makes hard and fast thrusts. One hand grips my waist, and I'm held still for him to take as he pleases.

I cry out with another orgasm and he rides me through it. His teeth are clenched as he says, "Come all over my cock, Gia."

My body does as he commands then he pulls out and flips me onto my back and thrusts right back into me. A burst of air is knocked out of my lungs with the force and I find him looking wild. "Ryker!"

HE BURIES himself inside me then makes little pumps, his cock is so deep inside and the small motion has his body moving in rapid pulses across my clit. Another orgasm takes me and he watches me. "You're so fucking gorgeous when you come for me, Gia."

I can hardly breathe as he continues his assault on my body. I place my hands on his broad shoulders and ride the wave of absolute pleasure until it ebbs. Trying to steady myself, I whisper, "I am yours."

He slows his furious pace and kisses me. Deep, sensual, and sexy, his kiss goes on and on until he pulls his head back as he stiffens and spills himself into me. "Gia!"

"Ryker!"

I wrap my legs around him as my body milks his with another orgasm. Our bodies shake as do our lungs as they expel large amounts of hot breath.

PANTING LIKE ANIMALS, he lies on top of me until the last shudder is felt. His heartbeat slows and returns to normal before he kisses my cheek and rolls off me, leaving me missing his weight. He gently rolls me to the side, to face him and pushes his leg between mine as he wraps his arms around me, holding me tight.

"I can't ever leave you," he mumbles with sleepy words.

My eyes, which had closed, open as I can't believe what he's said. "What does that mean?"

I'm met with soft snores as he's worn himself out, completely. I'll get no answer tonight and maybe not even tomorrow as he seems kind of love drunk.

Surely, he didn't mean he won't be leaving me and the Earth behind him!

~

RYKER

Half way through the test and it's going fantastic. The first birth has begun and soon we shall see how the mother handles that. The group is clustered around the outside area we've created, kind of like an outdoor bar. Sans the alcohol, which we don't have any of.

"You know, the trip to Mars is only eight months long," Allen, one of the engineers says. "I don't see why shipments of good food and drinks couldn't be sent to us. If we made more drones, do you think it would be possible to get more shipments?"

I play with Gia's hair that I've let down as she sits on my lap. She surprises me as she speaks up, "The drones, like the shuttles, will be out of fuel when they get to us. I mean, to Mars. I don't know how many we can get. Apollo Engineering will be building ships that never return and the people on Mars will have to figure out what to do with the massive vessels."

"We could build homes, like apartments, out of them," another woman offers.

Gia looks at me over her shoulder and I kiss the tip of her cute little nose as I totally caught her Freudian slip about her being on Mars someday. She smiles at me and runs her hand over my bearded face. "I think it should be of the utmost importance to see just what burns on that planet. So, we can make fuel of our own there," she says, further insinuating herself as a future Martian.

"And just how will revenue be created to make all these ships?" Gary, from logistics, asks.

"I have that under control," I say. "Not to worry, tons of money has already been invested to make sure Apollo Engineering stays not only afloat but prosperous. The last thing we want is for the company to go under while we're trapped on another planet. Plus, I've added on affiliate partners to make sure there's plenty of money."

Gia looks at me with a smile and mouths, 'Thank you.'

I added her family farm on as an affiliate partner. That way her family can sell their uniquely modified corn to us and after it's processed in the plant we built to do that, they are the ones who can sell that fuel under the wing of Apollo Engineering, making money for them and us. A few more affiliates like that and the company will be set.

With a laugh, Gia, says, "Hell, we may even be able to use all the extra hair you men seem to be growing to burn and make fuel from too."

I watch Donny, a certified genius, get a bright look on his face. "Hey, why didn't I think of that?"

"I don't really think you guys can make enough hair to have enough fuel for even one trip from Mars to Earth, Donny," Gia says with a laugh.

"No, not just hair," he says with a smile. "Our excrements too."

"Yuk!" we all shout as his idea just sounds nasty.

"No, NOT YUK," he says. "You'll see. I'm about to make an experiment." He looks at the other two men who have IQ's near his. "To the latrine!" They all get up and run toward the bathrooms as the rest of us shudder at the thought.

"You can leave me out of that experiment," Gia mumbles.

Everyone nods in agreement as I twirl a lock of her hair and leave a kiss on her cheek. "Do you want to go and see how Pam's doing? Maybe give her a pat on the back or whatever one does to help a laboring mother."

She nods and we get up to go see how things are progressing with the first birth in the dome. Holding hands, I swing them between us. "Things are so simple and yet so complicated, aren't they?" she asks me.

I nod. "Life is life, no matter where or when. Nothing is easy. And nothing worth having is ever easy, anyway."

A special tent was set up with laboring mothers in mind. Soothing sounds come from an audio box with a prerecorded track. A small blow up swimming pool was brought, just in case any of the women wanted to float in the water. Some say it helps ease the contractions or something like that.

I stop as we unzip the tent's door and find Pam in the water, naked as the day she was born. "Perhaps, I shouldn't be here?" I say, kind of shocked.

"Nonsense," her husband, Peter, says. "We're all going to be pretty damn close and things like vanity and being shy about one's body shouldn't be a thing we need to take with us to Mars. Please stay, Ryker."

Gia looks at me with a smile. "We can sit back there, if you're more comfortable with that. Then you'll only see her back."

Pam breathes in and out with slow breaths. "Yes, you're going to want to learn from this process, so you'll know how to handle it when you two have your babies."

Gia gives my hand a squeeze and then a smile moves over her sweet lips. "See, this is a teachable moment."

I TAKE a seat and pull her to sit back on my lap, so her body covers some of what lies in front of us. "Okay, let's learn." I lean up and whisper in her ear, "But I thought you wouldn't be going to Mars."

She looks at me and runs her hands over my beard. "I'm up in the air about that, at this time."

My eyebrows go up high, as she's not said a word about even contemplating it. But I have been trying my best to show her how great it'll be. Leaning in close, I whisper, "You should come to Mars, baby. I'd love to see how sex feels with you there. As opposed to how it would feel with someone else."

She pulls back and narrows her eyes at me. "Ryker," she hiss-whispers at me. "Don't you dare speak about you and another woman."

Jealousy!

So, I rub it in a bit more. "Well, if you won't come, what else will I be forced to do?"

Her body tenses in an instant then I rub her shoulders. "Let's never discuss that, please."

I shrug and continue to rub her shoulders and move my hands down her back, feeling the tension, slowly leave her body. As I half-watch Pam and Peter work together to help her ease her discomfort, I think about what I want.

Venturing further, I whisper to Gia, "I'd like to have the first baby born on Mars."

She looks at me as if I'm crazy. "The first one? And how would you even accomplish that? Tell the rest of the people to hold off while you impregnated your woman?"

"No, no one would listen to me, anyway. I've never thought about how I'd do it. I just want it, that's all. It would be nice, is what I'm saying. You know it takes eight months to get to Mars and if you were, say a month pregnant or a little less, then you could have the baby on Mars. Then, we'd most likely have the first baby."

She clicks her tongue at me. "You've thought about this, haven't you?"

I nod and run my hand over the back of her neck and pull her in for a brief kiss. "Extensively."

"But what about the fact, I haven't signed on for that yet? Also, let's just say I do sign up for it, am I to wait until we can go to Mars, to have a baby?"

. . .

I PONDER HER QUESTION. Getting to Mars is about five years away. That does seem like an awfully long time to wait. But then again, why would we have to. There're no rules saying kids can't go to Mars too.

"We could take whatever kids we already had," I say, earning a frown from her.

"And subject them to that kind of rough life?" She shakes her head and I try another direction.

"You'd be bringing a new baby into that too. But I don't think life will be rough at all. The first few days, while we set everything up, we'd live on the shuttle, just the way we'd have to as it takes us there. There'd never be any real hardship, like we had the first night here, in the dome."

She nods and looks like she's thinking about things. "You're most likely right. I didn't think about that."

PAM MAKES a little scream and Peter looks at the woman who's been trained to deliver babies, "What's that mean?"

"It means she felt a little bit more than she was feeling. Let me give her a check."

I close my eyes and bury my face in Gia's back as the woman puts her hands in a place on Pam, I'd rather not think about. "Tell me when this part is over."

"Will do," Gia says. Her hand moves over my back as she watches the process.

"You've effaced and are now at ten centimeters. When you get the urge to push, you can."

I open my eyes and feel a rush of adrenaline. "Is she about to have the baby?"

Margie, the midwife, looks at me with a smile. "She is. You two should come up here, so you can see this better. It's not nearly as bad as your imagination makes it."

With a tug at my hand, I find Gia has me in tow and off we go to get a better view of something I never imagined wanting even a bad view of. But here I am, watching a woman give birth in a blow-up swimming pool.

"Do you have to give birth in the water?" Gia asks.

The midwife shakes her head. "You can do it however you want. Some squat, some like to lie on the bed. It's whatever you feel comfortable with."

She nods and asks, "The baby can't take in a breath if it's under the water. Won't that be bad for it to come out like that?"

"They generally don't try to take in a breath until the air hits them," the midwife says.

Gia nods again. "I think I'd like to have our kids the traditional way. In a bed. Preferably, in a hospital with an epidural. Yeah, that sounds good to me."

When a horrible shriek comes out of Pam, Gia turns and buries her face in my chest. "Oh, my!"

I close my eyes as a streak of red has shot out into the pool. "Oh, my!"

"It burns!" Pam shouts. "Why does it burn so damn bad?"

"You're probably stretching very fast as the baby's head crowns. If you rip at all, I have the things I'll need to stitch you back up," Margie says.

"Do you have something to numb her if you have to do that?" Gia asks but doesn't pull her head out of my chest. Her arms are wrapped around me, holding me for dear life.

"I do. Not to worry," Margie says.

I open one eye and see her getting on her knees on the floor with a small blanket in her hands. "Do you see the head?" Peter asks as Pam grunts and pushes.

"Not yet. Patience, Peter."

My eye catches how red Pam's face has gotten and I stare in disbelief that anyone can go that shade without something terrible happening. "Is she going to be alright?"

"She is," Margie says as Pam grunts again with a massive push. "Oh, yes! Here we go. We're about to meet your baby, Pam, and Peter!"

. . .

WITH AN ODD SUCKING SOUND, a little mass comes out into the water and Margie picks it up and wraps it in the blanket. "Here you go, Daddy. Take your son, so I can get the scissors to cut the cord."

Gia turns around, taking her head out of my chest and opens her eyes. "He's not crying. Shouldn't he be crying?"

"He will, just watch," Margie says. "Ryker, will you do me a favor and hold the baby while Peter cuts the cord? I want to take a picture of this." She pulls out an old-fashioned camera and I move to take the baby from Peter.

"Man, he's really red and puffy, isn't he?" I ask as I take him and Peter nods.

"I suppose that goes away," he says.

"It will," Margie lets him know then hands him the scissors and snaps a few pictures as he cuts the cord that she's already placed a clamp on to stop us from being squirted with blood.

When my eyes leave the baby, I see Gia's moved to kneel behind Pam and is massaging her shoulders. "He's gorgeous, Pam.

No longer red in the face, Pam is beaming. "I can't wait to see him."

AS I JOSTLE him back into Peter's arms, he makes his first sound. A loud cry that tells us he's breathing. I follow him to take the baby to show Pam and find Gia with tears in her eyes as she looks at the little baby that's wailing away now.

She gets up and comes to me, wrapping her arms around me and wailing like the baby is. "Oh, Ryker!"

I hold her and hug her and take her out of the tent, so the new little family can have some time alone. "Baby, it's okay. Why in the world are you crying?"

We stop and I take her by the chin to make her look at me. "I want that! I want you and me to have a family!"

"Then let's do that," I say then pull her back into my arms. "Marry me. And tell me you'll come with me to Mars."

"I can't," she says then cries some more.

"You can," I tell her as I move us to a more remote area, so no one can hear us. "What if I make it possible to travel back to Earth too?"

With a sudden jolt, her head shoots up. "Could you?"

I really don't know if I can do that but here it goes, "I might be able to."

"If you could make that happen then maybe, just maybe, I could do that!" She jumps up and down and claps and now I feel bad.

Trying to slow her enthusiasm, I take hold of her narrow shoulders and look her in the eyes. "The important thing is me and you, being together. Can you agree about that?"

She looks at me for a long time, so long I think she might be about to tell me something I don't want to hear. Her lips part and she says, "I don't know what I'd do without you."

Pulling her in for a tight hug, I kiss the top of her head. "Me neither. Now that we're in agreeance on that, let's get some more things straight."

"Like?" she asks as she pulls back to look at me.

"Like, I want you to marry me when we get out of here. I want it official. And where I go, you go. Along with whoever we create along the way. I know you have your family here but I promise, I'll do everything possible to make sure you get to see them again. I swear to you, I will try. That's going to be my number one priority."

"You really want to marry me?" she asks with a sideways smile.

"This isn't how I planned on proposing to you, at all. But yes, I want to make you my wife. Change your last name. Put my ring on that finger. And every other cliché that goes with that." I laugh and she does too, making my heart pitter and patter.

HER SWEET SMILE fades away and she looks off to the side. "On Mars, Damien will be there."

"Not in our settlement, he won't. And what the hell does that matter? I don't care. He's not going to be able to come between us."

She pulls out of my arms and starts walking toward the tent, pulling me along with her. "It's just that I really didn't ever want to live in any kind of close vicinity to him."

"We can't let anyone stop progress, Gia." I pick her up as we get to our tent and carry her inside.

She giggles as I do and asks, "What's this for?"

"You and I are going to get married," I say then take her straight to our bedroom. "We have to celebrate that."

As I lay her down on the soft bed, she looks up at me with doe-like eyes. "Ryker, are we really going to do this?"

I nod as I unzip her jumpsuit and take it off her body that's just begging me to kiss it all over. "We're going to do this. We're going to do all of this and we're going to do it together. I knew from the moment I laid eyes on you that you were the one for me."

She laughs as I pull my jumpsuit off. "No, you didn't. You just lusted after me."

"Well, maybe a little."

"A lot," she says as she runs her fingers over her nipple, making it hard.

I watch her do that to herself and get an immediate boner. "A lot. Yes, I lusted after you a lot and I still do." Moving onto the bed, I take over what she's doing. "Here, let me help you with that."

She moans as I take over, placing my mouth on her pert nipple, giving it a hard suck. *I wonder if she'll let me tell everyone we're engaged!*

GIA

As I step out of our tent, I can hear the sound of a crying baby. It's a different kind of sound that's been added to life, here in the dome. Ryker comes out right behind me. With his hand on the small of my back, we make our way to the dining area to eat breakfast.

I stop and look back at him as he clears his throat, making everyone stop their chattering and look at him too. "Good morning, all. I'd like to make an announcement."

"Ryker," I whisper but he stops me as he runs his arm around me. My cheeks are already heating with embarrassment for some reason.

"Gia and I will be getting married when this test is over and we leave here. I want you all to know you'll be invited to our wedding. It will be a lavish affair with tons of great food, dancing, and drinking."

Cheers rings out and people come up to us, congratulating us and giving us hugs. I find it a little overwhelming, as I'm not used to being the center of attention.

THE LITTLE TRIO of people who've made a make-shift band come up to us after we take our seats. Their leader, Dylan, smiles at us as he tells us, "We'd love to play at your wedding, guys. Let us know what songs you'd like us to play and we'll start practicing them right away."

"How sweet," I say as I take Ryker's hand and hold it tight. "We'll discuss that and get back to you very soon."

With a nod, they leave us and Ryker pulls our clasped hands to give mine a kiss. "I caught you off guard, didn't I?"

I wag my finger at him. "You could've told me you were going to do that."

"I did tell you that last night, didn't I?" he asks me with a sheepish grin.

Leaning in close, I whisper, "You know damn well I'd have a hard time recalling anything that was said last night. You wore me out, completely."

He makes a low growl, igniting heat inside of me. "And more's to come later on."

"Ryker! You're insatiable."

"I am. And you're all I crave. Damn, who knew becoming engaged would make one so horny?"

Shaking my head, I say, "You're silly."

"Over you, I am." He pecks my cheek and we find Sabrina bringing our plates to us.

"For the happy couple, I've spritzed up your breakfast this

morning for this special occasion. I do hope you think about letting us cater the reception and the rehearsal dinners."

I FIND a few leaves of spinach on top of the freeze-dried, scrambled, fake eggs and give her a smile. "Thank you for the lovely breakfast, Sabrina. Of course, we'll consider you and your team. With some real food, you could do wonders."

Enthusiasm is bubbling in her eyes. "We'll have to get together sometime soon to make the menus."

"Yes, we will," Ryker says. "I'm setting the wedding date for 31 days after we leave the dome. We'll go get our marriage license and marry the day after the 30-day waiting period. I don't want to waste a minute."

Sabrina smiles. "How sweet. I'll catch up with you guys later. After you've had time to make your decisions. Just so you know, I make excellent chicken and beef recipes."

"Noted," I say and get to eating the tasteless food. "I wanted to talk to you about breakfast too. Do, you have a second?"

"I do."

"I think we should get away from the freeze-dried breakfast foods. The garden has come in well. Do you think you could come up with some vegetable based breakfasts, so we can get away from this other food? You know, something we don't think of as breakfast food? Maybe, roasted eggplant with a tomato and basil puree. Or yellow squash with pearl onions made soup style. We need to make up menus only using what we grow."

"I got you. Because we'll use up all the freeze-dried food on the trip out, anyway." She nods in agreement.

"Yes, and my team has been working on plans to grow the plants as we travel, so that when we get there we can transplant them. That'll help us to set up much more quickly than we did here. If I'm going to Mars, I'm going to be sure we can set up quickly and efficiently."

. . .

RYKER SIGHS. "You have no idea how great it feels to hear you say that."

"What? That I'm going to figure things out?"

"No," he says then kisses my cheek. "That you're going."

Sabrina gives us a nod. "I gotta get to work. See you guys later."

Ryker gives me a quick kiss on the lips. "You're making me happier than I've ever been and I wasn't a real sad individual."

Stroking his long beard, I feel lighthearted and happier than I've ever felt too. "I suppose we'll get even happier than this. The day we get married."

"The night after the wedding," he says with a little grin and a wiggle of his brow.

I blush as heat fills me. "And when we have our babies."

"And when we have our first one on Mars," he says then leans in and gives me a longer kiss.

Applause fills the air and I feel my blush deepen but he won't let me go. He won't end the kiss and the clapping just keeps on going. And I'm finding an odd feeling inside of me.

Pride at being who this man has chosen to live his life with!

RYKER

IT'S the last night in the dome, the lights have been dimmed. Gia and I have cleaned up after a long day, and she's looking like a goddess as she lies on the bed. I move in next to her and kiss the warm spot right behind her left ear. "Tomorrow, we'll get up and leave this place behind. First thing is to go home and change clothes, go to the courthouse and apply for that marriage license, then go buy you a fat engagement ring and our wedding bands."

She sighs, making her breasts heave. "Ryker, this is unreal."

"It's very real, baby." I take her mouth with a sweet kiss.

Her arms run around me, taking me close to her. Our bodies start to heat as they touch. Her breasts feel squishy as they press against my chest. The sweet kiss grows into something a bit more sinister. A bit more heated.

I move my tongue in a stroking motion and she ends the kiss with small pecks. "Get on your back."

KNOWING what kind of Heaven she's about to take me to, I roll over and let her have her way with me. Her soft lips move over my stomach, inching down to where I'm ready and waiting for her.

She makes a brief pause to tickle my belly button with her tongue, making me giggle a bit, which I hate to do in the heat of the moment. "Gia!"

With a giggle, she stops and proceeds to the promised land. "Party pooper."

She's in a playful mood, which can be worrisome at times. When her hands move around to grip my ass, I feel her pinky sliding toward a place I've told her to stay the hell away from, so I change things around.

Sitting up, I grab her around the waist and flip her over my shoulder, making her land on her back. She's lying face up, so I move back until her face is level with my straining appendage. "Feeling playful, baby?"

She bites her lip as I dangle myself just over her mouth. Her arms are pinned under my legs and she's at my mercy. She gives me a wink. "I was, but I think I'm done with that."

"Good," I say as I run my finger over her lips then push it inside. She sucks it as she looks at me and I find an evil smile moving over my lips. "So, you want it like this?"

She nods and I pull my finger out and move my cock into her open mouth. From this position, watching her take me in, I'm hot as hell for her right now.

I pump myself in a rhythmic motion, finding her mouth warm and the small amount of sucking she's doing feels better than it does the other way. Leaning over to hold my body up with my hands, I go at her a little faster, making her moan.

Her arms are freed as I move my legs. She moves her hands to my ass, squeezing it. After a few minutes, the sensations are getting to me and I'm about to explode, so I start to pull away from her but she holds me tight. "Baby, I'm about to lose it."

She sucks hard, letting me know she wants that. So, I get back to what I was doing and keep up the short strokes. Fucking her like this has me hotter than usual. "You like that? You like when I skull fuck you, Gia?"

Her moan vibrates me just right. One of her hands move to mess with my balls and I can't take it any longer. My orgasm rips through me and she groans as it all shoots down her throat. My groan matches hers as I feel it all come out.

Moving back, I pull my cock out of her mouth. She runs the back of her hand across her mouth. "My turn."

"Yes, it is."

～

GIA

HIS HOT, wet tongue glides down my body. The way he handles me has me shaking with passion. His forcefulness is something that drives me wild. With the tip of his tongue, he taps at my clit that's pulsing and throbbing. "Yes," I moan as he changes the tap into an intimate kiss.

His dark hair has grown long and when I move my hands into it, they get lost in the thick depth. One of his fingers dallies around the edge of my vagina, teasing it into a frenzy. Pushing in two fingers, he pumps them as he licks my folds all the way up my clit, over and over until I'm begging him to fuck me. "Ryker! Please, put your dick in me. I need it!"

He chuckles as he moves up my body and slams his hard cock into me. "Is that what you want?"

I arch up to meet his hard thrusts. "Yes! Harder!"

Pounding me with his body, I feel the orgasm he started, taking off even more. "Shit, you're so fucking tight and rippling all over me, baby!"

Grabbing his huge biceps, I try to steady myself as my body is on sensory overload. "It just won't stop!"

He grinds into me with a deep groan. "Baby, I don't want it to stop."

I'm quivering, my head is spinning. *I might pass out!*

HAS anyone ever passed out from an orgasm that's went on for a long time?

"Ryker!" I scream as somehow, he makes a deeper plunge, hitting a spot that sends my body into a different level of pleasure. It's so intense, I grind my teeth as my head falls back and I writhe underneath him.

"Oh, baby! Oh, baby!" The hot wet feeling, as his dick jerks inside of me, has me screaming with him. Our bodies are soaked in sweat as he's finally given in to me.

Ragged breaths, pounding hearts, and a slight sloshing sound is all I can hear as he keeps moving a bit as his cock shoots the last remnants of cum into me.

He stays inside of me as he kisses my neck and holds his body up. I pull him to lean on me. I love the way it feels when his heart is pounding. I can feel it through my chest. I marvel at the way our hearts beat at different times and speeds.

"Ryker, that was off the charts."

A gentle bite on my earlobe makes me moan. "You liked that, did you? My naughty girl."

My moan answers him. "You fuck like a pro."

"So do you," he whispers. "And I'm about to make you mine in name too. Mrs. Crawford. Mrs. Ryker Crawford."

MY BREATHING STARTS to calm as does my heart and the sound him saying the words I never dreamt I'd hear have tears stinging the backs of my eyes. "I'm going to be your wife. I'm going to go to Mars as your wife. It's not a thing I thought I'd ever decide to do. Not in a million years."

Soft kisses are trailed down my neck then over my cheek. His dark eyes catch mine. "Just because you don't imagine something, doesn't mean it can't happen. You're about to be my wife. The mother of my children. The first lady of Mars."

I have to laugh at his over the top way of thinking. "You know, Ryker, things will be very different there. There will be no one to enforce anything. That's scary."

He moves off to the side of me then moves his hand to rest on my stomach. "I'm not worried about that at all."

"Honestly, you don't seem to be worried about anything that has to do with leaving this world to go to another one."

"Because I'm not worried about anything. I'm excited and quite frankly, now that I'll have you with me, I can't wait to go."

Closing my eyes, I have to take a few deep breaths before I go on, "Ryker, I'm scared about so many things. The weather, for one."

"It's colder there. Okay, we know that. And there are people working on making clothing that's not so bulky. They're coming up with materials and they're testing them in the Antarctic. Don't worry about that at all."

"We have no idea if our temporary facilitates will hold up if a wind storm pops up," I say as I pull the blanket up to cover me as a shiver has run through me with all of my fears.

"Our ship will be there to shield us from any bad storms."

"And what about breathing? What if the air is too thin for us to get adequate oxygen?"

He leans up on his elbow to look down at me. "We will acclimate to the air, the same way we've done here, on Earth. You know the air is thinner at higher altitudes and people have adapted."

With a huff, I say, "Is there no worry I have that you don't have an answer for?"

He shakes his head. "No."

"At least you're honest." I have to laugh as he looks at me through his massive beard. "That hair is getting cut tomorrow too. Right along with that beard."

HIS BROWS RAISE then he rubs his thick beard over my cheek, making me laugh as it tickles. "You don't want to marry a caveman, Gia?"

I laugh as I push him back. "Stop! That tickles. And no, I don't want to marry a caveman!"

He stops rubbing his beard on my face and kisses the tip of my nose. "Okay, I'll get all prettied up for you, baby. Anything you want, you got it."

"Anything?" I ask as my mind starts working.

"Anything," he tells me then his lips touch mine and I melt with his light kiss. "I'll do anything for you, Gia."

"I'll have to think on what else I want you to do for me," I say as I snuggle into his wide chest.

He lies down and cradles me in his arms. "Would you do anything for me?"

"Like what?"

"Like anything."

"Um, I'm not as free-spirited as you are. So, if it's within reason then I will do most anything for you."

"Would you walk through fire for me?" he asks.

"If there's a fire and you're on the opposite side of it…"

HE PLACES his finger on my lip. "You know what I mean. I need to know before we do all this. Would you kill for me? Would you die for me? Would you do all you had to for me? Because I would for you."

Blinking back tears, I find my heart swelling. "I would. I love you more than I've ever loved anyone. And I would do all those things for you. You don't have to worry about my commitment to you. I already am committed, now all we need is the paper to prove it. I wouldn't go to Mars for anyone else. That's the truth."

His eyes go a little glassy as he leans over and kisses me. "I know you wouldn't. I love you. We're going to make big changes, you and I."

"We are, aren't we?"

With one more kiss, he makes the fear in me subside. How does he do it?

8

PART 8 - THE REDEMPTION

GIA

L ilacs and Gardenias tied into small bouquets, make a scent
that has me feeling calm. "You look amazing," my sister,
Fancy, tells me as she comes into the dressing room.

"I feel amazing. I can't believe this is happening. It seems fast and
insanely slow at the same time. Such an odd feeling." I look at my
reflection in the long mirror that's surrounded with lights.

Handing me a glass of white wine, my sister, Nancy, looks in the
mirror too, adjusting the blue ribbon in her dark hair. "It got messed
up when I walked to the car to get the wine. The wind's terrible
today."

"At least this is inside," Fancy says as she pours herself a glass. "A
toast, ladies."

I take my glass, as does Nancy, to meet our sister in the middle of
the dressing room. "Don't make me cry, Fancy," I warn her.

HER SMILE DOES nothing to convey to me that she'll keep her sentiment short and sweet, instead of long and sappy. "Not to worry, baby

sister. Now, let's raise our glasses to adding another member to our ever-growing family." She pats Nancy's bulging tummy. "Along with the newest baby to enter our family, Ryker Crawford will be joining us. Thanks to you, Gia, finding that man has meant great things for us all. I want to wish you many years of happiness with the man who has brought you back to us. You had been gone for a while and we love having the old you back."

Nancy takes over, as often happens when the twins have something to say, "To you, Gia. The savior of the family!" She taps her glass to mine then so does Fancy.

I find myself near tears and the things they said weren't even remotely sad. "Why do I feel like crying? Did you two feel this way?"

They laugh and hug me, then Nancy hands me a handkerchief. "It's nerves, honey. You're completely normal in that aspect."

I dab at my tears, so they don't go cascading down my cheeks, ruining my make-up. "I've felt so calm up until now."

Fancy hugs me then hands me over to Nancy who takes over the hug. The door opens and Mom comes in, taking me next. "Oh, my baby girl."

"Mom, please don't say anything to make me cry anymore." I sniffle.

"Now, why would I do such a thing?" she asks me then lets me go. "Your father is talking to your young man right now. Giving him the speech he gave your brothers-in-law on their wedding days."

"Oh, Lord," I say as I go and take a seat. "Why, Mom?"

"It's his way of making sure the men who marry his daughters know what he expects out of them. I think it bonds them all. Ryker will be a part of the pack now."

Nancy's beams as she adds, "My hubby likes him a lot. They had a lot of fun at the bachelor party."

"That's what my husband said too," Fancy says as she puts a necklace around our mother's neck. "Gia bought these for us, so we'll all match."

Mom's hand goes to the pendant that's dangling from the platinum chain. "Are these real diamonds and sapphires?"

"They are." I gesture to the earrings in the box on the vanity. "And don't forget to put the matching earrings on too. Those are to be kept forever and handed down, you guys. I don't like to talk about price but those cost me a pretty penny. I expect you all to do the right thing with them. I'd like to see my nieces wearing them on their special occasions."

"How can you do that?" Nancy asks me with a frown. "You're going with him to Mars."

"He's working on figuring out how we can make trips back and forth. Who knows? Maybe one day you all will decide to make a visit to us."

Mom laughs as she shakes her head. "Not me! Not ever! I'm afraid of heights. I don't know how I'd feel about looking out a window and seeing nothing but space."

"Nonsense, Mom. You ride in the jet. You'd do just fine." I get up and stand next to her and look at all of us in the mirror. "We all clean up, nicely, don't we?"

With a sigh, Mom says, "You three are my pride and joy. Gia, you have to start your family soon. I want to get to see those grandkids for a while before you take them away from us."

My heart aches with her words. "It's not a thing I really want to do. I wish like hell there was an easier way to do something like start life on a new planet while still being able to see the ones you love."

"Don't go," Mom says as she takes my hand. "Talk Ryker into staying here. You can do that. He loves you like crazy. He'll do it for you."

"Mom, he's so committed to going. You have no idea. He was so lit up the entire six months we were in the dome. He was born to do this. I swear he was. It wouldn't be fair to marry him then peck at him about not going. I know it'll be hard but I have to go with him."

Mom nods and looks sad, making me feel sad too. "I know."

Fancy hands Mom a glass of wine too. "Drink this and let's not talk about things that are in the future. By the way, Doug and I have talked about going too."

Mom's eyes nearly pop out of her head and she chokes on the wine she was taking a sip of. I pat her on the back as Nancy takes the glass before she spills it. "No! No, Fancy! I take care of your kids. I love them like they're my very own."

"Oh, we wouldn't go until the youngest is out of college, Mom. Not to worry about that," Fancy assures her.

Mom doesn't look reassured. "What if you two change your mind and do take off before that?"

"We won't," she says with a shake of her head. "Neither of us feel that it's right to take a child to another world. They should be allowed to make their own decision about that."

I sit back down, in silence. *That must mean she thinks Ryker and I are bad people for taking our kids to Mars!*

Nancy catches my expression. "Gia, you are your own person. You and Ryker are allowed to make your own parenting decisions. I can see it written all over your face. You think we'll judge you. We won't."

"We won't," Fancy echoes.

"Speak for yourselves," Mom says then takes a big drink of her wine.

"Mom!" the twins shout at her.

Nancy runs her arm around me. "Don't worry about her, Gia. We've got your back."

A knock comes at the door. "You ladies decent?" my father's voice comes from the other side of the door.

"Yes, Daddy," Fancy answers him.

He opens the door and comes in with a twinkle in his eye. "How's my baby girl doing?"

With a wobble of my hand, I say, "So-so."

"MOM'S GIVING her the guilt treatment over going away to Mars with any grandkids she might have. Help her out, Dad," Nancy tells him.

"I will. It's time for you three to skedaddle, anyway. Ryker and his best man are already standing in their places, waiting on this pretty young lady."

Heat flushes my body and I find my breath ceasing. "Already?"

Mom kisses my cheek. "It's going to be fine. He is the right man for you, sweetie. I'm sorry for being so selfish. Everything will be fine. You'll see."

With a wave from my sisters, they all leave me alone with my father. I get up and he pulls the veil over my face. "You ready, baby girl?"

I nod and feel a lump in my throat. "Did my sisters cry when it came to this part too?"

"Like babies," he assures me as he takes my hand and places it in the crook of his arm. "And here's what I told them to be sure I left a smiling bride for my new sons-in-law."

We start our walk to my future as I swallow the lump. "Okay, Dad. Get rid of these tears and the freaking lump in my throat, please."

"A long time ago, I met a woman who I loved more than life itself. She could kiss like an angel and cook like a master chef. But my goodness that woman couldn't carry a tune in a bucket. And Lord have mercy did she love to sing. And not quietly, either. No, she sang loud and proud, as if her singing was any good at all. I swear the cats scattered when she'd start up."

I smile as I know what he's talking about. "Mom does do that."

"And that's what love does to you. It helps you keep on loving someone, even through their faults. If I never got to hear her caterwauling again, it would devastate me. Crazy, huh?"

We get to the back of the large main church and I find a smile is covering my face. The lump is gone and I can see Ryker from here. "Oh, God, he's one handsome man, isn't he, Dad?"

"I'd say so. And he's getting himself a gorgeous bride."

"You might be biased, Dad."

"Not me," he says with a chuckle.

The wedding march starts up, filling me with chills. "I'm really doing this, aren't I?"

. . .

"YOU REALLY ARE. I'm going to miss this. You're my last kid I get to walk down the aisle. The end of an era."

"You're making me mist up, Dad."

"Oh, hell. Sorry baby girl," he whispers as we go down the aisle, one slow step at a time. "Just remember these words. Marriage is a compromise. Laughter cures most things. Men can be bigger babies than actual babies. Especially after they get married. Don't ask me why. It just happens that way."

My smile has returned and we're at the place where my father kisses my cheek and passes me off to my soon to be husband. "Take good care of her, Ryker," Dad says then looks at me. "I love you, Gia."

"I love you, Daddy."

When Ryker takes my hand, the calmness fills me again. I have no worries where he's concerned. And I doubt I ever will.

~

RYKER

FALLING ONTO MY BACK, I try to catch my breath. "I've never danced so much."

Gia falls sideways onto the bed, just like I have. "Me, neither."

Our hands meet between us, our fingers lace and my eyes close. "What do you say to a little nap?"

She giggles. "I'm almost there. I never knew how exhausting weddings and the receptions that follow were."

EVEN THOUGH I am thoroughly exhausted, I feel compelled to do the husbandly thing and make sure my wife is comfortable. Lifting my body off the bed, I pull my tux off and take her hands, pulling her up too. "I need to get this off you."

"But I'm tired," she mumbles.

Standing her up, I turn her around, so I can unlace the back of the blue dress she put on for the reception. "You'll be comfier with this off."

When I push the dress off her shoulders, it falls in a puddle at her feet. Turning her around, she finally opens her eyes when I pull her bra off. "Hey, you don't have any clothes on."

With a laugh, I say, "What did you think I was doing when I got off the bed?"

"I think I was asleep." Her eyes roam up and down my body. "But I'm kind of getting hot for you. You're my husband now, Ryker. Mine. All mine!"

Taking her by the waist, I pull her closer and wrap my arms around her. "I'm kind of getting hot for you too, Mrs. Crawford."

"Show me."

The exhausted feelings begin to fade into the background as our bodies touch and adrenaline starts pumping. Lying her on the bed, I rip her panties off, making her smile.

"I'm not about to let our first night as man and wife be sex-free."

"Good." She licks her lips as I move my body over hers. Her legs spread apart as I settle between them. I watch her beautiful face as I push my cock into her. Her heated depths caress me as I move, stroking her.

"We're married, Gia."

Her eyes sparkle as she looks into mine. "We are."

Grinding into her, I watch her eyes close as she moans. "I'm going to make you so happy, you won't believe it."

Her eyes open. "You already are."

"Even more." I kiss her, twirling my tongue around her mouth. *My wife's mouth!*

WHEN OUR MOUTHS PART, I look back into her eyes as I continue my slow movements. "For better or worse."

She smiles. "For richer or poorer."

"As long as I have you, I will never feel poor."

She runs one foot up the side of my leg, making me go deeper into her. "Through sickness and in health."

"Until death do us part," I finish the vows we recited to one another hours ago. "I hope you meant all that."

"Of course, I did," she says with a frown. "Why would you say something like that?"

Moving a little faster, I realize I said something very stupid. "I don't know why I said that. I'm kind of loopy, I guess. Ignore me. Let's not talk."

"Divorce isn't even in my vocabulary, Ryker." Her hands move to my shoulders as her eyes narrow at me.

"I said I was sorry. Come on, no more talking." I kiss her to try to end the stupid conversation I started.

Moving faster and harder, I keep going until she's breathing hard. Then I move my mouth to suck on her neck. She loves when I do that. "No marks, Ryker. Tomorrow we're going to Bali. I want to wear a bathing suit all the time. Without your marks all over me."

Easing the sucking, I kiss and nip her neck, gently. "Sorry, boss."

Hooking my hands under her knees, I pull them up high, so I can go deeper. The sound she makes lets me know she's through thinking at all. Plunging into her with hard thrusts, I pull her hair. "Ryker! Yes!"

"You're mine now, Gia. No one can ever take you away from me!" I pound into her, cementing our union.

"Nor you from me," she says as her eyes open. "We are one."

My heart pounds as we look at one another. It's as if our souls are actually connecting. The words we said were a start but this act is the real glue. My body goes into hers, making a connection that was intended to make two people into one magnificent creature.

"My God, you're gorgeous."

Her hand moves over my cheek. "I get to look at this handsome face from now on. I get to kiss this face whenever I want to."

With a smile, I make a very hard thrust, knocking the air from her. "Whenever I want, I can make you scream my name."

"Make me scream it now."

"You asked for it." I pull out and flip her over, pulling her back to me and ram into her from behind as I hold her waist.

SHE MOANS but doesn't scream. I push her shoulders to the bed, making her ass lift higher into the air. When I make harder thrusts, I can feel her getting wetter. Her moans continue as I pump away. When her walls start contracting, her moans get louder and when I don't stop as she climaxes, she screams, "Yes! God, yes! Ryker! Ryker!"

"Damn you sound sexy as hell when you scream my name, baby. You like it when I fuck you, don't you?"

"Yes!" Her body quivers as I don't relent. I watch her hands fist the sheets as she bears down with the orgasm. "Fuck!"

She's shaking like crazy now and I decide it's time to finish her, so we can get some rest. I pull out and flip her onto her back. Getting off the bed, I yank her until her ass is at the end of the bed, then I thrust into her again.

"I love to watch you cum."

She moans as I look at her. She's glowing with perspiration and passion. Her orgasm is waning, I can feel it. So, I give my finger a lick and run it over her swollen clit.

Her eyes spring open and she pants like an animal. "Ryker!"

"I want you to give me one more before I end this. Tell me you'll give it to me, Gia." I run my hand over my cock when I pull it nearly all the way out, wetting it and using our combined juices to lubricate my fingers that I use on her clit.

"I'll come all over your cock, baby. Keep fucking me hard and I'll come all over you."

I watch my finger as it moves in circles over her sex. My cock moves in and out of her, making me very close to meeting my end. With a glance at her, I see she's watching me touch her too. Her legs begin to quiver as they're hung over the end of the bed. "Ohhh!"

The contractions of another orgasm, ripple all over my cock and I can't take it any longer. I blow my wad as she screams my name. My head goes light with the action and I have to lean over to steady myself. My face is lying on her stomach as I jerk all I have into her.

Her hands move through my hair. "I love you," I mumble then press my lips to her flat belly. "I really do love you, Gia."

"I know you do. I love you too. Can we sleep now that we've consummated this marriage?"

With a silent nod, I pull my body off hers and we both climb under the blankets and cuddle up together. "Sweet dreams," I tell her as I'm nearly asleep already.

I'm met with her soft snore and can fall asleep, knowing I've got my wife by my side.

Gia is my wife!

~

GIA

A SHAFT of bright light hits me directly in my right eye. Rolling over to avoid it, I find the bed empty in the hotel room Ryker and I spent our first night as a married couple in. "Baby," I mutter.

No answer comes and I have to actually raise my head to see where my brand new hubby is. I see no one around. With a huff, I move my, still tired body, out of the bed, the soft, comfy, cozy bed, to get up and find my missing half.

As I get up on my feet, I realize that was a mistake. The night of dancing more than I've ever done in my entire life combined, has left my legs in a noodle-like state. When the door opens, I shriek as I see a maid coming in and I'm naked, "No!"

"Oh, sorry, ma'am. I thought the room was empty. The register says it is."

Blinking at her, I find it odd she hasn't left the room yet. *I am sitting here naked after all!*

"WELL, I didn't break in here! Do you mind?"

"I have to report this." She picks up a walkie talkie and I climb back under the blankets.

"Report away!"

"There's someone in the bridal suite."

"Excuse me." I hear Ryker say from the hallway. "May I help you?"

"That room is supposed to be empty," the voice on the walkie talkie tells her.

"It is not," Ryker corrects the voice.

The maid looks at him with a frown. "Who are you?"

"Ryker Crawford. The man who rented this room for the night."

"You checked out," she tells him.

"No. As you can see, I'm right here and my wife is inside. Pretty pissed I bet."

"She does look unhappy," she says. "But you did check out."

"Let me leave these things with my wife and I will be happy to go down to the front desk and fix this." She steps aside and he comes in. A bag from my favorite café is in his hand. "Bagels with cream cheese from your favorite breakfast spot, my esteemed wife."

My mouth begins to water, instantly. "My hero!" I hold out my arms to take the delicious breakfast he's provided for me. "Could I get any luckier?"

"No," he says with a grin. "Eat this." He pulls the pink tissue paper wrapped goodie out of the bag, along with a tall coffee cup. "I'll be right back. Once I clear this up."

AFTER A CHASTE KISS on top of my head, he and the maid leave the room. And I find my cell ringing. I look across the large room. The phone is on the dresser. The walk seems so far and my hot coffee and warm bagel are looking at me with soulful eyes, begging me to ignore the call and devour them.

My curiosity gets the best of me and I drag my body out of the bed and go to get the phone. I stop as my eyes catch the name on my screen. *Damien Markov!*

. . .

TAKING THE PHONE WITH ME, I don't answer it. I let it go to voicemail and slip back under the blankets. *He can suck it!*

CURIOSITY GETS the best of me, yet again, as the phone dings telling me he's left a message. I tap the screen to listen as his voice comes over my phone for the first time in over a year, "Gia, I know you weren't expecting this call from me. I wanted you to be the first to know this. We've planned our first mission to Mars. It will be in three months. I will be gone from here in three months and I wanted to let you know that Ryker will too. He and I talked and he said he wasn't going to tell you. I thought you should know."

I sit in complete silence and feel kind of numb. *Why would Ryker not tell me this?*

Will this not be public information? Is there some reason he doesn't want me to know? And what is this shit that he's going too? Is it on the Russian mission?

THE DOOR OPENS and Ryker comes in. "It was a weird mistake. Someone actually called in and said he was me. He told them I forgot to stop by the front desk and check out but that you and I had left. Crazy, huh?"

"Yep." That's all I can say. *I'm stunned.*

"HEY, I expected that bagel to be crumbs by now. What's up?" He runs his finger over the bagel that I'm not hungry for at all anymore.

"I feel sick."

"Hung over?" He grins.

"More like, run over." I give him a blatant stare.

He walks away from me, looking pretty guilty. "You seem kind of mad."

"I wouldn't call it that."

Sitting at the table, I notice he's staying away from me. "What would you call it?"

I toss my cell at him. *Well, toss is an understatement.* I throw it directly at his head.

"What the..." He catches the phone. "Gia, what the hell are you doing?"

"Press the voicemail."

He does and he hears the call I just got. I watch him go a bit pale. "That bastard!"

"What the hell happened? Why the hell didn't you want to tell me?" I pull the blanket up, even more, to cover myself, feeling naked and even violated for some damn reason.

"Gia, I wanted to. I was going to do it in my own time. And he knew that."

"Ryker, what's going on? Are you not going to take me?"

When he shakes his head, I pull the pillow over my face, so he doesn't see me crying. I feel lied to! I feel betrayed! I feel stupid!

His hands run up my arms, then he pulls the pillow away. "Baby, the World Space Exploration Center has made a mandatory decision. A group made up of only six men will be the first mission to Mars. Upon our arrival, if we can make a go of things, then others can come."

"No," I say with a soft voice. "You can't go."

"The men were hand-picked."

"Ryker, you can say, no."

"I don't want to."

I can only stare at him. My heart has stopped. "I'm asking you not to go."

"Don't."

"Damn it, Ryker! You'll be gone for eight months, just on travel time if everything goes right! Then you'll have a tiny team to get things going. No! No, you can't go! You can't!"

"It may take a year or more to make sure it's safe there. You see, a research craft came back with evidence of water. It also came back with evidence of what might be life. There may be life forms there. Hiding beneath the surface."

"And what would you do about that?" I ask as more tears are threatening me but I keep them at bay. "Ryker, if there are people or other creatures hiding under the surface, they may see your team as a threat and kill you all."

He nods and I can't hold the tears back any longer. "No! A thousand times, no!"

"I was born to do this."

"I was born to tell you not to." I hold his dark eyes with my stony glare. "You are my husband!"

"YOU ARE MY WIFE. You will stand by me as I do what I feel is my duty to do. This isn't about you or me. This is about the expansion of our race. The human race. Women and children have no place in a frontier that may have inhabitants that could kill them all. It's our duty, not only as men, but men who know a thing or two about the planet and how to make a life on it. Only men, who've been at the forefront of this mission to get to Mars, have been chosen. It's an honor and a privilege, Gia."

"And I may lose my husband to it!"

I watch his Adam's apple bob in his throat. I watch his eyes open wide. I watch him turn into a man I've never seen before. "You may."

"So, now you're a soldier, Ryker? I didn't marry a soldier. I married a very intelligent man. Not a mindless robot for the powers that be, to control. I want to be with you when you first step foot on that planet. I want to be with you when you take your first breath of Martian air. I want to be with you when you first lay eyes on the planet. You're stealing my dreams if you go without me."

"You're stealing mine, if you don't allow me to go, with your blessing, Gia."

I don't know what to think. All of what I thought has been turned upside down. My one, true love, my husband wants to go. Leave me. Maybe forever.

"I'm afraid." I bat back the tears, I've managed to reign in.

His arms close me in a circle and I feel the warmth of his body and wonder how I can possibly live without him for that length of time. Or maybe even forever. "So am I. But fears must be faced or nothing would ever happen."

"I hate your bravery." I run my hands up and down his muscled back. "I hate your need to conquer new worlds."

"But you knew I had those things when you married me," he says with a chuckle that pisses me off.

"Yesterday." I let him go and glare at him. "Yesterday, I married you. Yesterday, the plans were still the same. I would go with you on the first mission! And now look what's happened!"

"Would you not have married me if this would've come up one day sooner?"

I lie back on the bed and put my hands behind my head, which feels as if it might explode. Would I have married him? Would I have put myself in this boat? Would a day earlier of knowing this make a difference?

"Ryker, what if I get pregnant? Will you still leave?"

HE AND I both know I'm in a fertile state. He and I planned it that way. Our plan was to get pregnant right away. And now he wants to leave.

"I trust you to take excellent care of our child until you can come to me."

"And if that time never comes? What happens if you're killed by whatever is there, hiding under the ground?"

He stops, looking as if that's not occurred to him. "I suppose they'll give us weapons."

"Are you going to kill them all?"

He looks a bit unsure and sits on the bed. "Gia, help me. Help us to figure things out. I need your help, baby. I need it. You're brilliant. You think of things others don't. Help us all."

I cross my arms over my chest. "What if I don't want to help you go to a dangerous situation?"

"What if I need you too?"

I stare at him and wonder what the hell he's gotten us into. "I'm pissed right now."

"I know."

"Fuck! Ryker! Fuck! Everything has changed! God, damn it all to hell!"

"Gia, please don't say that." He takes me in his arms and holds me tightly against his chest. "Baby, I need you in my corner. Like never before, I need you. You said it before. You might be more help from Earth. I need you to be my help from here. Tell me you'll do it for me. For us all."

I have no idea of what I should say or do. I could get an annulment. I could move on with my life. I could try my best to forget Ryker Crawford. All of these options are mine.

"For better or worse," he murmurs as he kisses the place he loves to kiss, just behind my left ear.

"Till death do us part."

~

RYKER

THE FIRST MEETING of the team going to Mars is over. The plans are set and the information NASA retrieved has been given to us. Damien and I walk out of the conference room together. "She's taking it badly, isn't she?" he asks me.

I shove my hands in my pockets with a huff. "Badly isn't even strong enough for what she is. Gia is a mixture of disappointed, pissed, and scared to death. It makes for a shaky, cranky, erratic woman who cries, throws things, and screams like a banshee over things that don't amount to a hill of beans."

"Svetlana is unhappy as well. To make matters worse, I've had to issue her funds through a bank account my family knows nothing about. If she blows through the money, I don't know what she'll do." He looks worried and I feel bad for him for some damn reason.

"Thank God Gia can take care of herself. Now can you see how important it is to let your woman have her independence?"

"Do you think she'd look out for Svetlana and my son for me, while I'm gone?"

I STOP WALKING and stare at the man. "Are you kidding?"

"So, you think there's no way she'd help them out if they find themselves running out of money?"

Taking off again, I shake my head. "I don't know what she'd do. That's your deal to take care of, Damien. Gia is in no mood to be asked such a thing. She'd likely bite your head off if you did ask."

The glass doors slide open and we walk out into the bright sunshine. Both of us pull out sunglasses and put them on as we go to our cars. "Maybe I can find someone else to watch over them." Damien looks away as he heads toward his rental car. "You want to grab some lunch?"

"I've got to get back to my office. Gia asked me to meet her there after the meeting. She wants to know every little detail."

He stops and pulls his glasses down to look at me. "Except the one we were told not to disclose."

"Of course. I think she'd hog tie me and hide me away if she knew about that." Getting to my car I give him a wave and get in.

The secret we have to keep will be hard to do. Gia can be tenacious. But she can't know about this. *No one can!*

GIA

THE THREE MONTHS have passed far too quickly. In five days, the mission to Mars will leave, taking my husband away for God only knows how long. I lay on our bed, watching Ryker as he comes out of the bathroom, rubbing his head with a towel to dry his dark hair. "You look cozy." He tosses the towel away and it lands on the floor.

"Don't just leave that there," I snap at him.

I've been snapping at him a lot since he told me he was leaving. I feel a tiny bit of guilt as he goes to pick up the towel and places it on the back of a chair. "Sorry."

I hate how sad he's looked lately. But I also hate how sad I've been feeling. "When are you going to talk to me, Ryker?"

"I do talk to you, Gia." He climbs into the bed, pulling the blanket up then fluffing his pillows before he lies back on them.

"No, you don't." I huff then turn over on my side.

The fact is, I have something to tell him but I can't seem to make myself say it. It wouldn't change a thing if he knew it, anyway. I'm just so mad at him for going on this damn mission that it consumes me.

I feel his hand running over my shoulder. "Can't we get along these last few days, Gia? Can you pretend I'm not leaving?"

Flipping over, I look at him as tears trickle down my cheeks. "No, I can't pretend that. This is hard enough as it is, without adding in denial to this recipe for disaster. You've been dreaming lately. Talking in your sleep."

HE WIPES MY TEARS AWAY. "I have?"

"You have. You're hiding something from me. I deserve to know. I should know."

He looks at me for a while then says, "I am hiding something. And I'm not at liberty to discuss it with anyone, other than my team and our supervisors. If I could tell you about it, I would."

"It's dangerous. More dangerous than most people are aware of. And you want to walk right into it. Why?"

"Someone has to do it, Gia."

"They're training you all for battle. A battle cannot be won by six men. So, tell me why you'd go on a suicide mission. I don't understand."

"It's not a suicide mission. We're all being trained and given what we need to win the battle. If there is one. No one knows for certain if there will be one."

Sitting up in the bed, I cross my arms over my chest. "If there is one, how will you be able to retreat if necessary? No one has made any plan for that."

"Because you know there's no retreating. I wish you wouldn't worry. We do have plans in place and some things no one knows about. I feel confident in our training and our gear. Can't that be enough for you?"

"No."

My stomach growls and he looks at it. "Hungry? Did you eat anything at all today?"

I shake my head. "Food isn't sitting right with me, lately. I do take the capsules, though. I'm being nourished. As if you care." I huff and lay back down, pulling the blanket up.

"I do care, Gia." His hand moves through my hair. "I'm not going because I don't care about you. You know that."

"I don't know anything except you're leaving me and I may never see you again. That's all I know for sure." The urge to spit out what I should tell him fills my head as he runs his hands through my hair.

"I'm not really leaving you. You don't know you'll never see me again. For all you know, you may be following me sometime next year."

"I may be following you before that," I let him know. "You see, I've signed up for a mission too. I'm in the second group."

When his hand freezes, I know I've surprised him and he's not pleasantly surprised, either. "The second group? I wasn't aware there was going to be one. And how long have you been keeping this from me?"

· · ·

"A WEEK. I was approached a week ago. And you're not aware of it because a private company is funding the project. There will be twenty of us."

"You can't go, Gia. That private company isn't privy to the information we have from NASA. You can't go." He pulls me over, so I have to look at him. "There's more to Mars than others are aware of."

"I am going. If you're going, then I'm going too. I'll be right behind you, baby."

"I have to make a call," he says then gets out of bed. "No missions, other than ours can be sent."

"There is no governmental control over this, Ryker." I sit back up and watch him as he takes his cell and leaves the room.

I suppose he can't talk in front of me. I suppose there's a huge cover-up or secret about Mars that only a select few can know. And that tells me more about the danger that's lurking there.

My stomach goes tense and I jump out of bed and run to the bathroom. My nerves have gotten the best of me, lately. I've thrown up so many times in the last week, it seems at times like I have a virus.

I hear the bedroom door close as he comes back in then I hear him come into the bathroom. "Baby, are you sick?"

Flushing the toilet, I shake my head. "Nerves. This shit is getting to me. I'm having a hard time keeping myself together."

Wetting a washcloth in the sink, he brings it to me and helps me up off the floor where I ended up as I feel weak. Gently, he wipes my face then picks me up into his arms and carries me back to bed. "I'm sorry about all of this. I am."

Wrapping my arms around his neck, I bury my face in his chest as a sob escapes me. "Ryker, I can't take this. I can't."

"Shh, baby. It's going to be alright. You'll see. Everything is going to be alright. I'm going to make sure it is." Sitting on the edge of the bed, he cradles me on his lap.

"It's not going to be alright. You may stop me from following you with that mission but you can't stop me forever. If you go, so do I."

"Gia, it may be dangerous. You can come when we've found out if it's safe or not."

"Let someone else do that, Ryker. Let someone who doesn't have a wife do that. I'm begging you."

His hand moves up my arm then he takes my face in it and makes me look at him. "If I tell you what the secret is, can you keep it a secret?"

All I can do is look at him. I know I'll feel compelled to do something to stop the mission if it's really bad. But I have to keep that fact to myself and utter a lie, "I can keep it a secret, Ryker."

The way he looks into my eyes has my heart pounding. I wait and wait for him to tell me the big, dangerous secret. When his cell rings, I look away from him, finding the word, abort, blazing across the screen. "I'll be right back." He gets up, still holding me, then places me on the bed. Grabbing the phone, he walks out of the room.

I can't stand it any longer. I sneak out after him to hear what he has to say to the odd call. Just as I open the door, he's coming back in and gives me a look that tells me he's not happy about catching me coming after him. "What are you doing, Gia?"

"What are you doing?" I turn the question back on him. "Tell me what that's about."

"I can't. And I can't let you in on the secret, either. I had no idea the extent they've gone to, to make sure no one talks. The room must be bugged or my phone or something. They knew I was about to tell you the secret."

I step back into the bedroom, more than a bit shocked. "Ryker, do they have you over a barrel? Do you have to go on this mission or they'll do something to you?"

He just stares at me then blinks once, slowly. I can see they are using something to make him go on this mission. Taking his hand, I pull him back to the bed.

I've been so upset with this whole thing, I've hardly been intimate with him at all. He's been in training for hours every single day. And one weekend they kept them at the training facility for two nights. When he came back home, he was kind of stiff-necked.

I run my hands up his arms after I climb onto his lap as he sits on the bed. "Make love to me." Moving my hands over his shoulders, I send them on a path to check the back of his neck. When he reaches up, taking my hands in his to stop me, I know he must have some type of implant back there I'm not supposed to find.

"Baby, you don't know how good it is to hear you say that." His lips brush mine, sending sparks through me. "It's been so damn long since you've let me touch you."

"I'm not going to fight you about this anymore." I know now that he's pretty much at the mercy of the men who've set this whole thing up. I'm not about to put any more pressure on him about it. I'm going to stop them, though. I'm not sure how I'm going to do it but I am going to stop it.

He moves me off his lap and onto the bed. Unbuttoning my pajama shirt, he moves it off me as he looks at my breasts. His hands move over them then he leans over and takes one into his mouth. When he makes a gentle suck, it hurts like hell. I hold back a yelp and grit my teeth.

TRYING to send him on to better places, I reach out and grab the bottom of his T-shirt and pull it off, over his head, making him leave my tender breasts alone.

He smiles as he pulls my pajama bottoms off then gets rid of his too. My pink satin panties are all that's left between us and he grins at me as he rips them off me. I shudder with the action. It's been three months since he and I have done a thing.

"You've lost weight, Gia." He runs his hand over my flat stomach then over my hip bones which are jutting out. "You must eat."

"I will. I promise." I bite my lip as I've let things go as I've done little else, other than worry about him leaving.

Slowly, he moves his hands up my sides as he moves to cover my body with his. His lips meet mine and he gives me his sweet kiss. Desire rips through me and an instant need for him fills me.

His kiss grows intense in no time and our bodies grind together as they fight to get to the good stuff. I move my legs all over his then spread them wide for him. When he eases his hard cock into me, I groan with how good it feels and so does he. "Gia, my God."

"Ryker," I moan his name and run my nails over his back.

He moves in a slow rhythm, making my body heat and shiver at the same time. His lips press against my neck then he bites it with a softness that sends another set of chills over my body.

Every touch, every movement, further cements the idea in my mind that I have to do something to stop the mission he's seemed to be so down to go on.

Arching up to him, I spur him on until he's raging with an animal-like need for me. My hands move all over him, rubbing, clawing, raking. Then I move one of them in a circular pattern while the other moves up to the back of his neck.

I only get the smallest touch before he takes my hand and holds it down. But I felt something. A tiny bump, but he's trying his best to hide it. I know it's some kind of a device to track him or maybe even run him.

There's no reason to ask him a thing about it. I know now that he can't tell me or anyone else a thing. I begin to feel tremendous guilt over how I've treated him.

When I haven't been cold and distant, I've been bitchy and vindictive. A thing I'm ashamed of myself for now. I should've known there had to be extenuating circumstances for him going.

"Gia, baby, I love you so much," he whispers in my ear then bites my earlobe.

"Ryker, I'm so sorry." Tears flow like rivers as remorse tortures me. *I have to do something to help him!*

All the money in the world isn't helping him to do what he really wants. It seems maybe my mind, the thing he always saw as my best attribute, is about the only thing that can save him from this thing.

The waves of pleasure rumble through me and I'm shouting his name over and over with each surge. With a groan, he joins me, letting our bodies reconnect in the way they love to but I've denied them.

"Ryker, I love you."

"I love you, Gia."

Now I have to figure out what I have to do to save him.

RYKER

"You tell me how in the hell we're supposed to do this thing," I shout at the man in charge of our team, Captain Smithfield.

He looks at me with a frown so deep, his wrinkles have wrinkles. "Crawford, you know this mission is important to mankind. You were all in, up until a couple of weeks ago."

"After the implant was placed in us, I lost faith in this whole thing. I've felt weird since that moment. I've felt unlike myself. I want it removed. I want out of this. I think there's a lot of lying that's happening and I think we've been chosen to man this mission based on the fact the six of us are the top people who've made the discoveries that are needed to make life on Mars a reality. Get rid of us, get rid of the idea of going there."

"You don't know what you're talking about." His heels click as he turns away from me. "What's gotten into you?"

"The implant, possibly. I've had nightmares and thought things I've never thought about before. Things that scare me. I've also had thoughts about why all the governments want this stopped. I came up with a plausible reason too. Money."

"There's more than you six who pay taxes, Crawford. I think you're being paranoid." He takes a seat behind his large oak desk and takes out a pad of paper. "I'm sending you to the shrink. You need to be reevaluated."

"Send me to the clinic to have this thing removed. I won't be going on that mission. And I'm about to make sure it doesn't happen at all. You seem to think we're all idiots. I'm not talking about only our tax dollars, I'm talking about everyone who leaves this planet. This corrupt planet."

HE SIGHS and points at the chair in front of his desk. "Crawford, you're a smart man. All of you are. What none of you understand is the fact that I own you all. You signed a contract and I'm holding you to it."

"That's a contract that will ensure our deaths. Not only will you be able to get rid of us but all other missions will be stopped as the planet will be deemed too dangerous." I lean up and glare at him. "Do I need to go public with this?"

"With what, your conspiracy theory?" He laughs, infuriating me.

"With the truth, Smithfield. The truth about how you have us all made into highly trained assassins now. You took six men. All of us smarter than your average person and all of us with one wish. To see Mars and live there. Now, you tell me what the world would think about what you've done with us. Why make us into killing machines?"

"You saw the pictures of what you'll be up against. If we were to show the common people what's there, in their universe, there'd be chaos the likes this world has never seen before. Would you want that, Crawford?"

"There are only six of us and those things are huge. How can you expect us to take them all out?"

"WITH THE SPECIALIZED WEAPONS, we've made. You know that. It's almost like the last few months have ceased to exist in your head. Perhaps the implant is messing up. Maybe the clinic is where you need to go. This isn't like you. Not one bit. You've always been my best man for this mission. You were full of passion for it, in the beginning."

Shaking my head, I say, "That was because I thought it was real then. I don't anymore. I think it's a setup to get rid of us and the whole Mars program."

"Look, the discoveries you're combined industries have made can help more than people who want to live on Mars. They can help people here too. Yet, none of you want to share your discoveries with anyone here. Why is that?"

"Why is it you're just now asking this question? It cements exactly what I've been thinking. You get rid of us, the owners and CEO's of the top six space exploration companies, then what?" I hold up my hand to stop him from answering the question. "I'll tell you what. Then the governments come in and take over our companies that we've worked so hard for. They take our technologies and use them. Making the government's money that should belong to us and our shareholders."

"Wow, you really have an active imagination," he says as he writes something on the pad of paper. "Let me make a call to get you into the clinic right away. I'm afraid major paranoia is setting in. That implant needs to be replaced. I'm not letting you out of the contract you signed. If I have to keep you here for the next three days, until the shuttle leaves, then I will."

SITTING BACK, I cross my arms over my chest and smile at him. "You do that and my wife will tear this place apart to find me."

"I'm supposed to be afraid of a little woman?" he asks with a laugh.

"You should. She's kind of a pit bull when it comes to me." I can see he's not taking me seriously.

I know he can keep me here. I can't even leave this office without him opening the door, using his retina. But I can count on Gia to find me. She knows I'm here after all.

A knock at the door, has me looking back at it and he hits a button under his desk then leans over. A green light moves over his eye then the door opens. Two men in camouflage uniforms come in and I see where we're headed with this.

"These men will escort you to the clinic where a new implant will be inserted and the old one will be removed. I hope to see you back to your normal self soon, Crawford. Either way, you're going on the mission."

I look at the mindless goons and ask them, "Do either of you think it's right to send a man to outer space without his consent? And with possible mental issues, as the captain thinks I'm having?" Neither looks at me, both look straight ahead. I look at Smithfield and smile. "And you're going to tell my wife what exactly?"

"That we're quarantining you all until the shuttle leaves. For health reasons."

None of the other men are in the facility at this time. So, I have my doubts about him being able to get them to come in and submit to being held here for their last few days on Earth with their loved ones.

"You do that." I turn around and walk out of his office, flanked by the men who will make sure I get to the clinic.

No one has any idea that Gia and Damien have a past. She will call him when she gets this news, I'm sure. Then we'll see what happens.

I never thought I'd be happy about her having a past with that man but things seem to always happen for a reason!

GIA

"So, what you're telling me is that I can't see my husband before he goes on a mission he might not come back from?" I ask the man who's called me to tell me Ryker and the rest of the team will be kept at the facility until the shuttle leaves.

"There will be a brief chance to talk to him when they leave this facility to get on the shuttle. This is for their health, Mrs. Crawford."

"And why did this suddenly occur?"

"Our doctors decided this. You can come to the lift-off in three days at nine in the morning. See you then." He hangs up and I'm left shaking as I hold my phone in one hand and the pregnancy test I just took in the other.

I drop the phone and look to find out what the results are. *Positive!*

AND I CAN'T EVEN TELL the baby's father the good news!

Picking my cell back up, I call the only other man I know who's on the team with Ryker. "Hi," Damien answers his cell. "It's good to hear from you, Gia. I'm glad you've called."

"Um, okay." I hesitate as I'm not sure what the hell to say. "Damien, how come I can talk to you but not my husband?"

"What do you mean?"

"I mean, I just got a call from Captain Smithfield that said all of you are being kept at the facility for the next three days until the shuttle leaves. For health reasons. So, why are you able to have your phone but Ryker's not?"

Confusion is threaded through his deep voice, "What are you talking about?"

"I think something's wrong, Damien."

"I'll go up there and find out what's going on," he says. "I'll get back to you soon."

"Wait! What if they keep you too?" I ask him as I'm starting to get really worried about this whole thing. Even more, than I already was.

"I don't see how they could do that. I wanted to ask you something, though. Do you suppose it would be too much to ask you to watch out for Svetlana and Friedrich while I'm gone? And could you make sure they make it onto the Russian shuttle when it leaves?"

"Uh, really?" I ask him as that kind of is too much to ask of me.

"Yes," he says with a soft tone. "It's hard for me to leave here without them. Unfortunately, it's necessary for everyone's safety."

"Damien, what's the deal with Mars? What is it that you six are supposed to go and do what will ensure the safety of all others who will come after you?"

"I'm not at..."

I interrupt him, "...Liberty to discuss that. Yeah, I know. I just thought for a moment that you might want to let me in on it. I know you all have had some type of an implant placed at the back of your neck."

"I don't know where you'd get a silly idea like that, Gia." I hear another ringing sound in the background. "Can you hold on a minute? I'm getting another call."

"I can."

I CAN HEAR him as he answers the other phone. "Markov here. And why is that, sir? I am currently on my private cell phone with her right now. She's wondering why I'm not being kept at the facility, Captain Smithfield. When did you decide to do that? Is he okay now? I see. Yes, I can go in. Can you give me a little while to tell some people what I'm doing? A half hour. Yes, sir."

"Damien?"

"Gia, I have to go. I'm sorry about this. I really am. See if you can't find it in your heart to do what I've asked about my family. You're the only one who knows who they are to me. Try to get them to me on Mars."

"Damien, something's not right. What's happened to Ryker? What have they done to him?"

"I think you know I can't discuss that with you. He's alright. Just know that. I have thirty minutes to get to the facility. I have to get going. Please do as I've asked you to." He ends the call, leaving me hanging.

With another phone call, I make my way to grab my purse and head out to the facility that's taken over my husband. "Hi, I'm going to need your help with a situation. Are you still dating that news reporter?"

"Yes, why?" my colleague from work, Brittney, tells me.

"Can you grab him and meet me at 405 East Callahan Street? I'm going to need the media's help to get to the bottom of this mission

Ryker's been asked to go on. It seems he's been forced to go and now he's being kept at the facility under false pretenses."

"Oh, Lord!" she says with shock. "I'll get him and meet you there."

Ending the call, I get into my car and start it then I stop and think about how much time Ryker's been spending locked in his office and how his office is always locked now. Getting out of the car, I head back inside to get into his home office to see if he's been hiding anything from me.

Of course, I find the door locked, so I go get a knife out of the kitchen and run it between the door frame and the lock, jimmying it open. Taking the knife with me, I find the top drawer of his desk locked too and I stab at it until I get it open too. A file is in it and little else.

Pulling it out, I open it and find a picture of something that looks out of this world. A huge creature with giant teeth and sharp claws, the likes of which I've never seen before. And there are dozens more of them in the background. I pull it out and see a page behind it that reads, 'objective, get rid of these creatures before population begins.'

So, that's what they're sending them to do. Kill these things, so others can go there.

Not my man, not him!

9

PART 9 - THE DIFFERENCES

RYKER

Pain radiates down my spine as the doctor pushes a needle into the spot next to the implant on the back of my neck to numb it, so it can be removed. The two men, who escorted me to the clinic, are standing just outside the door of the small examination room they brought me to. My mind is a flurry of ideas about how the hell to get out of this place in one piece.

"There's a small amount of redness around the implant," he says as the numbing medicine begins to work. I can feel him pushing it but it doesn't hurt. "Have you been trying to take this out yourself?"

I keep my answer short. "No." But I have been trying to get it out. It's impossible to get at it on my own. A thing I'm sure that was thought of when they decided where to place these things on us, in the first place.

"This is an important device for you to have, Mr. Crawford. You have to be careful with this area. Captain Smithfield has written on this report that yours seems to be malfunctioning. Giving you paranoid thoughts. Can you explain to me what kinds of thoughts you've been having?"

. . .

HESITATING, as I think about what to say, I finally ask him, "How long have you been a part of this organization?"

"Not long," he says as he goes over to pick up a tray of surgical tools. A sharp scalpel catches my eye as the overhead light catches the silver object, making it gleam. "A bit over a year. When the team was formed."

"I thought the pictures from Mars with the creatures just got back to NASA four months ago." I watch him pick up the sharp scalpel and grit my teeth as I know he's about to slice my neck open.

"Oh, yes they did," he says and I think I've caught onto something.

"Then why would the team have been formed a year ago?" I feel the incision he's making. It's not painful but I can feel some pressure.

The sound of the metal implant clanks into a stainless-steel bowl behind my back and I know I'm free of the device. And this old man will play hell putting another one in me. He makes his way across the small room to leave the bowl on the counter top then he comes back with a bandage. "Let me cover this up to stop the bleeding. I have to run down to the supply closet to get another implant. I'll be right back, Mr. Crawford."

It's not lost on me that he doesn't answer my question. As I watch him leave, I reach back and touch the bandage covering the hole in my neck. *I'm free!*

THE TWO GUARDS are still right outside the door that has a glass window at the top of it, so I can see them clearly and they can see me. But they're looking straight ahead. I think I can use what I've learned to gain their weapons from them, rendering them useless to stop me.

Just as I get off the exam table I see Damien walking up to them but I can't hear a word anyone of them is saying. Then he comes in and I'm stuck. "Ryker, what's going on?"

"Damien, I need to get the hell out of here and I think you should too. This is a trap and..." I stop when he holds up his hand and points to the back of his neck then winks.

"Ryker, have you gone insane? What's happening to you? This is crazy talk. I heard your implant went haywire." He walks over to where the bloody scalpel is and takes it, cleaning it with alcohol. "After a new implant is inserted, you'll be back to normal." He comes to me and hands me the surgical knife. With a nod, he turns his back to me and holds up his hair.

Going along with him, I say, "You don't understand, Damien. They mean to kill us all. I think even the pictures are a hoax. It's as plain as the nose on my face what they want. They want us all dead, ending the plans to leave this planet, taking away citizens from every country, taking away tax dollars." I make a quick slit and use the sharp instrument to take the implant out.

"That's just insane, Ryker," he says with a pained sound to his voice.

I take the implant and toss it in the trash and get a bandage. Putting it on the wound on the back of his neck, I whisper, "You take the guard on the left and I'll take the one on the right. We need to get their guns and go to the nearest exit."

"Got it."

We move with quick strides to the door. When I pull it open, neither of them turns around, thinking it's just Damien leaving I suppose. With a quick slam of my fist to the side of the guard's head, I knock him to the ground and in no time, I have his gun out of the holster.

Damien and I stand in front of the men who don't even bother to get up off the floor, staying right where we laid them out. One of them shakes his head. "We're not about to try to fight you two. We know you've been trained."

"Good," I say then Damien and I turn to leave. The doctor meets us in the hallway. With one look at the guns we have, he turns around and goes into another door, leaving us alone.

"I say we get to Smithfield and set him straight," Damien says. "No reason to leave the others in harm's way."

.   .   .

WITH A NOD, we head that way and stop when we see an open door, leaking light into the dim hallway. A couple of women are inside, looking at a projection screen. There are pictures of the creatures from Mars that we've never seen before.

It's obvious they're unaware of us as they talk. The blonde says, "If we add in some red in the background, it'll look more realistic."

"I found this overlay of red dust blowing around. That'll give a good effect. These will be released to the media after take-off," the woman with dark hair says. "It's such a shame we have to lose some of those men."

"Yeah, the Russian's hot. I'm thinking about seeing if I can get a little taste of him since they're all being kept here for the next three days. I'm sure they'll all be seeking a little hot female interaction before leaving forever."

"I know Crawford is married but do you think he'd be desperate enough to give me a romp?" the dark haired woman asks.

My stomach is knotting and Damien puts his finger to his lips as we fall back to hide on the sides of the door, so we can listen some more.

"I overheard the Captain saying the boosters have been rigged to explode just before they reach the outer atmosphere. That's when the media will get these pictures, along with the explanation about why they were being sent. They'll all be labeled heroes."

"And the missions to Mars will stop there."

I look at Damien, 'I knew it.'

AND WITH WHAT we've just overheard, we move with stealthy silence to our Captain's office. Voices come from the hallway that's intersecting this one, halting us. "Markov's transmission has stopped. We have to find him," Joel, another man who's scheduled to be with us on the mission, says.

"The clinic is the last place where he was. Do you suppose Crawford took it out for him?" Clayton, another man slated to be with us on the fated mission, asks.

Damien and I slip into a room to hide. At this point we need to get to Smithfield then the other men can have their implants removed. Getting to the Captain is the number one priority at this point.

We hear their footsteps go past the door and wait until we can no longer hear the clicking of their shoes as they go down the hallway. Moving to a window, I look out into the parking lot and see a news van. Waving Damien over, he sees it too. "I wonder what's up."

"How much would you like to bet that Gia's behind that, some-how?" I ask him.

He nods. "She called me. That's why I was called in, I think. I wasn't on the phone with her but a few minutes when Smithfield called me and told me I had thirty minutes to get here. He knew I was on the phone with her. When I figured that out, I knew the implant was more than merely a tracking device."

"I feel like an idiot for falling for all this shit in the first place and even allowing them to put that thing in me," I say as I wonder what the hell I was thinking.

Why would I ever agree to leave Gia here, all alone? None of it makes any sense to me now. *Not any of it!*

GIA

Dust particles hang in the air as the news reporter, Dave Johnson, and his cameraman, stand in front of me and Brittney as we walk into the facility where Ryker has spent most of his time the last three months. "It's dark in here," the camera man, Gary, says.

"I'm sure they want it this way. It's hard to get accurate pictures in this light," I say as we find no one stopping us from coming in. We all expected a fight.

A fast set of heels, clicked down the hallway, coming toward us. Another set joins them and we stop as a couple of women, one blonde and one brunette, came to us. "You can stop there," the blonde shouts.

"I'm Dave Johnson with Channel Seven News. I'm here to ask Captain Smithfield some questions."

"No, you are not. He's not taking any questions. There will be a news conference on Tuesday. Just before the shuttle takes off," the brunette lets us know.

"We're here because of Ryker Crawford. He's been detained and his wife is worried about him. He hasn't even been allowed to call her. Things don't seem to be on the up and up here," Dave tells the two who look like they've been sucking on pickles, their lips are so puckered.

"Ryker Crawford is fine. I'm sure, when the Captain sees fit, he'll allow Ryker to call his wife," the blonde says.

THE BRUNETTE QUICKLY ADDS, "If that's a thing he wants to do. He may not be calling her of his own accord. The men will be leaving all their loved ones behind. Some are finding it difficult to be around them any longer with what's about to happen. If she loves him, she'd know how he's feeling."

"Excuse me," I say as I step around the men to face this crazy bitch. "I'm Gia Crawford. I do know my husband and I know he would never want to spend his last days on Earth anywhere but with me. So, where is he right now? I want to see him."

"That's impossible," the blonde says.

The camera man turns on his camera and sheds some light on us all. I find the women are much older than I could tell when the light was so dim. They shield their eyes from the light as the brunette shouts, "Turn that off. No videotaping is allowed in this facility!"

"Well, it's being done," I say and hold out my hand to separate the two and walk through them.

"You can't just go anywhere you want around here!" the blonde says as she grabs my shoulder. "This is a top-secret facility. Only people who are supposed to be here are allowed."

"You have my husband," I say as I shake her hand off me and move past them, with the other three people right behind me. "I see a light on under a closed door up here."

The women's laughter pisses me off as one of them shouts out at us, "You won't be able to get into any room that has anything you're seeking in it."

"Wanna bet?" I ask as I get to the door with the light on in the room. "You want to take it from here, Dave?"

With a nod, he steps up to the door and knocks. "Dave Johnson with Channel Seven News. I'm here to speak with a Captain Smithfield."

"No interviews until Tuesday," comes a man's voice.

"If you won't talk to me, we'll be back with armed forces," he tells the Captain. "You see, I've done some investigating. It's only a small sector of our government who's behind this. Not any other countries know a thing about what you're doing here. So, I'd like to know why you have six of the top men in the Space Industry leaving our planet to fight some very odd looking creatures that are supposedly inhabiting Mars."

THE DOOR FLIES open and an old man in a non-distinct military uniform is looking at Dave with a red face. "What in the hell are you talking about?"

Dave holds up a copy of one of the pictures I found in the file in Ryker's desk in his home office. "This is what I'm talking about. So, would you like to answer some questions now?"

"You need to leave here at once!" he snarls as he looks at us all. His eyes land on me. "Gia Crawford. I should've expected you'd be behind this."

"I found the file in Ryker's desk. I want my husband. Where is he?" I ask him and find him changing his snarling expression to an evil grin.

"Your husband is dead, Mrs. Crawford."

My heart stops but Dave shakes his head. "I doubt that. I've seen many liars in my day and you, sir, are a terrible liar. I don't know how you got so many intelligent men to believe you."

Chaos breaks out down another hallway, echoes of shouts and then gunshots, have us ducking for cover and scattering away to find somewhere safe to hide.

Dave finds a door that's not locked and we follow him inside, closing the door behind us. I shudder as I hear it lock and try to turn the handle, only to find that I can't. "He's trapped us in here."

Dave looks around the room. One window is at the top of a wall. "This is not a great place for us to be."

The little light there is out as the electricity has been shut off. "Great," Brittney moans. "Now what?"

"I have my camera light," Gary says. He points it up to the ceiling. "Air vents."

"That lead to air ducts," Dave says. "That can get us the hell out of here."

Brittney bumps my shoulder with hers. "He was in the Marines. Dave's a reporter with a few tricks up his sleeve and some military smarts that should help us, Gia. Not to worry."

"My only worry is Ryker and where he is. He can't be dead. I think I'd feel it if he was," I say and find my stomach clenching and knotting. *I cannot throw up right now!*

SHOUTS from just outside the door have my heart pounding. "He's heading toward the front exit, Damien!" *It's Ryker!*

Running to the door, I bang on it. "Ryker! Ryker, it's Gia! He's locked us in here!"

"Gia?" I hear him ask. "Bang on the door again."

I bang and bang until I hear him banging on the same door I am. "I'm in here."

The sound of him trying the door knob has me stepping back to see if he can figure out how to open it. Damien's voice is loud as he shouts. "I can't let him get away. I'm going after him, Ryker."

"Gia, you're safe in there. Stay put, I'll be back to get you. I promise you, I will!" I hear his footsteps leaving me here and find weakness enveloping me. "Wait up, Damien. You shouldn't go alone."

Brittney grabs me as I slowly fall to the floor. "He's coming back for us."

"WHAT IF SOMETHING HAPPENS TO HIM?" I ask as I hear more gunshots, more men's voices, and their shoes hitting the tiled floor as they run around in a chaotic manner.

"Look what I found," the cameraman says, drawing our attention as he points his camera light at a short file cabinet. "Let's get some footage of what's in here."

Dave hurries to open the cabinet but it's locked, of course. I pull out a little screwdriver I found at home and hand it to him. "Will this help you?"

"It might," he says then gets to work unlocking it. "Don't record this part, Steve."

WITH A NOD, Steve stops taping but keeps the light on Dave and what he's doing. In no time at all, he has the top cabinet open and pulls out files. Damien Markov's name is across the tab of the first one. When he opens it, we see pictures of Damien. Some have been altered, making it appear he's running from the same creatures that are in the pictures I found.

Each file he takes out has similar pictures. And behind them are reports of the fake mission on Mars. As if the world would really believe this shit!

Opening the next drawer, he pulls out one large file. Schematics are inside of it. "Okay, let's get footage of all this, Steve." He lays out the open files all over a table and the schematics too.

Brittney and I watch and listen as he makes his report about what we've found so far. Then shots ring out and our door is blown open. "Who the fuck put you in here?" Captain Smithfield shouts.

The gun in his hand is shaking as he points it at me. *And I don't know what the hell I should do!*

RYKER

Flashes of light, meant to disorient us, pulse around me and Damien as the other four men in our team surround us. "Drop, men. We just need to get you to the clinic to get the implants put back in. You'll be okay once they've been replaced," one of them shouts at us.

I look at Damien over my shoulder as we stand back to back. "Do you think they'll listen to anything we say?"

"We can give it a try," he says. "Listen, men. We've all been duped into this thing. And they plan on killing us all."

"No, they don't!" another man shouts.

"They do," I tell them as I hold my hands up over my head. "Listen to us. I do not want to shoot any of you."

"Nor us. But you have to stand down and allow us to take you to the clinic," one of them says. "It's our orders. We can't do anything different."

"You can let us cut that shit out of your necks and you will be able to think for yourselves. Your mind will become clear, instantly," Damien tells them.

"They told us you'd say that." The flashes get quicker and I can see they're moving in. "Drop the weapons and drop to the floor, now!"

"We won't be captured. If you come at us, you will have a fight on your hands," I let them know.

Sirens begin to leak into the corridor. "Shit!" Damien shouts. "We have to hurry!"

"They aren't here for us," I say and find the sound of gunfire coming from another area of the facility. "They aren't even here for you guys either. Put the weapons down and come with us. We need to get to them, they're here to protect us."

"From you, I'd bet," one of them says.

A loud screeching sound fills the air. Like a banshee. And I know that sound. "Gia! Stay where you are!" I shout out.

Something flies through the air and I hear the sounds of some of the men who are surrounding us grunting and groaning. "What the hell?" one of them asks.

Whack! Whack! Whack!

THE FLASHING STOPS and one large light comes up behind Gia, who's wielding a long pole with a red light on the end of it. The men she knocked down are staying down and perfectly still as if it has paralyzed them.

"Gia!" I shout and step over one of the men to get to her. She's shaking as I take her in my arms. Damien takes the stick out of her hand and holds off the one man who managed to escape the bad end of that stick. "Where the hell did you find that thing?"

"In the room, we were in. Smithfield came in, waving a gun and I jumped into a closet and found this thing. I found a button on the side of it, clicked it and when the red tip lit up, I jumped out of the closet and poked him with it. He fell and I came out to find you."

"I warned him about you. I told him you'd rip this place apart to find me." I kiss the top of her head and hold her tight.

The lights come back on and some man on a bullhorn is calling out, "Everyone on the ground. This is the Orlando Police Department. Place your weapons on the ground and shove them away from you."

"I guess we should all do what he says, so we can get done with this shit," Damien says as he takes the position and pushes the stick away from himself.

Out of the corner of my eye, I see the last man standing out of our group and he makes a dive to get the stick. Pushing Gia away from me, I lurch for the stick too and collide with the man who has been my teammate for three months. "No, Paul!"

When I fall onto the stick, I feel a jolt and go stiff. "Get him off it, Damien!" Gia screams.

I feel hands on me, turning me over and can't move. Damien picks up the stick as Paul tries to run and throws it at him. He drops as soon as it hits him in the back. "That'll stop the police from shooting your dumb ass, Paul. You can thank me later," Damien shouts at him then looks at me. "Does it hurt?"

I'M FROZEN. I can't even blink. Then Gia's face looms above me too. "I think it'll wear off, baby." She kneels down and touches my face, which I can feel.

"On the floor!" comes another loud shout from the police.

She and Damien lay on the floor next to me as the police come into the area. "We need you all to stay perfectly still while we cuff you and take you in for questioning."

"Most of them can't move," Gia tells them. "He and I are the only ones who can."

"Stand up, slow and easy," I hear one of the officers direct them.

They get up and Gia says, "This is my husband, Ryker Crawford. He and this man here, Damien Markov, aren't a threat. The rest are. Except for the cameraman, the reporter, and the woman with them, who are lying in the hallway down there. They're no threat, either. I'm the one who texted your office. I'm Gia Crawford."

I watch Damien put his arm around her and pull her close to him. "Damn, I never thought I'd ever say this but I'm damn glad Ryker stole you away from me. Shit, you're tough and smart as hell!"

"Thank you, Damien," she says with a bit of surprise. Then looks down at me. "Maybe a paramedic should come look at you, Ryker."

I'd like to nod but I can't. An officer picks up the stick and looks it over. "What's this?"

"Be careful with that," Damien tells him. "It shocks people into what seems to be a state of paralysis."

The cop looks around at the five men on the floor, myself included. "And who took all these men out?"

"He took himself out, on accident," Gia tells him as she points at me. "And I got the rest of them."

The cops all chuckle and one of them says, "Wow, are you a ninja?"

"No, just a wife who was determined to get her husband back. There's another man in a room near the front that I touched with that magic stick too. You might want to make sure that he's cuffed before he starts to move again. He's a major flight risk."

"Can you take me to him?" one of them ask her.

She nods then looks at me. "Damien will stay here with you. Don't worry, baby. I'll be back soon and I'll bring someone who might be able to help you."

Watching her walk away, I feel more pride than I can ever recall feeling. Then Damien takes a seat on the floor, wrapping his arms around his knees. "How is it, being married to her?" He looks at me as if I could actually answer him.

In my head, though, I say, 'It's like Christmas every day, being married to that woman.'

Because it is!

GIA

THE PARAMEDICS HAVE MANAGED to massage Ryker to help get his body moving again. He regained the ability to speak after thirty minutes, making him feel much better. His legs still need some work and they're wheeling him out to one of the ambulances to take him to the hospital to be checked out. Following behind him, I find Damien catching up to us. "Hey!"

I stop and wait for him. "Yes?"

"I've learned a lot from you, Gia. A hell of a lot. I just wanted you to know that I'm going to be marrying Svetlana. I'm coming out with the truth about my son and make my family get the hell over it."

"Wow!" *I'm stunned!* "That's awesome!"

"I'M glad you think it's a good idea." He opens his arms and I move in for a hug. "I really am happy I met you."

"Me too." I step back as he lets me go. "I think it's so much better to stop hiding them. For both their sakes."

"We need to head out, Mrs. Crawford," one of the paramedics calls out to me.

With a wave, I give Damien a smile. "We'll be seeing each other. Of that, I have no doubts. Give them my best, Damien. Make a wife out of her and treat her with respect."

He nods and I turn and get into the back of the ambulance where they've placed Ryker in his wheelchair. "You look happy. What did he say?"

"He's going to marry the mother of his son. He's done hiding them. It seems I've inspired him to do that." I take a seat on the long, padded area to the side of him as both paramedics take seats up front.

"You are quite inspirational, Gia." He wiggles his finger at me, so I lean over. One soft kiss melts me as his fingers hold my chin. "I love you."

Breathing out a long sigh, I find the words slipping off my tongue without even thinking, "You're going to be a father."

HE BLINKS at me as if he's not sure what I've said. "Huh?"

A smile breaks over my face. "A father. You're going to be one. I took the test earlier today. I'm prego, baby!"

"How?" he says then stops and shakes his head. "I mean, I know how. But we only had sex once in the last three months."

"We had it on our wedding night too, silly."

"So, you're like three months, already? We only have six months to get prepared for this. Is it a boy or a girl?" he asks as he's getting pretty keyed up.

"I have no idea. The test doesn't tell you all that," I say with a laugh.

"You're going to be a mom, Gia!"

"You're going to be a dad, Ryker!"

His eyes dart back and forth then he's asking, "What should we name it?"

"We should find out what it is first," I tell him and find his expression is priceless and I really wish I could've gotten a picture if it.

"Gia, you aren't messing with me, are you?"

"I'd never do such a thing! How could you even say such a thing?" I huff and cross my arms over my chest.

"Sorry, baby. Now it makes sense. All your bitchiness!"

My eyebrows raise to new heights. "My what?"

"Oh, shit!" He shakes his head. "I don't know what's wrong with me. I always say the stupidest things. I think it's the shock that had me saying such a dumb thing. I meant, that's how come my poor wife has been having a hard time and I'm going to rectify that."

"I'd love it if you'd spoil me a bit. I've been feeling so tired and moody."

"I know!"

My ire grows again. Then I laugh. "Ryker, you have little to no filter. Do you know that?"

"Did I say something wrong again? Damn, baby. You need to teach me," he says with a laugh.

As we pull to a stop, the paramedics get out and he wiggles his finger at me and gives me another kiss. "I love you, Ryker."

"And I love you, Gia."

RYKER

Sliding my fingers through her hair, I watch Gia as she lies back on our bed. "Swear it to me again, Ryker."

"I swear to you I'll never leave you or our baby behind for any reason in the world. Other than God…"

She places her finger on my lips. "I know about the one way out, you'll have no control over."

"You're a hero to me, baby." Pushing her hair off her neck, I lean in and graze my lips over the column of her throat. "You looked like a warrior angel, sent to rescue me, earlier today."

Her hand moves over my shoulder then up to my cheek. "Ryker, if you knew the anger that was coursing through me when I saw those men surrounding you, you'd probably be afraid of me."

I have to laugh. "I am, a little."

"You never need to be afraid of me," she says with a giggle. "I'll never turn my powers of destruction on you." She kisses me, sending me to the state her kisses usually do. A state of bliss and happiness.

When our mouths part, I find her looking at me. Moving my hand over her pink cheek, I whisper, "You're my world. I can't believe I ever thought, for one second, that I could live a year or more without seeing your sweet face. And now that you're going to be bringing our first child into the world, I know, without a shadow of a doubt, that I can't go a day without seeing you both."

"Are you saying that Mars is off the table for you, Ryker?" Her eyes dart rapidly as she searches mine.

"I'm saying, you and I will make that decision when the time comes. I won't be forcing anything on anyone. And my place is with you and our children. I'll never leave you. Not ever." Pulling her close, I kiss her again and feel her body warm under my touch.

The long, hot bath we took has left us smelling of lavender and coconuts. Her skin is smooth and soft beneath my hands that roam all over her body. Cupping her ass in my hands, I roll over, pulling her on top of me.

Her stomach is still flat as she's not eaten nearly enough in the last three months. A thing I know is my fault. I'll have to make sure she eats well from now on.

As her body moves over mine, my cock stirs and thickens, filling with a need for her. Her hands move through my hair as our kiss deepens. Her legs move to straddle me as she settles onto my erection with a groan, "Ryker."

When her mouth leaves mine, so she can sit up and move her body up and down my cock, I find her tits bouncing. I have to touch them and move my hands up the sides of her waist, making a trail to them.

Her stomach may still be flat but her breasts are already blossoming. They were never small but now they're getting even bigger. "I love the way these feel."

"WAIT until they're full of milk."

"Are you going to one of those stingy mothers who never let Daddy's taste what's baby's?"

She nods and I groan as she also makes a little swirling action that makes my dick hit a very deep spot inside of her. "I bet I can talk you into giving me a taste, every now and then."

With a smile, she leans over, her tits dangle near my face. "You can have a taste now. If you'd like."

Pulling one into my mouth, I run my hands to her waist to hold her, lifting her some to help her make longer strokes. When her body tenses, I release her scrumptious tit. "What's wrong?"

"It hurts a little. They're pretty tender. But do it anyway. I think the long period of keeping myself away from you has a lot to do with that too. Limber them up, hubby. I sure don't want them to go unused until little junior arrives."

"Can do, Momma." I pull one back into my mouth, being very

careful to be easy with her. When she moans, I know I've found the perfect amount of suck, lick, and nibble to satisfy her.

ALL I really care about is making her happy, pleasing her, worshiping her. With a sense of that, I roll her over on her back and change things up. She smiles and runs her hands over my cheeks. "I love you."

"I know," I say and give her a deep thrust that makes her eyes close. "And I love you."

One of her feet move up the back of my leg then the other does to and she wraps her legs around me. Her arms move up my neck, holding on to me as I make deep strokes.

Our bodies move up and down together until we're both shaking and breathing hard. When her body lets go, mine does too. Our sounds fill the room, making me think we're going to have to learn how to do this much quieter, once our little one comes along.

With a long sigh, I move my body to one side of hers, not wanting to leave my weight on our baby that's nestled inside his mommy. I stroke her stomach as I kiss her neck. "I can't wait to see him or her."

"Six months isn't a terribly long time to wait." Her hand covers mine as I caress her tummy.

"You say that but it sounds like an eternity."

She wiggles and moves around to face me. We hold one another as we look at each other. "I hope he has your eyes," she whispers.

"I hope she has your hair." I push a lock if it off her face.

"I hope he's blessed with your plump lips."

I smile at her. "I hope she's got your thick and lustrous eyelashes."

The way her hand feels as she gently touches my cheek, has me feeling sleepy and all too soon I'm taken over as we lie in our bed, basking in the glow of our love and how it's created another person, neither of us can wait to see.

GIA

Waddling to the kitchen, I find our new cook, Consuela, making some oatmeal. "How did you know I was craving that?"

She laughs. "You really don't know the answer to that?"

"I really don't."

"Around nine, every evening, you get hungry. It's either soup, oatmeal, or cereal. And I've figured out that you have a pattern. One night it's the soup, the next it's the cereal, and the one after that is the oatmeal." She taps the wooden spoon on the side of the small pot she's making it in. "After six months of making sure you eat right, I think I should be acutely aware of your eating patterns, Mrs. Crawford."

Sitting at the table, I pop a strawberry from the bowl of mixed fruit she's already placed on the table, into my mouth then take a drink of the milk she's put there too. "You do know me better than I know myself."

"And I love being able to help you." She places a bowl of the piping hot food in front of me. "Now you let that cool while I make you some wheat toast."

"Yes, ma'am."

The sound of footsteps comes down the hallway and into the kitchen Ryker comes in. "Sorry about how late I am."

"The drive from Orlando is a long one." He leans over and gives me a kiss then rubs my tummy.

"I missed dinner, due to a long meeting about that damn fiasco I was involved in," he says as he sits down next to me. "Is there enough of that for me, Consuela?"

"Of course," she says then brings him a bowl too and a glass of milk. "Let me get you some toast, Mr. Crawford."

He takes a couple of blueberries out of the bowl and eats them as he looks at my stomach. "You know, if he's not out by the end of the week, he'll be making his debut appearance on Saturday with the doctor's help."

"I know that, Ryker. I was just at the doctor's yesterday. It was me who told you that."

"What I meant to say is, maybe we should stay in a hotel in Orlando. We'd be much closer to the hospital and you just said it yourself, the ride from Sebastien to Orlando is a long one."

Consuela sits down a small plate with our toast on it and I look up at her. "How do you feel about having yourself a little vacation while we stay in town? We wouldn't need you to come back to work until we come home from the hospital."

Ryker claps his hands and gives her a smile. "I'll pay for you and your family to go wherever you'd like. And I'll send you there on the jet. I want you to know we really appreciate how well you've taken care of us both, and the baby."

She looks giddy as she smiles at us. "Oh, my! My husband and two daughters would love to see New York. It's Christmas in two weeks and they'd love to see the tree and shop in the fancy stores."

"A New York holiday it is for you four then," Ryker says with a huge smile. "Let them know that you will be going tomorrow. I'm going to take Gia into town with me in the morning. You can take off now, let the maid clean the kitchen up. And you'll have a hefty bonus in your account too."

"We really do appreciate all you've done," I tell her as she hops around with sheer delight.

"I can't wait to see their faces when I tell them the good news!"

I GET to eating my oatmeal and smiling away as I do. It makes me feel so good to get to do something for her for a change. The woman came in and took over the role of chef and chief nutritionist, like a boss.

Turning my attention to Ryker, I ask, "About the meeting, what was it all about?"

"The CIA had to get all of my information about what happened with the Mars mission. They're putting together all the evidence they can find on the people who were actually involved in that. Americans were the only ones involved. Corrupt politicians, mostly. A few ranking military people too. The thing is, the other countries are now thinking about doing no more business with the U.S. because of that."

"None?"

"Well, space business. That would put us having to figure out how to manufacture the boosters here. A thing I'm not looking forward to as I don't trust the American companies that can do that. Not anymore, I don't. They found out, it was several engineers from the main company that makes things like that, who fixed the boosters on the shuttle to blow up."

I shiver with the thought that my husband could've been killed. "So, what does that mean?"

"It means, I might need to see if Damien would build a facility here to make the boosters. I have no idea if he could pull that off or not. It means our race for space may be more of a crawl behind all the rest of the world. Thanks to greedy people, here in America."

My heart goes out to him. I know he's had this passion forever. "Things are falling apart, aren't they?"

He nods and takes a bite of his oatmeal. "If the space industry, here in America crashes, do you know what that will mean for Apollo Engineering and the companies that have joined us as affiliate partners?"

"Bankruptcy."

He nods and I find myself not so hungry any longer. The houses, the cars, the money, all would be history. All because of some greedy individuals.

"I've made wise investments for us, personally. We'll be fine, no matter what. I'll have my investment broker do the same for your family. The businesses might go under but we won't."

"What about all the employees?"

He shakes his head. "I can't take care of everyone, baby. They'll be on their own to figure things out."

With a nod, I put my spoon down and feel more than a bit sick. "When will we know about what the other countries will do?"

"I'm not sure. The government is scrambling to get every last person who was behind the scam. So far, only the people who were actually at the facility have been captured. But they know there's more behind it. Quiet individuals who cannot be trusted."

"This is not good."

"No, it's not."

~

RYKER

ARRIVING at the office after getting Gia squared away at the hotel, I find several members of my staff waiting outside. "Are we having an outside meeting I wasn't invited to?"

The receptionist, May, asks me, "Do you have something you'd like to tell us, Mr. Crawford?"

"No, not really." I look around at the eight people who are the first to arrive each morning and start to wonder about what's going on inside the building my grandfather purchased when he began this whole business. "Would anyone care to let me in on why you're all out here?"

Tony, the maintenance man, steps forward. "The CIA and the FBI are in the building. We all stepped out because they're going through everything and making us feel like criminals."

My eyes just about pop out of my head as I turn and haul ass inside to see why they'd be doing such a thing. I'm stopped as soon as I enter the door by a man in a dark suit and glasses. "Sorry, no one is getting in here today."

"I'M RYKER CRAWFORD. I own this place. I just had a very long meeting with the CIA only yesterday. Why is this happening?"

"I'm not at liberty to discuss that." His answer infuriates me and I storm back out.

"You all should go home. I have to make a visit to my lawyers," I shout as I go past the waiting employees.

"Are we getting paid for today?" one of them shouts.

"I sure as hell hope so. But I can't make any promises." I get into my car and head out, hitting the call button on the computer screen to call my lawyers.

"Davenport, Davenport, and Stephenson," the receptionist answers the call.

"I need to speak with any one of them."

"No one's come in yet," she lets me know. "If you'll leave your name and number, I'll have the first one to walk through the door give you a call."

"They have my number. Tell them Ryker Crawford needs to talk to them as soon as possible. It's of the utmost importance."

"Yes, sir."

JUST AS I end that call, I get one from the hotel I just left Gia at. "Hello?"

"I'm looking for Ryker Crawford."

"You got him."

"There's a problem with the credit card you left when you checked in earlier. Can you come back and give us a different one?"

"I'm pretty busy. My wife's in the room. She has all the same cards I do. Can you go up and let her know about the problem?"

"Of course. Thank you, sir."

Shaking my head to try to clear it, I decide to drive over to my lawyers' offices to meet them all in person. Something has to have happened to make the FBI join forces with the CIA and be looking at everything I have.

Making a quick call to my accountant, I try to figure out why that credit card isn't working. "Stimson's Accounting."

"Hi, I need to speak with Roger, please."

"One moment, sir," his secretary tells me.

"Roger Stimson here."

"Ryker Crawford here. I've had one of my credit cards turned down. Have you stayed up on all the bills?"

"Yes, sir. Which one did they turn down?"

"A platinum Visa."

"There's no reason anyone should ever turn that one down. There's no limit on it."

"Can you check into that for me? I'm pretty swamped today."

"Of course, I'll get right back to you, Mr. Crawford." I end the call.

And right away, another call comes in and I see it's Gia. "Ryker, you're never going to believe this."

"Try me." I tap the steering wheel as I sit at a red light. *My nerves are shot!*

"Our card was declined here at the hotel. The manager came up here with a credit card reader to get another one and every single one of mine was declined. Even the debit card from the bank. Ryker, what's going on?"

"I'm not sure, baby. You don't need to worry about a thing. You rest and relax."

"I can't. They said I have to leave the room. The bellboy is being sent up to get our bags."

"What the..." the light turns green and I have to make a U-turn to go back to the hotel to straighten this shit out. "I'm coming. Wait in the lobby if they make you do that. The bastards!"

"You sound pissed. Watch your speed, baby. Everything will be okay. You'll see."

"I hope so. Sit tight. I'll be there in fifteen minutes."

Ending that call, I make one to our bank in Orlando. An automated system answers the call, so I push zero to try to get to talk to a real person. Instead, I get this, "Hello, your phone number has brought up your account with The National Bank of Orlando. Our records indicate your accounts have been frozen. For more information, you will need to go into the local branch. Thank you and have a nice day."

How in the hell can anyone have a nice day after hearing that?

PULLING UP TO THE HOTEL, I stop as the valet comes to get the car. Rushing inside, I find Gia is sitting in the lobby with all of our things on a luggage cart. Heat flows through me as I hold out my hand to let her know to stay put and walk past her, to the front desk. "I need the manager out here now!"

"Ryker, stop," Gia's voice comes from behind me. "We need to go. We have more pressing matters to tend to right now."

Turning around, I look at her. "Just hang on. Let me deal with this. You'll be back in that room, relaxing in no time."

"No, I won't."

"Yes, you will," I tell her and put my hand on her shoulder to take her back to sit down.

"Ryker, my water has broken. I need to get to the hospital! Damn, stop and listen!"

"Shit!" I look back at the lady at the front desk. "Never mind!" When we get outside, I hand the valet the card the other one gave me. "Can you send someone inside to get our luggage? That's it right there." I point at it and he gives me a nod.

"Ryker, what the hell is going on?" Gia asks me.

"You just don't worry about that. I want you to think about you and our son and that's all. Noah is soon to be here. That's all that really matters, baby."

"Ryker, damn it! Tell me why our cards don't work!"

"I'm working on that as we speak. I have our accountant dealing with that right now. Not to worry. Most likely a weird glitch in the system."

THE CAR COMES UP and a bellboy brings our things and puts them in the trunk. When he waits a moment for a tip, I shake my head and feel like a complete fool. But I have no idea how much cash I even have on me. And I can't go giving away shit right now.

As I pull away, the phone rings and I see it's our chef. "Shit!"

Gia looks at me with confusion. "Why'd you say that?"

With a push of the button, I say, "Hello, Consuela."

"Sir, I hate to bother you. I really do. But we've arrived at the hotel in New York and they said the card number you gave them to pay for our room has been declined."

"Yes, I think there're some problems. Can I get you to hop back in a cab and get back to the airport? I'll call the jet and have them bring you back home. Things have turned a bit sour here. I'll explain things when I know more. I'm very sorry about this."

"Okay, sir," she says with a shaky voice.

"Honey, can you call the jet and tell them to pick them back up and bring them home?"

"I can certainly do that. And can you give me some idea of why this is happening to us?"

"It most likely has something to do with why the FBI and CIA are at Apollo Engineering, going through everything."

Out of the corner of my eye, I catch her eyebrows raising up high. "Damn."

"Yes, damn, damn, damn. Not to worry, though. There's nothing to find. I have no idea what kind of a tip they got but it's a false one. That will soon be found out and our accounts will be freed up."

"Freed up? Have they been frozen?"

I nod as the phone rings again. This time it's hers and it's her father. "Daddy?"

"HEY, sweetheart. We're running into a bit of trouble up here. Your mother went to buy some groceries and her card was declined. Then she went on over to the bank and found out our accounts have been frozen. Do you think you could get Ryker to see what's happened?"

"Ours are frozen too. The FBI and CIA are at Apollo Engineering. I'm not sure about anything. Well, that's not exactly true. I'm sure your grandson is about to be born today. My water broke and we're on the way to the hospital."

"That's good news! Send us pictures as soon as you can. I'll tell everyone else. Don't let this money business mess up such a great occasion. Your first kid only comes once, you know. Rich or poor, you won't feel a thing about that once you lay your eyes on your little man."

"Thanks Dad," she says then wipes a tear from her eye. "I love you. I'll keep in touch."

"I love you too, baby girl. And you better keep in touch." She ends the call and lies her head back on the headrest.

"Are you having contractions, baby," I ask her as she's not said a word about them.

"I didn't realize what they were. It's in my back. It hurts, then it doesn't. In all honesty, I thought I had to poop." She giggles and blushes.

Pulling into the hospital parking lot, I stop at the front door. "Let me grab a wheelchair and take you in. Then I'll park the car, once they're taking you up to where ever it is they'll take you."

Getting out, I run inside and grab one of the waiting wheelchairs and go back out to get her. She's still smiling as I help her out of the car and into the seat of the wheelchair. "I feel so much better being here, Ryker. Things will be okay. I just know they will."

With a nod to give her an idea that I'm on the same wavelength she is, which isn't true at all, I push her inside and go to the desk where a nurse is standing, waiting for us. "Are we having us a baby today?"

"We are," Gia says, cheerfully.

"I need to park the car. I'll be right back." I run out and get into the car and haul ass to park it. Then I grab the bag out of the trunk that we packed just for the hospital and run back inside.

When I get inside and see tears flowing over Gia's, now red, cheeks, I almost fall down. "Ryker!"

The nurse is no longer alone at the desk, there's a man there too and he's looking at me with a scowl on his face as he wiggles his finger for me to come to him.

"What's wrong?" I ask as I approach them.

"I'm afraid we can't check your wife in, Mr. Crawford. Your insurance company said they can't pay. The cards your wife gave us aren't working, either. I'm afraid you'll have to go to the county hospital to have the baby. This is out of my hands to fix."

"Her doctor delivers here and only here," I say as I look over and see Gia crying even harder now.

"Someone there will deliver the baby. Not to worry, sir. Sorry about this," he says as if he's really sorry.

"I guess there's no time to fuck around with you people." I turn around and wheel Gia out of the hospital, taking her all the way to where I've parked. "They can come pick up the wheelchair their damn selves! No compassion, mother..."

"Ryker, please just hurry. I'm uncomfortable and just want to lie in a bed. Or walk or do something!"

HELPING HER INTO THE CAR, I lean the seat back, so she can recline a bit. "I'll get you to the county hospital, baby. No worries."

"I'm sorry for being a bitch." She runs her hand over my cheek. "I'm just kind of freaking out now."

"You're not being a bitch at all. Just try to relax."

When I get into the car, I see her shaking her head. "Ryker, can you just call Margie, the midwife we were in the dome with, and see if she'll come out to our house and help us deliver this baby? I don't want to have him in the county hospital with some doctor I don't even know."

I nod and call Margie. "Hey, you. Long time, no hear. How the heck are you, Ryker?"

"Not great. But that can be talked about later. What are you up to right now?"

"Not much."

Gia pushes the button to bring her seat up into a sitting position. "Can we come get you and take you to our house? I'm having a baby. I need you, Margie."

"Gia, are you kidding? Are you having it right now?"

"I am. Well, I'm in early labor. Contractions are ten minutes apart. My water has broken already, though. The ride out to our place is about an hour. I'm sure I have plenty of time to get there and situated. Can you help me?"

"Of course, I can, Gia. I can take my car out there. No reason for you guys to go through the trouble of picking me up. Send me the address and I'll head out there right away."

I watch Gia breath out a sigh of relief. "Thank you. I'll send it to you."

"See you guys soon."

Looking at Gia as I stop at a light, I reach over and run my hand through her silky hair. "Hey." She turns her head to look at me. Her cheeks are a bit chubby and she looks absolutely adorable. "I hope he has your strength, Gia. You have it in spades, baby."

"No, I don't. I'm a wreck." She sniffles and wipes her eyes.

"You're not a wreck. You're level-headed and thinking clearly. You're a rock, baby. An absolute rock. I'm lucky to have you and Noah is lucky to have you as his mother."

"Ryker, what's going to happen if our accounts stay frozen for a while? How are we going to live?"

"You let me be the rock in that situation, Gia. I don't want you to worry one bit about that. First, we're going to take care of getting our son here. Then I'll take care of this financial thing while you take care of him."

"You're making it sound easy. I don't think it's going to be easy."

"Worse-case scenario, we have to sell some things for cash while this mess gets sorted out. See, I've already got an idea for money."

She smiles a weak smile. "My rock."

"Yeah, we're just a couple of rocks in this crazy world who

managed to bump into each other one, fateful night." I give her cheek a little pinch.

She closes her eyes and breaths in deeply. "They're getting a little closer together now. Maybe by five or six tonight we'll be looking at his little face."

"I can't wait. I will wait. But it's going to be hard."

Her laughter makes me happy and it becomes crystal clear. *As long as I have her, I have everything!*

GIA

HIS TINY ROUND head is lying on my breast. He's using it as a pillow and making little movements as he sleeps. "He's so precious," Ryker whispers as he runs his fingertip over our son's head.

"Isn't he?" I whisper too. I don't want to wake him. He's so little and needs his rest.

Margie looks in on us. "Last check before I leave. Is everything okay?"

"We'll be fine," Ryker tells her. "Thank you. When I get things figured out, I'll get you some money for being such a great friend and helping us through the delivery."

"No, you won't. I'm not taking a dime from you. When we all get to Mars, we won't have money to bother with. We'll all help each other, without any monetary gains. I'm living like that as often as I can right here on Earth. Now, if you need anything else, you just call me. And don't forget to get that little guy to his pediatrician soon."

"We will," I tell her then kiss the top of Noah's tiny head. "Thank you, Margie. I'll bake you a pie or something."

"Now, a pie, I'll take. See you guys later on."

RYKER MOVES his arm around me and gently pushes my head to rest on his shoulder. "Things will work out, Gia. I know they will."

"I have faith in you. I know you'll figure this whole thing out."

When his cell rings, we both cut our eyes to it as it lies on the nightstand next to his side of the bed. "That's the agent from the CIA, who's been running this case," he says as he just looks at the number.

"Are you going to answer it?"

"Nah. Right now, I'm going to gaze at my little boy and forget about everything but him and you. My perfect little family. Fuck the rest of the world, for right now."

A kiss to the top of my head, has me lying my head back on his shoulder. And I have to say, I've never found myself loving the man any more than I do right now.

But what will the future hold for us?

10

PART 10 - THE NEW LIFE

RYKER

W aking up to the sweet sound of my son's cries finds a smile on my lips. "I'll get him."

Gia moans a little as she wakes up too and tries to situate herself. I help her first, fluffing the pillows and helping her slide up, so she can feed him. I place a pillow under her arm to rest it on.

"Thank you, baby," she mumbles as she wipes the sleep out of her eyes.

Picking up the baby out of the bassinet that's right by my side of the bed, I place him in her waiting arms. "Here's Momma's little man." I kiss the top of his squirming head. "I'm going to go to the kitchen and grab you something to eat and drink. I'll be right back."

TAKING MY PHONE WITH ME, I see it's nine in the morning. Padding through the house to get to the kitchen, I check the messages that have come in. I put the phone on silent last night. I wanted to shut the world out for a while to let me get my bearings.

My lawyers are the first call I return. "Davenport, Davenport, and Stephenson," the secretary answers.

"This is Ryker..."

"Oh, yes! Mr. Crawford. Everyone has been trying to reach you. All day, yesterday we called and left messages. Are you okay?"

"I am. My wife gave birth to our first child yesterday. I had to take time for them."

"Oh, I see! How exciting for you two. Let me send this call to Harvey Stephenson. And congratulations, sir on the new baby. Did you have a boy or a girl?"

"We have a son. We named him Noah."

"How nice. Okay, sir. You have a great day."

I wait as the phone makes clicking noises then I hear a man's voice, "Crawford, we were worried sick about you!"

"Well, you can stop worrying now." I stop and think for a moment how some things do need to be worried about. "That's not exactly true. I need you to worry but over other things. My accounts have been frozen. The CIA and FBI were all over my office building yesterday. What can you find out about that?"

"Have charges been pressed?"

"Not that I know of."

"Hmm. Stay put and let me make some calls. Your accounts shouldn't have been frozen unless charges had been filed. Even if we're talking CIA and FBI. I'll give you a call back. Please answer our calls today, Crawford."

"I will. I just had to take a break from the drama to let the birth of our son take precedence in our lives."

"The birth of your son? That's why you weren't taking any calls?"

"Yes, sir. We had us a six-pound baby boy yesterday."

"Well, congratulations. What hospital are you in? Our office will send flowers and a gift basket."

"We're at home. The hospital wouldn't let us in. They told us to go to the county hospital. My wife wasn't keen on that, though. My wife and I know a midwife and we got her to come to our house to deliver the baby."

"Lord have mercy, Crawford. I'll get this straightened out ASAP! You can count on us."

"Thank you," I tell him then end the call.

I FIND the maid in the kitchen when I push the galley door open to walk in. "Oh, Mr. Crawford, can I get you anything? I'm not a great cook but I can make scrambled eggs."

Biting my lip, I don't exactly know how to tell her, she's not going to get paid and she should leave. "Um, uh, Patsy, we've hit some stumbling blocks. I hate to get you to work if I'm unsure if I can pay you or not."

She freezes as her mouth drops open. "Sir?"

"My accounts have been frozen by the government. I'm not sure how I can pay you for your work. So, as of right now, I'm sending you home. But I'll let you know as soon as this gets straightened out, so you can come back to work. And, if it all does get worked out, I'll pay you like you never missed a day. Okay?"

She shakes her head. "No, sir. That's not okay. I will stay on. Even if you can never pay, I will stay on. You both need me more than you ever have. I won't leave you in your time of need. I've been your maid for many years and you've been a generous and nice employer. Just because something has happened to your finances, doesn't mean you will lose me as your housekeeper. So, how about some scrambled eggs?"

The galley door opens and Consuela steps inside the kitchen. "That won't be necessary, Patsy. You can see to your work and I'll see to mine."

"I can't let you ladies work for free," I say as I look back and forth between them.

"I have faith things will work out and you will eventually be able to pay us again," Consuela says. "And even if you can't, that's okay too. You need me now. And I'll be damned if anything gets in the way of that."

My heart pounds with their generosity and I grab them both and give them hugs. "You two are the best people I know!"

WHEN I RELEASE THEM, I have to wipe tears out of my eyes. They both pat me on the back as Patsy says, "You go and take care of your wife and baby, Mr. Crawford. I'll bring in breakfast to you both, once she has it prepared for you."

Consuela goes to the fridge and takes out a bottle of water. "Have Mrs. Crawford drink this while I get the rest ready. It'll only take me a few minutes to whip up some omelets and toast for you two."

I turn and leave the kitchen, still wiping tears away and wonder how I got so lucky. My phone vibrates in my hand and I look to see the damn CIA agent's number. "Crawford," I answer.

"I need to see you in our offices today."

"No." *I'm not bending to these bastards!*

"YOU CAN COME on your own, or we can come get you," he threatens me.

"Look, my wife had a baby yesterday. That's why I didn't answer your call. Furthermore, I gave you all the information you asked me to. I held nothing back. But you did. You held a lot back. Why the search of my building? Why freeze my accounts? My baby was born here, at our home, thanks to you."

"What?" he asks.

"Don't act as if you give a shit. When you froze everything, even the insurance wouldn't pay. So, thanks a ton. As far as you talking to me anymore, you won't be. You can call my lawyers. Or better yet, sit tight and let them call you. I'll forward them your number, asshole!" I end the call and don't feel much better but at least I told him what I think about things.

Texting my lawyers the number, I let them know they need to call the prick. Going to our bedroom, I put the phone in my pajama pants pocket and take the water to my wife, who's nursing our son.

"Water, yes," she says as I sit on the bed beside her and open the bottle for her, holding it up to give her a drink as her hands are all tied up with feeding the baby.

"Consuela is here, making us breakfast. So is Patsy. I told them both to go, that I wasn't sure if or when I could pay them for their work."

"Let me guess, they both said they'd work anyway," she says with a smile. "Both of those women are so good. When we do get things straight, they're getting new cars!"

"And then some," I say as I agree, their loyalty should be greatly rewarded.

"He's eating better than I thought he would. Even though there's not much coming out. Margie said it would be like that for up to three days. I think I have enough cash in my purse for us to take him to the pediatrician today. I think if you call and tell them what happened, they'll get us in."

With a nod, I go and get her purse off the dresser. "I found a whopping sixty bucks in my wallet. Damn my habit of carrying so little cash." I open her purse and find three hundred in it. "Good, you have enough for the visit, I bet. I'll make the call."

"Once he's through eating, I'll put him down and you can watch him while I take a much-needed shower and get ready to go," she says as she gazes at Noah. "He's just so adorable!"

With a laugh, I say, "That he is, baby. Just like you."

Taking the card from the pediatrician we picked out, I make the call. "It's a Child's World Pediatrics," a young-sounding woman answers the phone.

"Hi, my name is Ryker Crawford. My wife and I came in for a visit a few weeks ago. We picked Doctor Wang to be our baby's pediatrician. We'd like to make an appointment for him as quickly as possible. He was born yesterday evening."

"Sure. What hospital are you in and I'll send him over?"

"We weren't allowed to have him where we had planned. We'll

come to you. Just give us a couple of hours to get there. And what's the cost for the appointment? We have limited cash."

"I'm looking at your file and money doesn't seem to be an issue. Would you care to explain what's happening, to me? Perhaps I can help you in some way."

"Our accounts have been frozen. I have my lawyers working on it and I'm sure they'll clear things up. But for now, we have a little over three hundred dollars to our names. And I'm not sure how long we'll need to make that stretch. But our son comes first. So, whatever the payment is, we'll make it."

"Can I call you back? I need to ask the doctor some things."

"Sure. Talk to you soon." I end the call and find Gia smiling as she looks at our baby.

I feel the weight of the world on my shoulders, so I walk over and sit down next to her and run my hand over our son's head as he sucks away at his mother's breast.

"Don't worry, Ryker. Everything will work out."

As I TOUCH our son and my wife leans her head on my arm, I feel the weight lift, like magic. "I hope so. Never, in my wildest dreams, did I see this coming. I thought I'd never have money issues. And for them to occur at the same time we bring our kid into the world, is insane."

"You know, it's teaching me things, though, Ryker. I was afraid to give birth anywhere but a hospital with all the capable doctors and nurses. Painkillers and all that stuff. But I did it. With a bit of help, mind you, but I did it."

"You did do it." I kiss the side of her head. "I'm so damn proud of you, Gia. You have no idea."

"And I'm proud of you. Ryker, you were right there every step of the way. Helping me and helping our son to get out into this world." She sighs as our son falls asleep at her breast. His mouth opens and his head lolls back a bit.

"So, here we are, a couple of people who are proud of one

another. I suppose things could be worse," I say then feel my phone vibrating in my pocket. "It's the pediatrician's office."

"Answer it," she says. "Hopefully they can give us a couple of hours to get ready and get there."

"Hello."

"Mr. Crawford, this is Angie, the nurse you just spoke to."

"Hello, Angie. Did you get us an appointment?"

"No, sir. I have the doctor coming to you. He's bringing a nurse with him and everything he needs to make sure the baby is in good condition. If, for any reason, he feels the hospital is the best place for his patient, he will bring you all in and place you in the hospital."

"Will they accept us?" I ask as I doubt they will.

"Yes, he said he'll use his personal money to make sure his patient is well taken care of. Not to worry, sir. He'll take excellent care of him. He'll be there in an hour and a half. We have your address on file. Thanks for choosing us to take care of your baby, Mr. Crawford."

"No, thank you! Bye now."

"What?" Gia asks as she looks at me.

"He's coming here. He's helping us. Gia, this is more than I could've ever asked for."

"Seems, with this little bundle of joy, came a bunch of miracles too."

We kiss our son's little head at the same time then each other. *Seems, miracles can happen!*

GIA

The sun is shining brightly as I sit in the backseat with Noah, who's resting comfortably in his car seat. Ryker's driving us into town for the meeting between him, his lawyers, and some government officials who think they have enough evidence on someone in the company to prove Apollo Engineering was part of the scam about the Mars mission. A preposterous accusation, in my opinion.

Ryker told me that I should stay home. The baby's only a week old. But I wasn't about to let him face this without me by his side. As he pulls into the parking lot of the law office the meeting has been scheduled at, I find myself getting a little nervous about things.

I brought a bottle of breastmilk, I pumped earlier. Just in case the baby wakes up hungry while we're here. Ryker parks and gets out of the car, coming around to my door, he helps me out first, then reaches in and gets the baby's car seat out and grabs the diaper bag.

"Hold on to me, Gia. I know you haven't regained all your strength yet."

I take hold of his arm and lean on him a little. He's right, I do feel a bit weak. "Thank you, Ryker. You're so thoughtful."

"You and Noah are my world, Gia." He opens the door and lets me go in first then comes in and nods for me to take his arm again. The smile that covers my face goes clear to my soul. It was no mistake that I met this man. *It was no mistake that he found me.*

When we step off the elevator on the third floor of his lawyers' offices, I find a couple of men in dark glasses and black suits, standing in front of the main door to the suite of offices. When we walk between them to go inside, I can't stop myself and say, "You look proud to be working for such a corrupt agency that would pull down hardships on innocent people. Bravo, boys."

Ryker snickers as he opens the door for me. "Don't worry fellas. I got the door. No need to offer any help here," his words are heavily laced with sarcasm.

"Being gentlemen must not be part of their training," I say as I step inside as Ryker balances the bulky car seat in one hand and opens the door with the other.

Neither move a muscle as Ryker kicks the door closed. The receptionist hurries to us. "Oh, my! Can I see him?"

Ryker pulls back the blanket, showing off our handsome son. "This is Noah Ryker Crawford."

"What a little cutie," she gushes. "Follow me. They're all waiting on you."

She pauses at a small fridge in the hallway. "Anything to drink before I take you in? We have a little bit of everything."

"I'd love a soda," I say.

Ryker shakes his head. "A couple of waters, please. No caffeine for Momma."

"I forgot." I kiss his cheek. "Thank you for remembering."

"It's my job as Dad." He smiles at me and kisses the tip of my nose.

The receptionist smiles as she gets the waters then leads us to the meeting room. "You two are adorable."

"Thank you," I say as I love it when people say things like that about us. I too think we're adorable.

WHEN SHE OPENS THE DOOR, we find three men obviously, lawyers as they're all wearing expensive suits. And two men obviously, government agents who have on suits that look as if they came from JC Penney's.

She places the bottles of water on the table where we're supposed to take seats at, then excuses herself and leaves.

"Mr. and Mrs. Crawford," one of the lawyers says with a nod. "I've never met you, Mrs. Crawford. It's a pleasure." He leans over to shake my hand. "Call me Pat."

"Hello, Pat. Nice to meet you."

He shakes Ryker's hand and greets him as the other two lawyers introduce themselves to me. Harvey and Leon are the other two. The government officials have yet to speak. They're looking down at their files.

Harvey gestures to them as he takes his seat. "Allow me to introduce you both to Agents, Booth and Danner. They're from the CIA."

The man he pointed to when he said, Booth, stands up. "Let's get these proceedings under way. I'm not a man who dallies about with things."

"Great. Time is pretty critical to us too," Ryker says.

Danner stands up too. I suppose this is a tactic used to dominate the room. He adds, "Good, then here's the first question we have for you, Mr. Crawford. When you took over the CEO position of Apollo Engineering, is it true you ousted a man who was your grandfather's right-hand man for the last ten years of his life?"

"Frank Holiday?" Ryker asks. "Is that who you're talking about?"

Danner jots down his response as he nods. "Frank Holiday was the man your grandfather had told many people would be taking the CEO position when he was no longer viable to do the work. You swooped in when your grandfather became ill and took that over. No formal vote was ever made by the board. Is, that right?"

"Not a written vote. The vote was spoken and the secretary has the notes from that meeting, stating everyone's oral vote," he says.

"And how does this pertain to you freezing our accounts?" I ask.

RYKER PLACES his hand on my leg and looks at the men too. "Yes, how in the world does that justify such an action?"

"The money you've made by being the CEO of that company should've been Frank Holiday's. He's given us information on you that had us justified in freezing those accounts," Booth says. "You see, he told us about overhearing you and Damien Markov talking one late night at your office. He told us about you and Damien meeting at a hotel while he was in town. He told us about the booster agreement."

"I have no idea what he thinks he heard. Markov and I are not into anything unethical," Ryker says as he sits up straighter. "He and I had a few conversations that might have seemed odd but that was because he and I were fighting over this woman, right here." His thumb hooks at me. "Not that it's anyone's damn business."

"Mr. Holiday has written a statement that says he overheard you and Markov talking about setting up the whole scam and finding others who wanted the same thing to happen," Booth says. "And it's odd that only you two had the implants removed. His story is that you and Markov did that to ensure you two would be left here and the others would get on that shuttle and blow up, leaving you two the top space industry leaders. Making it so you two could get to Mars first. Something you both craved."

"You couldn't be more wrong about any of that," Ryker says. "We were going to die, if we had to, to stop the whole thing. You can ask anyone."

"We did ask them all. The other men in your team," Danner says as he tosses out four pieces of paper. "These are your team members' statements. All had ideas that you and Markov were in on something together. All had distrust for you two."

"There was no reason to," Ryker says. "Markov and I have a history, is all. That may have been why they thought the things they did."

Booth takes a seat as he says, "Holiday thinks you've always had a plan to win the race to Mars. He's told us, in his statement, that you've had the plan to be on the first mission since before your grandfather passed away."

"That's not a crime," Ryker says.

"Stealing the CEO position is," Danner says.

ONE OF THE lawyers clears his throat and I look to see Pat holding up one finger. "The position wasn't stolen. I'm sure we can get the notes from that meeting to prove that."

"The files have been confiscated," Danner says as he looks at the file in his hand then he takes a seat too. "And here's what we found, no file that says anything about the meeting your client is claiming took place. We didn't find one shred of evidence that any type of vote was taken. And that too makes Crawford seem suspect of being one part of the mastermind behind this murder plot to kill off the competition. With Markov's help, he nearly killed those men. We've been instructed to strip him of his office as CEO of Apollo Engineering."

"By what authority?" Pat asks.

"The United States President," Booth tells him and tosses another piece of paper, he takes out of the file that's on the table in front of him, to Leon who's sitting closest to him.

I can see the presidential seal from here and I cringe. "That aside," I say, quickly. "You've frozen everything. My money is in those accounts too. All the deposits are not his."

BOOTH SMILES as he looks at me. "Your small amount will be unfrozen and you can take that and open another account. I wouldn't put his name on it, though."

I look at him and smile. "Great. I expect that to be done by tomorrow. It shouldn't be hard to see what deposits are for me and what are for him." I look at Pat who's across the table from me. "Can you handle that for us?"

"Well, um, there is the matter of our attorney fees," he says as he threads his fingers together. "With this presidential order, I'm afraid those assets are gone. Ryker Crawford is no longer the billionaire he once was. I don't know how we can represent him any further."

"What does this all mean for me?" Ryker asks Booth. "Exactly what's going to happen to me?"

"We don't have enough evidence to charge you with a crime. You've managed to cover your tracks there, Crawford. Being that other countries have threatened not to do business with one of America's top space companies, the President is within his rights to take that company away from you and place it in more trustworthy hands."

Danner takes over as he pulls a paper out of his file and pushes it toward Ryker. "This paper states that you can no longer serve in any capacity at Apollo Engineering. It states that all of your cash assets will revert to the company. And no criminal charges can be made at this time with the evidence we have."

"Essentially, I'm broke and jobless," Ryker says.

I pat his leg. "Don't let that worry you, baby."

"You're taking all I've done and flushed it down the drain. You know there's every chance that Frank Holiday got rid of the minutes from that meeting. He took advantage of the scam that happened. A scam that I too was a victim of. He took advantage to gain control of something he has no business having control of. And our president gave it to him."

"Look at it any way you want to. You're no longer the CEO of Apollo Engineering. You can't step foot back into the place. Your personal effects have been packed up and are in the trunk of our car," Danner tells him. "You should feel grateful that you're not being charged with a crime."

RYKER'S HAND moves over my leg. "The only thing I'm truly grateful for is this lady at my side and this child. All the rest if this Earthly shit can go to hell. So, I am free to go on about my life then, right?"

With a nod, Danner says, "Yes. Just stay out of Apollo and all will be okay."

"Not a problem," I say. "Since I have no legal team, how long do I have to wait for my part of the bank accounts to be freed?"

"It's our policy to have them freed within twenty-four hours, ma'am," Booth says.

"Good." I look at the attorneys and give them all nods. I won't be employing them. "And what about the smaller affiliate companies that were working with Apollo?"

Pat looks at Danner who says, "Their accounts have had the holds taken off them. It'll be up to Holiday to decide to keep any contracts with them or not."

"Good," I say. "We're done here, then." I get up and Ryker does too, picking up the car seat.

"I want a file of all that you have," he tells them all. "I want a copy of everything in both of those files."

"You'll have to wait for that," Pat says. "Let Stephanie, in the front, make copies. We can no longer do business with you, Crawford. You understand, I'm sure."

. . .

MY HUSBAND'S head drops and so does my heart. He's never been treated this way. It's humiliating to him, I can feel it radiating off him. I turn back and push all the papers together and hold out my hands for the files the CIA agents have. "Let me get these to her. We don't have time to fuck around. Our son will be waking up to eat in half an hour. You all seem like time-bandits. Time, we don't have."

They let me take the papers and files and I follow Ryker out. "Thanks, baby."

"You really don't have to worry, Ryker."

"I know. I know you have money. I just feel terrible. I feel deflated."

Dropping the stack of papers on the receptionist's desk, I say, "Can you make copies of these really quick for us before Noah wakes up and wants to eat?"

"Of course," she says as she hops up and gets busy doing that.

"Frank Holiday?" I ask Ryker as we take seats to wait for the copies. "Who the hell is he? I've never even heard anyone talk about him."

"An old as shit man who knows so little about modern technology, it's not even funny. But, apparently, he's quite a good bull shitter and an excellent man with paperwork." Ryker rubs his temples, telling me he has a massive headache. *And who wouldn't with this news?*

"WHAT DOES HE DO AT APOLLO?"

"Um, I think his official position is something like vice president of accounting or something like that. I'm not sure, really. I know it holds no real responsibility. It's more of a paid job until he retires. Which I don't know why he hasn't taken retirement already."

"Don't worry about him. That would take more time than we care to take. Okay, he's got the company. You have the brain. I have money. And Damien is our ally."

For the first time since this shit began, Ryker smiles. "We do have all of that, don't we?"

"That and Mars isn't inhabited by a damn thing." I pat his leg then lean over and kiss him, sending us to that place only we can take each other. When the kiss ends, he and I are both smiling.

"Here are the copies. I put them in this large manila envelope for you," the secretary says.

"Great," I take it and we both get up. "See ya."

I keep my mouth shut as we walk out between the two CIA pricks and go to the elevator. As the doors close, Ryker puts the car seat on the floor and wraps his arms around me, giving me a real kiss. When the elevator stops, he ends the kiss. "Baby, you really are my hero."

"AND YOU ARE MINE," I tell him. "Never doubt that for a second. We're a team, you and I. What you want, I want. And I want you to see Mars."

The glazed look in his eyes does something to me. "Gia, you don't have to..."

I stop him with another kiss. "Shh. I want it too."

We step out of the elevator with our arms around each other as the doors close. "The baby!" we both shout.

He throws out his arm to stop the doors from closing and grabs the car seat with our son in it. "That was close!"

I clutch my chest and try to calm down. "Damn, baby!"

"I know," he says as he shakes his head.

Walking out of the office has us knowing things are very different. But not so much so that we can't handle those changes. Nothing worth having is ever easy. And neither of us mind working hard.

The future doesn't scare me. I hope it doesn't scare him, either.

RYKER

"I'M BROKE, GIA," I say as I drive my wife and son home. "For the first time in my life, I am dead broke."

"How does it feel?" she asks me from the backseat as she looks at me through the rearview mirror.

"I'm still breathing. It doesn't cost a dime for the air I need to stay alive."

"Are you feeling worried at all?"

DIGGING DEEP INTO MYSELF, I look for worry, dread, fear, and I find none. "I'm not. You know I think I can deal with this."

"And it doesn't hurt that you're married to a pretty rich chick, either," she says with a laugh.

"Oh yeah, you have money. I kind of forgot about that. Funny, huh?" I stop at a red light and look back at her. "Guess you can be my sugar-momma."

"I got you, Big Daddy."

We both laugh then quickly shut up as the baby starts to move. "We almost woke him up," I whisper.

She pats his little leg to settle him. "We don't want to do that. He's going to want to eat as soon as he wakes up and I can't take him out of this car seat."

Driving home in silence, I think about how I really feel. I've had everything I've ever worked for taken away from me. By a man who doesn't deserve it. A man who's lied about me and stolen from me.

I should be furious. I should be seething with anger. But all I can be is happy. Looking in the rearview mirror, I see my gorgeous wife, dozing and the car seat with my son in it. Happiness is all I can feel.

So what if I'm not a powerful CEO anymore. So what if I have only a few dollars in my wallet. So what if I have no clue what I'm going to do in the future. I have people to love and they love me.

That's all I need!

. . .

THE SKY IS STILL BLUE. I don't have money and the sky is still blue. The breeze still blows, the birds still chirp. Life goes on. Money or not, life goes on.

"Baby, I'm starving," Gia says as she shakes her head in an effort to stay awake. "I've got money in my purse. Can you pull through somewhere and get us something to eat?"

"Dollar burgers?" I ask with a chuckle. "Anything off the dollar menu, Gia."

She laughs and sighs. "You're hilarious."

"I think I'm going to be good at being poor," I tell her.

She wrinkles up her nose as she shakes her head. "You're not going to be poor. Not a damn thing is going to change. We'll keep the staff at the house. The cars, the house, all of it will remain the same."

"But I'm not going to be paying it. It won't be me keeping us wealthy." Then it hits me like a brick wall. "I'm going to be a kept man. I really am going to be kept. I'll have to ask you to give me money. I'll have to rely on you, Gia."

"So?" she says like it's not a great big, huge, deal.

"So? So, Gia? That's not cool!" I pull into the drive-through of a fast food place and have to reach back for money to pay for the cheap stuff. "I need some cash." The words feel thick on my tongue.

SHE PLACES a twenty in my palm and runs her fingertip over it as well. "Don't ever think about this money as mine. This is our money. The way it's always been. Now order me a burger and fries and a bottle of water, please."

I think about what she's said as I look over the menu. Our money. Her money is now, our money. *Nope, it still feels bad!*

"TWO CHEESEBURGERS, all the way with mustard. Two small fries and two bottles of water, please."

"That'll be twenty-five dollars and seventeen cents," the man in the box tells me, freaking me out.

"How much?" I ask as this has to be a mistake. *It's a couple of burgers and some fries and water, for God's sake!*

"TWENTY-FIVE, seventeen, sir. And do you need extra ketchup?"

"How many ketchups come with it?"

"One small packet. Most people want extra," he explains.

"Baby, do you need more than one packet of ketchup?" I ask Gia.

"Please," she says.

"Yeah, give me some extra ketchup."

"How many?" he asks.

"Um, how about two or three more?"

"You want two or three?" he asks, annoying the crap out of me.

"What does it matter? Put in a couple or so."

"There's a thirty-cent charge for each one. So, give me an exact number" he says, sending me into a tizzy.

"Thirty cents each? For little tiny packets of fucking ketchup? Are you fucking serious right now?"

"Ryker!" Gia hisses at me. "No cussing! They're going to spit in our food!"

"Sir! You can't speak to me like that! You know what, I'm deleting this order. Find somewhere else to eat. I'm refusing you service," he tells me, sending me into a rage.

"Listen here, dipshit! You can't refuse me service because I'm deleting this order. That's highway robbery, anyway! So, fuck you, prick!" I peel off and then I hear the baby crying and Gia's glaring at me and I think I may have just messed up.

"Pull over. Now that you've woken him up, I have to get him out and feed him. Way to go!"

PULLING INTO A PARKING LOT, I spot a little pizza place. "I'm sorry. I am, Gia. But that guy was crazy."

"No, you were the one being crazy," she tells me, making my jaw drop.

"Me?"

She nods as she gets the baby out. Spotting a little pizza place in the strip mall I've pulled into, I get out of the car. "Where are you going, Ryker?"

"To get us a couple of slices of pizza and some water. I'll be right back."

I can feel her icy stare pummeling my back as I walk away from the car. *Am I really the crazy one?*

GIA

ICICLES ARE FORMING on the trees as I look out the window of my parents' farm house. "Ryker, can you see if Noah needs his diaper changed? I smell something funky."

Ryker gets off the bed and goes to check on our son, who's sleeping in his little playpen at the foot of the bed. "Yep, he's ripe. But won't it wake him up if I change him?"

"If you don't, he'll get a rash. We certainly don't want that to happen. Not when we're about to leave."

"It's hard to believe that we're really doing it, Gia," he says then shushes our one-year-old as he wines about being moved around. "I know, Buddy, but you went stinky and Daddy has to get you all cleaned up."

"The house and cars have been sold. The plane tickets have been paid for. We're really doing it, Ryker."

"Damien sure pulled it off, didn't he?"

"It's hard to believe, but he certainly did. Giving you a job at Markov Global is the best thing to happen to us since Noah." I get out of bed and stretch as I watch a cardinal perched in the tree outside my childhood bedroom window. It looks back at me and flies away when I wave at it.

"There will be no birds. No trees. No barking dogs."

"No, roosters to wake us up," he adds. "Mars is thankfully, void of those things. Is that the same damn rooster from when we came here the first time?"

"I'm not sure," I say as I take the dirty diaper and go throw it in the wastebasket. "Why do you ask that?"

"Because it's as stupid as that bird was. It's not dawn at four in the morning." He snuggles Noah back up, and he falls right back to sleep.

WIGGLING HIS FINGER AT ME, he whispers, "Come here, pretty momma."

I giggle and go to him. He wraps his arms around me and kisses me with a long, sweet kiss. "In a few hours, a plane will start our journey to Russia."

"A few years after that, a shuttle will take us to Mars," I finish his thought. "Things are still moving in the direction you've always been going. Just a few speed bumps got in the way."

He sways with me as we look into each other's eyes. "Losing Apollo was a great loss. But it helped one thing. It helped us all to realize we need to be working together instead of apart. The program that Markov Global came up with, where we all work together and stop the segregation of different countries, is pure genius."

"It is," I say and kiss his cheek. "And you were the mastermind behind that idea. Damien had the ability to get it done. You two actually make a great team."

"Weird, huh?" He kisses me again. "I stole his girl and now we're partners."

I give him a frown. "You didn't steal me. I left him. I hate when you say that."

"That night, when I saw you for the first time, I knew I had to have you. I stole you then and there." He kisses me again.

"I suppose you're right. You got into my head that night. That's for sure."

"And your heart," he says then gives me another kiss.

. . .

LAYING BACK DOWN on the bed, he and I snuggle down under the thick blankets. "It took you a bit longer to burrow into there, Ryker. But once you did, you made a real home for yourself in there."

Rubbing his nose to mine, he says, "You've created quite the homey spot for yourself in mine too."

"I think losing Apollo Engineering was the best thing to happen to the space industry, Ryker. Sure, you lost your shit for about six months but when you came back around, you kicked ass and made things happen. I didn't know I could be any prouder of you than I already was but you made it happen, somehow."

"You know I hate it when you bring up my six-month meltdown. Stick to the good parts. Like when I came up with the idea for conglomerating the tops minds in the field. Now that was sheer genius."

"It was." I kiss him again and feel a stirring in his pajama bottoms.

His hand moves down to the waistband of mine and he moves it on in, finding my little pearl and giving it a swirl. Our tongues dance as his fingers ignite a heat in me. *What a great way to warm up!*

SOMETHING THUMPS THE BLANKET, followed by a grunt, stopping us. We look up and see Noah, standing in the playpen and he's thrown his empty bottle at us.

"Breakfast time," Ryker says with a laugh. "Mommy will have to wait."

I moan as he gets out of bed and trots past Noah, making Noah let out a sharp sound, commanding his daddy to come back and get him. I climb out of bed and pick him up. "Daddy's going to go make his little man a bottle. You want to snuggle with Momma until he comes back?"

I take him with me back to our bed and lie him down then get in and snuggle with him. His dark hair needs a trim and a lock of it has fallen into his face. I brush it back and gaze at our little boy. He's a perfect mixture of us. Our little creation.

He pinches my cheek as he looks at me and I think about what life will be like for him. Growing up on Mars will mean he'll never see some things we have here. It'll mean he won't get to do a lot of things we all take for granted. But he'll have experiences no one on Earth will ever have.

I battle myself at times about taking him away from this Earth. His grandparents are people that he might never see again. That's why we're here now. So they can know him and him them.

But today we'll leave here. Only sporadic visits to them will be made. But at least they will all have some time together before we leave this place forever.

The decision was made that those who leave cannot come back to Earth. Primarily for health reasons. We might bring back viruses that could wipe out the planet. There are so many little reasons for us not to come back.

The decision to go wasn't easy. But the urge to do it was always there. So, we will start the first leg of our journey to Mars today. And Noah will be right there with us.

I just pray we're doing the right thing!

RYKER

THE MORNING SUN is bright as we walk to the launch pad. Noah's holding his little sister's hand as we make our way down the long corridor. Gia and I walk behind them, watching our children take steps most other children will never get to do.

The first group of settlers has three hundred people going to Mars. And Gia has one in the oven, just the way I wanted it to be. Only two weeks pregnant, we have high hopes the space travel won't interfere with the pregnancy.

I take her hand and swing our clasped hands between us. "You ready for this, Gia?"

Damien walks up on the other side of her with a huge grin on his face. "She's more than ready, Ryker. Can't you see it written all over her face? She never planned on making this journey but here she is, just the same."

"I am ready. I'm so ready. The little family gathering we had this last week let me know that my family will always reside in my head and my heart. And it's important to move forward and not allow anything to stop progress. With their support, I know I'm doing the right thing."

Damien's wife and three children come up behind us and he gives us a nod and steps back to walk with them. "See you all on board."

Photographers are taking pictures of the people as they stop just before getting onto the giant shuttle. We pause for a photo with the kids then step through the door.

"Wow!" Noah says as he looks around at the entry.

"You want to really see something, keep walking, son," I tell our five-year-old.

Gia picks up Maggie, our two-year-old and carries her as she's frozen in place. "I think she's a little afraid."

"Not Daddy's girl," I say and tweak her little nose, making her giggle.

Taking the seats that have our number on them, I strap in Noah as Gia straps in Maggie. Then she takes a seat and I strap her in too. "I like how these bonds look on you, baby."

"Ryker!" She gives me a wink. "Wicked man!"

WITH THE KIDS seated between us, I go to my seat, next to Noah. "Your dad has dreamt of this day what seems like forever, Noah."

"Are you scared? I'm a little scared," he says.

"Sure, I'm a little afraid." I buckle the last buckle and tussle his dark hair. "But all great adventures start with being afraid. It's part of the lure of it all. Only the strong of heart and mind will do something like this. Not everyone has this strength in them. You're special, Noah. You have your mother's strength."

"So do you, Dad," he says as he holds his hand up for a high-five.

I give him one and say, "She did give me the strength I have today.

She sure did. She's my rock, you know."

"Yeah, mine too. I'm not worried about Mars. Mom can take care of all of us. She's great at it."

I look past the kids to find Gia resting her head on the headrest with her eyes closed. "You see what she's doing there, Noah."

He turns to look at his mother. "What's she doing, Dad? Sleeping?"

"No, son. Your mother is praying. That's her secret. That's how she stays so strong."

"Oh, then we should do that too, Dad." I watch him close his eyes and lay his head back. His lips move as he prays, silently.

LAYING MY HEAD BACK, I start praying too. When I finish my prayer, I find the cabin we're in is now full and take off will be very soon. My heart speeds up as the speakers fill with soft music.

They're getting ready. The sound of the music is supposed to keep everyone calm and not so focused on the sounds of the rockets that will project us into space.

But I focus on the sounds beyond the music. The eerie silence in a cabin full of people. Then the clicking of the ignition and the roar of the engines.

Noah takes my hand and I look over to see Gia taking Maggie's hand. Noah takes her other one, making our family chain complete. "Can I have everyone's attention?" a man's voice comes over the speakers. "I'm Captain John Stevens. I'll be one of the people flying us all to the first manned mission to Mars. I'd like everyone to sit back, relax, and get prepared to start this eight-month journey. Once we get out of the Earth's gravitational pull, you will be free to move around. Check out your quarters for this trip. This place is your home for now. You all share a common bond as the first settlers of another planet. So, let's relax and enjoy this part of the ride. It's going to be the roughest part, except for when we land. But in the middle, will be a whole lot of nothing. Once we reach the outer atmosphere, our internal gravity system will kick in, keeping us on the floor. You will hear a countdown, followed by a pretty loud explosion. Some of you may want to cover your ears. Here we go."

A woman's voice fills the speakers, "Ten, nine, eight," I look at Gia and give her a smile. She beams one back at me. "Seven, six, five." Noah gives my hand a squeeze and I give his one back. "Four, three, two." I brace myself for the sound. "One."

And here we go!

GIA

THE ROUGH LIFT-OFF has my body feeling very odd like a heavy weight is covering it. I want to look at Maggie, to see how she's taking this but my head won't move. The sound is so loud and I want to cover my ears but I'm stuck in the position I was in when the shuttle blasted off.

Holding Maggie's little hand, I try to breathe normally but can't seem to take in any kind of a decent breath. This seems to be taking forever. The woman who made the countdown comes back on the speakers, "Fifteen seconds."

I don't even know what the hell that means but I count to fifteen in my head and nothing happens. Then I feel it. The weight is gone in an instant and so is the loud sound of the rockets. I hear sighs coming from everyone and let out one myself.

Looking at Maggie, I expected to see her crying but she's grinning like a lunatic. "Fun! Do it again, Mommy!"

"Wow, you liked that?" I ask her as I'm shocked.

Ryker gets out of his safety harness and comes to help me out of mine. "Your face is so red, baby."

"I couldn't breathe. I'm okay now," I tell him as he sets me free then picks me up and gives me a big kiss.

A tug on my jumpsuit has me ending the kiss and turning to find Noah, is the culprit. "Can you guys let us out of these things before you start making out?"

"Noah!"

Ryker chuckles as he lets me go. "Sure, Buddy." He gets to work setting him free while I free Maggie.

Excited murmurs are everywhere then Damien is at my side. "Did you enjoy the lift-off, Gia?"

"Not really. But it's all good now."

"The living quarters are back this way. Come, I'll show you," he says as he leads my family to where we'll call home for the next eight months.

Ryker steps up beside me, putting his arm around my waist. "I purposely didn't come on the shuttle, so I could see it all for the first time with you guys."

"Are you excited?" I ask him as I pick up Maggie.

"More than that." He leans in close to whisper in my ear. "And I can't wait to christen our new bed."

Heat moves through me and I find myself blushing. "Ryker, naughty, naughty."

I feel a pinch on my ass as he gives me a devilish grin. "Yes, I am."

Turning down a narrow hallway, I see doors along both sides, just like in a hotel. Numbers are on each door. Each individual traveler or group of them, were given a number. That number designates where you live, sit, and even when you eat. Our number is seven and we find our door, easily.

With no material objects to covet as everyone was issued what they need, there is no need for locks on the doors, so Damien opens ours and we see a small living area with three doors off of it. "Your suite."

We walk in while Damien stays in the hallway. "It's small," I say as I can reach out and touch each person in the room.

"Cozy," Damien says. "I prefer to think of it in that way."

"You'll get used to it," Ryker says then kisses my cheek. "And I like being close to you, anyway."

Not happy about how small it is, I make my way to the first door and find an even smaller room. A set of bunk beds that are built into the wall is there and only enough room to walk in and get on the beds. "I suppose this is the kids' bedroom."

"Of course," Damien says, still standing in the hallway. "These quarters are generally for sleeping and not much else. There are large areas around the ship where you can spread out. The dining areas, the entertainment areas. The observation area is very nice and adult beverages are served there. You two should join Svetlana and me for drinks later. You could leave the children in the play area."

"Sounds good," Ryker tells him. He points to the watch-like thing we all wear on our wrists. "Tap me when you're there."

With a nod, Damien leaves us alone and closes the door, making the main room feel even smaller.

Ryker opens the door in the middle of the three of them and we find a tiny toilet area. "Bathroom. Look, Maggie, the potty is in here."

SHE CLAPS and comes to look. "Potty!"

We just recently potty trained her. Her joy at seeing a toilet makes me laugh and Ryker leaves that tiny room to open the door to what must be our bedroom. "The master..." he stops talking as he looks inside.

I can't imagine what has rendered him speechless but when I look in too, I find out. "Oh, Ryker!"

A twin bed is all there is in the room. Tiny amounts of space are on each side of it. Barely enough room to walk. *And my pregnant body will be expanding all the way there!*

"GIA, this isn't a problem. This is great, we'll get to be so close."

"I'm going to be on top of you! And I'm only going to get bigger! I didn't think about this. I should've jumped in and had a hand in designing this space."

"It'll be okay," he says as he pulls me to sit on the bed. Our combined asses take up every bit of the space.

"Tight quarters aren't so bad. Think about it, Gia." He gives me a kiss and I fight back the urge to cry.

"Can we go in our room, Mom?" Noah asks me. "I want to lay on my bed. I'm taking the top bunk. I've never had a bunk bed before."

I nod and watch him take his little sister's hand and lead her the five steps across our living room and they go into their new room and both seem very happy and excited. When I look at Ryker, I see the same damn expression on his handsome face. "You love this, don't you?"

"Close the door and come to bed. I think we need a naked nap."

I close the door, using my foot and lie back on the bed. "Take me away, Ryker. Only you can take my mind off how small everything is."

Unzipping my jumpsuit, he pulls it off me, tossing it to the little floor area next to the tiny bed. I watch him as he pulls his off and has more difficulty doing that than he had taking mine off. "We'll get used to these close quarters. I know we will. When we have the wide-open spaces on Mars, we won't know what to do."

"I'll know what to do," I say as he lays down on one side of me, stroking my tummy and looking into my eyes. I cradle his face in my hands and kiss him. Letting my mind go, feeling only his lips on mine.

His hand makes slow strokes over my stomach then he dips it into my pleasure pool, stirring up sensations that take my mind even further away. Playing with me until I ache to have him inside of me, he finally gives me what I need. Moving his body to cover mine, he makes one hard thrust into me.

I arch up to him and he moves his mouth off mine to kiss along the length of my neck. I moan a little as he gives me a good bite then thrusts into me harder.

My body is quivering before I know it. My heart is racing as the wave washes over me, leaving me writhing under his attention. *I'm home!*

RYKER

A RED SKY greets us as we step off the ship. A gentle breeze blows and I take in a deep breath of the cold air. Steam forms when I blow my breath out.

"Steam, we can make water just like we planned," Damien says as he and I take the first steps onto the loose red dirt. "We made it, Ryker."

"We did," I say as I look all over at the vast open space where we will make our new home. I tap my communication device. "Gia, bring them out."

Damien calls his wife too and they come out of the door as we watch their faces. Steam floats around them all as they walk out with much hesitation. Gia gets to me and I find her smiling. "Ryker, we're here. We're finally here!"

Taking her in my arms, I kiss her as our children cling to my legs. "We're home, baby."

I run my hand over Noah's head and reach down to pick up our daughter. "Daddy, it's windy!"

"It sure is." I carry her away from the shuttle, so everyone else can get out too. The eight months went by like molasses but we're finally here. And here is where we'll stay.

GIA

THE BABY WAITED a whole week before coming out to see his new world. Zane Ryker Crawford was the first-born citizen of Mars, just how Ryker wished for.

Life on Mars is hard work. Diligence and patience are required here. We've managed to make things easier as time has gone by. Five years have passed. Ryker and I have had another child in that time, a girl named Cindy.

The people here are from all over the world. We are but one race now, the Human Race. No divisions are made here. We all work hard and we all share the fruits of our labors, evenly.

Money will never come into play. If we, the founders, have things our way. We've penned a constitution that makes everyone equal and set basic rules for society.

No murders have occurred, knock on wood. We have had one death but it was from natural causes. Mr. Chadwick was eighty-seven when his heart gave out on him. He came here alone. He had no one left on Earth anyway and he was proud when he told us, he'd make a name for himself here, as the first person to die on Mars.

It seems most people want to be remembered for something, no matter where they are. I want to be remembered as the woman who once was lost but found her way and ended up as a founder of Mars.

Ryker wants to be remembered as the man who didn't let adversity stop him from achieving his very large goal of getting here. And he's also happy he'll be remembered as having the first child here too. His planning paid off for him.

Planning, preparation, and follow-through are important things to remember when you want to reach your goal. Any goal. And most goals aren't easy to get to. Most have a road filled with hard work, trials, tribulations, and even disappointment. In the end, though, when you reach that goal that seemed like it would never come, how you feel is beyond amazing.

Focus is the key. One must remain focused if they want to see their dreams come true.

I wasn't lost when Ryker found me. I was hiding from greatness. He forced me to come out of hiding and grab the brass ring, joining him in a future most can only dream about.

The time has come for us to settle in and just live now. And I think it's safe to say, we will all live happily ever after...

THE END

ABOUT THE AUTHOR

Mrs. Love writes about smart, sexy women and the hot alpha billionaires who love them. She has found her own happily ever after with her dream husband and adorable 6 and 2 year old kids. Currently, Michelle is hard at work on the next book in the series, and trying to stay off the Internet.

"Thank you for supporting an indie author. Anything you can do, whether it be writing a review, or even simply telling a fellow reader that you enjoyed this. Thanks

❀ Created with Vellum

CPSIA information can be obtained
at www.ICGtesting.com
Printed in the USA
BVHW041405100221
599801BV00005B/94